ALMOST HUMAN

Degrees of freedom - book 1

Anne Cleasby

Almost Human
Copyright © 2018 by Anne Cleasby

Acknowledgements

Thanks to Mandy Bannon for editing Almost Human and to Helen Dunning for producing the cover art. A special thanks to Inés G Labarta for providing feedback and useful criticism.

ALLIANCE NEWS CORP – keeping you informed

June 7ᵗʰ, 2452.
News Update – International Division

Military

Fighting continues to escalate around the north-western border of the Indian Republic, as the Eurasian Alliance acts to prevent expansionism on the part of its neighbours. Political analyst, Dr. Takim Redditch, told NewsCorp that 'Population explosion and lack of reproductive legislation by past and present regional governments have turned parts of the Indian subcontinent into a rumbling volcano of discontent'.

Yesterday evening, Alliance Speaker, Sifia Hong, issued a statement declaring that the Council will not allow the carefully established stability of the Allied nations to be threatened by the reckless behaviour of neighbouring countries. Speaker Hong insists that 'while the Alliance would prefer to reach a diplomatic compromise, all potential solutions are under discussion'.

~~~

Weather

Temperatures throughout Eastern Asia are expected to reach record highs this summer, bringing environment restoration projects to a temporary halt. Predictions suggest that Central Europe will also suffer from the heatwave. Water levels in many central rivers are at an all-time low, while in parts of the north, winter flooding has persisted into spring and early summer.

Chapter 1

Eight o' clock.

Sabre-Tooth frowned at the illuminated display on the panel opposite his cage. Temperature 293K, time 08.00; the numbers were clear; it was daytime, so where were the labtecs? The lights had woken him at seven when they flickered into life as they did every morning. Why had no one come?

His stomach grumbled. The duty tec should have been here half an hour ago with his breakfast. On the white wall across from the row of cage units, the large flatscreen had switched to active mode, and now displayed the morning news. Small Alliance soldiers moved silently through the images of dry, broken landscapes, bare mountains and ruined settlements. In the bottom right-hand corner of the screen a serious female reporter mouthed a commentary.

There would be no sound until someone arrived and manually activated the controls, but as far as Sabre-Tooth could tell, the news rarely changed. Weather, fashion, political gossip, and news from the various combat zones ran on a cycle, interrupted occasionally by sales pitches from an assortment of corporate groups. A cursive script snaked along the bottom of the screen, the words appearing on a similar repeat to the pictures.

Sabre-Tooth spared them a cursory glance. India might as well be a fantasy land as far as he was concerned.

Five past eight.

He slid his hand beneath the waistband of his exercise shorts and scratched his grumbling stomach. For as long as he could remember, his days had revolved around an axis of regularity. The whitecoats *always* arrived at seven thirty. So where were they? The morning felt all wrong. He was ravenous. The heavy steel handle on the inside of the lab door remained in its default closed position.

"Sugar?" he called. "Are you awake? Tygre?"

A faint snore drifted from the cage on one side of him. No point in trying to talk to Tygre; he had to be physically shaken awake. Every morning, the tec on duty beat him out of his bed with an inactive shockstick. Sabre-Tooth flinched at the violence. Tygre only yawned, blinked and sleepwalked to his breakfast bowl.

5

"Sugar?" Sabre-Tooth called again.

"Yesss." Her breathy voice came from the cage on his other side. She peered through the window, her small face screwed up in annoyance. "Of course I'm awake. It's late. What do you think's happening? Where is everyone?"

He sat on the edge of his bed. The last time anything changed was five years ago, when the three of them were moved out of their big communal cage into smaller separate ones in a different laboratory. This lab contained a row of wire-fronted cages along one wall. On the opposite wall, separated from the cages by a wide, white-tiled expanse of floor, was the entertainment unit and the labstat panel. Each cage-unit had a bunk, a water-fountain and a private hygiene cubicle at the rear. Sabre-Tooth had the central unit. Standing up, he could see both his companions through the plasglas windows, but he still missed the comfort of curling up to sleep next to their warmth. Since then, breakfast, exercise on the treadmills and lessons filled the mornings, always in the same order, always at the same time. In the afternoon, there were more lessons, and once a week, the physicals. He could do without the physicals, especially the ones where needles stuck into him. It would be nice if the tecs forgot to do those. In the evenings, after the last exercise session, the three of them could watch the entertainment channels on the flatscreen, or read stories on small palmunits. That was the best part of the day. Sabre-Tooth loved stories, especially the ones about adventure and heroism in exotic places. Occasionally he realised he was bored, but the feeling never lasted long. Sugar often complained about boredom. She claimed it would kill her in the end.

"I don't know." He stared at the door, willing it to open. "I'm hungry. I want to get out of here."

The wire front of her cage rattled. "Me too. Do you think—" She gave the bars a final thump as the steel handle swung through a half-circle and the lab door slid silently open. "About time."

Sabre-Tooth pulled his knees up to his chest and wrapped his arms round them, sniffing at the air. No food smells, just the nostril-stinging chemical odour of the corridors.

Two of the whitecoats walked in; Professor Rizzi, the chief scientist, and Tom Chang, one of the senior labtecs. Tom was a frequent visitor, but Sabre-Tooth usually saw the professor in one of the labs, if he saw him at all. He sniffed again. A faint sour smell of man-sweat mixed with other scents. It came from Tom, who stood aside to let two strangers into the room, his shockstick tapping against his leg.

Both strangers wore military uniforms and flat hats; sleeker versions of the soldiers still running across the flatscreen. Both towered over the scientists; one tall, lean and tanned, the other, dark-skinned, dark-eyed and built like one of the cage fighters from the sports vids. Maybe he was the reason Tom stank of fear.

Tom switched off the news and increased the light levels in the cages.

Sugar hissed at him. She hated Tom and his shockstick, almost as much as she hated Rizzi.

Sabre-Tooth flinched, anticipating her punishment, but today Tom ignored her and stepped back to allow the visitors to pass him. The two soldiers scrutinised the interior of the cages, peering through the thick wire on the fronts.

"These are the three you told us about? They've got better quarters than most conscripts." The bulkier one leaned on the door of Sugar's cage, head cocked as he listened to the hostile sound of her hissing. "I like this one. She's lively. A bit small though. Couldn't you have made her bigger?"

Tom smacked the front of Sugar's cage with his shockstick. "Shut up."

She jumped back, her hiss rising to an outraged yowl.

The soldier laughed.

The thinner soldier glanced at Sabre-Tooth, who dropped his eyes. "The big one's a bit quiet."

"That's Sabre-Tooth," Professor Rizzi said. "He's on a low sedative dose to keep him docile. We started him on the regime a couple of years ago when he got a bit troublesome."

"Troublesome? He's aggressive?"

Sabre-Tooth peered through his lashes at the soldier's raised eyebrows. He knew they gave him and Tygre something in their food. He'd known it for years. Whatever it was, it made him not care. It made Tygre sleep all the time.

"He didn't want to go back in the cage. It took three of us to force him. We couldn't have that. Someone might have been hurt." Rizzi dragged a hand through his thinning overlong hair. "It was only teenage tantrums. He's not particularly aggressive. The drugs just make it easier for us. For him too."

Sabre-Tooth remembered, even though it felt like a long time ago. He hadn't wanted to be locked up again. He'd knocked one of the labtecs over, and snarled at the other. A third one arrived and shot him with something. He'd woken up in his cage and since then he was too tired to argue with the tecs.

"He needs to be aggressive," the bulky soldier said. "That was on the list of desirable traits."

Professor Rizzi frowned. "Wait till you've seen what he's like when you stop the sedatives. He'll probably be okay. Physically he's the most mature of the three. They were all started at the same time, seventeen years ago, but they've developed at different rates. Sugar's small and Tygre's still not reached his full growth. It's interesting how—"

"Good names." The lean brown soldier interrupted him.

"One of the labtecs came up with them." Rizzi gave a short snort of laughter. "Or they'd still be called Sample 132 and so on."

"132? How many attempts did it take?" The soldier peered into Tygre's cage. "Is there anything in here?"

Tom banged his stick on the bars. "Come on out, you lazy waste of space."

"He'll be hiding under the bedding. He's useless at the moment and he's slower to mature than the others. All he does is sleep, and the sedatives don't help. He'll grow out of it. Never mind him. This is the one you want." Rizzi pointed at Sabre-Tooth.

Both soldiers joined him in front of the cage, their interest making Sabre-Tooth's skin itch. He hated being watched and turned his back on them, crawling to the back of his bunk to sit cross-legged, facing the white wall of the hygiene cubicle. His ears flicked as he tuned in to the conversation.

"Those are all the chimeras you have?" The soldier with the deeper voice spoke.

"Not all of them. You can look at the others later. These are just the first batch. They're the most advanced ones." Professor Rizzi's footsteps moved closer. "What do you think?"

"Not very friendly, are they?" There was a clank as one of the men kicked at the door of Sabre-Tooth's cage. "And they look human. Except for that one."

The sound of something thudding to the floor, and the subsequent shuffling of feet made Sabre-Tooth's ears twitch as several people moved at once. Tygre's distinctive morning grunt emerged from the next-door cage. He must have woken up at last.

"They're supposed to look human." Annoyance coloured Rizzi's voice. "I did play around a bit with... I just wanted to see what we could do with fine-tuning. I admit we made a small error with Tygre. It was in the DNA splicing. It shouldn't matter. He's fully functional."

Sabre-Tooth had learned to interpret nuances in voices, and Professor Rizzi sounded defensive. Tygre did look different; he had thick tawny fur over parts of his body, though why that should irritate Rizzi was something Sabre-Tooth couldn't understand.

"He's hardly going to fade into the background is he? He won't be much use to us, not looking the way he does." The soldier's footsteps moved away.

"Regimental mascot?" The other soldier sniggered.

Sabre-Tooth squirmed round as Tom opened the door. The visitors moved towards it.

"I suppose, in that sense, Tygre's a failed experiment. On the other hand, I think he'll come in very useful as a control and baseline." Professor Rizzi ushered the soldiers out of the room. "Your commander specified only one specimen in the first instance, so Tygre and Sugar are extras. You'll take him tomorrow?"

"Commander Diessen will decide. He couldn't make it today."

The voices disappeared as Tom followed the rest of the group, sealing the door behind him.

"What was all that about?" Sugar asked. "Who were those soldiers?"

"I don't know. They were talking about us though."

"I didn't like them."

"You don't like anyone," Sabre-Tooth pointed out.

"What's happening?" Tygre's lisp sounded half-asleep. "I'm hungry."

"We're all hungry," Sugar said.

Ten minutes later Rashelle, the lab manager, arrived with breakfast and, after that, the day progressed as usual but Sabre-Tooth couldn't shake off the sense that something bad was going to happen.

At twenty o'clock, when the security guards came round, Sugar jumped off her bed and leaned against the front of her cage. "Do you know who those men were today? The ones in uniform?"

Sabre-Tooth dragged his attention from his palmunit digi-book and the world of outer space, propping himself up on his elbows to watch. Sugar was a shameless manipulator.

Frank, the guard with no hair and a tattooed face, liked her. He told her she was sweet, cute, a precious kitten, and would often stop to chat. He never bothered with Tygre or Sabre-Tooth.

"They must have been those DFD blokes," he said. "Alliance Military pays for this place. They've been here before haven't they?"

"DFD?"

"Department for Defence," Frank said.

"I know that, but I've never seen them before? Why were they here?" She could be persistent when she wanted something.

"No idea." Frank yawned. "I'm just a hired grunt. Look kitty, I've got something for you." He reached through the bars to hand Sugar a small piece of chocolate.

"Thanks." She peeled the covering off and sniffed at it.

Sabre-Tooth's nostrils twitched. Chocolate was a rare treat.

"They were soldiers weren't they?" Sugar said. "Do they shoot people?"

"What on earth…?" Frank glanced at the violence showing on the flatscreen. All three of them liked action films, but Sugar loved stories of war. "They're not going to shoot you, kitten. That's all you need to worry about. You shouldn't watch that sort of rubbish."

"I'm not worried." Sugar sucked the melting chocolate off her fingers. "I just want to know what they wanted with Sabe and Tyg. And why's Tyg a baseline?"

Frank's smile faded. "I don't know anything about that. Enjoy the chocolate. I've got work to do." He disappeared, locking the door behind him.

Sugar broke the chocolate into three, handing two pieces through the bars to Sabre-Tooth. "I don't like it when I don't know what's going on."

Sabre-Tooth passed one of the squares to Tygre. "Me neither."

Dissension – the campaign against injustice

June 8th 2452

India's punishing heatwaves and cataclysmic storms threaten the lives of many of its citizens. Refugees, fleeing the continent via the northwest boundary, find their escape blocked by the border guards of the Eurasian Alliance. Many are murdered by Alliance troops, while the majority are sent back to almost certain death. There have been no protests from the Indian authorities.

Journalists from Dissension have interviewed reliable witnesses of this politically sanctioned massacre and believe that their stories are true. There is no doubt amongst right-thinking people that this is deliberate extermination of a vulnerable populace, and a form of genocide. We, the members of Dissension, will resist such inhuman Alliance policies to our last breaths. Our legal representatives are in close discussion with the ruling council as to the lawfulness of its actions.

ALLIANCE NEWS CORP – keeping you informed

June 8th, 2452.
News Update – London Division

Socia

The New British Island's King, Valerio Stuart I, escorted consort, Liljas Oroz-Stuart, to a performance of traditional Chinese dance theatre yesterday evening. The consort wore a cloak of faux feathers in blush pink, work of London designer, Sen Watson. Afterwards, the royal couple attended a reception held in honour of the highly regarded dance company. Increased security personnel patrolled the streets of central London. Chief Civilian Enforcer, Commander Ludwig Turle, told News Corps, that the patrols were a formality and a courtesy to the King. 'There is no escalation in the threat of criminal, or terrorist, activity,' he claimed.

~~~

Science

Today, Alliance Chief Scientist, Odin Mishurin, released up to date information on the completed first dome on Mars. The dome is now sealed and independently viable. Nearly nine thousand individuals make their home under its protection. Four hundred genetically engineered pansy constructs support the external labour and maintenance teams. A mock holo-construction can be viewed in the National Museum in New Beijing, where a series of lectures is planned for the coming year. Sifia Hong sends her congratulations to the exploratory teams and is considering names for the new settlement. She told News Corps journalists 'This first successful colony, outside Earth, strengthens the ability of the human race to survive any challenges the natural world can throw at it.'

Chapter 2

The morning after the soldiers' visit, the alarm sounded as usual. Sabre-Tooth pulled on his exercise shorts and knelt at the end of his bed, eyes fixed on the door.

At seven thirty, one of the junior labtecs brought his breakfast of toasted oatmeal, vegiprotein and mixed nuts. Afterwards, the labtec removed the empty bowl and disappeared again. Normally all three of them would have an hour of lessons and then exercise on the treadmill.

"Something's definitely going on," Sugar said.

"I know. I wish they'd tell us." The lab staff never told them anything, just instructed and ordered, and pushed them about.

"Do you ever wonder why they do this to us? Why we have to live in cages?" Sugar jumped off her bunk and leaned against the barrier between her cage and Sabre-Tooth's, small face pressed against the plasglas. Her energy radiated through the room, making Sabre-Tooth tired. "No one on the vids lives like this. They aren't locked up."

"I suppose not." Thinking about the things he was meant to think about was hard enough. The lessons in maths, history, politics, citizenship and geography filled his brain. If he didn't concentrate on those, he was punished with the shockstick. He rarely bothered with things he didn't need to know. Too much rumination made his head ache.

Sugar sniffed. "Normal people don't live like this. Only criminals." She nodded her head towards the flatscreen, where a political trial was the major news story of the day. "Like them."

"We're not criminals." He shifted so he could see her through the cage's window.

She rolled her eyes. "I know that. So why…? Oh never mind."

Sugar's curiosity hadn't been dampened by drugs. Sabre-Tooth had heard one of the labtecs tell another that the pharma aids wouldn't work on her. The one time they'd tried, she'd convulsed and passed out. Professor Rizzi had discontinued the programme. Her aggression wasn't dampened down either. She might be the smallest of the three of them, but the labtecs took more care around her than they did with him or Tygre. Sugar was fierce and he loved her for it.

Eventually Tygre, who had crawled back under his blanket after eating, emerged from his bunk and jumped down to the front of his cage. He would have slept for twenty-three out of twenty-four hours if he'd been allowed. He clutched the mesh with clawed hands and rested his face against it. Tygre was as averse to change as Sabre-Tooth. "Why haven't they come?"

"You keen to run?" Sugar asked.

Tygre growled. He hated the forced exercise.

Sugar climbed back onto her bunk and huddled in the centre, dressed in her exercise singlet, pointed chin resting on her bent knees. Her shock of tawny hair covered her eyes. "Why has everyone disappeared this morning?" She sounded as though she was talking to herself.

Sabre-Tooth shifted his attention to the flatscreen, where a news presenter interviewed one of the ten governing Councillors of the British Islands about the political trial and its implications. "I don't know."

A frisson of unease rippled down his spine. He shivered and focussed on the news vid. The Councillor had disappeared, and now images of a swollen Thames alternated with those of a flooded housing complex. The presenter, who stood on the deck of a small boat on the river, spoke earnestly about rising water levels, future-proofing the city, and a possible relocation of London.

I wonder what it's really like out there. The thought passed through his mind and floated away.

"I think it must be something to do with the people who were here yesterday," Sugar said. "What else could it be?"

The presenter disappeared and a female vid star took his place, twirling in a circle to display the new season fashions. It was hard to believe people actually wore garments like the ankle-length feathery thing dominating the screen. Sabre-Tooth tugged at the waistband of his shorts.

"Sabe?" Sugar's voice rose impatiently. "Will you stop staring at that and talk to me?"

At nine o'clock, the door leading into the lab finally opened and Professor Rizzi walked through, accompanied by the two senior tecs, Tom and Rashelle. Rizzi wasn't wearing his usual white coat; instead, he was dressed formally, in a dark skinsuit and a loose jacket, with his thin black hair slicked back from his face. He keyed in the door code and gestured to his assistants.

Rashelle pulled her goad from the belt of her white coverall and pointed at Sabre-Tooth. "Out."

All three doors slid open.

She lifted her shockstick, holding it at a threatening angle. "Just Sabre-Tooth. You two stand back."

Sugar ignored her and pushed ahead of Sabre-Tooth. She stared up at Professor Rizzi from a safe distance. "What's going on? Why do you want Sabe?" Her upper lip curled, revealing her tiny fangs.

Rashelle aimed the goad at her. "Did you hear what I just said?"

Sugar backed away, almost bumping into Tom. Her hostility scented the air, bringing goose-bumps to Sabre-Tooth's bare arms. She hated Rashelle the most out of all the staff. Rashelle returned the dislike with interest. The scar on her cheek came from Sugar's claws and stretched from under her short dark fringe to the corner of her mouth. Instead of having it removed, she'd had it cosmetically enhanced, so that now it was a metallic gold flash, bisecting her cocoa-brown skin. Sabre-Tooth thought it looked good. Rashelle looked good. She was horrible, but sometimes he couldn't help thinking about her.

Once Sugar retreated to the door of her cage, Rashelle beckoned to Sabre-Tooth. "Come on you, don't keep me waiting."

He shuffled forward slowly, reluctant to leave the safety of the cage. The feeling that something bad might happen hadn't gone away. With one eye on the goad, he edged past Rashelle, who could be trigger-happy. Her strong chemical perfume filled his nostrils. He sneezed. Rashelle's reality had a tendency to ruin all his fantasies about her.

"Get her back in the cage." Professor Rizzi pointed at Sugar, before turning to the door. "And Tom, make sure it's locked. We don't want any problems today. Get someone down to fix it as well. All three shouldn't open at once. Hurry up. We've got a lot to get through this morning."

Rashelle ushered Sabre-Tooth out of the room. He dragged his feet, turning back to look at Tygre and Sugar, who remained at the front of their cages, faces pressed to the wire.

The door slammed, cutting off his view of them.

Tom followed him into the corridor and shoved him forwards, cuffing him across one ear before pushing him ahead, out of the way, as he caught up to his colleagues. "Move."

They took him along a passageway, through another security door, and into a room he'd never seen before. He tensed on the threshold, relaxing when he saw it wasn't a laboratory. Needles, injections, blood-sampling, skin biopsies and tissue extractions happened in laboratories. Often the whitecoats locked him into a chair and hurt him.

This room was colourful, not white and monochrome like the labs. It had a wooden desk, dark shelving around the walls and a strange sort of clock, like something out of an old story vid. Regular clicking sounds came from it and parts of it moved. He inched forward, fascinated. It was taller than he was and, for a moment, he forgot his fear, reaching out with one finger to touch the circular face.

Tom tapped him with the goad. He jumped away from the clock, expecting the punishing pain, but the goad was inactive.

The sound of a cough dragged his attention back to the room's occupants. A soldier, not one of the ones from yesterday, sat behind the desk, illuminated by a bright, floor-standing lamp at his shoulder. His fingers tapped impatiently on the desk's surface. Rows of medals decorated the front of his black uniform. He had no hat, no hair, very little neck and a mean mouth at the bottom of a round red face. Rising to his feet, he crossed to the front of the desk and slowly circled Sabre-Tooth, coming to a halt directly in front of him.

He rubbed one hand over his chin. "This is it, Professor Rizzi? Eighteen years work?"

Sabre-Tooth squirmed as narrow grey eyes assessed him. The soldier's bulk invaded his personal space, flooding the air with the scent of chemical hygiene products, smoke and the lingering sweetness of fruit. He rubbed his nose.

"Longer than that, if you count all the prep work. It's the most advanced experiment." The professor took hold of Sabre-Tooth's upper arm, pulling it straight. He shifted his grip to the wrist. "You can see the improved musculature. And he's got the claws and teeth as well as enhanced vision. He's a work of art."

"Show me." The soldier wrapped his hand around the biceps muscle, squeezing to the point of discomfort. "He's a bit skinny, isn't he? Puny?"

Sabre-Tooth hissed and stepped backwards, shaking the man off.

"He's still growing. He'll fill out. You can see his potential already." Rizzi's voice rose in command. "Sabre-Tooth? Show Commander Diessen your teeth."

Sabre-Tooth eyed Rashelle's goad and lifted his upper lip.

"Nice." The soldier touched a finger to one fang. "I can see why he got his name."

Sabre-Tooth pulled away, closing his mouth. He ran his tongue over his teeth, ridding himself of the flavour of soldier.

Professor Rizzi released his wrist. "Let the commander see your claws."

Sabre-Tooth obediently flexed his fingers, revealing sharply curved claws, which glistened, oyster pale, in the light from the floor-lamp.

"Is he dangerous?"

"He's sedated slightly. He's not aggressive anyway." Rizzi shook his head. "Your problem's going to be toughening him up."

"He'll toughen up if he wants to stay alive." Diessen's eyes narrowed. "And what do you mean, he's not aggressive? Wasn't that our number one requirement?"

"Yes. But…"

"Don't bother with excuses." Diessen barrelled into Professor Rizzi's personal space and jabbed a forefinger into his chest. "We'll see what he's like when the drugs wear off. He'd better be as good as you claim."

Sabre-Tooth shifted his attention from Rizzi to Diessen, unsure what was happening.

"We've got a collar for him." The shake in Rizzi's voice was almost imperceptible.

Sabre-Tooth's ears twitched. Why was the professor nervous? He was in charge, wasn't he?

"It'll keep track of his whereabouts once you let him out. It's also active, so you can use it to punish him, even kill him if necessary."

Sabre-Tooth's gaze jerked back to Rizzi. The conversation felt unreal.

"Not a chip?" Diessen asked. "It would be less visible. We don't want him looking like a convict."

"No. You wouldn't get the killing power in something that small. Not yet anyway, and not if you want fine control."

Killing power? Sabre-Tooth shuffled his feet, flexing claws inside the running shoes he wore. He'd wanted out of the cage. Now he just wanted to go back. To Sugar and Tygre and safety. Why would anyone want to kill him? His heartbeat pounded in his ears.

"Right." Diessen nodded impatiently. "Let's get on with it."

Professor Rizzi turned to Rashelle who handed him a silver metallic strip. "This is the control collar. It's simple to use." He walked towards Sabre Tooth, who backed away until the wall pressed against his spine, halting his retreat.

"Rashelle?" Rizzi nodded at his assistant, who came over and lifted the goad.

Sabre-Tooth froze.

"Keep still and I won't have to hurt you." She moved the stick a fraction.

He held himself as stationary as possible, heart banging against his ribs. Rashelle liked to use the stick.

Rizzi fastened the metal strip around his neck. The ends clicked into place. "It's locked." He picked up a small laser pointer. "Press this button and it releases the collar seal."

Diessen peered at it. "What's this button do?"

"That gives him an electric shock. You can use it for training."

"Show me."

Sabre-Tooth flattened himself against the wall.

"Jesus, Rizzi. He doesn't look much. I hope you haven't wasted our money."

Professor Rizzi pressed the button.

The room exploded in bright pain.

Sabre-Tooth sprawled on the floor, retching in the aftermath. The shock had been a hundred times worse than anything he'd ever felt from the shocksticks. He pulled himself to his knees, whimpering in distress. He'd done nothing wrong. Why had they hurt him?

"Bit of a pussy isn't he?" Diessen's voice held amusement. "The gadget seems to work though. What's this red button?"

"That's the destruct button," Rizzi said. "If you have to terminate him, that's the one you press. It's disabled at the moment, in case you touch it by accident. You'll need to reset it from a comm. I'll show you how before you go, but I'd advise you to keep it inactive. Accidents happen."

"I've seen these things before," Diessen said. "We use them on dangerous prisoners."

Professor Rizzi nudged Sabre-Tooth with one foot. "Sabre-Tooth?"

Sabre-Tooth kept his head down, rolling his eyes up to look at the professor. His arms and legs spasmed with remembered pain.

"You'll do as you're told. This collar has a long distance detector. Wherever you go, you'll be tracked, so if you annoy your handlers you'll be punished. Even if you're miles away."

Sabre-Tooth crouched lower. Nausea still cramped his stomach and flashes of light played behind his eyes. He knew what words like kill and destroy meant, but it was hard to apply them to himself. His breath came in pants; fast and shallow. The collar was strangling him.

"Do you understand?"

"Yes." Sabre-Tooth squeezed his eyes closed.

"Does he really understand?" Diessen asked.

"He's pretty bright," Professor Rizzi said. "They all are. We've educated them along standard government guidelines and he's in the top percentile of intellectual ability. All our chimeras are. He's just led a limited life and as I said, he's on sedatives. You'll have no problem training him."

Sabre-Tooth opened his eyes. The flashes on the edges of his peripheral vision grew dimmer; red instead of diamond white. He risked another glance upwards through his lashes. The professor's narrow tanned face and the soldier's big red one filled his view.

"Not with that as a motivation." Diessen nodded at the collar.

"Don't use it too much. It can cause nerve problems and Sabre-Tooth's an expensive creation. Years of work went into making him." Professor Rizzi moved away. "You don't want to damage him unless you have to. Rashelle, clean that up, would you?" He gestured at the thin puddle of vomit. "And give Sabre-Tooth some anti-nausea pills before he goes. Commander Diessen won't want him messing up the back of his transport."

"Right. Better get him loaded." Commander Diessen walked over to where Sabre-Tooth crouched on the floor and kicked him in the side. "On your feet. You're a soldier now. Act like one."

Sabre-Tooth wriggled away from Diessen's boot and pushed himself upright. His legs didn't want to support him. Raising one hand, he sucked hard on his knuckles.

"We stopped his sedation programme last night. He might have some adverse reactions from the withdrawal." Professor Rizzi examined Sabre-Tooth, who averted his eyes and stared at the floor. "Tomorrow or maybe the next day. Watch out for mood swings and other potential side-effects. They'll only last a day or two, but they might be unpleasant."

ALLIANCE NEWS CORP – *keeping you informed*

June 8th 2452
Recruitment advert

A Call to Arms

The Alliance Military divisions are the biggest employers in our group of nations. Recruitment levels for the army are at their highest in decades, and a career in the armed services is a sure fire way for any citizen, or even non-citizen, to improve his or her standing in the hierarchy of Alliance society.

Opportunities abound for YOU!
You lack citizenship?
Enlist as a soldier cadet.
Do it NOW!

'Two years of service will put you on the rung to Level One registration as a bona fide, benefit-earning citizen'
– General Henry Myerton. The army is an honourable and fulfilling career for those with limited options.

Protect your borders. Police your cities
Keep your people safe. Patrol your environmental resources.
Become a Hero of the Alliance!
What are you waiting for?
APPLY NOW!

Chapter 3

The quiet hissing of the engines died as the transport slowed and came to a halt.

Sabre-Tooth huddled in the darkness, still clutching the strap on the vehicle's side, his blood racing. He didn't know how much time had passed since they'd taken him to the basement garage and pushed him into the back of the armoured groundtran. It felt like days. His joints ached and his muscles squirmed under his skin from the aftermath of the punishment collar. He'd fallen against the edges of the vehicle as it hurtled along so his right hip throbbed where he'd landed on it. He hummed to himself, in an effort to drown out the discomfort.

The rear door slid open with a screech, sending his pulse rate sky high. He squinted into the electrifying brightness as his enhanced eyes quickly adjusted.

"Come on." Commander Diessen stood, feet apart, a wide shadow outline in the sunlight. "Out with you. And stop that fucking awful noise."

Heaving out a shaky breath, glad that the loud rattle and shudder of the journey had stopped, Sabre-Tooth rose to his feet, testing his legs.

"Move."

The loud voice irritated his ears. He edged towards the door, rubbing them.

"Hurry up."

He jumped down from the back of the groundtran, blinking in the natural light.

Outside.

His misery dropped away, overwhelmed by a tidal wave of new sensations. The air was warm and heavy, the fresh smell completely different from the stinging odours of his old home. He could barely believe he was truly outside. Secretly he'd wondered whether the outside existed anywhere but on the vids. The unfamiliarity of his surroundings rooted him to the ground.

Commander Diessen's voice continued to babble away in the background. Sabre-Tooth tuned it out. Everything was so much sharper than he was used to. He took a deep breath, savouring the unfamiliar scents, and turned his head to stare across the flat expanse of plascrete to the hills rising beyond the perimeter.

The world was green, even greener than on the vids. A hundred different greens.

High wire fences kept the encroaching woodland from spreading over the cleared area. All around him, chirps, warbles and high-pitched piping sounds mixed with the rustle of the trees on the slopes.

Bird noises. Birds singing.

Something small and brown flew from a patch of shrubs on the other side of the wire. His eyes followed its path, until it disappeared into the tangled branches of a small tree. The sky was a clear blue, the colour reflected in puddles on the ground. He concentrated on them, wondering how the water had got there. It must have rained. He took a deep breath, linking what he'd seen on the vids with this new reality.

Behind him, tall plascrete walls loomed, dwarfing the narrow gate his transport must have passed through.

Outside.

He began to hum again.

Diessen smacked him hard across the back of his head. "You'll have plenty of time to gawp later. And I told you to shut up."

Sabre-Tooth curled his upper lip to reveal his fangs. He rubbed his scalp.

Diessen's thin lips stretched into a smile and he fingered the control for the collar. "Do you know how to obey orders?"

"What?" Sabre-Tooth focussed on Diessen's stubby fingers. He closed his mouth.

Diessen sighed. "I can see there's a lot of work to be done with you. You'd better be as bright as Rizzi claims." He tossed the collar control in the air, and caught it again.

"What are you going to do with me?" The movement of the torture device in Diessen's hands mesmerised him.

"Make you into a soldier. All you need to know at the moment is that you obey your superiors instantly."

"Me? A soldier?"

"Do as you are told and you'll be alright. Deliberate disobedience will be punished. I don't think you want that, do you?"

"No." The collar pain was the worst thing that had ever happened to him. His throat constricted at the thought of it hitting him again.

"You address me as 'Sir'." Diessen gestured as a man in camouflage printed coveralls approached. "Corporal Obi will take you to your quarters. He's your immediate superior. You call him 'Sir' too. Do exactly as he tells you and you'll be fine."

Sabre-Tooth sneaked a quick glance at the man, who gazed back at him with cold flat eyes. He was one of the soldiers who'd visited the lab yesterday. The big muscular one.

"You are dismissed." Diessen waited.

Sabre-Tooth shuffled his feet.

"The correct response is 'Yes, Sir'."

"Well, say it." Corporal Obi leaned forward, snapping the words into his face.

"Yes Sir," Sabre-Tooth muttered, edging away.

Diessen spun on his heel and marched off, disappearing through a door in one of the walls. Sabre-Tooth took a step after him; he didn't want to be left alone here, without Sugar and Tygre. He might have wanted to get out of his cage; he might have wanted his freedom.

19

Not like this though. This wasn't real freedom. Diessen was scary, but he was the most familiar thing around.

"Where do you think you're going?" Obi stepped in front of him.

Sabre-tooth froze. "Nowhere."

"Nowhere, Sir. Say it." Spittle sprayed over his face.

"Nowhere, Sir." He repeated the words.

"Don't stand gawking." Obi punched him in the arm. "Follow me."

Sabre-Tooth rubbed his arm, not understanding what he'd done wrong.

"What do you say?"

"Yes, Sir."

"Quick learner, eh?"

He jogged ahead of the soldier, across the plascrete to a long single storey building. Obi pushed him through an open door, into the dim interior, where a corridor stretched from the entrance to another door at the opposite end. More doors lined the sides of the passage, some slightly ajar, most closed.

"Lucky you. You get your own cubi-unit." Obi opened one of the doors, shoving him into a small space. "You'll be training with three other cadets, two men and a woman. The other men share. They're seasoned veterans and normal."

Sabre-Tooth wrinkled his brow.

"You'll find a uniform in there." Obi pointed to a cupboard. "Change into it. You can't go around like that." His gaze raked Sabre-Tooth from head to toe, taking in his exercise shorts, lingering on his naked chest and finally resting somewhere around waist level.

Sabre-Tooth scratched his bare stomach nervously. People looked at him a lot; the scientists photographed him, weighed him, stuck needles in him and measured everything about him. It was familiar and had never made him feel more than slightly irritated. This soldier made him feel as if he was doing something wrong.

"Yes Sir," he said.

"Good." The soldier grimaced. "Your name's Sabre-Tooth?"

"Yes."

"Yes, Sir."

"Yes, Sir." Sabre-Tooth scraped at the bare floor with one foot and stared at his training shoes. All this 'sirring' was a stupid waste of breath. Sugar would have told them so, but he wasn't like Sugar.

"Good name for a soldier." Corporal Obi said.

"What?" He glanced up. "Sir."

"Are you stupid?" Obi patted him on the cheek, hard enough to sting. "I hope not, for your sake. I'll be back to collect you in an hour. Make sure you're in uniform."

Sabre-Tooth stared at him.

Obi's eyes narrowed and he shook his head. "How long do you think you'll last in the army?"

"I don't know, Sir."

"I give you three months," Obi said, "and that's because the commander wants you. I can't see you making it past September."

Obi marched away, leaving Sabre-Tooth alone in the entrance to his new quarters. To his amazement, they hadn't locked the door, just left it ajar. Lifting his hand, he touched the collar, realising he couldn't go anywhere while he was wearing it.

The room was almost as tiny as his cage at the lab, with just enough space for a single bunk, a small desk with a communit, and the clothes cupboard. Inside, the air was still and warm, even hotter than it had been outside. The lab cages had always been kept at the same temperature, one that was much lower than this. Sabre-Tooth wiped a bead of moisture from his forehead, unsure how he felt about the heat. Behind the bed, an open window looked out onto the outside world, framing a patch of sky. A faint breeze brushed his skin. Climbing onto the bed, he rested his elbows on the sill and leaned out, gazing across the expanse of the square.

Directly opposite, beyond the wire fencing and the plascrete walls, rough pasture sloped gently to the foot of a hill, where the grass turned into scrub and woodland. The sky was blue and the sun shone, creating a dark shadow-net from the fence. The fierce light forced him to squeeze his eyes closed until he could focus again. All the colours were brighter than he'd ever seen. He hung out of the window, looking from side to side, letting the warmth caress his bare shoulders. A small group of single storey, black buildings clustered on one side of the square and, on the opposite side, high wire fencing enclosed a flat grey field.

So many shades and colours. Real daylight was different from the lab's 'natural light'. The damp warmth of the day soaked into his skin, filling him with a pleasurable languor. He definitely liked the heat. The air was a complex mixture of intriguing smells.

What would Sugar and Tygre be doing now? Had they realised that he'd gone yet?

Several men marched past, dressed in the same camouflaged coveralls as his soldier escort, and it occurred to him that he wasn't sure how long an hour was. The lab clock, on the wall opposite his cage, had measured out his day without him having to think about it. He looked around the tiny room to see if there was one here.

There wasn't. He examined the communit, but the activation button was locked and the screen dark.

He opened the cupboard. Three piles of clothing lay on one of the shelves and two thin towels on another. Each set of clothes looked identical. He shook out the nearest, finding a dull green all-in-one coverall, padded socks, underwear, a belt with lots of loops and a pair of ankle length boots. It took him a few minutes to work out exactly what went where, but eventually he felt he was satisfactorily dressed in the military garment. Tugging the belt into position, he knelt on the bunk to wait, gazing out of the window and flexing his toes in the unfamiliar boots. He stroked one hand down his new uniform, wondering if he looked anything like the soldiers in the vids.

No one came.

He turned from the window to stare at the open door. They'd have locked it if they'd wanted him to stay in the room, or at least closed it. Outside siren-called to him. He rose to his feet and tiptoed into the corridor.

The sound of a closing door, and approaching footsteps registered at the back of his consciousness.

"Hey."

Sabre-Tooth snapped out of his trance, and shot back into his room, to perch on the edge of his bunk.

Two strangers loomed in the doorway; both male, both almost as young as he was, and both dressed in similar clothes to the ones he wore. One was as tall as him, the other shorter and wiry. Their attitude screamed confidence and arrogance, just like the vid soldiers. The tall blonde one propped a shoulder on the doorframe, blocking the exit. The other, whose dark head was covered in darker stubble, squeezed past into the room. Both looked cool and dangerous in their military green. Sabre-Tooth flexed his fingers nervously.

"Shit. Are those real?" The dark stranger stared down.

"Real?" Sabre-Tooth made a conscious effort to retract his claws.

"Did you grow them, or are they cosmetic?" Dark Hair's eyes widened as the claws disappeared beneath their nailbeds. "Not cosmetic. What the hell are you?"

"I'm Sabre-Tooth." He wondered whether he needed to call these people 'Sir'.

"Cool name, wrong answer." The taller man edged into the room. "Not who are you. What are you?"

Sabre-Tooth scrunched up his forehead. "I don't know what you mean."

He had met more strangers in one day than he usually saw in months, and spoken to most of them. Not many of the lab visitors ever bothered to talk to him. Sugar was the chatterer in their little group and neither Tygre nor Sabre-Tooth had felt much need to converse when she was there to do it for them.

"You're fucking weird. Or stupid. Both I should think." The man sat in the chair by the desk, twisting sideways to face the bed and stretching long legs out in front of him. He bared his teeth in a wide artificial smile, before raising one hand and pointing to his mouth. "Flat teeth." He jabbed his finger at Sabre-Tooth's face. "Pointed. And you've got animal eyes. You're an animal, aren't you?"

Sabre-Tooth lifted one hand and touched his needle-like canines.

"See," Blonde Man said. "And your ears are all wrong. What the hell are you?"

He rubbed his ear. It lay flat to his head, just like the stranger's. It was pointed and covered in fine hair, but it wasn't that different. Anyway, Blonde Man's eyes were just as weird as his; a blue so light they were almost colourless. As far as Sabre-Tooth was concerned, they were more wrong than his. He decided not to say so.

"Come on. Deviant? Mutant?" Blonde man's unblinking eyes were scary. "Some sort of construct?"

"They called me a chimera. Back in the lab."

"A chimera? You mean like a cross-breed? Or a mongrel? Obi said you'd be different. He didn't say you were a fucking mongrel." The short, dark-haired man reached out and twisted the pointed tip of Sabre-Tooth's ear until it hurt. He made a noise of disgust. "It's hairy."

Sabre-Tooth jerked his head away."

"Well?" Dark Hair persisted. "Are you too stupid to know? You're a mongrel aren't you?"

"I suppose so."

"Hey, Laszlo? It's a mongrel." Dark Hair's tone made 'mongrel' sound like a bad word.

Blonde Man dug his hands into the pockets of his coverall and leaned back in his chair. "You were made in a lab? Cool. I thought that was banned."

"Didn't you hear me? We'll be working with a fucking mongrel. Sleeping in the same place as a mongrel. It should be in a kennel, not living with civilised people."

"Cool," Blonde Man said again. He smirked at Dark Hair.

"Cool?" Dark Hair reached for Sabre-Tooth's ear again. "It's fucked up, is what it is."

"What do you mean?" Sabre-Tooth wrinkled his forehead as he automatically dodged the grabbing fingers. "I lived in—"

"Never mind," Dark Hair interrupted him. "We all know the army doesn't have much use for the law."

"Let me guess." Blonde Man narrowed his eyes. "Claws? Fangs? Pointed ears? Half cat?"

"Can't be half," Dark Hair said. "He might be a mongrel but he looks almost human. If he kept his mouth shut and wore lenses and a hat, you wouldn't be able to tell." He reached forward and roughly rubbed Sabre-Tooth's head, pushing it to one side. "Do you purr?"

Sabre-Tooth hissed, his attention moving from one to the other. He couldn't keep up with what they were saying. His claws were fully extended. They'd come out all by themselves and he hid his hands behind his back. If he'd shown any aggression in the past, he was usually punished with a blow from a shockstick. Some of the labtecs had been just as horrible as these strangers, but they hadn't lasted long once Professor Rizzi found out they abused his experiments.

"Looks like you don't." Dark Hair tugged hard on his ear again.

Sabre-Tooth jumped to his feet and edged away. Blonde Man's extended legs blocked his way.

"You're a pussy." Dark Hair sniggered. "Moggie, not mongrel."

"We'll be training together." Blonde Man examined Sabre-Tooth again. "I'm called Laszlo." He reached around Dark Hair and held out his hand.

Sabre-Tooth had seen people shake hands before. He gingerly took the offered hand.

"Wow." Laszlo grasped his hand, turning it palm upward. His voice was wistful. "Claws. What I could do with claws."

"You don't do so bad without them," Dark Hair muttered.

Sabre-Tooth made another effort to retract his claws. Rashelle smacked his hands with the live goad if she saw them. Rashelle was mean, but at least she was familiar. He felt a pang of longing for Sugar and Tygre.

"I'm Cyrus." Dark Hair gave up trying to grab at him and moved backwards.

Sabre-Tooth exhaled in relief. Dark Hair confused him; his instincts hovered between retaliation and wanting to run for cover.

"So you were brought up in a lab?" Cyrus rubbed a hand over his cropped, wiry hair. "Where was it?"

"I don't—" Sabre-Tooth was about to answer when the stamp of heavy feet distracted his audience.

Dissension – the struggle against injustice

June 8th 2452

A new independent study suggests that less than ten percent of bottom level military recruits leave the army with their promised citizenship. Many recruits never leave, the vast majority dying in action or from the consequences of exposure to chemical or radiation hazards. Entry-level cadets perform the most dangerous and unpleasant jobs existing in our developing society. Only the lucky or the skilled survive long enough to take the first step towards citizenship. Only the lucky or the skilled achieve postings that enable them to progress.

Desertion levels are at their highest on record. This is a travesty and a betrayal of the less advantaged members of the populace. Dissension urges the Alliance Council to tackle this unjust and worrying issue.

Safety for our soldiers must become a priority. It is unacceptable to treat them as disposable assets. More legal protection exists for the common ground beetle than for non-citizens. This situation must change.

Chapter 4

"Out, now, all of you." Corporal Obi halted outside the door, his bellow echoing off the opposite wall.

Sabre-Tooth flinched at the assault on his ears, but followed the example of Laszlo and Cyrus who exited into the corridor where Obi waited. A woman stood to attention against the wall, dressed in a similar coverall to the one that Sabre-Tooth wore. She appeared tiny next to Obi, so was probably of medium height, thin and sallow-skinned. Her hair was glossy black, short and straight, and her eyes suggested that East Asia figured somewhere in her ancestry.

"March." Obi snapped the words out.

"Yes Sir." The two men answered instantly, and Sabre-Tooth chimed in a second later, not wanting to make the corporal angry.

All four marched down the corridor, into the brilliant sunlight. Sabre-Tooth slowed, turning his face up to the sun again. Clouds had begun to form, casting darker patterns on the dark plascrete. The light slipping through was still bright.

Obi halted. "You." He pointed at Sabre-Tooth. "Keep up. Are you trying to annoy me?"

"No Sir."

"I'll be watching you." Swinging round, he led them across the compound to another building and into a square dining room where groups of men and women, dressed in either green military coveralls or camouflage skinsuits, sat at long tables, eating and talking. Sabre-Tooth had never seen so many people before, all in one place. A cacophony of noise filled the space. He sniffed, realising how hungry he was. It must be much later than his usual lunchtime.

Obi shoved his shoulder hard. "Don't dawdle."

Sabre-Tooth stumbled. He hurried after the other three, watching them carefully, copying their actions. He didn't want Corporal Obi to shout at him again.

After picking up trays of food from the counter, they carried them to an empty table and sat down, Sabre-Tooth at the end, with Laszlo on one side and the woman on the other. Cyrus sat next to her. Obi took the seat opposite him. The food smelled very similar to the vegetable protein stews he'd eaten in the lab.

"Same old shit," Cyrus muttered to Laszlo, poking at his meal with a spoon.

Corporal Obi gave him a sharp look and he subsided into silence, clearing his plate with no more complaints. Laszlo finished his portion before leaning back to stare at the woman. After giving him a dismissive glance, she ignored him.

When everyone had finished eating, Obi escorted them to a large room with a sloping floor and tiered rows of seats. "Wait there." He disappeared back through the door.

The room was empty of other people. Cyrus and Laszlo squeezed along the front row to the seats in the centre. Sabre-Tooth followed them. The woman made her way along the row behind.

Cyrus twisted in his seat to face her. "I'm Cyrus."

Sabre-Tooth turned his head as the woman nodded.

"You?" Cyrus waited.

"My name's Tessis." She was young, younger than Rashelle, and her dark hair was short enough to make her eyes and cheekbones stand out. She still looked hungry.

"Regular army?"

She shook her head. "Not anymore."

"How long—"

The door to the theatre slid open. Cyrus stopped in the middle of his sentence as Corporal Obi strode into the room, followed by the other soldier who'd visited the lab.

"There's just the four of us," Cyrus muttered to Laszlo. "I wonder why. I thought there'd be more." He and Laszlo stood up, slowly followed by Tessis, then Sabre-Tooth a second behind the others.

The second soldier leaned towards Obi, muttering in a low voice. "Eighteen years of research? For that? Rizzi's asking to get his funding cut."

Sabre-Tooth frowned. It didn't look like the other three had heard.

Obi glanced at the front row, his mouth tilting in a small grin.

"Bloody scientists," the second soldier continued. He stepped to the front of the platform. "My name's Sergeant Murkhal. I'm in charge of your training. You can sit down now."

They sat.

Sabre-Tooth scratched his shoulder absently. The new clothes irritated his skin.

"This is a Military Intelligence training site," Murkhal said. "Proficiency Enhancement Camp 1, where you'll be trained in skills useful in your new roles. Three of you have some experience with the army, so you know the basics. However, you've all got a lot to learn, you've all screwed up, so you've all been reassigned to cadet level."

Next to Sabre-tooth, Cyrus muttered, "Another bloody demotion."

"Did you have something to say, Cadet?" Murkhal frowned at him.

"No Sir."

"Good. Keep it that way."

Sabre-Tooth missed the next few words. He mulled over what he had just heard.

Military Intelligence?

He hoped he wouldn't have to shoot anyone. He hoped no one would shoot him. Scratching his thigh, he sneaked a sideways look at Cyrus. He tugged at his uniform belt.

"Are we boring you?" Corporal Obi stamped down from the platform and bent forwards, leaning over the shallow desk, until his face was inches away from Sabre-Tooth's.

Sabre-Tooth recoiled. He wished the man would keep his voice down. The shouting hurt his ears. And his teeth smelled bad.

"Well?"

"No, Sir."

Obi's dark eyes bored into his face. "Pay attention. You treat Sergeant Murkhal's words as gospel. As far as you're concerned, he's God and I'm his avenging angel. Understand?"

"Yes, Sir." Sabre-Tooth was bewildered, but he had an idea that he'd better not show it. Gospel, God and angels were bad, dangerous words. People were put in prison for using them. It had been on the news vids. Sometimes people were executed.

Obi straightened, eyeing the other three with distaste, before turning his attention back to Sabre-Tooth. "Don't give me a reason to tell you again. Don't expect special treatment. You're not special. You're just a mutant." He returned to the platform.

Cyrus dug a sharp elbow into his ribs. "Mongrel."

"Shut up." Sergeant Murkhal paused in his speech to glare at Cyrus for a long second. "Any more interruptions from you and you'll spend the next week on minimal rations." He stepped forward and pressed a small techstick. The screen behind him lit up, displaying a picture of a soldier in uniform, dripping with weaponry. Murkhal proceeded to give the four listeners a list of the qualities a soldier should possess. Sabre-Tooth was fascinated.

Next to him, Cyrus squirmed restlessly. We've seen this before." He muttered under his breath. "Loads of times. Fucking boring."

"Do you have something to say, Cadet?" Murkhal pointed his techstick at him.

"No Sir."

"Then let me repeat myself. Shut the fuck up." Murkhal kept his eyes on Cyrus as he continued. "You'll have physical training every morning, the same as you would in any inactive military unit. In the afternoons, the next three months will be occupied by instruction in weaponry, technology, artificial intelligence, location analysis, strategic thinking and…"

Sabre-Tooth zoned out. He didn't mind the idea of physical work in theory, but the rest all sounded new. He didn't even know what strategic thinking meant.

The screen display changed, showing stick figures running, swimming, climbing and fighting with each other. Putting his hand to his throat, Sabre-Tooth ran his claws around the collar.

Corporal Obi descended from the platform again. "Are you paying attention?"

This time the words hissed moistly into his ear.

Sabre-Tooth's ear-tip twitched at the discomfort. "Yes Sir."

Obi stood next to his seat for the rest of the presentation, his massive presence intimidating. Sabre-Tooth tried to concentrate, but it was a relief when Sergeant Murkhal deactivated the screen and finished talking.

He clasped his hands behind his back. "Your desk communits will be active when you return to your bunks. They're keyed to your wrist chips and will explain your timetables. That's all."

Afterwards, Corporal Obi gave the four of them a tour of the site, the parade ground, the lecture theatres, the gym, the exercise rooms, weapon training areas, the running track and the computer rooms. All of them were situated on two sides of the camp, with the central area taken up by the fenced plascrete square. Finally, he took them to something he called the

Junior Mess Room. "There are usually between one hundred and two hundred recruits on site at any time," he said. "Most of them are here to train in some specialisation, and work in groups of between four and ten. You can mix with them when you're off duty."

"Sir?" Cyrus asked. "Is all of this a Military Security site?"

"It's a Security training site. Commander Diessen is head of Military Security."

"What's Alliance Security, Sir? I've never heard of it."

"It's the group who run Military Security. You might know them as Security Services. The name changed. Is that all?"

"Yes Sir." Cyrus still looked puzzled.

Once he'd gone, Sabre-Tooth inspected the Junior Mess. He'd seen the same sort of thing on the flatscreen; it was a basic looking bar, with flexichairs at one end and plastic tables scattered about the rest of the room. A small group of men and women, in uniform coveralls, clustered round a table at the far end of the room. They glanced up as Sabre-Tooth's group arrived.

Cyrus headed for a circular table, where he sat down and waved the others over. Sabre-Tooth followed Laszlo. Tessis hesitated.

"Come on." Laszlo turned back and grabbed her arm. "We'll be working together for the next few months at least. We should get to know each other." He blew into her ear before pushing her at the table.

Tessis staggered forward. She jerked her arm free of Laszlo, pulled out a chair, spun it round and straddled it. "Keep your hands off me."

Laszlo moved a chair next to her and slapped his hand on her knee.

She pushed it away. "Stop it."

He sat back and stared at her with flat, unreadable eyes.

Cyrus watched them both. "Or else what?"

"Or else I'll kill him."

"Kill him?" He started to laugh, stopping when Laszlo reached for Tessis again. "No. Laszlo, you know what they said. They told us what would happen if you screwed up again. And I'll be blamed as well. Leave her alone."

Laszlo shrugged and leaned back in his chair.

Sabre-Tooth glanced from Tessis to Cyrus to Laszlo and back to Tessis again. Her lips thinned as she glared at the two men. Wariness emanated from her, and the sweaty smell of her fear drifted around the table.

"Don't wind him up." Cyrus pointed a finger at her.

"Me?" Tessis's eyes widened.

"He likes little girls," Cyrus said. "They don't like him so much though. So leave him alone. I don't want to face a firing squad because you've wound him up."

"Make sure he leaves *me* alone, then." She leaned her arms on the back of the chair and rested her chin on them. "Why do you think I'm here? Try pushing me around and you'll find out."

Cyrus shrugged. "You're not his type anyway. Too skinny. Too dark."

Laszlo nodded. "Much too skinny. You've got shit hair as well. I'd rather fuck the mongrel and I'm not that desperate."

Sabre-Tooth edged away. Tessis's expression didn't change.

"Okay." Cyrus rested his elbows on the table. "Laszlo and me. We were regular military. Our officer strongly suggested we apply to join this sort of group. The mongrel," he nodded dismissively at Sabre-Tooth, "came from some sort of lab. What about you?"

Tessis shrugged. "I was in the ragtag. Entry level, conscripted straight from my institution."

"You're only eighteen? How did you end up in this shithole? You didn't volunteer, did you?"

Her pale skin flushed. "I made a mistake. They could have executed me. Instead, they offered me this."

"A mistake? What—"

"Mind your own business." She sat up straight, her face flushing with rage.

Cyrus raised his eyebrows. "Okaaay." He turned his attention to Sabre-Tooth. "Let's hear more about you."

"There's nothing to tell." Sabre-Tooth's head throbbed with confusion. Tessis's inexplicable anger discomforted him. Undercurrents swept through the conversation. "Are we going to be soldiers? What's ragtag?" He scratched his scalp.

"Are you completely fucking stupid?" Cyrus rolled his eyes. "We're already soldiers."

"I don't think I am," Sabre-Tooth said. Annoyance made his claws flex. It was an unfamiliar feeling.

"You are now." Cyrus blew out an impatient breath. "How come you know nothing? Ragtag's the conscript force. The bottom level of the army. Me and Laszlo were ragtag, but we're four-year men now. We should have got our level one citizen licenses for service rendered, but—"

"We were sent here instead." Laszlo glowered at the tabletop.

"Whose fault was that?" Cyrus said.

"You should have cleaned up after me. That's what you do."

"If you'd told—"

"Just drop it," Laszlo said.

Sabre-Tooth was more confused than ever. Tessis was a ragtag? Cyrus and Laszlo had been ragtags. They'd all been in trouble? None of them were citizens?

"What's Alliance Security?" He rubbed at the skin of his arms. Underneath, a muscle twitched.

Cyrus shook his head. "Never heard of it before today. You heard what Obi said, same as I did. If it's the same as Security Services, it covers everything from civil enforcers to the army. Anyway, they change the names of things at least once a week."

It made no sense to him. He frowned at Cyrus.

"It's just words," Cyrus punched him in the arm. "Come on Mongrel. Tell us your story."

"There's nothing much to tell. Like I said, I lived in a lab and then I came here." Sabre-Tooth's back muscles twitched and he twisted to scratch at them.

"What the fuck is wrong with you?" Cyrus snapped. "You got fleas or something?"

Laszlo guffawed. "Fleas? The mongrel's got fleas."

"It's not funny," Cyrus said. "He's living in the same building as us. We should give him a bath."

"I haven't got fleas." Sabre-Tooth had no idea why his skin itched.

29

"You've never been anywhere else but here?" Laszlo asked.

"No. I'd never seen the outside before today." He wanted to go back outside, not sit in this boring room with these horrible people.

Tessis frowned. "Sounds worse than my institution."

Sabre-Tooth rubbed his eyes, squeezed them tightly closed and blinked. They felt dry and itchy. He scratched his wrist, stopping when he sensed Cyrus watching him. "It was boring. I hated it. I wanted out. We all wanted out."

ALLIANCE NEWS CORP – keeping you informed

June 9th 2452
News Update - Local

Domestic - London

Queen consort, Liljas Oroz-Stuart, visited the Krewchek manufacturing base in North-west London yesterday, for the unveiling of the latest all terrain army vehicle. This innovative military transport uses ground-breaking algal photosynthetic technology in its power cell (more in our science reports). The Queen consort arrived in her private airtran, wearing the latest in utility skinsuit design and accompanied by the King's personal guard. She stayed to lunch with chairman, Andrei Krewchek, in the site's visitor dining room.

~~~

The use of recreational drugs has escalated amongst Level One and Level Two citizens over the last five years. A representative from the Department of Health told Alliance News that this is a matter of grave concern to the ruling Council. The Justice Department has joined with Health to issue a forceful statement. 'Degenerate behaviour of any sort will not be tolerated in our civilised society.' Criminals who deal in prohibited substances will be executed for crimes against humanity. Casual users will receive the maximum sentence presently allowed by law.

~~~

Two days ago, during high tide, the Thames breached its barriers east of the inhabited zone. The weather conditions were particularly unfavourable, but the river authorities assure us that no lives were lost.

Chapter 5

Sabre-Tooth jerked awake, every nerve in his body flaring at the same time. His skin burned and his feet twitched. Sitting up, he swung his legs to the floor. He scratched his bare chest, then his head, his groin and his eyebrows. Returning to the bed, he knelt on the thin mattress, leaning out of the window and trying to catch a cooling breeze. The horizon was beginning to brighten where the hills met the sky, and the main sound was the raucous morning cacophony of a multitude of birds. The dissonance scraped against his nerves. He rubbed his ear and then his stomach, raking fully extended claws over blazing skin. His heart thudded painfully against the walls of his chest. Wet heat crawled up his body and settled in his head.

Hissing to himself, he jumped off the bunk and ran to the hygiene facility where he stood under the shower faucet, hoping it would cool the fever raging through his blood. The cold button dispensed a weak stream of lukewarm, slightly brown water. A thin trail of blood trickled from where he'd scratched his upper body, turning the water pink as it swirled down the drain.

His vision blurred. Panic settled into his gut. He returned to his cubicle, naked and wet, with a body that still flamed as though it had been dipped in acid.

When he pulled his clothes on, they chafed his skin so badly that he hummed in distress. He tugged at the collar circling his neck, sure it was about to choke him. No one else appeared, so he headed out of the building, pacing up and down the plascrete outside his room. He dragged his hands through his hair, tugging on it in an effort to stop the prickling sensation.

He rubbed his eyes with the palms of his hands before walking blindly towards the archway at the end of the plascrete road. Two uniformed men guarded it; big men with no hair, each hung with a whole arsenal of weapons.

"Halt." The command came from miles away.

He ignored it.

"I said, 'halt'."

This time the shout was loud enough to make him wince. Sabre-Tooth slowly turned his head towards the guards. It looked like there were four of them. As he blinked, they turned back to two. The two blurred into one. The one loomed at him. He rubbed his eyes again, dragging in a raspy breath, and with it, the scent of fresh sweat and laundry liquid. He sneezed.

"Last chance."

He kept on walking.

The blurred amalgamation of men pulled stunguns out of their belts. Pain flashed through him, lasting a long second, before his already limited vision narrowed and the world disappeared.

~~~

Pain woke Sabre-Tooth. His muscles ached, his teeth ached, and the itching made him feel as though worms were burrowing into joints, ears, eyes, even the skin between his toes. He tried to raise a hand to scratch at his face. It didn't work, so he turned his head sideways and rubbed his face against the scratchy blanket beneath him. The moment he stopped, the irritation came back worse than before.

His hands were trapped behind him and he couldn't sit up. He wriggled desperately before realising his wrists were tied together. He squirmed into a sitting position and looked around. The room was just as small as his barracks cubicle, but stank of stale urine, underlaid with fear-stained human. The light was artificial. The bunk was a hard slab underneath the thin blanket, and a bucket stood on the floor by the wall. He slung his legs over the side of the bed and leaned against the wall, rubbing against it. The room had no window, just a small barred gap in the door.

It was a prison cell.

He jumped off the bed. Pressing his face against the bars, he tried to see what was outside. "Hello?"

No one came.

He raised his voice a little. "Hey!"

Still no one came.

Panic swelled in his throat. Worms crawled between his skin and his bones, drowning out the residual pain in his muscles and he flung himself at the wall, wriggling down it, pressing as hard as he could. He strained at the bonds on his wrists, trying to twist his hands to scratch. Even when he flexed his claws, he couldn't reach his skin. He howled, high-pitched and loud.

Long minutes later, he was pulled out of his misery by the snap of a familiar voice.

"Sabre-Tooth?"

Panting, he looked up. A large dark face appeared at the gap in the door.

Sabre-Tooth pushed himself to his feet and leaned against the door. "Let me out."

"He's a mess." Corporal Obi moved aside.

"Make it stop." Sabre-Tooth's voice rose to a wail. Obi was leaving him.

Sergeant Murkhal's thinner face appeared. He frowned at Sabre-Tooth without answering.

"Please," Sabre-Tooth begged. "My skin – I need to…" The itching was unbearable. He sank to his knees, squirming against the wall again.

"He's going to fuck himself up." Murkhal had turned away from the window. "Diessen didn't say the withdrawal would be this bad. His skin's moving by itself."

"Makes me want to hurl, but he should be okay," Obi said. "These cells were designed to stop any idiots who thought they could escape by killing themselves."

Murkhal paced down the corridor and paced back, the thud of his boots an assault on Sabre-Tooth's ears. "Sabre-Tooth. Stop that. I'm giving you an order."

"I can't." Fury consumed him, at the stupid request.

"I'll have you whipped. Stand up now."

Springing from his crouching position, he bared his fangs at Murkhal, before turning his head sideways and snapping at his own shoulder. He couldn't reach, but the movement gave him an idea. He sank to the floor again and bit at his thigh. The taste of blood and fabric flooded his mouth, making him gag. Pain made the itching go away. He bit again.

"Shit." Murkhal's voice rose. "Stop it. Now."

Sabre-Tooth turned his attention to his other leg.

"Sedate him." Murkhal snapped. "I don't care if the stupid fucker bleeds to death, but there'll be trouble for us if he cripples himself."

Something stung his shoulder, a minor inconvenience amongst all the sensations pounding at him. He glanced up. A needle stuck out from just below his collarbone.

Obi blew out a loud breath. "Look at his legs. I know Diessen said he'd have withdrawal, but—"

"They'll heal if he stops biting them," Murkhal said. "Those scientists gave him the tranquillizer they made for the troops in the nuclear clean-up zones. Only a mild dose, Diessen said, but it was bad stuff. Fucking idiots. It killed the men who didn't die from radiation sickness. They don't use it anymore."

"Scientists." Obi spat the word out. "Useless know-nothings."

"If he dies, Diessen will make sure that boffin wishes he'd never been born," Murkhal said.

"He'll do the same to us."

"Keep an eye on him." Murkhal's voice faded. "We don't want Diessen blaming us for losing his pet."

~~~

Sabre-Tooth lay on the floor, twisted and uncomfortable. He slid his eyes sideways and stared at the spongy white plastiles beneath his cheek. His muscles hurt, his joints hurt and a stinging pain in both his thighs made his eyes water. He wished he could go back to sleep. Rolling over, he struggled to a sitting position and examined his legs. Dark stains spread over the torn fabric of his coverall. His hands were still bound behind him. He was still in the small cell. The itching had almost disappeared, but he remembered the desperate need to scratch and bite his own skin. His legs hurt.

How long had he been locked up?

He wanted out. His tongue was dry and tasted disgusting. He wanted water. Someone must come soon. He took a few deep breaths, trying to direct his thoughts in a less disturbing direction.

He was going to be a soldier. Soldiers on the entertainment channels were often heroes. Cyrus and Laszlo weren't heroes. They reminded him more of the villains. Tessis was harder to figure out, but she didn't look much like a hero either. Soldiers often died. They had to kill people.

He leaned his head back and closed his eyes.

Outside.

34

He was out of the lab. He'd been outdoors and that was good. He'd felt the sun on his skin for the first time in his life.

He was alone. He might never see Sugar and Tygre again. What were they were doing now? Did they know what had happened to him? Again, he changed the focus of his thoughts before the loss overwhelmed him.

He had the collar round his neck and that was very bad. He wasn't free. They could make him do anything they wanted.

He folded his legs close to his chest, stretching the wounds he'd inflicted. He couldn't lie on his back without discomfort; he couldn't even lean against the wall properly, with his hands bound behind his back. He'd been restrained before, but it hadn't made him feel as panicked, powerless or annoyed as he did this time. Hunger and thirst gnawed at his throat and stomach. A riot of emotions wrestled for control of his mind.

He shifted uneasily, rested his head on his knees and began to hum quietly to himself.

"Cadet."

Sabre-Tooth raised his head.

Corporal Obi's face appeared in the small window. "Are you rational?"

"Yes Sir." Sabre-Tooth suppressed his fury. It wouldn't do him any good.

The door swung open. "You're lucky you won't be up on charges for yesterday's behaviour."

"Yes Sir."

Obi pressed a small fob to the plasmetal bindings on Sabre-Tooth's wrists and they sprang open. He sighed with relief and rotated his shoulders backwards and forwards in an attempt to loosen them up.

"Get back to barracks and clean yourself up. You're a disgrace."

"Yes Sir." Sabre-Tooth hesitated. "What happened? Was I ill?"

"You were insubordinate." Obi shoved him out into the light. "If you weren't completely new, you'd get a taste of the taserwhip."

It appeared to be early morning. Maybe he'd missed a whole day. No wonder he was hungry.

"Go on. You've got physical training in an hour. Don't be late." Obi spun on his heel and marched off.

Sabre-Tooth watched him go, picking over the fragments of conversation he'd heard before they shot him with the dart.

He walked slowly back to his quarters.

The water in the shower was as tepid as before, but it took the last of the irritation and heat out of his skin, and he scrubbed the dried blood from his legs with the bar of stinging antiseptic soap. He'd done a lot of damage; the gouges were deep, and when he rubbed at them, they oozed dark, sluggish blood. Bending forward, he ran his fingers over the wounds before letting the thin cascade of water flow through his hair and over his face. His eyes were still sore, but he could see. He stopped the water and stepped into the drying area, where the cold blasts of air made him shiver. At least the morning was beginning to heat up. Taking a deep breath, he pushed the remnants of his rage to the back of his mind.

He returned to his room, pulled a clean coverall from the cupboard and dressed, sitting on the edge of the bunk to fasten his boots as the door swung open.

"Where've you been?" Cyrus pushed his way into the small space. "For all of yesterday?"

Sabre-Tooth tugged the bottom of his trousers into place and glanced up. It was none of Cyrus's business. An unfamiliar wave of irritation washed over him. "What do I do about that?" He inclined his head towards the torn and bloodstained coverall.

Cyrus frowned. "I asked you a question, Mongrel."

"I was in a cell somewhere," Sabre-Tooth said. "What about my uniform?"

Cyrus poked at the heap of cloth. "Is that blood?"

Sabre-Tooth nodded.

"Who'd you kill?"

"It's my blood."

Cyrus's frown deepened. "We'll miss breakfast. Come on. There's a laundry chute by the showers."

Sabre-Tooth picked up his discarded clothes. Missing food would be bad. His stomach felt like it was rubbing against his backbone.

Breakfast was in the mess hall and consisted of a generous portion of a smooth beige paste along with a small bowl of nuts. Sabre-Tooth dug his spoon into the paste and licked tentatively around the rim. It was almost identical to the food he'd been given in the lab, an oat base with a hazelnut flavour. His stomach groaned as he realised he hadn't eaten for nearly two days.

"So where've you been?" Cyrus pointed a spoon at him from the other side of the long table. His bowl was much smaller than everyone else's and he had no nuts.

"I told you. In a cell."

Laszlo glanced up from his breakfast.

"What did you do?" Cyrus grabbed Sabre-Tooth's bowl and pulled it away. He dug his own spoon into it.

"Give me that back."

Cyrus took another spoonful. "Why were you bleeding?"

"Bleeding?" Laszlo spoke round a mouthful of food.

"I scratched myself."

"What with?" Cyrus jerked the bowl away from Sabre-Tooth's grasping fingers.

"My teeth. Give me my breakfast."

"Too late, loser." Cyrus pushed the empty bowl back across the table. "Did you try and kill yourself?"

Tessis gave Sabre-Tooth a quick glance. "You'll let him get away with that? Stealing your food?"

Fury burned through him. He opened his mouth, closed it again. Even small displays of temper had meant a blow from the shockstick. Not that he'd much energy for anger in the last few years. He squeezed his eyes closed for a second, as he wondered why things had changed.

Cyrus smirked. "I'll have the nuts as well." He made a grab for them. This time Sabre-Tooth was ready and snatched the small bowl back.

Cyrus turned to Tessis. "It'll have to be yours then." He reached across for her food.

36

She lifted her spoon and slammed the edge down into the back of his hand. He yelped. The spoon was blunt, but Tessis had put a lot of effort into the blow. She carried on eating her breakfast while Cyrus examined his hand.

"Good move." Laszlo eyed her.

"All right for you to say." Cyrus rubbed at the weal on his hand. "I'm going to have a hell of a bruise. It might be broken. And I'm starving."

"Serves you right." Tessis picked up a handful of nuts. "If you weren't such a dickwit you wouldn't be on minimal rations."

"Bitch." His tone mixed disbelief with admiration.

At least he'd given up questioning Sabre-Tooth, who still wasn't sure what had happened or why he'd been locked up. There would be time to think about it later. Now he was ravenously hungry, too hungry to make sense of anything. He quickly finished off the nuts, keeping a wary eye on Cyrus. Why did he have less food than everyone else? What had he done?

"So you scratched yourself?" Cyrus turned his attention back to Sabre-Tooth as they left the mess. "Why? Are you a fucking mental case as well as a mongrel?"

Sabre-Tooth flexed his claws. Cyrus was annoying, but not worth risking punishment for. The anger churning in his gut was something he hadn't felt for years. He forced himself to ignore it.

"Well?"

"I itched."

"They locked you up because you itched?"

"I tried to leave the site." Sabre-Tooth said.

"AWOL? Why didn't they shoot you?"

Sabre-Tooth shrugged.

Cyrus jabbed him in the ribs with his undamaged hand. "You're a pet pussy. They must love you."

Behind them, Laszlo sniggered. Cyrus slowed down to walk with him.

Sabre-Tooth increased his pace.

"You shouldn't let him get away with it," Tessis muttered as he caught up with her. "He'll just get worse. I've met his type before."

"Why's he like that?"

"He's a bully. Fight back or he'll make your life miserable. Or don't. It's up to you." Tessis left him behind as she stalked off in the direction of her quarters.

Sabre-Tooth thought about what she said. He didn't like being pushed around by Cyrus. It made his pulse race and gave him a sick feeling in his empty stomach. Hopefully there would be more food at midday.

He growled under his breath as he entered his room. He could deal with Cyrus; force him to leave him alone. Like Tessis had. Was it allowed though, or would he be punished?

Sugar did a good job on Rashelle's face just by using her claws. Sabre-Tooth could do the same to Cyrus. That would teach him a lesson. They'd beaten Sugar for it though.

He ran a finger around the collar. Perhaps he shouldn't mark Cyrus's face, but if he didn't cause visible damage, he might get away with marking other parts.

Tessis was right. He should fight back.

ALLIANCE NEWS CORP – keeping you informed

June 11th 2452
News Update

Society

Unlicensed births are down to a ten-year minimum, thanks to decisive action on the part of the Alliance Council. According to Representative Sirelli (Department of Environment, subdep Population), lack of population planning is as great a threat to civilisation as worldwide rising temperatures. In her latest interview, she points out the indisputable fact that habitable regions are still shrinking and, until this has been reversed, populations cannot be allowed to increase. Over the next generation, the number of Alliance citizens must remain stable or decrease. To ensure that this is the case, reproductive licensing will be strictly enforced. Rep. Sirelli states that she will insist on maximum penalties for any reproductive transgressions. In addition, Speaker Hong intends to raise the subject at her forthcoming meeting with the Chief Minister of the Indian Republic. India is not alone in having no official laws on population growth, but it is the nearest neighbour of the Eurasian Alliance and the greatest threat to efforts to rebuild a civilised society.

Chapter 6

Cyrus held Sabre-Tooth's breakfast bowl just out of reach, protecting it with his forearm and shovelling the cereal paste into his mouth with the other hand.

Sabre-Tooth kept his gaze on his stolen food while he wolfed down his bowl of mixed nuts. When he'd finished, he glanced upwards through his lashes, meeting Cyrus's eyes.

The other man smirked at him.

Sabre-Tooth looked away. The pulse in his temple began to pick up pace. This was the last time Cyrus would get away with taking his food.

Back in the barracks, he followed his tormenter into the cubi-unit he shared with Laszlo and pushed him against the wall. "I don't like you stealing from me."

Cyrus's eyes widened. He dug a hard fist into Sabre-Tooth's side. It was his left fist. Black and yellow bruising bloomed across the back of his right hand, a reminder not to mess with Tessis. "Tough."

"Stop hitting me."

Laszlo and Tessis watched from the doorway. It didn't look like Laszlo was going to defend Cyrus.

"I don't like that either." He lowered his head until his nose was an inch from Cyrus's.

The rage rising through him was an old friend; he had a vague memory, from years ago, of losing his temper with a group of labtecs. That hadn't ended well. He took a deep breath.

"Yeah?" Cyrus made a mock kissing noise and punched him again, speaking in a singsong falsetto voice. "You're such a pretty pussy. And you're going to give me your breakfast. Every fucking morning from now on. If you're lucky, I'll let you keep the scrapings."

The stupid voice grated on Sabre-Tooth's nerves, but he forced his temper back down his throat. "Shut up." He wrapped a hand round Cyrus's neck and held him against the wall while he used his free hand to open the top of his uniform.

"What the fuck are you doing?" Cyrus's good fist pounded into him. At such close range, it didn't have a lot of impact. "Get off me, pervert."

Sabre-Tooth pulled the uniform away from Cyrus's shoulders. Underneath the coverall, he was almost as hairy as Tygre.

"I want you to stop pushing me around." Sabre-Tooth flexed his fingers and drew a careful claw down one side of Cyrus's exposed chest, leaving a shallow red line.

Cyrus inhaled sharply. Blood welled up and dripped down towards his stomach, trailing deep crimson across his light brown skin.

"You leave my food alone. I'll hurt you worse if you don't." He drew his claw down Cyrus's other side.

Cyrus yelped, more surprise than pain in his voice.

"Don't kill him." Laszlo leaned against the doorframe, making no attempt to stop Sabre-Tooth or to help Cyrus.

"I could slit him open if I wanted to." He thought about scenes he'd seen in vids on the flatscreen, back in the lab. The violent ones Sugar liked to watch. "I could gut him. It wouldn't bother me to see him die. I'm an animal, remember?"

He'd lain awake the night before, weighing up what he could get away with. Murder would be a step too far. Anyway, the thought of killing made him sick to his stomach. Sugar might have been able to do it; he couldn't. He'd had to close his eyes during the gory scenes in the vids but Cyrus didn't need to know that.

"I'd slash his throat for him," Tessis said.

"I wish I had those claws." Laszlo said.

Cyrus lurched away from the wall as Sabre-Tooth loosened his grip, touching his bruised right hand to the blood running down his front. "Thanks for the help." He glared at Laszlo who shrugged.

"Don't push me around again." Sabre-Tooth bared his teeth at Cyrus.

Cyrus snarled back. "Wouldn't dream of it, Mongrel. You're meaner than you look." He rubbed the blood into his skin. "Now I'm going to have to clean this up. We'll be late." Studying his stomach, he sucked the blood from his finger. "I hope you keep those claws clean."

"Don't call me Mongrel."

He didn't care what they called him. He knew he was human. He'd fixed Cyrus and it felt good to fight back against somebody. Maybe he should have tried it before. Those drugs though…And the shockstick… "And you'll be late. I won't."

"Get a move on." Laszlo gave Cyrus a hard shove. "You'll make us all late. You don't want to be on minimal rations for another week, do you?"

~ ~ ~

Over the next few weeks, Cyrus made a few more attempts to intimidate him but after Sabre-Tooth pushed back, he gradually gave up. Cyrus was bored, annoying and a bully. He wasn't stupid.

Most evenings after the official day ended, all four members of the small group headed over to the bar in the junior mess. Non-intoxicating drinks were freely available, and served by human staff rather than an auto-dispenser. They came in a mixture of artificial fruit flavours and spicy mixtures. Sabre-Tooth preferred water. The flavoured drinks left a chemical aftertaste on his tongue.

As well as the bar, the mess had a mixture of games, a news screen and an entertainment screen. Cyrus and Laszlo spent most of their evenings at the games tables, where Cyrus swapped war stories with some of the other more experienced recruits while Laszlo watched everyone with a pale, unblinking stare. There was definitely something weird about Laszlo.

Tessis rarely lingered for more than half an hour; she would have a drink, glance at the news on the flatscreen and head back to her quarters. She hid it well, but Sabre-Tooth could tell that Laszlo made her uneasy.

Sabre-Tooth sometimes stayed for the flatscreen entertainment. The films brought back memories of evenings in the lab, with Sugar and Tygre. He liked that; it gave him a warm feeling. Occasionally, if Cyrus annoyed him enough, he retreated to his cubicle to read his favourite space operas and thrillers, or to use his communit to find out more about the life he was living. Every day, he was aware of his own lack of experience. Connections between his lessons in the lab and the realities of life began to form in his brain; too slowly for his liking.

If he was destined to be a soldier, he wanted to know who he was fighting and why, but as far as he could tell, the reasons for conflict were simple. Too many people and not enough land or food. His mind worked much better now the drugs had washed out of his system.

The drugs had messed with his body too. Every morning now, he woke with an erection, and his sleep was disturbed by fragmented dreams. Sometimes he would wake, aroused and restless, sometimes he orgasmed in his sleep. He'd never done that before, and he checked on his communit, relieved when he discovered it was normal. Sometimes he would lie on his bunk fantasising about horrible Rashelle while he masturbated. He found himself watching the other recruits with interest, mostly the female ones, but some of the men as well. His communit gave him access to a variety of porn vids, but he couldn't imagine anyone letting him do those things to them. Cyrus and Laszlo made moves on some of the support staff, but Sabre-Tooth didn't think they'd had any success.

Everything was changing. It was hard to keep up.

He watched the other three cadets carefully, basing his own actions on what they did and what they said. Cyrus especially liked to talk. Over breakfast one morning, he told Sabre-Tooth and Tessis that he and Laszlo had grown up in the same North London Institute for unlicensed children.

Sabre-Tooth had always thought unlicensed children were thrown out as infants, and abandoned to starve. The idea of institutions where they lived was new to him.

"I looked out for Laszlo," Cyrus said. "He's a menace on his own. He needs a keeper."

Laszlo's smile didn't reach his icy eyes. "That's shit."

"He's okay most of the time." Cyrus ignored him. "But sometimes he loses it. I don't think he'd be able to hurt you, but Tessis should watch out."

Tessis folded her arms. "I can take care of myself."

"She's in the team," Laszlo said. "I don't hurt my own people."

"What about that time—?" Cyrus stopped as Laszlo focussed his pale stare on him.

Sabre-Tooth shivered at the expression on his face. It wasn't directed at him, but even so...

"Okay. But... Okay." Cyrus held up both hands in appeasement.

Laszlo relaxed.

"When we were seventeen, we both registered for the army," Cyrus continued. "It was the only realistic option for us. If you've got a talent, some corporate group might offer you probationary citizenship. I don't know anyone it happened to, though. Laszlo's good-looking enough to get work at one of the entertainment agencies, but he'd be a disaster as a sexscort." He shot a nervous glance at Laszlo. "He'd kill somebody on his first time out. The army was our best bet. If we managed to stay alive through our two years, we'd get level one. That's what they promise you and it's enough to get another sort of low-level job. One with a better chance of survival and maybe advancement to Level Two."

"It's dangerous?"

"Lots of the ragtag end up at clean-up sites," Cyrus explained. "Chemical and old nuclear reclamation zones. I knew a couple of recruits who got sent straight from training to the north of the Euphrates basin, round where Azerbaijan used to be. They say it glows in the dark."

Sabre-Tooth decided he'd look it up next time he had a chance. He'd heard about the nuclear disasters of three hundred years ago, it was one of the compulsory history modules, but he hadn't been taught any more than the basics.

"There isn't much protective gear," Cyrus continued. "Not for us anyway, and the casualty rate is high."

It didn't sound like the war films or even the recruitment ads that Sabre-Tooth had watched on the flatscreen. "So how did you manage to stay alive?"

"We got sent to repair river defences," Cyrus continued. "In central Spain, near an abandoned city. León, I think it was called. Some of the landless from the southern deserts tried to divert the flow. Don't know why they bothered, it was barely a trickle. One of the heavy divisions was training in the area. They obliterated the uprising and, afterwards, we were brought in to do the labouring."

"So did you get your Level One citizenship?"

Tessis snorted.

"There were a few problems."

"I bet there were." Tessis rolled her dark eyes at Sabre-Tooth.

Sabre-Tooth smiled. She'd become a little more talkative and he liked her better than the other two. She wasn't as pretty as Rashelle, but he still enjoyed looking at her.

"We were there for four years," Cyrus said. "Then Laszlo went off the rails a bit. I tried to cover up for him, but we got caught."

Sabre-Tooth glanced at Laszlo.

"So we were offered this posting."

"Last chance, was it?" Tessis asked.

"Mind your own fucking business," Cyrus said. "And why don't you tell us why *you* didn't go the sexscort route? You might be skinny, but you could probably do exotic. I'd do you. Once at least. With my eyes closed."

"Same problem as Laszlo," Tessis said. "I'd have killed you."

Cyrus sneered. "So you joined the army and failed basic training? I'd like to hear about the crime that got you here."

Tessis pushed her empty bowl away, stood up and walked out.

"Come on." Cyrus waited for the others. "We'd better go."

They followed Tessis out to the parade square, where the entire company of recruits gathered every morning in preparation for a run, or a heavily laden march. Sabre-Tooth took his place between Cyrus and Laszlo.

Physical training took up a lot of his day. Cyrus said that the only purpose of all this exercise was to keep them too exhausted to cause trouble, but Sabre-Tooth didn't think there was much trouble they could get into in the fenced compound. It wasn't that taxing anyway. Not for him. He enjoyed it.

Physical contentment made him happier than he'd ever felt before. He especially loved the cross-country running and the challenge of rock climbing, when he was almost alone and dependent on his own skills. Learning to swim was okay, even though immersing himself in cold water would never be one of his favourite things. Outdoors was wonderful. Even the torrential rain, which happened regularly at midday, made him happy. The weather heated up as summer progressed, the humidity rising to wrap round him like a warm, damp blanket. He liked that too, although his companions suffered.

He was better than the other three, at everything he tried. He was stronger than Tessis, Cyrus or even tall, lean Laszlo; he could run faster and for longer, his reaction speeds were swifter, and once he had learned to keep his claws sheathed he was more accurate with every kind of projectile launcher he was given.

"Hybrid vigour. It's because you're a mongrel." Cyrus glowered at him and turned to Laszlo. "It's not fucking natural. They can fuck off if they think I'm going to compete with that."

Cyrus hated being beaten.

Sabre-Tooth smiled, baring the tips of his pointed canines. "You're no challenge. Not even an appetiser. Fighting you is like playing with a kitten."

"You don't know how to be a real soldier," Cyrus sneered. "I bet you've never killed anyone, never even been in a proper fight."

"I could start with you."

Cyrus's face flushed and he clenched his fists.

Laszlo shoved him. "Don't be stupid."

By July, the weather was almost tropical, the mornings heavy with promised rain. After his run, on one of these days, he stretched out on the grass at the edge of the camp, basking in the heat and humidity, letting it lull him into drowsiness. The loud buzz and hum of insects merged with birdsong. It was a good thing he had his military coverall as protection against the stingers. He half-closed his eyes, wondering about his old lab-mates.

He missed them. He hoped they'd left the lab too. Outside was much better. It hadn't taken him long to work out that he'd been drugged into a state of complacency and resignation. Years of his life had been spent with a zombie-like mind-set. It had been the same for Tygre. No wonder Sugar always sounded frustrated with them.

He rolled onto his back as a pang of longing for his old companions hit him.

Tessis waved as she walked past, returning from her own run. Her hair was damp with sweat, and dark patches of moisture stained the back of her exercise singlet. Sabre-Tooth's gaze followed the sway of her narrow hips.

During the afternoons, after the physical training, he learned advanced computer skills, and strange things such as code breaking, and how to get places without a locator unit. He learned how to make minor repairs to weapons and equipment. He practised driving three different types of transport.

Sometimes he could even forget the collar around his neck. So far, no one had used it.

ALLIANCE NEWS CORP – keeping you informed

July 14ᵗʰ 2452
News Update

Political

Councillor for Foreign Affairs, Andrei Krewchek, has publicly accused his fellow councillor, Viktor Einerson, of a failing in his duties as Councillor for Defence. Krewchek and Einerson have strongly opposing views on the Eurasian Alliance's approach to its neighbours. Krewchek has long voiced the opinion that both the Indian Republic and the Union of the Americas pose a threat to Alliance safety. If they won't comply with Alliance demands voluntarily, he says, they should be forced to do so. Einerson is reluctant to engage in a conflict, which may rapidly spin out of control, at a huge financial cost to the Alliance. News Corps sources believe the Council is split on the matter, but it is unfortunate for Einerson that many in Military High Command agree with Councillor Krewchek. This matter is unlikely to go away.

Chapter 7

"I'm bored out of my skull," Cyrus said. "We've been stuck in this dump for six weeks."

"I'm not bored." Sabre-Tooth finished off his vegetable and protein bake, scraping the last morsels from the bottom of the bowl. He was always hungry nowadays.

"You're unnatural. What about you, Tessis?"

"No." Tessis didn't bother looking at Cyrus.

"Laszlo?"

"What did you have in mind?" Laszlo's ice-blue eyes sharpened.

Cyrus put his chopsticks down. "A trip into town. It's only about five miles away. Yamen told me there was a decent bar there."

"Who's Yamen?" Laszlo asked.

"One of the cyber trainees. You know – from that group we saw the other day."

"The useless ones?"

Sabre-Tooth put his own chopsticks down and listened. He'd never seen a real town, except from a distance or on the flatscreen. The top of the hill outside the camp gave a view of the nearby walled settlement. He wondered how many people lived there, and what they did.

"I'll ask Murkhal," Cyrus said. "I can't see why he'd say no."

"Have you any credits?" Laszlo asked.

"Only our cadet allowance."

"That won't get us much of a good time." Laszlo's pale eyes turned thoughtful.

"It'll be a change." Cyrus slapped him on the back. "Come on, at least we can see what's available."

"We know what's available," Laszlo grumbled. "Fuck all. Oh well, I suppose it's better than another night in the mess."

"There'll be beer at least," Cyrus said.

Laszlo stood up. "I'm going to the mess. They're showing that execution tonight."

"What's that?" Sabre-Tooth asked.

Cyrus rolled his eyes at Laszlo. "Those four god-botherers. You know? The ones who were preaching 'go forth and multiply'. They got execution by firing squad. It's being broadcast tonight, as a warning."

"Go forth and multiply?" Sabre-Tooth frowned.

Laszlo pushed his chair under the table. "They've been telling people to have loads of children. Talk about stupid. Anyway, I want to see it."

"Vacuum for brains. Deserve what they get," Cyrus agreed.

"I'm not watching a public execution." Tessis turned towards her quarters. She glanced over her shoulder. "You're sick, Laszlo, you know that?"

Laszlo licked his lips and smirked at her.

~~~

On the Friday evening Obi gave the four of them passes to visit the town. Sabre-Tooth fizzed with excitement. Like the others, he had accumulated credits. Not many, but he could buy things. A chip in his wrist contained his personal information, including his credit rating.

He jumped into the army groundtran after Cyrus and Laszlo. Even Tessis had eventually decided to come along. She strapped herself in, next to him, the warmth of her thigh sinking into his.

Six other recruits were already inside, crammed along one of the side benches. Sabre-Tooth knew them by sight but he'd never spoken to any of them. He inspected them discretely. All six stared back at him.

The closest, a thin man with short light brown hair, leaned forward, resting his elbows on his knees. "You're the mutant. We've heard about you."

Sabre-Tooth blinked.

Before he could respond, Cyrus nudged him. "He's not a mutant. He's a mongrel. Show some fucking respect."

The thin man sat back. "Who are you?"

"Name's Cyrus."

"Tomas. So what's with the *mongrel* then?"

"I can talk." It hadn't taken Sabre-Tooth long to realise he could deal with men like this. His razor-sharp claws bought him a lot of respect. Cyrus had talked about him and shown the wounds Sabre-Tooth had inflicted. "Not sure I want to talk to *you* though." He jerked his head towards Cyrus. "Carry on."

"Huh." Tomas returned his attention to Cyrus. "What's your specialism?"

Cyrus shrugged. "They haven't told us yet. What about you?"

"We're being trained in old-fashioned explosives. Blowing shit up. Stopping shit blowing up. Making big-bang shit."

"Wouldn't mind doing that myself." Cyrus grinned. "You getting all that physical stuff as well?"

"Yeah." Tomas grimaced. "They say we'll be working in challenging territory." He sat back as the transport slowed down and stopped. "I think they just want to make us suffer."

"Figures," Cyrus said. "That's the army for you."

Sabre-Tooth followed Tessis as she jumped to the ground. He spun in a circle, examining his surroundings. Heavy iron-grey clouds obscured the sun, making it feel much later than it was. At his back, the groundtran stood next to another identical one. Both were parked against a high plascrete wall, the town's fortified barriers rising behind it. Ahead of him, low buildings surrounded a small square, which centred on a white plastone statue. One dim, energy-saving light illuminated the statue but shed little extra visibility on the rest of the square. Food smells drifted past his nose, overwhelming the metallic odour of the transport vehicles and mixing with the humid evening air.

"What a dump," Cyrus said.

"Told you." Laszlo folded his arms.

"We need to start thinking about getting more credit," Cyrus said. "Anywhere's okay if you—"

"What's that?" Sabre-Tooth walked towards the statue. It was a man in army uniform, standing wide-legged on a plinth. It was twice the size of any normal man.

Cyrus gave it a cursory glance. "Fuck knows. Some war hero? Politician? Who cares? Come on."

The explosives group had already moved off and were disappearing down a narrow street on the opposite side of the square. Sabre-Tooth dragged his eyes away from the statue. A couple of tables stood behind it, the owners taking advantage of its light to serve food.

He sniffed. The rich scent of chocolate filled his nostrils. The last time he'd tasted chocolate had been in the lab with Sugar and Tygre, the night before Diessen came for him. Nostalgia made him take a step towards the tempting smell. A pot of liquid chocolate stood on a portable heater.

"Come on Mongrel. You don't want to waste your money on that." They'd all been paid the same small amount of credit. Very small, according to Cyrus.

"It's good value." The man selling it called out.

Sabre-Tooth sniffed again, wondering if security guard, Frank, still brought chocolate for Sugar.

"Not now," Tessis said. "We can always come back. Cyrus is right though – it'll take most of your credit."

He turned away, dragging his feet.

"We're closing up." The vendor called after him. The square was almost empty of people. "Later will be too late."

"What's the name of this place?" Sabre-Tooth caught up with the others. There were so many things he didn't know. He felt dizzy sometimes, with the effort to take everything in.

"Nowhere much," Cyrus said. "It's called Colunn."

"Oh right." He'd seen it marked on maps of the area around the camp. "I know it."

"Why ask the fucking question then?"

"What's it for? Who lives here?"

"It's here to serve the army bases. I've been in loads of places like this. They wouldn't exist without the army. They're all shit. Full of losers." Cyrus walked away, towards the small street the other group of men had disappeared into.

Sabre-Tooth dawdled, still interested in the town. It was summer. It should be daylight for at least another hour. The towns he'd seen on the entertainment screen were always brightly lit. Despite the energy saving laws, he hadn't expected it to be so dark.

Two men in the black safesuit uniforms of Military Enforcement emerged from the alley behind the parked transports, heavy weapons strapped across their bodies.

Sabre-Tooth hurried after his companions. The armed enforcers made the town look like some of the warzones he'd seen on the flatscreen, back when he'd been a lab rat.

"What are they doing here?" He drew level with Cyrus.

"Security." Cyrus gave an exaggerated sigh. "Do you never stop with the fucking questions?"

Sabre-Tooth ignored him. "Who would attack this place? It's full of soldiers."

"Some fucking nutter. You get gangs of illegals out here. They end up raiding food production complexes. None of them last long, but they're desperate and there're enough of them to be dangerous. A lot of illegals make their way to Wales as well, so they'll have to come this way."

"They'd climb over the walls?"

Cyrus shrugged.

Sabre-Tooth turned in a circle. There was no one who looked remotely like a threat. The only people he'd seen, apart from the enforcers, were the vendors in the square. This place was nothing like the towns in the vids.

"Those two are watching us." Laszlo glanced over his shoulder. "Most trouble round here probably comes from the barracks."

"There's always someone watching us. Sometimes I wonder if it would have been better to run," Cyrus said. He threw out his arms. "Live as an illegal."

Laszlo punched his shoulder. "You're so full of it." He turned to Sabre-Tooth. "Don't listen to him. The Council does periodic cleansing. They send the army out to tidy up anyone who isn't licensed, force them into conscript gangs, sterilize them or shoot them. Sometimes rich high-level citizens come along for the hunt. It's a sport to them."

"Why?"

"Fuck knows. They don't want people living outside the cities? Unlicensed people break the population laws? They just like killing people?"

"Bit like you, Laszlo," Cyrus said.

"I can't run anyway." Sabre-Tooth touched his collar. "Not with this."

"Haven't you been anywhere except London?" Cyrus nudged Tessis, who stared around as curiously as Sabre-Tooth.

"Recruit camp." She scowled. "I wasn't there long enough to get a pass to outside."

"What did you do exactly?" Cyrus had tried to find out why Tessis had been thrown out of ragtag ever since he'd met her. Apparently there wasn't much you could do that would warrant dismissal, let alone execution. And even less that would get you transferred to an elite group. Cyrus had told Sabre-Tooth that they were all lucky. Most new recruits lived under much more repressive conditions, while they were beaten into unthinking obedience. Everyone at the training camp was a specialist of some sort.

"None of your business," Tessis snapped back at Cyrus.

"Who did you kill?"

She scowled and kicked at the ground with the toe of her boot. "Where are we going?"

"Yamen said there isn't much here." Cyrus gave up. "Just a couple of drinking clubs and the supply depot. There's the army brothel as well, but you need a different pass for that. He said to try the second bar we come to."

"What sort of entertainment do they have?" Laszlo grumbled. "I bet it's not—"

"It'll be better than the mess," Cyrus said.

The two clubs were close neighbours at the far end of the narrow street. One was directly opposite the other. Cyrus pushed the button below the almost illegible sign. The door opened and a heavily armed man with a naked chest waved them through into a wide, dimly lit space.

A bar stretched along one end of the room. Two people waited behind it, a man and a woman, both young and thin, and both dressed in brightly coloured thigh length tunics. They looked up as the newcomers entered.

Behind the bar, an archway opened into another room. Flashes of multi-coloured light emerged from it, accompanied by muffled music. Sabre-Tooth liked music. He drifted towards it.

Cyrus grabbed his arm. "Where are you going?"

"I want to hear—"

"Later. We'll get a drink first."

Tables were scattered around the edges of the room, most of them occupied by people in uniform. There were more men than women. The explosives trainees already had drinks in front of them. Tomas waved at Cyrus.

Very young entertainers circled the customers, occasionally joining a group at a table, or disappearing through a narrow door with an individual or a small group.

"Minimally classified sexscorts," Cyrus muttered in Sabre-Tooth's ear. "Leave them alone. The army has its own. You can't afford them anyway."

"Sexscorts?" Sabre-Tooth had seen them on the flatscreen entertainment channels in the lab, but he'd never been interested. Now he followed them with his gaze, wondering about them. His new knowledge made him wonder if the drugs had subdued any inconvenient sexual urges he might have had when he was in the lab. He stole a sideways glance at Tessis. "How much do they cost?"

"More credits than you've got," Cyrus said. "You've never had one?"

Sabre-Tooth shrugged. He was beyond being embarrassed by the things he'd never done. His previous life hadn't lent itself to new experiences. This one was much better. He touched the cool metallic plastic of his collar and followed Laszlo and Tessis to one of the empty tables.

Cyrus watched a thin dark girl walk across the room to one of the other tables before raising his hand.

The male bar attendant came over immediately.

"You've had beer before?" Cyrus drew an analytical fingertip over the surface of the table before leaning his elbows on it.

Sabre-Tooth shook his head.

"Beer for all?" Cyrus checked with Laszlo who nodded.

"This is a shithole," he said, after the waiter left. "I don't call it entertainment. Diluted drinks and sex we can't afford?"

"What did you expect?" Laszlo said. "Synth players and mood enhancers?"

"Something better than this."

"I told you what it would be like."

The waiter came back with a jug of cloudy yellow liquid and four glasses. It looked like piss to Sabre-Tooth and didn't smell much better. His nose wrinkled.

49

"It's starbrew2," the waiter said. "Perfectly good stuff." He poured the liquid into the glasses and slammed the half-full jug down on the tabletop before stalking away.

Sabre-Tooth picked his glass up, sniffed it and took a tiny sip. It was horrible. Why hadn't he spent his credits on the chocolate?

Tessis copied him, her face screwing up at the flavour.

Cyrus and Laszlo both took big gulps and swallowed with satisfaction.

"It's not that bad," Cyrus said. "Not the best, but it's a proper drink. Down it." He gestured at Sabre-Tooth and Tessis. "It'll relax you."

"I'm already relaxed." Sabre-Tooth picked his glass up again. He wasn't convinced.

"And I don't want to relax." Tessis pushed hers around the table, watching it leak over the sides of the glass and drip down onto the stained surface.

One of the entertainers appeared behind Laszlo, leaning over his shoulder. She looked like a dilute version of Tessis, skinny and pale with shiny black hair covering her shoulders, oriental eyes and a strip of blue cloth tied around her hips. Sabre-Tooth stared.

"Hey, Blondie. Can I join you?"

Laszlo didn't move. "No. Fuck off."

"Laszlo. Don't be rude." Cyrus leaned towards the girl. "Sit down."

"I thought we weren't going there?" Laszlo raised an eyebrow as the girl sat next to Cyrus. "We've no credit, remember?"

The girl glanced from one to the other. "I'm not expensive." She crossed one thin bare leg over the other. Her movements enthralled Sabre-Tooth; he stared at her slender foot swaying backwards and forwards, before letting his gaze drift up her body to her small exposed breasts.

"My name's Flower." She leant towards Cyrus.

"Weed, more like," Laszlo muttered. He stared unblinkingly at the girl, who shifted nervously.

"What do you think?" Cyrus stroked one hand along the girl's side. "Pool our credit?"

Sabre-Tooth opened his mouth, closing it again when he couldn't think of anything to say.

The girl's mouth curved into an insincere smile. "I don't cost much. And I do cheap deals for mouth jobs."

A man rose from his seat at a table on the opposite side of the room and strolled towards them. At the halfway point, his pace changed into a threatening swagger. Grabbing Flower's arm, he pulled her out of her chair. "What do you think you're doing, bitch? I told you we wanted your services."

"And I said no." She jerked away, sinking back onto the seat. "Not five of you. Not for that price."

The man hauled her to her feet again.

"Let go of me." She glanced towards the bar.

The male waiter put a glass down and folded his arms. He took a step towards the table. His female colleague bent and picked up a heavy cosh, swinging it loosely at her side.

"Did you hear her?" Cyrus rose and inserted himself in front of the man.

He dropped the girl's arm and clenched both fists. "Do you want to argue over her?"

Cyrus narrowed his eyes. "Hell, yes." He glanced at Laszlo who dipped his chin in a small nod.

The stranger waved at his companions who pushed their seats back and rose to their feet.

Sabre-Tooth frowned. "What's he doing? There're five of them."

"Posturing," Tessis said, her voice a mixture of disgust and resignation.

The other four men sauntered towards them.

"Stupid bastards." Tessis's voice dripped contempt.

Sabre-Tooth glanced at the men, unsure whether she referred to her own companions or the strangers. Both Cyrus and Laszlo smiled wide smiles. Flower edged away and hurried over to the bar where she whispered something in the waitress's ear.

Laszlo kicked her chair out of his way and circled the table to stand next to Cyrus.

Tessis leaned back and blew out a sigh.

"Hey, look at that." The first man leered at her. "She's a bit skinny, but I'm not fussy. You'd do five of us, wouldn't you?"

Tessis rolled her eyes.

Cyrus glanced at Laszlo.

The stranger smirked. "How about we swap yours for ours?"

Tessis picked up Laszlo's empty glass and smashed it on the edge of the table. She held the broken end towards the man. "I'd love to get acquainted."

The male server hurried towards them. "You'd better pay for that."

Tessis pointed her improvised weapon at him.

He backed away.

Across the bar, the other group of recruits, the ones who'd travelled in on the same transport, stood up and drifted towards the action. A small crowd congregated around the archway behind the bar.

The original man turned away from Tessis and her broken glass. He shoved Cyrus hard.

Cyrus staggered, drew back his fist and punched. The man dodged and his friends surged forwards.

Laszlo leapt on his back.

Sabre-Tooth checked Tessis, who slouched forward, one elbow propped on the damp table. She clutched the base of the broken glass.

The men all merged into a big pile. The six explosives recruits watched, arms folded, not interfering. Laszlo and Cyrus were outnumbered. What if they got hurt? Or killed?

Sabre-Tooth's fingers flexed and his claws came out. He trembled with a mixture of excitement and indecision. He stood up, glancing at Tomas who shrugged.

"Sabe? Don't…" Tessis's voice faded out.

"Look at the freak." One of the men pulled away from the melee and sneered, while the ones who weren't occupied with Cyrus and Laszlo moved closer to look.

Sabre-Tooth hissed.

The man punched him in the jaw.

He let out a yelp of surprise and clutched at the sore place with one hand.

The man laughed.

Sabre-Tooth took a deep breath, wincing at the sharp pain in his face and the constriction of his collar. A new rage burned through him. Before he could think, he hit his assailant with an open hand.

Blood spurted from the man's face, flying over the table in crimson drops. He staggered backwards. More blood ran from his face and pooled on the floor.

Sabre-Tooth stared at his claws; they were wet and red. The anger drained from him, leaving him nauseous.

The man's hand pressed against his cheek, blood leaking between his fingers. The fight between the others had halted as they realised everyone else in the bar was staring.

Sabre-Tooth backed away, his legs shaking; he'd never done anything like that before; he'd never retaliated when someone hit him. He never lost his temper. Even when he wounded Cyrus, he'd done it carefully. This man was badly hurt and it was his fault.

"Shit." Cyrus sounded stunned. "Good work Mongrel, you've taken his fucking face off."

The man wobbled, his eyes unfocussed. One side of his head was red and wet.

The male server ran forward with a medigun and sprayed the wound. Sealant spread to cover the left side of the man's face. The blood flow stopped and the man sank down to sit on the floor, his head resting on his knees. He moaned. One of his companions crouched next to him.

The server pulled a cloth from his belt and wiped the blood off the floor with it. "You'd better get out of here. All of you." He nodded at the waitress. "She called the Military Police."

The waitress tapped her weapon against her thigh. Flower had disappeared.

"Shit," Cyrus repeated. He glanced at the entrance. "Too late."

Two military enforcers approached. Both carried loosely held weapons. Both looked down at the wounded man and then at Sabre-Tooth's bloody claws.

"What the fuck happened here?"

The soldiers all spoke at once. Tomas and his colleagues slowly retreated, returning to their drinks.

"You." One of the enforcers pointed his gun at Sabre-Tooth. "Talk. The rest of you - shut the fuck up."

"I hit him."

"What with, for fuck's sake?" The man stepped into his space.

Sabre-Tooth retreated, the backs of his thighs banging against the edge of the table. "Just my hand." He held up his hand, flexing the fingers to show his bloodstained claws. "I forgot." Everyone had seen what he'd done so there was no point in trying to lie.

The second enforcer had taken a first-aid kit from his backpack and was busy finishing the repairs to the man's face. He glanced upwards, eyes widening as he registered Sabre-Tooth's hand. "You can't have hit him directly. You'd have torn his face right off or ripped his jugular open with those. What the hell are they?" He straightened and spoke to Sabre-Tooth's victim. "There you go. You won't bleed to death, but unless you can afford a high end medic, you'll have an impressive scar."

"I can't afford any medic." The man's voice slurred as the painkillers in the sealant took effect.

"I tried to stop," Sabre-Tooth said.

"You can explain that to your commanding officer." The first enforcer surveyed them all. "That goes for the rest of you too. Get yourselves back to camp." He glanced around the rest of the room. "And you all. Get on with your business."

Two men, from the group of strangers, helped their comrade to his feet and half carried him to where a troop carrier waited in front of the bar. Laszlo, Cyrus, Tessis and Sabre-Tooth followed the rest of the strangers. A few heavy raindrops plopped onto the roof of the vehicle, the preliminary to a heavy downpour, and all nine soldiers scrambled hastily into the back. Sabre-Tooth sat on a bench opposite the man he had wounded.

"I'm sorry. I didn't mean to—"

"No prob." The man's pupils swam loosely in his eyes. "I won't be picking a fight with you again, though."

"You ruined our fun, Mongrel." Cyrus jabbed his forefinger at Sabre-Tooth. "Laszlo likes a good fight."

"Sorry." It had felt good to fight back, even if his gut cramped with guilt. He still fizzed with the remains of the adrenaline rush. Maybe he was a real soldier. Nausea rose to the back of his throat and he swallowed, pressing the back of one hand against his mouth.

"You're all pathetic," Tessis said. "I hope they lock you up for years. They'll whip you at least. Serve you right."

Back at the training camp, Sergeant Murkhal paced up and down in front of them. "No more passes for you lot for the next month." He stopped in front of Sabre-Tooth. "You're grounded."

Sabre-Tooth stared straight ahead. He'd never been whipped. Would it hurt as much as the collar?

"And an extra hour's run every morning with weights before your official day starts."

That wasn't a punishment in Sabre-Tooth's mind. That was a reward.

"Who started the fight?"

"They—" Cyrus started to answer.

"Shut up. I'm asking him." Murkhal jabbed a finger into Sabre-Tooth's chest.

"They did, Sir."

"I'll ground you all till the end of training if you do anything like this again." Murkhal moved his attention to Laszlo and Cyrus. "I know your reputation. Any more trouble and you'll both be whipped."

Cyrus paled. Laszlo stared straight ahead. His mouth twitched as he suppressed a smile.

"And the cost of that glass will come out of your credit." Murkhal glared at Tessis who remained expressionless. "Well?"

"Yes Sir."

Murkhal shook his head. "At least you showed you could fight," he said to Sabre-Tooth. "We worried you were a complete pussy. Just save it for the right time."

"Yes, Sir."

Sabre-Tooth relaxed, realising he wouldn't be made to suffer for losing his temper. The last time he'd done it, when he was still a child, he'd been beaten with the shocksticks.

The others weren't so pleased.

"I hate fucking running," Cyrus said. "Still, it could have been worse. I think he likes us."

"Who? Sergeant Murkhal?" Sabre-Tooth didn't believe it.

"He could have pressed that button you told us about. On your collar."

Sabre-Tooth thought about that.

"I've an idea," Cyrus said. "How would you like to earn some more credits?"

"Me?"

"Yes. You're a good scrapper when you want to be. How about entering one of the Friday night bouts? You'd be paid and you could bet on yourself." Cyrus eyed him. "You'd be a definite contender. I'm going to help organise the fights. I could fix it for you."

"No." Sabre-Tooth didn't need to think about it.

"We'd all make a profit."

"No."

"We could all use some more credit. For fuck's sake Mongrel—"

"No."

Dissension – the struggle against injustice

August 29th 2452

Rifts in the government over future international strategy become more evident as Defence and Foreign Affairs in the Alliance Council confront each other. The International Council of the Eurasian Alliance is split down the middle on the subject of border policies. Dissension maintains that corporate interests are the motivating forces for both sides. Andrei Krewchek, chairman of the world's largest armaments manufacturer, has close links to many senior figures in the military high command. His role as Councillor for Foreign Affairs is a clear conflict with his business interests. Viktor Einerson's reputation as a massive procrastinator is well deserved, and Dissension's opinion is that he is the wrong leader for the Alliance Defence Forces.

ALLIANCE NEWS CORP –keeping you informed

August 29th 2452
News Update

Breaking News!

An attack on Military Camp 17 took place earlier today. A stolen airtran flew, unpiloted, into the accommodation wing, where it exploded. At least fifteen soldiers are reported to have been killed with many others injured. The perpetrators have not been identified, and so far, no one has claimed responsibility for this incident. The public may rest assured that the Alliance will leave no stone unturned in their search for the authors of this atrocity. There will be no mercy for the cowards who killed defenders of the Alliance while they slept.

Chapter 8

"All of you." Sergeant Murkhal's voice echoed through the speaker system and bounced off the walls of the cubi-unit, his bellow loud enough to give most people concussion. "In the lecture theatre. Now."

Sabre-Tooth winced. Enhanced senses had definite disadvantages. He put his digi-reader down and rolled off his bunk, sliding his feet into his boots in one smooth movement. He stretched, shaking off the evening's lethargy. The cubi-units were uncomfortably humid, as the temperature climbed higher and higher. It was the end of August; surely the heat must reach its peak soon.

Almost three months had passed since he'd left the lab he'd grown up in. Sugar and Tygre were an ache in the pit of his stomach when he had time to think about them, but he didn't often have the time. Sometimes it felt as though his old life was a dream. He kicked his door open and stepped into the corridor.

Tessis emerged from her cubicle almost simultaneously with him. There was no sign of the other two. "Still in the mess," she said. "Come on, let's go."

The two of them walked across the square to the other side of the compound. Sabre-Tooth glanced down at her, his eyes lingering where the cloth of her uniform coverall clung to her small breasts. If he tried hard, he could almost imagine the shape and colour of them. She would look better than the sexscort in the town bar. If she took her coverall off…

Her sharp elbow jabbed into his ribs.

He grunted.

"I know what you're doing. Just stop it before I have to hurt you."

"Sorry." He couldn't help himself. This sort of interest had never bugged him when he'd lived in the lab cage. His fantasies about Rashelle had been feeble in comparison.

Tessis lifted one hand, flapping it at the swarm of small biting insects buzzing around her face. Her coverall tightened across her chest.

"Sabre-Tooth." Her voice was low and threatening.

"Sorry." He fixed his gaze on the plascrete.

Overhead lights activated as he shouldered the door of the lecture theatre open. The room was empty. Tessis edged along the second row after him and sat down, leaving a seat between them.

The door swung open again. Laszlo and Cyrus entered, sliding into the front seats. Corporal Obi followed, taking a position at the end of the row.

Sabre-Tooth frowned. None of the other teams were present and they'd encountered no one on the way. It looked like it was just the four of them.

"What's happening?" Cyrus turned his head to check the back entrance then leaned forward, resting his elbows on the bench in front of him. He shifted restlessly, tapping one foot on the floor.

"Will you stop that," Tessis hissed. "You're driving me mad."

Cyrus sat up straight, holding a finger up in a rude gesture, but he stopped tapping.

The door opened again and Commander Diessen strode in, his heavy figure followed by Sergeant Murkhal. He stamped up the steps to the speaker's platform and folded his arms while he scowled at the four cadets. Behind him, Murkhal stood at attention.

Sabre-Tooth's interest sharpened, along with his concern. He hadn't seen the commander since the day he'd arrived in the camp. He touched the edge of his collar.

"Good evening." Diessen let his gaze move from Laszlo, across Cyrus and Tessis, to Sabre-Tooth. "Sergeant Murkhal tells me you've all successfully passed the first stage of your training. Congratulations."

"Thank you Sir." Cyrus and Laszlo spoke in unison.

"Tomorrow, most of the recruits will be moving on, but you'll stay here for the remainder of your instruction. I want you to go out with the patrols from the regular camps when they do control operations in Wales. After the attack on Camp 17, we're coming down hard on illegals."

What did that mean? Sabre-Tooth glanced at Tessis. She was as unreadable as ever.

"I'll speak to you all individually, tomorrow, after parade inspection. I've heard good things about your progress. Well done." Diessen stepped down from the rostrum and approached the benches, halting in front of Laszlo. "I take a very personal interest in this team. I'm looking forward to working with you." He saluted Sergeant Murkhal and moved off, followed by the two instructors.

"What the hell was that about?" Cyrus pushed himself to his feet. "We still don't know where we'll be deployed."

"Why would Diessen be looking forward to working with us?" Tessis chewed on her knuckles. "We're the bottom rung and he's the man in charge. He hobnobs with Council members. We're nothing, just disposable nonentities. It's weird."

~~~

The following morning everyone in the camp marched out onto the square and lined up for inspection. After Diessen checked each group, the cadets left to pack up and move on to their next base. Sabre-Tooth's small group were last. Diessen dismissed them and told them to go to the mess.

Corporal Obi collected them immediately after lunch and marched them to the small lecture theatre. "The commander has a big investment in this group," he said. "He's taken a gamble on you all. He'll be watching you carefully, so make sure he's happy with you."

"Why, Sir?" Cyrus asked. "There's nothing special about us. Except the mongrel." He jerked his head at Sabre-Tooth.

"You don't need to know why." Obi waited until they all sat on the front bench. He leaned on the end of the desk. "You just make sure he's impressed. If you do want a future, that is. Now shut up and pay attention."

Diessen entered the room with Sergeant Murkhal and climbed onto the podium. "I'm sure you all want to know where you fit into the army's structure." His bloodshot eyes focussed on each of them in turn. "Well?"

"Yes Sir."

The sour taint of last night's alcohol drifted from the commander. Sabre-Tooth stifled a sneeze.

"If you pass all your final tests, you'll report to me directly," Diessen said. "You'll take your orders from me."

Next to Sabre-Tooth, Cyrus stirred, but didn't say anything.

"You'll form a small team outside the regular hierarchy. You'll handle problems I think are too sensitive to take to any senior military committee. You're *my* experiment. Do you understand?"

Sabre-Tooth let his voice join the others.

"Any questions?"

Cyrus shifted in his seat. "What sort of problems, Sir?"

"Any problem I point you at," Diessen said. "Any problem that needs to be handled swiftly and discretely. Is that a *problem* for you?"

"No Sir. Which section of the army will we belong to?" Cyrus asked. "Where will our pay come from?"

"Military Intelligence."

Sabre-Tooth felt the tension in his companions. The news must mean something to them, but while Sabre-Tooth had heard of the different security forces, he didn't see why this was bad. Commander Diessen was head of Military Intelligence. Surely it was normal that they'd be placed in his department. He wondered whether they would be enforcers. He wasn't sure if he liked the idea.

The commander paused, waiting for more questions. When none of them spoke, he continued. "Your group will be one of several squads of elite soldiers and agents who perform tasks we don't like to publicise. As you know, the National Council and the Eurasian Alliance are involved in struggles both with external forces and with internal terrorist organisations. The attack earlier this week is just one example. The teams trained here will have the function of neutralising threats to our settlements, with least cost to the government and its regular army. They'll be ready to move immediately they get the call." He inspected his audience. "That's why we have trained specialists in cyber security, explosives, interrogation and so on. You understand that?"

"Yes Sir."

"You'll be a little different though. I won't make you wait for fifteen levels of approval. You'll act at my direction. Anyone want to say anything?"

All four remained silent for a moment.

Cyrus stood up. "Will we be saboteurs? Assassins?"

Sabre-Tooth gaped at him. How had he come to that conclusion? Laszlo didn't look surprised and Tessis stared ahead, her small face fixed in its normal expression of gloom. Corporal Obi turned a reproving frown on Cyrus.

"That's probably not an accurate description of the majority of your future work." The commander pursed his lips. "However, there are sometimes tough decisions to be made, and sometimes tough jobs to do. We need tough operatives to do them, and you were all chosen because of your abilities, as well as your psychological profiles. I'd describe you as maximum force operatives. Information gatherers. Possibly provocateurs. Stealth operatives. Do you have a problem with that?"

"No Sir." Cyrus's face was expressionless.

"Laszlo? Sabre-Tooth?"

"No Sir." Sabre-Tooth's voice rang out at the same time as Laszlo's. He couldn't help thinking that the job description was very vague. Unease rippled beneath his skin.

"Tessis?"

"No Sir."

Sabre-Tooth's mind raced. He fixed on one word.

Assassins.

He understood what an assassin was. Would he have to murder strangers? He didn't like the term 'maximum force operative' at all. And provocateur could mean anything.

He knew better than to argue with the officers, but his collar felt as though it might strangle him.

"You'll be helping to keep the world safe for most people," the commander continued. "You'll be doing a job you can be proud of."

Sabre-Tooth swallowed the moisture pooling in his mouth. He could smell his companions' worry.

"I'll talk to you all individually now," Diessen said. "Wait here until you're sent for." He left with Murkhal.

"Right," Obi said. "Cyrus. You're first."

Cyrus stood up and pushed past Tessis and Sabre-Tooth to follow Obi.

After a long pause, Sabre-Tooth leaned across Tessis. "Do you know what's happening?" Laszlo had been with the army for four years, so surely he must have an idea.

"Not a clue," Laszlo said.

Sabre-Tooth sat back again.

"The whole thing stinks," Tessis muttered, "but nothing about this setup surprises me anymore." She folded her arms and slouched against the back of the bench.

Obi collected Sabre-Tooth last, marching him down the corridor and into one of the offices. He left, closing the door behind him.

Diessen sat at a small round table by the wall. He glanced up from his communit. "Take a seat."

Sabre-Tooth sat on the other side of the table. He flexed his toes against the inside of his boots. Commander Diessen made his skin crawl.

Diessen finished whatever he had been doing on the communit and looked up. "Sergeant Murkhal tells me you're showing promise. I heard about your fight in the bar."

"I'm sorry, Sir."

"You need to keep your temper under control," Diessen said. "Learn to focus your aggression. I don't want you behaving like a malfunctioning weapon."

"No, Sir." Sabre-Tooth didn't want to lose his temper again either. The minute of euphoria wasn't worth the subsequent guilt, or the worry about possible fallout.

"A soldier directs his aggression at the enemy, not his own comrades," Diessen continued.

Sabre-Tooth's eyes widened in incredulity. Cyrus and Laszlo weren't the only people in camp who liked to pick fights. A small group of soldiers organised combat matches, but most of the camp liked to watch. He'd been to one himself. Seeing the loser pounded into bloody unconsciousness had given him nightmares. Why would anyone do that? Even the officers placed bets sometimes, ignoring the fact that serious injuries could happen.

"We'll provide you with targets for your aggression," Diessen said, "but if you attack or kill anyone without permission, you won't like the consequences."

"I won't kill anyone, Sir," Sabre-Tooth said.

"You'll kill whoever I tell you to." Diessen leaned across the table. "That's what soldiers do. Obey orders." He pushed a small object to the middle of the table. It was the collar control.

"Yes Sir." Sabre-Tooth couldn't look away from it. He clenched his jaw, suppressing the need to bare his teeth.

"I'll be passing this to Sergeant Murkhal, so think carefully before you do anything to annoy him."

"Yes Sir." Hatred heated his blood, flooding him with a mixture of rage and impotence.

"You have skills which will come in useful in infiltration, sabotage and extraction. You'll learn to use those over the next few months. Each of you will follow a training programme that plays to your strengths." He squinted at Sabre-Tooth. "You've filled out. You're not as scrawny."

"No, Sir."

"Good. Your officers will keep me updated. Don't disappoint me."

"No Sir."

"You know what happens if you fail."

"Yes Sir." When he swallowed, he felt as though the collar would choke him.

"You can go."

~~~

"Assassins? Saboteurs?" Cyrus's voice rose. "Provocateurs? Reporting to Diessen?" He pounded the bar with his fist. "I signed on to be a soldier, not some high-up's personal fucking hit squad."

"It's not just that though, is it?" Sabre-Tooth said.

Cyrus ignored him. "A job we can be proud of? Like fuck we can. We'll be under the radar and if we become inconvenient, Diessen will just get rid of us."

"I don't mind being an assassin," Laszlo said.

"You wouldn't," Cyrus snapped. "See how you feel when Diessen has *you* terminated."

"I don't want to kill people," Sabre-Tooth said.

"Don't be such a pussy. That's what soldiers do," Laszlo said. "That's what we signed on for."

"A soldier is different from an undercover assassin though." Cyrus slapped viciously at a mosquito as it landed on his arm. "Especially one who does Diessen's dirty work. I don't mind killing people, you know that, but I don't see why I should do it for Diessen's benefit. It stinks. I didn't take the oath to push someone else up the career ladder."

"I didn't take any sort of oath." Sabre-Tooth placed his hand on his collar. His claws were fully extended. "I wasn't given any choice. I had to obey or they hurt me."

"Pretty much the same as the regular army," Laszlo said.

"It was the same for me." Tessis ran one hand through her short hair, flattening it over her skull. "Execution or this. And I know if someone's got to die, I'd rather it wasn't me." She sighed. "I don't think any of us have any choice now. I can't see us being allowed to walk away. I wonder what Diessen's really up to. He must have something going on."

"Shit. Shit. Shit." Cyrus kicked the bar. "All I wanted was a chance to move up the hierarchy quicker. Get my citizenship, make a few credits and get out. That bastard, Diessen..."

"I don't like Commander Diessen," Sabre-Tooth said.

"Who does? We're screwed." Cyrus's voice dropped. "I wonder what our psychological profiles showed. What did he say to you, Mongrel?"

"Do as I'm told and control my temper." Sabre-Tooth ran a finger round his collar. "He'll hurt me if I don't. Nothing new."

"He told me to stay out of trouble." Cyrus glowered and kicked the bar again. The thud echoed around the room. "Threatened me with drugs if I didn't and told me I'd be locked up between assignments. He told me I was scum. Fucking evil bastard. What about you, Laszlo?"

"I'm scum as well. I get drugs or execution if I step too far out of line. Chemical castration." He didn't sound concerned. "Same old, same old."

"Tessis?" Cyrus raised an eyebrow.

"My business." She folded her arms defensively.

"I wonder if everyone else passed," Laszlo said. "The explosives lot and so on. Those cybermen were useless. They might be pursuing a career as compost on one of the farms by now."

Sabre-Tooth glanced at him. He was smiling.

"Don't be so negative," Cyrus said. "They might be shovelling defunct nuclear cores out into holding blocks."

"They might just be fixing communits." Tessis rolled her eyes.

Laszlo grunted. "I suppose we'll know we've passed if we survive the next few months."

"What the fuck does it matter?" Cyrus said. "I can't see us ever getting citizenship now. A bullet in the back of the skull. That's our future."

ALLIANCE NEWS CORP – keeping you informed

September 12th, 2452
News Update

Social

Members of the Eurasian Alliance will be pleased to hear that Speaker Sifia Hong's office has formally announced that she plans to marry General Manuel DeWitte, Head of the Swiss Branch of Alliance Defence, later this year. Speaker Hong, daughter of Rohan Hong and Sucheng Lo, has led the Councils of the Alliance for ten years and shows no sign of retiring in the near future. General Manual DeWitte comes from one of the most influential families in the Swiss area and is an active figure in the Alliance's strategic team. Alliance News Corp wishes them both a long and happy marriage.

Chapter 9

The camp was quieter than usual in the week following Commander Diessen's visit. Cyrus's complaints turned into background noise. The next lot of trainees moved in. Things returned to normal.

Sabre-Tooth received his new training schedule. Active Duty was a new category, but otherwise it was similar to the old one with extra classes in intelligence gathering. Tessis attended these as well, along with a small cohort of the new recruits. Cyrus and Laszlo spent the time in more physical training.

"The pair of you are lazy fucking bastards," Corporal Obi told them. "You can't afford to be in less than perfect condition. Not in some of the places you'll find yourself." He studied them for a brief second. "I'm scheduling you for an extra cross-country run twice a week. In your free time."

"Thank you Sir." Cyrus watched him leave. "Fucker." He spat onto the plascrete square.

"Evil fucker," Laszlo agreed, with no heat at all.

Sabre-Tooth's physical programme changed as well; serious combat training was added into the mix, together with practical exercises in military electronics, explosives and poisons. Every evening, he spent an hour practising with weapons such as taserguns, small ballistics and the lethal needle lasers. He flew an airtran; just a simple one, but it did cruise above the treetops. It was amazing, but he only got to do it a few times. He practised stealth killing on dummies, interrogation techniques on other recruits, and chose to study various forms of unarmed fighting, from simple wrestling to obscure martial arts. He even had fencing lessons.

"When on earth are we likely to get into a sword fight?" Cyrus muttered after one session. None of the physical stuff was voluntary on his part or Laszlo's. "Talk about a waste of time."

"You'll learn to handle blades," the instructor told him. "It helps you think strategically. Next week we'll have a look at the use of knives in close hand-to-hand combat. Nothing's wasted."

Cyrus grunted. "I've used knives before. I don't need fucking lessons."

"I'd say you need to study strategy more than anyone else here," the trainer retorted. "You've got a brain, so use it. You'll be working with the regulars in the next week or two. They won't tolerate any of your whinging."

"I've *been* a regular," Cyrus muttered in an aside to Sabre-Tooth. "Whinging's almost a religion with them."

Sabre-Tooth enjoyed the mock fights. It helped that he always won. He loved winning. A few of the new recruits sneered at his differences. They stopped after he confronted two of them, leaving the front of their uniforms stained with blood.

Cyrus applauded, as the bully and his friend retreated. "What a waste. Mongrel, are you sure—?"

"Yes. Don't call me Mongrel." He was human.

The rhythm of the days lulled him into forgetting about the collar. He tried not to think too much about the future. Nothing could be worse than the years spent in a cage.

Two weeks into the new training schedule, Sabre-Tooth and Laszlo were summoned to Sergeant Murkhal's office.

"What do you think he wants?" Sabre-Tooth asked.

Laszlo shrugged. "No idea. I haven't done anything."

Sabre-Tooth searched his memory for anything he might have done, but came up empty. "Me neither."

"You're both on active duty." Sergeant Murkhal came out from behind his desk. "We've a group of illegals set up camp just over the border. One of the squads from camp A is going to deal with them. Make sure they don't get too comfortable. The two of you will accompany them. You'll report to Captain Sindre, at 07.00 tomorrow." He jabbed his forefinger into Sabre-Tooth's chest. "Understand?"

"Yes Sir."

He moved onto Laszlo. "Do you have any questions?"

Laszlo said nothing.

Sabre-Tooth took a deep breath. "Yes Sir."

Murkhal raised his eyebrows. "What?"

"Why do we need to deal with them? They aren't harming anyone, are they?"

Murkhal stabbed his finger into Sabre-Tooth's chest again. "You don't need to ask why. Your role is to get on with it and obey orders."

Sabre-Tooth waited.

"Our governing Council doesn't want them there," Murkhal said. "That's the reason. They don't want them breeding indiscriminately, because registered citizens might start asking questions about their own breeding rights."

"Thank you Sir." He could think about it later.

Murkhal hadn't finished. "They're living off the land. They're damaging the new growth, they're eating the wildlife, they're upsetting the ecology. They encourage terrorism. They're breaking the law, so they've got to go. Satisfied?"

"But where are they supposed to go to, Sir?"

Unregistered people had no right to live in residential areas such as London. If they couldn't live off the land either, what were their options?

"They aren't supposed to go anywhere," Murkhal snapped. "They shouldn't exist. They're unlawful. The Alliance needs to be protected from them. Dismissed."

"I don't see they're harming anyone." Sabre-Tooth grumbled as he followed Laszlo back to the mess.

"Not the point," Laszlo said. "They're outside government control. Governments don't like that. Like Murkhal said, we don't need to know why; we just have to do as we're told. It'll be fun, anyway."

"It's stupid," Sabre-Tooth said.

Laszlo shrugged.

"Where've you been?" Cyrus appeared as soon as they got back to the mess. He grabbed Laszlo's arm.

Laszlo shook him off. "Camp A are going to clean out some illegals in Wales. We're going with them. Active duty."

"Just you and him?"

Laszlo nodded and collapsed into one of the flexichairs, stretching his legs in front of him. He crossed them at the ankle and folded his arms across his chest. His eyes closed.

"Fuck." Cyrus turned to Sabre-Tooth. "Keep him out of trouble."

"Me? What sort of trouble?"

Laszlo opened one eye. "He wants you to stop me killing anyone I shouldn't. For fun."

Sabre-Tooth frowned.

"I'm not going to do that." Laszlo opened both eyes, uncrossed his ankles and kicked Cyrus. "I'm fine. I know what the penalties are. Stop messing with my head."

"Yes, but—"

"I said I'm fine." Laszlo pushed himself out of his chair and stamped off.

Cyrus's gaze followed him. "He's wound up. Sabre-Tooth?"

"What?"

"Watch him," Cyrus said. "If he steps out of line, I pay for it as well."

"Why?"

"It doesn't matter why. That's what they told me."

"Why would he kill anyone? He hasn't—"

"Stop asking bloody questions. Just do it."

~~~

Laszlo and Sabre-Tooth joined the camp A squad the next morning, reporting to Captain Sindre.

Ten regular soldiers clambered into the troop skycarrier and sat in rows along each side. Sabre-Tooth copied their actions, pulling the stability belt across his body. Laszlo did the same in the opposite seat. The captain climbed in last and took the end position, next to Sabre-Tooth. He was a tall, lean man, with a face coloured by a mixture of sun and wind. The skycarrier lurched into the air as he fastened himself in.

He twisted sideways to examine Sabre-Tooth. "I've heard about you. You're one of MI's special operatives aren't you? Privileged?"

"Sir?" What was he talking about?

"You attacked a soldier in one of the town bars, didn't you? Got away with it?"

"I didn't—"

"Do that while I'm in command, and I'll make sure you regret it. Understand?"

"Yes Sir." He'd defended himself, that was all. The unfairness made his mouth taste sour.

"And you." The captain jabbed his forefinger at Laszlo. "I've heard about you too. You should have been shot. Any trouble from you and I'll shoot you myself."

"Yes Sir." Laszlo's mouth twitched.

Sabre-Tooth stared at him. What had he done?

Less than an hour later, the skycarrier set down on a small patch of plascrete in the middle of a tangle of young trees.

Sabre-Tooth jumped out after Captain Sindre. The ground underfoot was wet enough to feel spongy beneath his boots, and he was glad of his weatherproof army coverall. Rain battered the ground and the trees, while the dark grey sky, swollen with more rain, turned the gloomy woodland to monotone. Sounds of dripping water filled the air, forming a counterpoint to the clamour of running water. There must be a river close by. The air was warm.

"I hate this place," One of the soldiers grumbled as he pulled his kitbag out of the transport.

"Stop moaning," Captain Sindre said. "We won't be here long. The weather watchers are predicting severe flooding within the next few days. We'll need to be out before it starts." He splashed through the swampy undergrowth to speak to the driver of the skycarrier.

"Must be bad if they call it severe," one of the other soldiers said. "This place's got some sort of flooding most of the year. Look at it? And it's not even fucking October yet. I've never seen rain like it. Why anyone would try to live here is beyond me."

"Poor bastards." Another of the soldiers wiped the water from his face with the back of one hand. "We're doing them a favour really."

"It's worse up north," a third said. "Or so I've heard."

"Come on." Captain Sindre organised them into a compact group and led the way through the wet branches. "There're some flat rocks about a mile away. We'll set up camp there. At least the ground will be drier."

The skycarrier lifted into the air as they left, and the soft hum of its progress disappeared into the distance. It would return in two days.

The woodland was wetter than anywhere Sabre-Tooth had been before. Sporadic flurries of wind whipped sodden branches backwards and forwards. The trees dripped, the sky spat out water, the ground underfoot was soggy. Small streams carved out paths between tree roots, and created temporary cascades over rocks and small shrubs as they tumbled downhill. The noise from the river grew louder as the group headed diagonally up the hill. When it eventually appeared through a gap in the thickening forest, it was a wide torrent of water in a shallow gorge.

Captain Sindre stopped at the brink and peered over.

"We've got to cross that?" Laszlo whispered to Sabre-Tooth. "I'd say it's already in flood."

Sabre-Tooth shivered.

The captain scowled over his shoulder at Laszlo. "Yes. We need to cross that. We'll do it in groups of three, roped together. It's only a stream, for fuck's sake. It looks fast, but it's not deep yet. You and your friend can go first. With me. We'll fix up a rope on the other side for everyone else." He dug in his pack and pulled out a thick coil of plascord.

Laszlo swore under his breath.

Sabre-Tooth entered the water last. His orders were to stabilise the crossing for Laszlo and the captain. Two of the soldiers knelt at the top of the gorge, playing out the rope, which they'd anchored around the trunk of a sizeable evergreen. He closed his ears to Laszlo's cursing and stepped into the foaming torrent. Close to the bank, the river was shallow and rocky underfoot. The captain was already waist deep, the water breaking against his body.

"I don't think it gets much deeper." His face was red with effort. "Hurry up. The current's stronger than I thought."

Sabre-Tooth braced himself as the water swirled around his thighs.

Water came up to Laszlo's waist as well now, and his normal expression of cool detachment had warmed to concern. The captain was almost at the far side, stretching towards the bank. He pushed forward, lurching as his foot slipped and he disappeared under the foaming surface of the river. The plascord jerked as Laszlo was pulled after him.

Sabre-Tooth staggered. Behind him, the rope held, but the weight of his two companions, added to the force of the river, dragged him downstream. He managed to stay upright.

Laszlo struggled to regain his feet against the torrent, and ahead of him, the commander thrashed desperately.

Sabre-Tooth grabbed the plascord tether in both hands, leaned back against the force of the stream and dragged himself towards Laszlo. He seized him under the arms, pushing him forward until his feet found purchase on the bottom.

"Just hang on." He released him. "Keep moving towards the bank."

Laszlo coughed out a mouthful of water.

Sabre-Tooth thought about how much he hated cold water. There was no way he was going down in this. He pulled himself along the linking rope until he reached the captain, who still thrashed at the limit of the plascord. He grabbed him by one arm.

"Laszlo? Can you brace yourself against him?"

"No."

Sabre-Tooth risked a quick look over his shoulder. Laszlo was still on his feet in hip-deep water, fighting hard to stay that way. His hair, darkened by the water, clung to his skull and his normally pale face was scarlet with effort.

Sabre-Tooth moved forward carefully, feeling his way. The riverbed was rocky underfoot, a maze of rocks and small chasms. He didn't want to copy Captain Sindre and fall into a deep hole. The water should be shallower closer to the far bank, but he was taking nothing for granted. He dragged the captain behind him, ignoring the tug on the rope that was Laszlo. One thing at a time.

The water level fell to his hipbones. Hauling the other man forward, he waited while Sindre struggled to connect with the bottom.

Swearing under his breath, the captain spat out a stream of river water as he finally managed to find his footing. He drew himself upright and forged forward together with Sabre-Tooth. A second later, both of them were knee deep. All three staggered out and hauled themselves up the bank. Laszlo and the commander collapsed to the ground, breathing heavily.

"Are you all right?" Sabre-Tooth hovered over them, nostrils twitching at the smell of blood.

"I will be. Just give me a moment," the captain said. "I don't remember the stream being this full before." Taking a deep breath, he unfastened himself from the plascord, waiting while Laszlo and Sabre-Tooth did the same. He wrapped the end round the trunk of a tree and pulled it tight over the stream. "At least we've made a handhold for the others. That was a near thing."

"You're bleeding." Sabre-Tooth pointed at Captain Sindre's thigh. A jagged tear in his coverall exposed a similar gash in his skin.

The captain glanced down and rubbed his leg absently, squinting at the blood staining the palm of his hand. "Just a cut, I think." He waved across the stream. "Right you lot. Get moving."

The rest of the group managed to cross by clinging to the thick plascord, using it to save themselves when their feet slipped.

"How the hell are we supposed to get back if the weather's worsening," Laszlo muttered. "Another hour or so and that thing's going to be impassable."

The commander rummaged in his pack, extracting a tube of disinfectant gel and rubbing it into the wound on his thigh. "I hope that water's clean." He put the tube back, wiped the back of his arm across his face and answered Laszlo's question. "We'll think of something. If we leave the plascord in place it'll help." He nodded at Sabre-Tooth. "Well done."

Sabre-Tooth glowed with pleasure; praise rarely came his way.

Laszlo shivered. "It's fucking freezing. And I'm wiped out."

"I'm warm," Sabre-Tooth said.

Laszlo turned his head slowly, pale hostile eyes narrowing.

Sabre-Tooth bared his teeth in a smile.

Half an hour later, they reached a rocky outcrop, which reared up in the middle of a group of trees. Ferns and rich moss grew in the cracks, but most of the ground was solid. Sabre-Tooth sat on a flat rock, ignored the water trickling down it and chewed on an energy bar. He was ravenous.

Captain Sindre limped over to join him, lowering himself to the ground with a wince. "I hear you have superior hearing, great eyesight?" He rubbed his leg.

"Yes." Sabre-Tooth knew he outclassed his companions.

"Anyone ever tell you what happens when you do a good job?"

"No Sir."

"You're given another one."

Sabre-Tooth glanced at him.

"I need someone to do a recon. You need the experience."

"Sir?"

"Do you think you can manage without getting yourself lost?"

"I think so, Sir."

"You'd better," Captain Sindre said, "because we won't be coming out to look for you. I want you to do a scan of the area. Spend the afternoon looking for signs of habitation. Our intelligence scouts did an aerial search last week, and found heat signatures of quite a few humans. Make a note of locations, numbers of people, if you see any. I particularly want to know what sort of weapons they might have. Can you do that?"

"Yes Sir." Sabre-Tooth examined the area around the camp. The forest thickened downhill, and sounds of water filled the air. He hoped he wouldn't encounter any more torrential streams.

"Fahreed will go with you." He beckoned to a group of three soldiers who clustered together on a nearby rock.

One of them stood up, brushed the water from his coverall and joined them. He was a lanky, long-limbed man with short dark hair, a straight nose, and brown skin, which already showed the shadow of a beard. Captain Sindre stood up awkwardly, favouring his damaged leg.

Sabre-Tooth scrambled to his feet.

"Fahreed's good with weapons," the captain said. "No sense of direction though."

The corner of Fahreed's mouth tilted in amusement. "I always come back. Don't I, Sir?"

"Eventually. I want you both back here before dark."

"Yes Sir."

"Go on then."

Fahreed jerked his head at Sabre-Tooth and headed out into the woodland.

Sabre-Tooth followed, making mental notes of the landscape and the location of the rocks relative to his passage. The only sound now was that of the rain and the muted brushing of Fahreed's body against the trees. The conversation of the other soldiers disappeared into the distance. He rubbed his throat above the collar. He wondered if Murkhal still had the control, or whether he'd given it to the commander of A squad. How far did its range really stretch?

"I do know where I'm going." Fahreed slowed down and glanced over his shoulder. "I won't get you lost."

"Why did the captain—?"

"I went missing after a mission at the Eastern border," Fahreed said. "Not my fault. I fell into a mantrap. A pit. They had to come back for me. I was in there for two days though. They've never let me forget it."

"I've got a good sense of direction," Sabre-Tooth said. "I won't get lost."

After a couple of miles, the trees thinned to scrub and short wet grass. A cluster of grey, soggy sheep huddled together, appearing too depressed to eat.

"I've never done this before," he said to Fahreed. "How are we supposed to find people? They could be anywhere."

"Just look for signs that people have passed," Fahreed said. "You learn to notice anything out of place. The captain said your eyes were good."

"Yes." Everything looked out of place to him.

"Modest, aren't you?"

Sabre-Tooth frowned.

"Anyway, we haven't got long. We need to be out of here before the storm starts. It gets pretty hairy in the hills once the weather gets going, feels like the whole world is about to land on you." He kicked at the grass. "We might not get much done this time, but top brass had a knee jerk reaction to that attack on Camp 17."

Sabre-Tooth stared at the ground. "Is that out of place?"

Fahreed squinted at the streak of mud that split the grass. "Mmm."

"It looks like someone slipped," Sabre-Tooth crouched down, inspecting it more closely. "Not an animal."

"Yeah. Maybe we'd better be quiet."

The trees thickened again, and the sliver of an acrid odour reached his nostrils.

"Something's ahead," he whispered. He followed the scent, stealing through the undergrowth as quietly as possible. The weather, with its constant drip, drip, drip of water gave good sound cover. Behind him, Fahreed was almost as silent.

A group of men, six in total, sat under a makeshift canopy.

It didn't look much like an attempt at settlement to Sabre-Tooth, more like a temporary waystation. The canopy had holes in it. The men were gaunt-faced and dressed in tattered coveralls which must once have been coloured the same green as standard military issue. Maybe they were army deserters.

Despite the damp, they'd managed to build a fire and were cooking something. Sabre-Tooth sniffed, wrinkled his nose and squinted at it. It looked like the body part of some animal. The smell was burning flesh. His mouth watered at the same time as his stomach revolted.

It must be one of the sheep.

They'd killed a sheep.

They were going to eat a dead animal.

It was hard to get his head round this. Food was grown in vats. Fresh food was cultivated in fields and in plasglas controlled environments. People didn't eat animals. That must be what Murkhal meant when he said that illegals killed the wildlife. It was disgusting. He stared for a moment longer before touching Fahreed's shoulder and silently backing into the trees.

Once they were well away, Fahreed slowed. "I think we should look round the edge of that sheep herd. I bet there's more. What do you say?"

Sabre-Tooth nodded, happy to get away from the illegals. The stench of burning flesh drifted away on the breeze. The two of them turned back to where they'd seen the sheep, and circled the herd, hunting for signs of human life.

Light was fading from the sky when they joined their companions. The remainder of the group had erected a canopy over the camp, giving shelter from the worst of the weather.

"Well?" The commander handed out energy bars.

"You talk." Fahreed prodded Sabre-Tooth.

"Two groups of people. Skinny and miserable. They didn't look like they planned to stay long," Sabre-Tooth said, through a mouthful of pressed protein mix. "And a herd of wet sheep."

"How many?"

"Six men in one group, one man, three women and a child in the other, and fifty-two sheep. There were fifty-three but the men killed one of them." He waved one hand, trying to discourage the cloud of small insects around his face. Rain had stopped, and the biting insects had come out from wherever they hid during the downpours.

"Armed?"

"Small personal protection guns, but only one in each group. They've got weak stunguns as well, but that's all."

"Good." The commander sat cross-legged on one of the rocks. "We'll deal with the men tomorrow."

"What about the women?" Laszlo sat up straight, his pale eyes gleaming. "And the child?"

"Leave them for now. We won't be taking prisoners back with us either. The weather's too bad."

Laszlo grimaced. He slapped his arm, squashing a marauding mosquito.

"And the sheep?" one of the soldiers asked.

"I said no prisoners."

The soldier laughed.

Sabre-Tooth chewed on his energy bar thoughtfully. "Sir?"

"Yes?"

"Why don't we go after them tonight? In case they move on? They won't expect us and it would be easier in the dark."

Fahreed raised his eyebrows.

"It might be easier for you," Captain Sindre said, "but the rest of us would have problems in the dark. Even with night vision goggles. The illegals won't have night vision, so I doubt they'll go anywhere before tomorrow. Even then, I'd guess they'd hang around the sheep. They're easy prey."

Sabre-Tooth swallowed the last of the food bar and tried not to think about the sheep.

Dissension – the struggle against injustice

September 22nd 2452

Dissension finds itself alarmed by the Alliance's ever tightening legislation around reproductive rights. Tying citizenship to the legitimacy of birth is bound to lead to undeserved suffering. This legislation affects those who have no power to fight it – unplanned children. Dissension realises the dangers of unfettered population growth - history has given us many examples of the tragedies resulting from it – but tragedies also result from the marginalisation of the disadvantaged. Already, the Alliance is seeing increased suffering through its hard-line border policies. Does it really want to create more disaffection amongst its own citizens? Where is the sense or the justice in this? All our children deserve a future.

Chapter 10

As soon as the sky lightened, Captain Sindre moved his team out of camp and into the grey miserable day.

"Sabre-Tooth, you take the lead. You know where you're going?" Captain Sindre beckoned him forward. "Fahreed? You stay with me."

The rain had started again in the night. It forced its way through the trees, pasting his hair to his skull, and running into his eyes. Underfoot, the ground squelched as Sabre-Tooth followed the path he'd travelled the previous day.

As he'd expected, the illegals had left the site where they'd cooked the dead animal. Only a pile of sodden ash remained, but the disturbed plant growth and trampled mud made the direction of their passage obvious. They were circling round, back to where he'd seen the sheep. Before long, the sound of distant voices competed with the dripping water and loud birdsong.

Captain Sindre pushed ahead and raised a hand. Everyone halted.

"We'll set a trap and ambush them once they're pinned." He pointed at half of the group. "You. Get ahead of them. The rest of us will take them from the rear. Fire when I tell you. Not before."

The first half of the group disappeared into the trees.

Sabre-Tooth drew back to stand next to Laszlo. "What are we going to do?"

Laszlo shrugged. "Kill them. We should have gone for the women. They're a smaller group. They'd be easier. More fun too." He followed the first group into the woods.

After a moment, Sabre-Tooth tagged onto Captain Sindre's team, frowning over Laszlo's strangeness.

Voices drifted from the path ahead before the illegals appeared. They talked in normal tones as they walked through the trees, apparently unaware of their trackers. Each of them carried a backpack. The scent of blood drifted past Sabre-Tooth's nostrils, weaker than yesterday and mixing with the sour smell of unwashed human. He wrinkled his nose in distaste.

The captain waved them forward. All six of the illegals trekked carelessly along a poorly made path through the woods.

"Stop." Captain Sindre's voice was absorbed by the forest, but the last man on the trail spun round, mouth gaping in shock.

He pulled out his weapon and fired it at his pursuers, missing by a wide margin as the captain stepped off the path.

"Drop your weapons," the captain shouted.

The man ignored him as two of the other illegals grabbed for their stun guns.

"Kill them."

The soldiers raised their weapons. Sabre-Tooth touched his, hesitated and left it in his belt. He didn't want to kill starving strangers.

The three leading illegals dropped their packs and ran into the trees, crushing ferns and mosses underfoot and splashing through the swampy ground. The three who faced the soldiers backed away, stunguns still pointed at their assailants. One of the soldiers intercepted a beam; his camouflage armour bouncing it harmlessly into the vegetation. He aimed his own hand laser at the man who'd shot him, and hit him in the centre of his forehead. The target's eyes widened; his mouth opened, but no sound came out. He fell to the ground. The other two turned to run. The soldiers let them stumble through the trees for a few yards before shooting them in the back of their heads.

Two of the soldiers jogged along the path after the three who'd fled.

Sabre-Tooth, rooted in position, stared.

None of this seemed real. The illegals had fallen with no sound, no struggle, no blood. He forced himself to move, crouching down next to one of the bodies. The odour of burning tickled his nostrils. Around the tiny hole in the back of the man's head, tendrils of charred hair drifted, He turned the body onto its back. Mud streaked the shabby coverall, splashed the naked skin of the face. The hole between the man's eyebrows was at least an inch across, neat and circular, and surrounded by dried, cauterised blood. He dragged in a breath, panting for air. His chest had a band of steel around it.

"What are you doing with that?" Captain Sindre rested a heavy hand on his shoulder. "Leave it alone."

Sabre-Tooth stood up. Everything had happened so quickly. The man had been alive one second, dead the next. He forced himself to take one deep breath after another. Captain Sindre's eyes burned into his face, before he muttered under his breath and turned away.

The half of the team who had circled ahead, appeared further along the path together with the men who had chased the escaping illegals. One of them nodded at the captain. "It's done. We let one get away as usual."

"Do we go after the women now?" Laszlo asked.

Captain Sindre frowned at him. "Not today. We need to get back to the pickup point before the weather turns bad. We'll have to take a longer route 'cos that stream's going to be too high where we crossed before." He kicked at one of the backpacks. "Check what's in there, will you?"

Laszlo bent down and opened the pack, pulling out a bloody object. "What the hell?"

"They were cooking dead animals last night," Sabre-Tooth said. His voice had finally returned. "I think they were sheep."

"That looks like sheep to me," the captain said. "A sheep's leg. Bring it along. We can roast it while we wait for the pickup."

Blood dripped from the leg before Laszlo thrust it back into the bag. Sabre-Tooth swallowed the pooling liquid in his mouth. There was no way he would eat that, and he didn't think the others should either.

~~~

"How was your fieldtrip?" Cyrus sounded sour when he met them in the mess.

"Boring," Laszlo said.

"What?"

"Wet, uncomfortable, even worse food than we eat here, and I didn't get to kill anyone. Not properly."

"What do you mean, not properly?"

"He was already dead when I shot him," Laszlo said. "And it was over in seconds."

Cyrus blew out a long breath and turned to Sabre-Tooth. "What about you?"

"I didn't get to kill anyone either." He still couldn't believe he'd seen men falling dead in front of him. Like Laszlo said, the whole massacre had taken less than a couple of minutes. It felt like a vid; distant and unreal.

"I've never been to Wales," Tessis said, from the depths of her flexiseat. "What's it like?"

"Wet." Laszlo and Sabre-Tooth spoke simultaneously in a rare moment of harmony.

"*Just* wet?"

"We nearly drowned crossing a river," Sabre-Tooth told her, "and that was before the storm even started. No wonder it's not settled. The government doesn't have to destroy illegals. If they leave them alone, they'll all be washed away."

"We did get real meat though," Laszlo said. "The illegals killed a sheep, so we ate it."

"Some of us ate it," Sabre-Tooth said. "Some of us thought it was revolting. Part of a dead animal? It was all burnt and bloody. How they could—"

"Some of us should have tried it before criticising." Laszlo smirked at him.

"Sounds like it was interesting." Tessis interrupted before an argument started in earnest.

"We'll get our chance," Cyrus said. "Murkhal said next week."

Sabre-Tooth sank into the flexichair next to Tessis. It was good to be dry.

"Don't get too comfortable." Cyrus folded his arms and smirked. "You've got to report to Murkhal as soon as you get back. You as well." He nodded at Laszlo.

"Why didn't you say so?" Laszlo turned his back and stalked to the door.

"Did he behave?" Cyrus lowered his voice.

"He didn't harm anyone," Sabre-Tooth said.

Laszlo's focus on the small group of women had made him feel uncomfortable. Sabre-Tooth jumped from the chair and followed him out of the mess.

"Captain Sindre was pleased with you." Murkhal stood in front of a rigidly attentive Sabre-Tooth, a small smirk on his face. "Although he was a bit worried by your interest in one of the dead bodies. He said he thought you were going to eat it."

Eat it? Sabre-Tooth swallowed. That would have been worse than the sheep.

"He did say you showed promise as a stalker. A regular bloodhound's what he called you. Said you were slow to attack though. And not suited to ambush or clearing campaigns."

"No Sir."

"Bit of a pity really, considering why you're being trained here. You showed well as a team player though. He told me how you got him and Laszlo out of the water."

Sabre-Tooth had thought that was normal behaviour. He wrinkled his brow as Murkhal moved on to Laszlo.

"Sindre reported that you showed enthusiasm," he said. "He wasn't sure it was the right kind though. I'll be watching you."

"Yes Sir." Laszlo held himself still. Sabre-Tooth sensed his annoyance.

ALLIANCE NEWS CORP –keeping you informed

News update
November 5th 2452

Crime

The Council of the Eurasian Alliance is increasing its efforts to weed out terrorists in the New British Islands. Security has announced a no tolerance policy, and its military arm is sweeping over large parts of the outer regions of London and the Midlands. The days of organisations such as Dissension are numbered. The Council has always encouraged open discussion, even criticism of its policies, but it will not allow any group to openly support terrorism within its own borders.

~~~

Social

Andrei Krewchek's most recent political gathering almost ended in violence this week after Viktor Einerson took visible offence during an intense conversation with his host. Fortunately, Councillor Krewchek's formula of perfect food, copious alcohol and charming staff defused the situation. As our readers will know, Krewchek's Friday night parties, at his Hampstead mansion, are a regular fixture in London's social scene. Top figures from the military have become frequent guests, but possibly Einerson had not expected to meet General Rivera, General Mookjai and Commander Diessen in his rival's house. We have sincere hopes that the two Councillors will learn to work in harmony.

Dissension – the struggle against injustice

November 8th 2452

Security forces are patrolling many areas outside the London Walls, murdering anyone who can't provide evidence of citizenship. Other non-citizens have been taken and brutally questioned in a quest for knowledge they don't have.

Illegals are not terrorists.

Most of those captured or killed are disadvantaged victims struggling to survive.

Members of Dissension are not terrorists. We do not support acts of terrorism. We admire freedom fighters and campaigners for justice, but we don't encourage illegal activity. We are the voice of the disenfranchised. We will not be silenced. Our lawyers are working round the clock to end this exercise in social cleansing.

Chapter 11

Cyrus and Tessis got their own active duty assignment in Wales. The weather wasn't quite as bad as it had been for Sabre-Tooth and they were away for six days.

"Terrorists in the border region," Cyrus said. "We got them all. There were eleven of them. Seven men and four women."

"They were unlicensed citizens," Tessis said. "That doesn't make them terrorists."

"Did you kill them?" Sabre-Tooth asked, wondering if that was the only way of dealing with illegals.

"Four of the men and one of the women," Cyrus said. "The rest were brought back in a security transport. I don't know what they'll do with them. Put them to the question, maybe?"

"They'll send them to some sort of labour camp," Tessis said. "Sterilize them. I don't think they'll waste an interrogation on that bunch. They weren't organised, they were just pathetic outcasts."

~~~

During the next month, Sabre-Tooth had two more active duties. The first took him to outer London, where he worked for a week as a checkpoint guard on the external wall. It should have been exciting. He'd seen so much of London on the vids. Disappointment flooded him when he realised he wouldn't see any more of the city than its fortifications. The other trip, much more interesting, was to an almost dry river system in central Spain. He and Tessis joined an army squad whose role was to protect the environmental restoration team as they worked on the river. It was very hot. Hardly anything grew in the region, and the plants that did manage to survive were spiky and sparse. Sabre-Tooth thrived while, despite the protective wear, Tessis wilted. They saw no hostiles, and killed no one. The people they were supposed to protect were hostile enough for him. Tessis said she wasn't surprised by their belligerence.

~~~

On a morning at the end of November, Sergeant Murkhal summoned them to the parade square, lining the four of them up in front of him. The camp was quiet. Another batch of recruits had moved on to the next stage of their training and the new group hadn't arrived, so only a few soldiers, mostly instructors and admins, went about their business on the other side of the wire.

It was raining again. November had been both warmer and wetter than usual and when the rain stopped, clouds of tiny bloodthirsty insects instantly appeared. Sabre-tooth preferred the rain to the insects. Marginally.

Murkhal paced along the line, staring into each soldier's face. "I am pleased to tell you that you've all successfully completed the major part of your on-site instruction programme. You'll be moving out next week. Well done." He didn't look particularly pleased. The expression on his face was sour.

"Thank you, Sir." A small drop of water slid down Sabre-Tooth's nose. His eyes crossed as he tried to track its path.

"Congratulations. Now you move onto the next stage. You need more field experience but today we are going to see if you have what it takes to kill a person up close and personal, in a non-combat situation. Fail this and you fail the entire programme. I'm sure you remember what the consequences of that will be."

Sabre-Tooth frowned at him. Of course he remembered. He still hadn't had to kill anyone, although he felt partly responsible for the deaths in Wales. If he hadn't tracked the illegals, they might not have died.

"What do you mean, Sir?" As usual, Cyrus asked the question.

"What I said." The sergeant stepped into his personal space. "We have a few prisoners who've been condemned to death. They were brought here last night so you can carry out the sentence. We've one each for you."

Cyrus opened his mouth.

"Do you have a problem with following orders, Cyrus?" Murkhal spat as he hissed the words.

"Me Sir? No Sir." His face flushed. "Not me Sir."

"I know *you* aren't new to killing." Murkhal slapped his stick against one thigh. "You're not new to murder either, are you Laszlo? Or you, Tessis. All of you have experience." He halted in front of Sabre-Tooth. "Maybe not you, but it's no different from the dummies you practised on. You're a fucking animal anyway."

Sabre-Tooth felt his breath leave him. The drop of water clung to the tip of his nose. He took a gulp of air and the drop fell. He really needed to scratch the itch. A quick glance sideways showed him that the flush had faded from Cyrus's face and he had relaxed now that Murkhal's attention had moved on. Laszlo appeared unmoved, but a small smile curved his mouth. Tessis stared straight ahead, her stillness radiating tension.

"Kill prisoners, Sir?" Sabre-Tooth forced himself to speak. Murkhal's foul mood spun outwards, filling the square with unease. He smelled bad. What was wrong with him today? "Defenceless prisoners, Sir?"

"Of course they're fucking defenceless, you idiot. Do you think we'd give them weapons? We don't want them hurting you." The sergeant's voice oozed sarcasm as he sidestepped until he was immediately in front of him. "They're fucking criminals." He spat the words into Sabre-Tooth's face. "DFTs. Dangerous Fucking Terrorists. They might kill thousands if we didn't execute them. Starting with you, if we give them the chance. Good riddance I'd say. If it was up to me."

"But…" Sabre-Tooth couldn't finish his sentence. He felt sick.

"I would have thought it would be easy for you." The sergeant smiled at him, baring discoloured teeth. "With all those predator genes they gave you. Or did the pussy ones win out?"

"I can't kill an unarmed man. Not unless I'm mad at him." He'd never felt the need to kill anything. Except for the man who'd hit him in the bar and, even then, he'd felt guilty for days afterwards. The memory of the blood on his fingers, and under his claws, made his skin crawl.

"You'd better get mad then." The sergeant's face was inches from his and the fetid scent of stale alcohol saturated the air. "Those scientists made a pretty poor job of you, didn't they?"

He forced himself to stay in position. Something was wrong with Murkhal. He never showed up on duty, smelling of alcohol like this. He always sounded angry, but usually it was a performance. Today it looked and smelled real. Sabre-Tooth couldn't think of anything he'd done to make him this mad. "Yes Sir. But—"

"Are you taking the fucking piss?" Sergeant Murkhal's sallow skin flushed as his voice rose to a bellow again. "You don't argue with me. You need to remember why you're here. Why you're allowed to live. Remember who controls your collar." He pulled the console from his belt, held it up and pressed the button.

Sabre-Tooth choked, gasped and his legs crumpled under him. He lay on the ground for a second, panting and unable to move. The pain was even worse than he remembered. When he raised his head, he couldn't focus. At least he hadn't thrown up this time. Or pissed on himself. And he'd managed not to whimper. He pushed himself to his knees, teeth clenched, jaw aching.

"Don't argue with me again." The sergeant pointed the laser control at him, before kicking him in the ribs. "I don't like it. Your job is to do as you're told. All I want to hear from you is 'Yes, Sir'. Now get up, you fucking pussy."

He staggered to his feet, muscles still twitching, his body throbbing with pain.

"And you three," the sergeant said, turning his attention to Laszlo, Cyrus and Tessis. "I really don't want to have you court-martialled for refusing to obey a direct order. You know what the penalty for that is?"

The three stood absolutely still, a new tension in their postures, eyes focussed over the sergeant's shoulder. Laszlo's expression was as blank as ever, but both Cyrus and Tessis looked shocked.

"Well?" He fixed on Tessis. "You know. Why don't you tell us all?"

"Exe…" Tessis stuttered, swallowed and started again. "Execution, Sir."

"That's right. If you're lucky. You know what you'll get if you're unlucky."

The colour drained from Tessis's face.

The sergeant stepped back. "Is that clear?"

"Yes Sir." Cyrus and Laszlo spoke together, their eyes avoiding Sabre-Tooth. Cyrus's eyes slid sideways, tracking a movement at the far end of the field.

Corporal Obi closed the gate behind him and marched a man towards them. The corporal marched slowly, while the man shuffled, with a half walk, half-jogging motion, helped along by constant shoves from Obi. Small and thin, he was dressed in an oversized fluorescent yellow coverall. The sleeves sagged over his hands, and with every few steps, he stumbled on the ragged hems of the trousers. His face had the unhealthy pallor of someone who had been confined indoors indefinitely, and his pupils were enormous, consuming any colour his eyes might have held.

The corporal had a large, muscular dog on a short leash; one of the army's specially bred, genetically enhanced attack dogs. Several of them were chained in a compound in a corner of the training camp. Dogs were used in crowd control, and by military enforcement patrols. Not many troublemakers wanted to risk an encounter with their impressive teeth. Apart from its size, this one didn't look like a dangerous tool of oppression. Its pink tongue lolled out of its mouth as it strained against the leash, snapping at the drops of rain and wagging its plumed tail.

Murkhal jabbed a finger at Sabre-Tooth, then at the prisoner. "There you are. All yours."

"No." Sabre-Tooth couldn't kill that pathetic cowering figure. He wasn't even in a state to fight back. It would be like stamping on some small beetle. He braced himself for the debilitating pain.

The sergeant heaved a melodramatic sigh. "Show him the consequences of disobedience."

Obi dragged the dog forward and grasped its collar, twisting it.

The dog whined.

"Just like yours." He raised his free hand to show a small unit identical to the one that controlled Sabre-Tooth's collar.

"Look at me, Sabre-Tooth. You know this has a kill button?" Sergeant Murkhal turned the collar control in his hands, and stroked the red button. He held Sabre-Tooth's gaze. "If you defy me, then tonight I'll activate this and press it. You're no good to us if you can't obey your handlers. Like that useless dog." He turned to Obi. "Go on, Corporal."

Obi released his grip on the animal's collar and pressed a button on the control unit.

The dog leaped into the air, howling. Sparks flashed around its throat. It convulsed and fell to the ground where it lay on its side twitching for thirty seconds. A whining sound emerged from its mouth.

Sabre-Tooth took a small step forward, mind and body blank.

"Keep your position." Murkhal bellowed at him.

Sabre-Tooth froze, his legs weak from the double shock.

Foam dribbled from the jaws of the dog. One paw jerked.

"Failed obedience training." Sergeant Murkhal returned his attention to Sabre-Tooth. "Follow your orders, or tonight you'll be where that fucking useless mutt is."

Sabre-Tooth swallowed the moisture in his mouth, and fought the urge to vomit.

The dog finally lay still; lips drawn back over white teeth, and eyes bulging. Its shaggy fur already looked dull. That was death, messy and painful. And smelly. The scent of urine, faeces and charred fur clogged his nose. It was nothing like the instantaneous ending of the illegals in Wales.

Sabre-Tooth didn't want to be dead. He cast a desperate look at the other recruits. All three kept their eyes fixed straight ahead. Laszlo's expression was more blank than usual.

"We don't have all day." Murkhal nodded at the prisoner, who drooped next to the corporal, mute and uninterested in anything happening around him. "Just get on with it."

"How?" Sabre-Tooth took a step backwards.

"What have you learned?" the sergeant demanded. He slapped Sabre-Tooth's face with the flat of his hand. Hard.

"For fuck's sake? You've all got hands, knives, and you, you useless fuck, have claws and teeth. Remember what you did to that soldier in town? Just do that again. Now, do you want me to press this button? Because once I start, I won't stop until you're a dribbling wreck."

"No Sir."

What Sabre-Tooth wanted was to slap Sergeant Murkhal back. With his claws extended. He wanted to rip out his throat and watch him die. He wanted him to go away. He wanted him to be a bad dream. He took a single step towards Obi.

His prisoner didn't resemble a murderer or a terrorist in the least. If he'd ever been dangerous, it had been drugged or beaten out of him. The oversized coverall made him almost childlike. His head sagged forward onto his chest. He *must* be drugged; he couldn't have listened to the command for his death so peacefully otherwise.

Sabre-Tooth pulled a knife from his belt and took another small step forward. There was no way he'd use his claws again. Absolutely no way. The memory of all that blood, sticky on his hands and down his nailbeds, made him shudder. He looked round at his companions. There was no support there. Cyrus and Tessis looked very wary, and even Laszlo was uneasy, although Sabre-Tooth guessed that he, at least, was enjoying the spectacle.

He lifted the knife; wishing he could bring himself to sink it into that sadistic sergeant. And then into Corporal Obi, who was idly pushing at the dog's body with one foot. Only the memory of the crippling pain stopped him. That, and what had happened to the dog.

"We're waiting." Sergeant Murkhal fingered the collar control. "Get on with it."

He was trapped. Sabre-Tooth clenched his teeth, ignoring the pain as his pointed canines sank into the inside of his cheek. Stepping forward, he slipped behind the prisoner, pulling the man's head backwards and holding him in position with the palm of one hand across his forehead. The man's body was warm and soft, and much smaller than his own. He was completely submissive. Sabre-Tooth wanted to hug him protectively, but instead, he drew the sharp edge of his knife hard across his throat, from ear to ear, exactly as he'd been taught. He jumped backwards again, and circled round.

Blood spurted from the wound. The prisoner didn't react. His gaze was distant and unaware and he didn't seem to have noticed he'd been stabbed. His life pumped out from the gaping hole, coating the plascrete with a crimson sheen.

"Good job," Murkhal said. "I knew you had it in you."

The prisoner's legs gave way and he collapsed to the ground, his eyes losing even the limited awareness they had had before. Sabre-Tooth took a deep breath, almost choking on the cloying scent. He blew it out, trying hard to rid himself of the taint. It was easy to kill; there was such a small gap between life and death.

"Fetch the next one, Corporal."

Fresh blood odours mixed with the smells from the dog. Sabre-Tooth staggered away to the corner of the field, his hands rubbing at the spots of blood staining the front of his uniform. As the adrenaline drained away, he sank to his knees on the bare earth and vomited. When he looked up Murkhal loomed behind him.

"Get back in line. And you can clean that up later." The sergeant shook his head. "Pathetic."

Sabre-Tooth walked back, legs still trembling from the after effect of the shock collar.

The same scene was played out three more times by his teammates. Between them, they killed two more men and a woman. No one argued. Cyrus struck as efficiently as Sabre-Tooth. Laszlo smiled as he used his knife on the woman. Tessis clenched her jaw and dispatched her prisoner quickly. After it was over, the sergeant lined them up again and ran his eyes over their features. "You're all pathetic. I hate to think what you'd be like if any of them tried to fight back."

No one answered.

"The first one is always the hardest, but the next ones won't be drugged." He paced to Tessis and inspected her.

She stared straight ahead.

"Next time it will come more easily. You don't like them to fight back though, do you?"

"No, Sir." Her expression didn't change.

Murkhal moved to Laszlo. "Easy for you, this time, wasn't it? Well?"

"Yes Sir."

"And you?" Murkhal glared at Cyrus.

"Yes, Sir."

Heavy breathing from his companions filled the space on either side of Sabre-Tooth. It echoed in his ears. The metallic smell of blood saturated his nose and mouth.

"You've all got a free day tomorrow, and free passes for the brothel tonight." Murkhal sneered as he glanced at Tessis. "You'll move out to more permanent barracks on Monday."

"Sergeant?" Obi tipped his chin towards the four dead prisoners and the dog, all sprawling in a lake of blood and dirty rainwater.

Sergeant Murkhal nodded. "Clear that up before you go. The Corporal will show you how." He marched off, leaving Obi to supervise the disposal of the bodies.

As Sabre-Tooth dragged his victim towards the gate, he realised that a small audience of uniformed men watched from the other side of the wire. One of them raised his hands and clapped.

~~~

"What the hell's wrong with him?" Cyrus growled when they were back in barracks. "I think we did a fucking good job. Killing drugged unarmed prisoners though? Where's the fun in that?" He glanced at Sabre-Tooth. "And if that one of yours was a terrorist of any sort, I'll eat my boots. Mind you, he has given us those passes. It's a while since…" He glanced at Tessis's rigid expression and didn't finish the sentence.

"Murkhal?" Laszlo said. "Something must have rattled his cage. What he did to you?" He nodded at Sabre-Tooth. "That was fucked up. And he enjoyed it."

Sabre-Tooth sat on Laszlo's bunk, shaking; the aftermath of the electric shock still thudding through his body, the sourness of vomit on his tongue.

"He lost a month's credit last night," Cyrus said. "In a bet. Not one I organised. I don't even know what it was, but maybe that was it."

Laszlo let out a low whistle. "No wonder he was pissed off."

"He had no fucking right to take it out on us. And calling us pathetic? It's not like I mind doing my job," Cyrus continued. "They probably deserved to die and anyway, they shouldn't have been caught. That dog though…"

No one answered and Cyrus sat down next to Sabre-Tooth. "What's with the collar? I know you said it was for control, but would they really kill you with it?"

"You saw the dog," Sabre-Tooth said. "I'm pretty sure they wouldn't do that to me at first. I'm an expensive piece of kit. At least that's what they say I am. I say I'm human. But if they can't control me I'm worthless to them." He stared at the floor, weak from the horror of the dog's death, as well as shock from the collar and the killing. He looked up at his companions. "You volunteered for this?"

"Not exactly, but it was either this or court-martial. And if anyone has to die it's not going to be me." Cyrus grimaced. "The worst bit was that dog though. I've never heard anything like the noise it made."

"That's shit." Laszlo shrugged. "You've heard a lot worse. They were condemned anyway. It was easy to kill them. I'd do it again. I just wish we could have taken a bit longer. Savoured the moment."

"Lovely." Tessis pushed herself away from the wall and stalked towards him, her face one fierce scowl. "And rewarding you all with the brothel?" She jabbed him in the chest with her forefinger. "I suppose you think it's a great idea to screw some poor woman who's got no choice."

Laszlo's pale eyes narrowed. "I like killing. It makes me horny."

Tessis backed away, her hand descending to the knife in her belt.

"Tessis, don't..." Cyrus jumped up and stood between her and Laszlo.

Laszlo smirked.

"I'm going to kill him." Tessis pulled the knife out. "Filthy bastard. Get out of my way."

"It makes me want to do *baaad* things to people." Laszlo licked his lips. "Killing's a turn on."

Tessis tried to circle round Cyrus.

"Laszlo..." Cyrus started to say something.

"Well it is."

Sabre-Tooth pulled himself out of his introspection. Leaning forward, he grabbed Tessis's wrist, twisting it.

She dropped the knife.

"Don't do it. They'd shoot you."

She strained against his grip, jaw clenched, face flushed. Finally, her shoulders sagged.

"Finished?"

She gave a small nod.

Sabre-Tooth released her, bending down to pick up the knife.

"Brothel." Tessis slipped the knife back into its holster before kicking the edge of the bed, hard. "That's the other alternative I was offered. Join this unit or become a resource for the army. That's where I'll end up if I fail."

"You're one of us now." Cyrus sounded defensive.

"Why are you making such a fuss? They have males in the brothels as well," Laszlo said. "And herms. There'll be something to your taste."

"I wasn't even offered the death penalty." Tessis paid no more attention to him. He'd completely missed her point.

"What did you do?" Cyrus asked.

"Mind your own business." She kicked the bed again.

Sabre tooth winced as the clang of her reinforced toecaps on the bed frame rattled through his aching joints.

"I volunteered for the army," Laszlo muttered, watching Tessis from half-closed eyes. "I knew I'd probably end up dead." He raised his pale eyes to meet her angry stare. He smiled. "This is better."

ALLIANCE NEWS CORP –keeping you informed

Social

Officials have decreed a week of celebration in New Shanghai, the home city of Alliance Leader, Sifia Hong. Our long-serving head of government will marry this weekend, in an important political alliance. This, her second marriage, unites her family, which includes influential council members for the Eastern region of China, with that of General Manuel DeWitte. De Witte heads the Swiss military arm of the Alliance and is Chief Executive of his family corporation, Hydroenergie. Throughout the countries of the Alliance, citizens have been awarded an extra day's holiday to celebrate the wedding. News Corps joins with the citizenship to congratulate the happy couple.

Dissension – the struggle against injustice

November 8th 2452

Speaker for the Eurasian Alliance Council, Sifia Hong, is scheduled to marry Manuel DeWitte later this week, in a blatant display of power grabbing. Readers of Dissension News will remember the rumours of Speaker Hong's first marriage and the suspicious death of husband number one. General DeWitte would do well to watch his back.

Chapter 12

The military brothel squatted in the centre of town; a square three-storey building constructed from black plascrete and sited on the side of the square next to the military enforcement offices. There were no windows on the ground floor and the main door was the same black as the plascrete walls.

"This is supposed to be a pleasure house?" Cyrus cast an incredulous glance at Laszlo. "It's like a mini-model of Security Central."

"It's not bloody London." Laszlo shrugged. "Come on, Cyrus. You've been in worse places."

"Not for fun, I haven't."

"You have."

"I don't like it," Sabre-Tooth said. "It's like a prison. And Tessis—"

"Will you shut the fuck up about Tessis? She could have come if she'd wanted to." Cyrus sounded uncharacteristically defensive. "There's something for all tastes in these places."

"But she—"

"Will you just shut up? So she might have become a chained whore. We might have become dead," Cyrus said. "Anyway, as long as we're careful, none of that's going to happen. Not to any of us."

Sabre-Tooth gave up. He was here, so he may as well dump the guilt. There was no way he wanted to spend the night alone in his cubicle. He'd never sleep; sparks still jumped at the back of his eyes from the collar shock and every time he closed them, he saw the dog.

"You've never done this before, Sabe." Cyrus forced cheer into his voice. "You're not a man till you've fucked something."

"According to you I'm not a man anyway. I'm a mutant mongrel. You keep telling me that." Against his will, he was interested.

He forced the image of the drugged prisoner out of his head. It was hard to think of pleasure when that man would never feel anything again.

And the dog.

He regretted the dog's death far more than that of the zombie-like prisoner. It had been so pleased with its life, not like the man who was half-dead even before Sabre-Tooth touched him.

The door opened and a woman appeared in the dimly lit entrance. "Your passes, please?"

She had skin as dark as Obi's and her well-muscled body was covered only by combat boots and a heavy belt that circled her waist. It dripped offensive weapons and concealed as much of her as a skirt would have done. She blocked the door as she examined the passes by the light of a wristunit. Even her forearms were sleek with muscle. Moisture pooled in Sabre-Tooth's mouth.

Finally, she stepped back and let them through, pointing them in the direction of a door at the other end of the corridor. "Any trouble and I'll shoot you."

Sabre-Tooth looked back over his shoulder as he followed Laszlo though the door. If they had women like her…

She was better than Rashelle. Better than Tessis. He cut the thought off; Tessis wouldn't like him thinking of her in that way.

"Come on." Cyrus waited for him. "For fuck's sake, Mongrel. Don't stare at her like that. She's not a sexscort. She really would shoot you. She'd cut your balls off first though."

Sabre-Tooth flinched.

"With a blunt knife. So leave her alone."

The room was poorly lit, with a drinks bar at one end, a small booth next to it, and a selection of tables scattered around the floor. Five young women stood on the narrow platform opposite the bar, along with three youths and a person who could have been male or female. Dim spotlights illuminated them. They all looked bored despite the wide smiles they directed at the newcomers. None of them were as exciting as the woman on the door.

A small group of men dressed in regular army coveralls lounged round one table, drinking heavily and talking. Two naked women sat with them. Sabre-Tooth recognised one of the martial arts trainers from his base. Strong perfume filled his nostrils as a bare-chested, shaven-headed young man dressed in low-cut silky black trousers glided up to them. A scar ran from his right shoulder, bisecting the brown skin from his chest to his navel, narrowing before it disappeared under the silk of his waistband.

Sabre-Tooth sneezed as the chemical fumes assaulted his senses.

The man ignored him. "What can I do for you? I'm your host, here to make sure you have a good time. Would you like drinks now? Or afterwards? Your passes cover the cost of one drink only. If you want any drugs, legal of course, you need to pay extra." His voice was a monotone.

"Afterwards," Cyrus said.

The host pointed at the platform. "All these are available tonight, and covered by your passes. Between them, they'll cater to most tastes. They're all motivated to please."

Laszlo fixed his gaze on a small blonde woman, who looked even younger than Tessis. He licked his lips. "I like her."

Cyrus nudged him. "Not that one."

Laszlo turned his head and glared.

"You know you—"

"Fine." Laszlo pointed at one of the youths on the platform, a slender brown-skinned figure wearing only a strip of pale cloth around his hips. "He'll do."

Cyrus let out a breath that held a lot of relief.

The host nodded at the youth, who stepped down and smiled at Laszlo. Taking him by the hand, he led him across the room, through a door and out of sight.

Cyrus watched them go, a frown crossing his face. "I hope Laszlo remembers he's been given limits. At least he's chosen..." His voice trailed off into silence.

"What do you mean?" Sabre-Tooth asked.

Cyrus shook his head, still looking worried. "Nothing, I think. I hope. He's been warned. Anyway, he likes small blondes best. Females usually. I'm sure he'll be careful." His frown deepened.

"What does Laszlo—?" Sabre-Tooth had occasionally wondered why Cyrus was so concerned about Laszlo. He talked about killing, and had threatened Tessis. It was all talk though, wasn't it? Surely, he wouldn't follow through? They'd shoot him.

"Never mind." Cyrus shrugged off his concern and turned to the host. "My comrade here's an absolute beginner; never had a woman or a man. Who would you suggest?"

Sabre-Tooth flexed his fingers nervously, realising his claws were out.

The host's eyes widened. "Is he dangerous?"

"We're all dangerous." Cyrus smirked. "Stone cold killers, that's us."

The host folded his arms, unamused. "Male or female?"

"What do you want?" Cyrus asked. "Any of those appeal?" He nodded at the platform.

"Female," Sabre-Tooth said. The two remaining youths and the herm did nothing for him. None of the women were anything like the impressive doorkeeper either, but he was reluctantly interested.

"I don't want any of them damaged. They're all good earners, and a pass doesn't pay enough to cover downtime." The host pursed his lips thoughtfully. "I think I have what you want though. If you'll follow me?"

Cyrus nudged Sabre-Tooth. "Go on. I'll check he's not trying to rip you off." He lowered his voice. "Laszlo's the one he should really be worried about if he's concerned about damage."

The host glanced over his shoulder. "Are you both coming?"

"I want to see what you're offering. The Mongrel's got a proper pass, so you'd better give him his money's worth." Cyrus followed them through the door and up a flight of stairs.

The lights were low and tinged with an orange hue, giving a look of warmth to the smooth white walls. There were no windows. He was reminded of the lab.

"Are you alright?" Cyrus whispered. "I mean, after that electric shock. Will it still work? You don't want to waste your pass if it doesn't."

It took a moment for Sabre-Tooth to understand what he was talking about. It was none of Cyrus's business, but his body had definitely responded to the woman on the door. "I'm fine."

The host stopped in front of a door. "Here you are. Try not to damage her." He didn't sound too bothered.

Cyrus reached past him and pushed the door open, activating the low lighting inside. Sabre-Tooth peered over his shoulder at a pale naked girl who lay on the narrow bunk, arms folded behind her head to form a pillow. Her head jerked as the door opened.

"She's chained to the bed." Cyrus turned an enquiring eye on the host. "Why?"

"She tried to attack a client," he said. "Last week she got a knife from somewhere. We haven't decided what to do with her yet, but she's clean and up to date with all her vacs. Your man looks like he can take care of himself. Anyway, she's practically worthless, so if he does get violent…."

Cyrus inspected the girl again. "What do you think? She's alive and female. Mongrel?"

Sabre-Tooth shrugged, uncomfortable with the situation. Why didn't Cyrus just go away and leave him to it?

The room was small and hot. Did the girl lie in the dark when she was alone? An acrid scent of urine drifted past his nostrils, almost overwhelming the stale odour of old sex. The smell was awful. Surely, the others must have noticed?

A narrow collar encircled the girl's neck securing her to a metal bar on the bed. Her thin body tensed as he ran his eyes over her. She was nothing like the awe-inspiring doorkeeper.

He suppressed his disappointment. "I suppose so."

"Okay." Cyrus backed out of the door. "I'm off to find one of my own."

"Come down to the bar when you're finished." The host followed Cyrus. "And please? Try not to damage her. It makes a lot of paperwork." He closed the door behind him, leaving Sabre-Tooth with the girl.

She still said nothing.

Sabre-Tooth fingered his own collar. He didn't want to touch this girl; he could feel her waves of frustration and smell her despair. Every one of her ribs pressed visibly against her skin.

His claws were still out and he gazed at his hands while he concentrated on retracting them. "Why did you try to knife someone?"

The girl pushed herself to a sitting position, a shock of messy light brown hair falling in tangles over her shoulders. He darted a glance at her. Small breasts sat on her skinny frame and as she turned to look at him, the light caught a halo of darkening colour around her half-closed left eye.

Despite himself, Sabre-Tooth was reluctantly aroused. And ashamed.

"He deserved it," she muttered. "I'm sorry I didn't kill him. It was his own knife. He shouldn't have brought it in here."

"Was it worth ending up a prisoner?"

"No." She caught her lower lip between her teeth. "Anyway, I was already a prisoner. We're all prisoners here. What's that round *your* neck?"

Sabre-Tooth hooked his claws in the edge of his collar "A control collar. It's used to punish me." He examined hers. It was a plain plastic circle, designed to restrain rather than punish, and tight enough to abrade the skin of her throat. "Are you drugged?"

"I wish." She lowered her eyelids, concealing her expression. "I'm just hungry. Well? Are you going to do what you came for?"

"I don't know." It wasn't right to fuck a chained woman, one who had no choice and had obviously been beaten. That was rape, wasn't it? Life was just too complicated. "I don't think so. What's your name?"

She sighed heavily. "What business is that of yours?"

Sabre-Tooth stepped forward, flexing his claws.

The girl scrabbled backwards on the bed. "Alina. I'm sorry. I—"

"I want to take that collar off. It's making your neck all red." He frowned at her. "I'm not going to hurt you."

Her pupils were huge. She nodded.

He slid the tips of his claws behind the plastic round her neck and jerked. The collar split easily. The rapid beating of her heart echoed in his ears.

She pushed it off the bed. "Now what do you think I'm going to do? It's not like I can get away. There's nowhere to go."

The collar was a symbol. Sabre-Tooth raised his hand to his own throat, absolutely sure he shouldn't take advantage of this woman. A raised welt circled her neck, where the collar had rubbed the skin. She winced as she scratched it.

Twisting round, she slid off the bunk and stretched her arms above her head. The light caught the marks of other bruises as she moved.

"They'll probably kill me, you know? Or chain me up again. I'd be better off dead." She glanced up at him, checking his reaction.

Sabre-Tooth shrugged; eyes focussed on her movement. That was what Tessis said too, but his status was almost as bad as the girl's. He hadn't wanted to kill that pathetic little man, but he wanted to die even less. "*I'm* not going to kill you."

"Pity. You'd better fuck me then."

"What? I don't want to. Why?"

She moved her gaze down his body. "Looks like you do to me. It's what you came for isn't it?"

"I suppose. But…" He hadn't realised the woman would be a prisoner. He hadn't realised her room would smell so bad. A rank scent rose from her skin.

"Come on. You can tell them I co-operated. Tell them you liked me." She stalked towards him, breasts thrust forward. "Tell them you'd like to see me again. And make sure you tell them who broke the collar. If they think I did it, they'll beat me." She smiled, revealing teeth that were a little crooked.

Sabre-Tooth backed away. "I can't—"

"I don't *really* want to die." She stroked both hands over his chest, desperate eyes meeting his. "They might not kill me if you say nice things about me. They might let me out of here one day if I look cowed enough. Please?" Her fingers trembled against his body and moved downwards.

He grabbed them with his own hand. "Stop it." He squeezed his eyes closed, aware of his growing arousal. Even the sour smell rising from her body didn't stop it.

"Please?"

ALLIANCE NEWS CORP – keeping you informed

News Update
November 9th 2452

Political

Intensive lobbying is underway at government level as the Council prepares to vote on the issue of the Indian Border area. The Council is more divided than ever, with Viktor Einerson, the Councillor for Defence firmly against 'wasting more money, at a time when the Alliance faces multiple challenges within its own boundaries.' His opponents claim he is a weak figurehead, both for the army and for the security forces, while his supporters praise him as a cautious and efficient leader. Both arguments have merit. According to Councillor for Foreign Affairs, Andrei Krewchek, the civil uprising in India has the potential to cause disturbances throughout the neighbouring Alliance countries. Sifia Hong states that the Alliance cannot afford to display weakness, but has given no indication of which way she intends to vote.

Chapter 13

Tired of Cyrus's incessant chatter, Sabre-Tooth ate his lunch late and alone. A day without the constant yelling of superior officers was a true luxury and he didn't want it marred by his irritating teammate, who was keen to talk about the previous night. Sabre-Tooth didn't need to hear about Cyrus's experience and he certainly didn't want to share his own.

He picked up a cup of caffa and carried it back to his table. Propping his elbows on the tabletop, he let his chin rest in his hands. He was miserable and his head hurt; a residue from yesterday's collar shock. However hard he tried, he couldn't get the image of the dying dog and the chained woman out of his mind.

Closing his eyes, he started to spin fantasies in his head; he'd avenge the dog and rescue the woman, like in the old vids he used to watch.

He'd liked the sex, but not as much as he'd expected. It had been over quickly, almost as soon as he was in her. He knew he'd done it right. It just felt wrong; the woman was desperate, and afterwards he kept thinking about what Tessis had said, about how she'd been threatened with imprisonment and servitude in an army brothel. Maybe all the workers there were in the same situation, maybe none of them would ever see the outside world again.

Why did everything have to be so difficult? He couldn't even rescue himself, let alone a heavily guarded, indentured sexscort.

Nursing his cup between his hands, he took a small sip. The drink was lukewarm and unappealing. He put it down as Obi approached.

"Sir." He pushed his chair back and stood to attention.

Evil fucker, he thought, borrowing one of Cyrus's favourite phrases.

"Day off's over," Obi said. "For you, anyway. Commander Diessen wants to talk to you."

Sabre-Tooth followed him across the square to the administration building. The morning rain had stopped and the plascrete gently steamed in the late autumn sun.

Obi let out an unconscious sigh of relief as they entered the cooler gloom of the office block, wiping the sweat from his forehead before knocking on a door, opening it and pushing Sabre-Tooth through into a roomy office.

Sergeant Murkhal stood at the window looking out. As Sabre-Tooth and Obi entered, he pressed the button controlling the shutter. It swept across the plasglas, blocking the daylight. Artificial lights blinked on and Murkhal turned round.

A wave of mixed apprehension and hatred deprived Sabre-Tooth of breath. He coughed.

Obi waved him towards a desk, and adopted a parade rest position just inside the door.

"Commander Diessen wants to speak to you." Murkhal approached him, pushing him roughly into the desk's chair. "Sit down." Reaching over Sabre-Tooth's shoulder, he touched the control panel. "Pay attention."

Sabre-Tooth kept one eye on Murkhal, who loomed over him from the other side of the desk, smelling strongly of fresh sweat and stale alcohol. Still? His other eye focussed on the opposite chair, which brightened as an image took shape.

Commander Diessen's face and shoulders appeared first, before his body solidified into an impression of reality. A holo-image. The real Diessen must be in his London office.

"Good afternoon Sabre-Tooth." The image smiled at him.

"Good afternoon, Sir." He didn't know what to do with his hands. Slipping them under his thighs, he sat on them.

"You did well yesterday," Diessen said. "I watched your performance. For a first attempt, it was a good clean kill. You need to be more decisive though."

"Yes Sir." It was a pity he hadn't killed Murkhal and Obi instead of the pathetic prisoner.

"Corporal Obi, Sergeant Murkhal. Leave me with Sabre-Tooth for a moment." Diessen waited until the door closed behind Obi. "Right, Sabre-Tooth. I want you to do a job for me. It'll be a test of your abilities."

Sabre-Tooth frowned. "Sir?"

"I need to know that you're worth keeping. You're expensive. Are you worth future investment and training, or is it more economical to stop the experiment now and get rid of the other chimeras? Do you understand what I'm asking?"

"Yes Sir." He wasn't an idiot; he knew a threat when he heard one.

"I want you to terminate a man who has become a danger to the country and to the Council of the Eurasian Alliance."

"What man, Sir?" Sabre-Tooth pulled his hands out from underneath him, clenching his fists and letting his unsheathed claws dig into his palms. The pain stopped him losing his calm and punching the desk console. He still didn't want to die and he definitely didn't want the collar shock again.

"This man is in a position to destabilise the whole Alliance," Diessen said. "He could cause major civil unrest. It's my job to stop him. I want you to kill him. As efficiently as you killed the terrorist."

"Sir?"

"Yes?"

"Why me, Sir?" If the man was that dangerous, surely there were more experienced operators? Even among Diessen's chosen four, he wasn't the most obvious candidate. Laszlo enjoyed killing, Cyrus was indifferent, and Tessis was more efficient than he was. They all had more experience. "The others—"

"Because that's what I've decided." Diessen's already pink face darkened. "If you can't follow my orders, you're done."

"Yes Sir." He wondered whether Diessen would really kill him if he disobeyed.

"You have an advantage at night and in places you've never been," Diessen said, with an exaggerated air of patience. "Those enhanced senses you were given have to be useful for something. Besides, I told you you're a gamble, so this is a test of your technology. This is the sort of job you were designed for."

"Yes Sir." He hesitated. "What if I can't do it?"

"You won't fail," Diessen said. "But if you do, and if you allow yourself to be caught, you won't live long enough to be questioned. If you don't make the rendezvous point on time, I'll press the termination button. Understand?"

"Yes Sir." Sabre-Tooth's heart started to race.

"Do you have any questions?"

"Is this another terrorist, Sir?"

"You don't need to know who it is," Diessen snapped. "You don't need to know anything, other than that I've given you an order."

"Yes, Sir." So, why did he bother asking? Sabre-Tooth's fists tightened round the pain in his hands.

"I've had the necessary details documented for you," Diessen said. "Location, target information and so on. They'll be on your desktop unit for the next hour; after that they'll be deleted. You'd better get on with it."

"Yes Sir." Sabre-Tooth pushed his chair back.

"I'll talk to you again once you've read your instructions. Don't let me down."

"No Sir." Sabre-Tooth dug his claws further into his palms, letting the pain hold him in position while Diessen's avatar faded.

Murkhal had gone, but Obi waited outside the door, propped against the opposite wall. He straightened as Sabre-Tooth came out. "You need to memorize your instructions. I don't know what they are, so you have to make sure you understand them. I've been told to take you to your start location tonight."

"Where is it?"

"It'll be in your instructions. Make sure you don't fuck this up," Obi said. "My job's on the line here. You don't want to fail. Remember yesterday? Fido?"

"Yes Sir." Sabre-Tooth turned across the square to his cubicle.

Obi's voice followed him. "What happened to your hands?"

A drop of blood fell to the plascrete. Sabre-Tooth closed his fists around the wounds. "Nothing Sir." He kept walking.

ALLIANCE NEWS CORP – keeping you informed

News Update
November 9th 2452

Environment

Reports from climate scientists based at the North Pole indicate that the warming of the planet is slowing. This is good news, although the temperature will continue to climb the upward curve for at least a hundred years. Updated predictions for sea level rises will be released sometime in the next week. This year has been fractious as far as weather patterns are concerned, with an increased number of super-hurricanes reaching further into former temperate zones. Northern Europe has escaped the worst of the damaging storms, but news from the Americas has not been good. The most positive data comes from Southern Europe, where desert encroachment appears to have reached its peak.

~~~

Low Countries – Breaking News

Over the past week, heavy winds and high seas have battered The Floating Cities of The Netherlands. Two housing complexes are known to have broken loose from the mother city. The authorities are hopeful that they will be found intact. Searches will start as soon as the winds die down.

Chapter 14

Obi dropped him at a location an hour away from camp. As soon as Sabre-Tooth climbed out of his seat and jumped down to the road, the groundtran jerked forward, leaving for wherever it would wait until he returned.

The sun had completely set, but the night was bright with a thin sliver of moon and a sky full of stars. Pushing his way through the roadside vegetation, he followed a narrow animal track into the woodland. He visualised the map he'd been given and began to jog. An image of his target flickered at the back of his mind.

Middle-aged man, stocky, medium height, no enhancements. Should be asleep.

"You don't need to know who he is," Diessen had said. "Just what he looks like."

Sabre-Tooth had watched the news vids on the lab flatscreen every morning for as long as he could remember. The target was a household name. How could Diessen think that he wouldn't recognise him? Did he imagine Sabre-Tooth was stupid?

Diessen was the stupid one.

Lack of cloud cover gave the air a fresher feel, even in the dense woodland. The trees were spindly, many of them leafless deciduous species, and bare branches allowed enough moonlight to leak through for Sabre-Tooth to see where he was going. Half his mind was sufficient to pick his way along the trail; the other half mulled over his assignment.

Councillor Einerson.

Councillor Einerson was Councillor for Defence, not only for the New British Islands, but for the whole of the Eurasian Alliance. He was a very important person. That's why it had to be so secret. That's why Obi and Murkhal couldn't know.

It must be why Diessen had chosen him. If anything went wrong, Sabre-Tooth could be terminated before he had a chance to reveal Diessen's involvement. He wondered whether Diessen might kill him anyway, just to keep the secret.

Obi had organised the transport though; surely he would be able to work out who the target was, especially if Sabre-Tooth succeeded. There'd be uproar from the media. Diessen was delusional if he thought he could keep that sort of secret. Hopefully he was delusional enough not to realise that Sabre-Tooth recognised the image of his target. He had been very clear. Sabre-Tooth wouldn't be allowed to talk. Hairs on the back of his neck rose as he remembered the charred smell of the dog's fur.

He had to lose the image of the dog. There was no point in dwelling on it. For all his fantasising, he couldn't do anything about it, but it was too easy to imagine himself in its place. He raised one hand, to touch the collar. Without it, he could disappear. With it, he was helpless.

Rustlings from the woodland broke the silence from time to time, and at one point something large rippled through the undergrowth to one side of the path. Probably a boar, disturbed by his passing. This far from London, the countryside appeared to be empty of humanity, and the only sounds were the natural sounds of the night. Sabre-Tooth paused, squinting into the darkness and hoping to see something more exciting than the half-drowned sheep in Wales.

The woods at night held no horrors for him. If only he didn't have the collar, he could live in this forest. Sighing, he pulled an energy bar from his belt and crammed it into his mouth. Even if he didn't have the collar, they'd come after him. The army would hunt him down. It was what they did.

Eventually the trees thinned to a mixture of tall shrubs, thorny undergrowth and ferns. A high wall loomed ahead of him. Someone had made an effort to clear the growth around the base of the wall, but it hadn't been cut back for a while and a few fast-growing shrubs would give Sabre-Tooth enough shelter. His chameleon skinsuit turned him into a shadow.

The security was pathetic, especially for a member of the Council of Government. Sabre-Tooth had learned how it should be done in the first month of his training. There ought to have been at least fifty metres of clear ground between the forest and the wall. The new moon illuminated patches of rough grassland along the base of the barrier, but young trees sprouted up as well. He couldn't see any signs that the security guards had ever patrolled along this part of the boundary.

He halted, listening. Small sounds in the darkness told him he wasn't alone. His enhanced eyes caught sight of a tiny shrew meandering through the thorns.

Why the hell did Diessen want the Defence Councillor dead?

Smooth black plastone walls, nearly four metres high and topped with a tangle of spiked wire, surrounded the estate. Sabre-Tooth crouched in the shadows at the bottom of the wall, assessing the barrier. It was exactly as it had been described in his infopack. Every few metres a tiny camera eye peered out from the wire. He wondered how carefully they were monitored.

Einerson had to be personal to Diessen. If he survived the job, Sabre-Tooth intended to find out why. He didn't like not knowing and his mind ran in circles while his other senses checked the landscape.

Diessen said this was a test; his first real mission. If he failed, he would die. If he succeeded, he might still die. Diessen threatened Sugar and Tygre as well.

He *had* to kill Councillor Einerson.

Einerson was a corrupt enemy of the state, according to the information on his communit, but Sabre-Tooth suspected that the man was just an enemy of Diessen, an enemy in the top layer of government. This weekend he was supposed to be alone in his country house; an easy target, according to Diessen. Of course, he'd be surrounded by servants and security guards, not to mention his own private army. Apparently they didn't count. They would be 'dealt with'.

Sabre-Tooth wished it were Diessen he needed to kill. The savagery of his mood took his breath away. He leaned against the wall, out of sight of the cameras. Tonight, he'd been told, only two sentries were on duty, manning both the gate and the security cameras, ready to alert their team if the estate was attacked. He started to wonder if Diessen had anything to do with the scarcity of security personnel; after all, he had the power and the influence. Even so, the Councillor should have been more cautious. Councillor for Defence? He shouldn't be trusted to defend a chocolate stall, let alone the whole of the British Islands and the Eurasian Alliance.

The shrew moved along the side of his foot, oblivious to his presence. Sabre-Tooth shifted less than a millimetre and the small animal froze, nose twitching, before it spun round and fled into a gap between tree roots.

Sabre-Tooth turned back to the wall.

He flexed his leg muscles, bouncing on the balls of his feet for a moment. His stomach lurched upwards and he retched, wiping his hand across his mouth afterwards. He hoped it would rain later, as leaving vomit behind was probably something Diessen would frown on. Of course it would rain; torrential downpours were as reliable as the dawn.

Cyrus told him he'd become hardened to killing.

Laszlo told him he should just enjoy it but Laszlo was not normal by any standards.

The smell of blood, the messiness of death, the way the light had faded from his victim's eyes, haunted Sabre-Tooth. Images of the spreading crimson puddle, the shock in Cyrus's eyes, the lifeblood draining from the drugged man ran round and round his head, and he only just stopped himself humming with distress.

He was procrastinating. It was time to move.

The plastone wall towered above him, so he took a few steps back, crouched down and sprang upwards, thrusting with all the power in his calf muscles. He grabbed the base of one of the spikes and pulled himself to the top, landing amongst the sharp edging. The skinsuit protected him from the worst, but he wasted no time in jumping down from the wall; backing into its shadow while he assessed his surroundings. A selection of small eyes swivelled on top of the wall, turning their imaging systems on him. All they would record was his skinsuit, or so he'd been told. Programmed to fit in with any background, it was indistinguishable from the shrubs and the wall.

His heart pounded against his chest, heavily enough to hurt. It would be bad if he had to kill any of the guards as well. Worse if they killed him. He couldn't see any though, not even around the house. He examined it very, very carefully.

House was probably not the most accurate description of the building. To distract himself, Sabre-Tooth toyed with other descriptions: *manor house, estate, citadel.*

A strip of grassland, a hundred metres wide lay between the wall and the house.

Villa, mansion, fortress.

He closed his eyes, leaning back against the plastone perimeter wall.

Memory rose up, swamping him in a wave of confusion. Last night, after he finished with the woman, he'd left her on the bed and returned to the bar, wondering what would happen to her. Would they put a new collar on her? He'd told the host that he was very satisfied and maybe that would be enough. The metallic taste of blood flooded his mouth as he bit the inside of his cheek.

He was procrastinating again.

Castle, stronghold…

If he didn't get on with the job, he'd be in a worse place than that girl.

He pushed himself away from the wall and sprinted across the garden, planning his entry as he went. Landscapers had been hard at work in the grounds, and the stretch between the wall and the big house (*mansion*) was roughly clipped lawn. Shadows around the edges resolved themselves into huddles of small sheep. Maybe *they* were the landscapers. Whatever their function, they paid no attention to Sabre-Tooth as he passed.

His instructions said that a window on the bedroom corridor would be left open for him. When he looked up, a window stood slightly ajar on the second floor.

A plasteel downpipe helped him to steady his careful ascent up the side of the house to his target window. He pushed it wider and slipped into an empty bedroom. All was quiet. The darkness was almost absolute, but Sabre-Tooth's eyes adjusted quickly. He left the bedroom and padded along the corridor, picking out the doors as he went. Under his feet, the floor was soft and springy. Carpet. He'd never encountered it before and crouched down to run his fingers over the surface.

No security guards disturbed the quiet. It was hard to believe that the owner of this house was an important man.

Sabre-Tooth was grateful no one was around, but…

Why didn't Einerson have better protection? What was the point of a private army if it was asleep?

He paused, took a deep breath, and approached the bedroom door he wanted. Turning the knob, he stepped inside. The room was as dark as the corridor. His eyes picked out the shape of an oversized bed. His ears picked up the sound of breathing.

Two different rhythms?

He froze in surprise.

Einerson wasn't alone; there was another body asleep in the bed. No one had mentioned a second person. The instructions were clear. The target was supposed to be alone. Diessen had said so.

Both bodies breathed as though deeply asleep, and one of them let out a soft, rumbling snore. Sabre-Tooth pulled his knife out of his belt, but stayed close to the door.

Did the presence of someone else change things? Should he still kill his target? What if he killed the wrong one?

Einerson was a middle-aged, stocky, florid-faced man, soft, overweight, and no physical threat to anyone. His expression was dour, his mouth turned down at the corners. According to Diessen, he should be an easy kill. The pictures of him didn't shout out 'one of the most powerful politicians in the New British Islands'. They didn't state 'important representative of the Eurasian Alliance' but maybe, in person, he had more charisma.

Sabre-Tooth moved closer to the bed, trying to work out which of the sleeping bodies matched the description. Both were mounds, covered by light bedding.

Should he kill both?

He chewed his lip as he thought what might happen to him if he returned without performing his task. The closest body stirred in its sleep, huffing out a small grunting noise.

Sabre-Tooth turned the knife in his hand, indecisive. Would he be expected to make the kill under these circumstances? What if neither of them was his target?

An image of the dog played through his mind again and he swallowed, feeling the pressure of his collar under the skinsuit. Taking a deep breath, he leaned over the bed, squinting at the two shapes. The man nearest to Sabre-Tooth lay on his back, mouth half-open. He was substantial in shape and size.

Sabre-Tooth sniffed.

Two distinctive scents. Male and female.

On the other side of his target, a woman slept on her side, her back to the man.

The man had to be Einerson.

He slid his knife vertically along the first of the carotid arteries in the man's neck, then plunged it into the second, jumping back as blood sprayed out. Job done, he backed away. No one could survive that sort of wound.

He flung himself through the door, sprinted back down the corridor and was half out of the window when the screaming started

ALLIANCE NEWS CORP – keeping you informed

News Update
November 10th, 2452

Breaking news!

Viktor Einerson, Head of the Department of Defence of the British Islands and Defence Councillor for the Eurasian Alliance, was murdered on Saturday night while he slept in his own bed. His long-term lover, Sybil Rante was asleep next to him, but apparently saw nothing. Miss Rante has now been taken into custody for her own protection.

The majority of Einerson's household appears to have been drugged, the finger of suspicion pointing at the servants' kitchen. The Councillor's personal guard is in the custody of the Security Services and will be closely questioned over the next few days. At the present moment, the Intelligence services are not prepared to implicate anyone. The field of suspects is open.

Chapter 15

The following morning Obi took him back to the office where Commander Diessen talked to him by holo-link.

"You should have killed them both." The life-sized avatar jabbed at him with one forefinger.

"Yes Sir. Sorry Sir." Sabre-Tooth stared at the blank wall behind the commander's image, hands clasped behind his back, hiding the fact that his claws flexed in agitation. His palms, where he'd clawed himself at his last meeting with Diessen, still stung.

"Suppose she saw you?"

It was a stupid question. Sabre-Tooth didn't answer.

The skinsuit had been designed to provide the perfect disguise, as well as enabling him to come and go, leaving nothing behind. It had been too dark for purely human eyes anyway. She wouldn't have even seen his shadow.

"You can't afford to be squeamish." The avatar paced round to the front of his desk and fixed its narrow gaze on Sabre-Tooth. It looked and sounded exactly like Diessen, except it left no footfall and had no scent at all. "Not if you want to stay alive. Understand?"

"Yes Sir."

"Good. It wasn't a bad first job. Next time though, kill anyone who's with your target."

"Yes Sir." Next time?

"Still, you did well. You've made the world a safer place."

"Thank you, Sir." Sabre-Tooth kept his voice flat. Rage burned at the bottom of his throat. He wanted to scream it out into Diessen's bloated red face.

He'd made the world safer for Diessen, maybe.

He wanted to rip the commander's throat out. That murder wouldn't cost him much soul-searching. There was the collar, though, and anyway, he didn't think it was possible to kill a holo-image.

"Don't talk about this to anyone." Diessen's avatar folded its arms and leant against the corner of the desk. "You'll find a small reward in your credit listing when you check it."

"Thank you, Sir," Sabre-Tooth repeated.

"You're dismissed." The avatar faded into nothingness.

Sabre-Tooth held himself straight until he was out of the building, and then he slumped, his awareness of the collar around his neck choking him. He was on a tighter chain than the murdered dog. He almost wished he was dead, but whenever he thought of the dog convulsing as the soldier pressed the kill button, he shuddered. Like Tessis, he wanted to live.

Unwilling to talk to anyone, he headed straight for his room. He hadn't slept when he returned from the mission and his head spun with exhaustion.

"Mongrel?"

Sabre-Tooth groaned under his breath. He waited until Cyrus caught him up.

"Where've you been?"

Sabre-Tooth shrugged.

"Obi said you had a test," Cyrus said. "What happened?"

"I had to kill someone," Sabre-Tooth said. "I'm not supposed to talk about it."

"Someone else? Who was it? Another prisoner?" Cyrus's eyes widened. "Why just you? Come and have a drink." He had a secret source of alcohol, as well as a stash of other forbidden drugs.

"I can't talk about it," Sabre-Tooth repeated. "Anyway, it's not midday yet."

"Have some coffee at least. We're all moving out tonight, so we're free until then," Cyrus waited. "Come on."

Sabre-Tooth sighed. He was sure he was still too wired to sleep. "Okay."

Laszlo and Tessis were in the mess, both sprawling in battered flexichairs in front of the entertainment screen. Laszlo's eyes were glazed.

Probably illegal painkillers, Sabre-Tooth thought, wishing he knew where they came from. Both Laszlo and Cyrus had contacts they wouldn't share.

He collected caffa from the duty waiter and slumped onto the sofa.

Cyrus sat next to him. "So, Mongrel—"

"Shut up Cyrus," Sabre-Tooth snapped. "I said I'm not allowed to talk about last night so just shut the fuck up." He stretched his legs out and focussed on the news, ignoring Cyrus's irritation.

The screen filled with the face of a man. A familiar face.

Sabre-Tooth lifted his cup to his lips.

"They got a Councillor," Cyrus commented. "At his country house. He was Councillor for Defence. There's absolute uproar. No senior government rep has been assassinated for more than five years. It's all over the media."

Sabre-Tooth made a non-committal noise, still not quite believing what he'd done. He'd murdered a Councillor. The New British Islands were ruled by the Councillors, in the name of the overarching Eurasian Alliance. They were the most powerful people in the union of nations, answering to Sifia Hong herself. It shouldn't have been so easy to kill one.

"I wonder who did it." Cyrus wasn't going to let the subject drop. "There're so many terrorist groups. It could have been practically anyone." He leaned forwards, eyes on the screen. "I thought all those people had private guards though. Personal armies. That's the sort of job I need. If I could get citizenship that's what I'd go for."

"Maybe his small army turned on him?" Laszlo mumbled. "Maybe they're all slated for execution."

"Why would anyone assassinate him?" Sabre-Tooth muttered.

Why would Diessen want the Councillor for Defence dead? However hard he thought, he couldn't come up with a reason that made sense.

"Apparently all military as well as civilian police have been called in." Cyrus repeated the vid presenter's words as though everyone else was deaf. "They're arresting anyone they catch without ID."

"Who do you think did it?" Sabre-Tooth asked, testing the water. Would Cyrus connect his disappearance with the assassination?

His heart jumped when Cyrus pointed a finger at him. "Maybe that's where you were last night."

"What?"

"I'm joking." Cyrus and Laszlo both laughed, and after a brief second, Sabre-Tooth joined in.

"Opinion's split between a squad of home-grown terrorists and a team from the Americas," Cyrus said. "The media think it's an American plot. The personal guard squad has to be involved though. They've all been arrested. They say the squad leader died during the arrest."

Sabre-Tooth sipped his drink. If he had to guess, he would have bet the squad leader had played a part in the poor security. At least *he'd* been paid in credits, rather than with the business end of a gun.

"I'm not surprised," Laszlo said. "Talk about major incompetence. I bet they execute the lot of them."

That was on his conscience too.

ALLIANCE NEWS CORP – keeping you informed

News Update
November 10th 2452

Breaking news - update!

Despite the horrific murder of Councillor Viktor Einerson, the planned day of celebration for Speaker Sifia Hong's marriage will go ahead. 'We thought very hard about the situation,' Chief Aide Deyo Chang told our journalist, 'but in the end, our advisors decided that it would be wrong to let the action of terrorists despoil a joyous occasion'. Alliance News has been told that Speaker Hong sent personal condolences to the Einerson family. Challie Einerson, daughter of the murdered Councillor, and a diplomat working at the centre of government in New Shanghai, thanks the Speaker, adding that her father will be greatly missed.

Chapter 16

The new camp, Woodgreen Barracks, lay on the outskirts of London, just within the outer wall, and a two-hour journey from TEC1. The transport was an army airtran, a lumbering, solar-charged flyer that had room for fifty passengers on the benches in its interior. Sabre-Tooth peered out of the narrow window as the vehicle began its descent. Night had fallen and the site was almost dark. Dim lights around the perimeter suggested major development.

A single officer, dressed in the solid black of Military Intelligence, marched into the landing bay to meet them as they scrambled out of the transport. He waited for them to line up in front of him.

"Welcome to WoodGreen. I'm Sergeant Cooper. I'll be your direct command in Commander Diessen's absence. If I shout, you jump. Do you understand?" He spoke in a monotone, as though he'd said the words more times than he cared to remember.

"Yes Sir." Sabre-Tooth heaved a mental sigh as he joined in with the response. Sergeant Cooper might as well be an Obi-clone.

"You'll be in ME4 barracks. That's Military Enforcement number 4. Do you understand?"

"Yes Sir."

"Follow me."

All four of them had single cubi-units in Building 4 in the Intelligence and Enforcement part of the site. Sabre-Tooth's quarters were even smaller than his room at TEC1 but he'd been with the army long enough to realise he was privileged. Regular soldiers at his level got a narrow bed in a crowded bunkroom. His minimal space had a pull-out bed, a cupboard, a small communit that could be flattened to the wall, and a fold-up chair. Tessis's quarters were on one side of him, Laszlo's on the other and Cyrus's across the corridor. Ten soldiers shared each pristine hygiene facility. Two hundred shared the building. His cubi-unit had a door with a secure fastening. He could close himself away from the rest of the world if he wanted to. There would be no more Cyrus bursting into his space without an invitation.

"Tomorrow you'll be given details of your duties when you aren't working in the field." Sergeant Cooper ran his eyes over them. "Nine o'clock at assembly point three. Understand?"

"Yes Sir."

"You'll be issued black MI dress uniforms in the next couple of days, but when you leave the site, you wear army green unless told otherwise. Understand?"

"Yes Sir."

"Dismissed." He marched off into the darkness and the four recruits turned back into their accommodation. Sabre-Tooth closed his door firmly behind him, hearing clicks as his companions did the same. He collapsed onto the bunk, every bit of his body heavy with fatigue.

~~~

An hour later, he lay on his back, head pounding from sleep deprivation. He squeezed his eyes tightly together and blanked his mind, but images from the past couple of days burst through the barrier to dance on the back of his eyelids. Corporal Obi's furious face, with its bulging eyes, the convulsing dog, the spray of blood from severed throats. He still felt the constriction around his own throat, and smelled the pernicious metallic odour. He hadn't had an opportunity to dwell on the high-profile murder he'd committed, or to untangle it from his feelings about the test-killing. The scream of his target's companion echoed around the inside of his skull. Turning onto his side, he pulled the thin cover over his head and forced his brain into stillness. The screams followed him into sleep.

The next morning, after early parade inspection, Sergeant Cooper announced that everyone had a free day and a travel pass for London Central. A day's holiday had been declared throughout the Alliance, in celebration of its leader's marriage to some influential businessman.

"You have to be back by nineteen hundred," Sergeant Cooper told them. "And keep a low profile. The whole city's on high security alert after the assassination so don't get into any trouble." He dismissed them with a salute.

Cyrus's face crumpled with frustration. "What's the point? We can't afford to go anywhere good. We're still not being paid more than entry-level cadets. They should pay us properly. I've been in the fucking army for four fucking years.

Laszlo smelled as angry as Cyrus, but he smirked. "Maybe you should have thought about that before. Before you got demoted."

"Whose fucking fault was it I got demoted?" Cyrus kicked at the smooth surface of the plascrete.

"Not every time. Anyway, I want to look around the base. It's big enough."

Sabre-Tooth interrupted. "I'm going. I've never seen London except on the screen. I want to see the river." He had the extra credits Diessen had given him for murdering the Councillor, but he wasn't going to let Cyrus know that. He needed a distraction; something to help him keep the last few days penned at the back of his mind.

"Bloody tourist." Cyrus kicked at the wall. He was still annoyed with Sabre-Tooth's refusal to tell him about his disappearance. "You can go by yourself."

"I'll come," Tessis said. "It's got to be better than sitting here with this pair. Anyway, I've only been in the city a couple of times and I wouldn't mind going down to the river again. It's worth looking at even if you can't afford anything more than real coffee."

"What happened to all those credits you saved?" Sabre-Tooth knew both Laszlo and Cyrus had managed to accumulate a small fortune from the gambling ring Cyrus set up. They must have made something from the fights as well. And the drug dealing. Where had it all gone?

"That bastard, Murkhal." Cyrus's mouth twisted into a frown. "Confiscated the lot. Just before he loaded us into the AT."

Tessis stifled a snort of laughter.

Cyrus glared at her. "Fuck you."

Tessis raised her middle finger to him. "I bet that cheered him up. I hope he drinks the lot and it poisons him."

"Slowly and painfully." Cyrus kicked the ground again. "We'll get more credits. It'll just take a while."

"I had plans for those credits." Resentment bleached most of the colour out of Laszlo's odd eyes.

Cyrus regarded him nervously.

"Come on," Sabre Tooth said to Tessis. "Let's leave them to it."

~~~

WoodGreen military hubstation was the last port of call on the main north-south London transport line, and their military passes granted them unlimited travel on it. The Skytran link, or SkyTee or bubbletrain or bubble (depending on who was naming it), was the major form of travel between London Central and the outlying regions as, outside the inner wall, the North Road was the only ground-level route suitable for anything other than foot traffic. It was widely used by the military, but apart from official vehicles, only the top levels of society had their own personal transport. The Skytran link operated a regular service, which consisted of a variable number of linked plasglas compartments for standing passengers.

"Wow." Sabre-Tooth clung to an overhead strap, swaying as the bubble train leapt into the air. Two women in the green military coveralls of the regular army balanced easily at the other end of the compartment. Officers, Sabre-Tooth thought; they both had silver embroidery on their sleeves. After an initial glance, they ignored Sabre-Tooth and Tessis and continued discussing the murder of Councillor Einerson, and the subsequent political fallout. They both expressed surprise that Sifia Hong's wedding celebrations hadn't been cancelled, or at least postponed.

"Who do you think's going to replace him?" the taller one said.

Her shorter, plumper companion shrugged. "No clue. No one's thrown their hat in the ring yet. It's only been a day. Give them time."

"It could have—"

Sabre-Tooth deliberately closed his ears.

The morning was gloomy, the sun obscured by iron-grey clouds and the air heavy with the prospect of rain.

The last few days felt more like scenes from a horror-vid than real memories. Sabre-Tooth glanced at Tessis. She'd said she forced herself to forget, to compartmentalize. He wondered if she'd already forgotten she killed someone. Her introspective profile didn't invite confidences and Sabre-Tooth turned back to the view. He didn't want to ruin the day by making her angry. Her moods were difficult to predict at the best of times.

After five minutes the skytee descended, stopping briefly at a hub where a small group of enlists waited. They were all young and male. They smelled weird. Chemically weird.

109

"Where are we?" He glanced at Tessis who shifted to make way for the newcomers. Once they'd pushed into the bubble, he was crammed against strangers but there was no space left to retreat to.

She peered round his shoulder. "It's Camden Gate. At least that's what the sign says."

"Oh." Now she pointed it out, it was obvious. "Why aren't we moving?"

"I think there'll be a check of our passes," Tessis said. "We'll cross into inner London next."

Three uniformed and heavily armed men pulled two of the enlisted men out of the skytee, scanned their wrists, and climbing inside, checked the other passengers. After they finished, they jumped down to the platform, waving the two men back into the cabin.

Sabre-Tooth leaned his face against the plasglas, watching as the bubble rose again, clearing the black plastone of London's inner wall and passing over the lushly wooded outskirts of the city's centre, before descending towards the river hub. The area after they passed the checkpoint at Camden Gate was more heavily populated then anywhere he'd ever been.

Multiple narrow paths criss-crossed the ground below, lush with foliage and dense with residential buildings. Some of the rooftops had energy harvesters on them; some were flat and covered with rich green plantings and social spaces. At least two had café-bars, where people clustered around small tables. Flags in Sifia Hong's colours of gold and green fluttered above many buildings. Further south, the wide Thames snaked through the tall river walls that protected the ornate buildings of the North bank, and the more functional constructions on the south side. Beyond the river, the buildings shrunk in size before disappearing into marshland.

"What's that?" He pointed out of the window. "That black building on the other side of the river." A pole on the roof supported a huge green and gold banner.

Tessis elbowed her way to his side, slipping under his arm. "That's Central Security, SecCen. Civil police, military police, the intelligence agencies, law enforcement, justice and anything else you can think of. All the higher-ups in all the security forces have offices there. They've got a prison there as well. People get executed in it, and worse, I've heard. People disappear." She rested the palms of her hands on the plasglas. "We got a tour of the place with school. I was fifteen. It scared the shit out of me. You should see the interrogation rooms."

"I don't think so." Sabre-Tooth was quite happy for them to remain a mystery.

The security building loomed over the south bank of the river, its walls constructed from a matt black plastone that appeared to suck all the light from its surroundings. A heavily loaded passenger ferry docked in front of it and a line of ant-like people, many in the black uniform of MI, disembarked.

"I thought they executed people in the Tower of London." Sabre-Tooth had seen it on the entertainment screen. He'd heard about it in the history modules he'd been forced to study.

"Only the ones they want to use as an example. Public punishments."

"What?" He'd learned a lot in the past six months, but sometimes Sabre-Tooth felt defeated by what he still didn't know.

"People disappear quietly over there." Tessis nodded at the South Bank. "Everyone knows that. There's no fanfare."

They watched the stream of people vanish into the building.

"It's a big employer," Tessis said. "Good benefits, I've heard."

The bubbletrain descended to its terminal and slowed to a halt. The doors slid open.

Sabre-Tooth followed Tessis out onto the wide path that ran parallel to the river. Behind him, one of the enlisted men slammed into his back. He stepped out of the way automatically. The man barreled into him again.

Deliberate.

Sabre-Tooth sighed and swung round to confront the annoyance. "What's your problem?"

"You." The man folded his arms and sneered. "Just look at you. Poseur."

Sabre-Tooth folded his arms in a mirror movement and raised an eyebrow. Next to him, Tessis did the same.

"Those ears. They're ridiculous. Fucking stupid. How much did they cost you?" His assailant pulled a knife out of his uniform belt. "And what's with the eyes?"

Sabre-Tooth kept one eye on the knife.

"Ignore him," Tessis muttered. "You can't afford to get into a fight here."

She nodded towards two men in the uniform of Civil Enforcement, who strolled towards them from the far end of the block of buildings.

"You need to lose the ears." The enlisted man tossed his knife from one hand to the other. He didn't appear to have noticed the approaching presence of law enforcement. "I can't do much about your eyes, but I'll help you with the ears."

From the corner of one eye, Sabre-Tooth registered the two female officers from the bubble-train. They hurried towards the potential scuffle, nodding in acknowledgment of the Civil Enforcers, who had their taser stunners ready for use.

The shorter of the two officers held up one hand, halting the Enforcers. She drew her own stungun.

"You." She pointed it at the man with the knife. "Put that away."

The man angled the knife towards her.

"Uh-oh." Tessis winced dramatically.

The officer fired and the man folded to the ground.

Her tall companion nudged him in the stomach with the toe of her boot. He whimpered and curled into a tight ball.

She turned to glare at his friends. "All of you – get back to your base and report to your officer-in-charge."

The group faded away, back towards the hub-station, leaving the ringleader huddled on the ground.

The tall officer kicked him again and beckoned to the Civilian Enforcers. "Have him shipped back in restraints. To WoodGreen military camp. Compliments of Captain Verdeer."

The Enforcers dragged the moaning man away.

The short officer turned to Sabre-Tooth. "You really should get rid of those. They make you a target." She rolled her eyes. "What were you thinking of?"

Tessis watched her walk off to join her companion. "They all think you've got cosmetic enhancements."

"Where do they think I found the credits?" Sabre-Tooth bared his teeth. "And why do they care? Why don't they just leave me alone?"

Tessis frowned. "Didn't you see his eyes? All of their eyes? That little group were screamer freaks."

"What?"

"Screamer. The recreational drug? He'll be in deep shit when he gets back. Another thing we learned in school. Illegal drugs and what would happen if anyone caught us using them." Her frown deepened. "I don't know why they do it. They'll all be sentenced to a whipping at least. Stupid."

Sabre-Tooth rubbed his face hard, thinking about Cyrus's recreational drug scam. He didn't know where his stock came from or what it was, but he was sure Cyrus boosted his credits by dealing, as well as gambling. No wonder he and Laszlo had been so pissed off. They'd taken a big risk and gained nothing from it.

"Come on." Tessis started walking. On one side of the walkway, the river wall was a low barrier between the city and the water. In some places, it was wide enough for small cafes and bars to cluster along its edges, in others it was just a wall. On their side of the walkway the buildings of north London rose.

More people than he'd ever seen in one place before hurried purposefully along the thoroughfare. He and Tessis weren't the only ones wearing military coveralls, but most of the crowd were civilians, taking advantage of their extra day of leave. To Sabre-Tooth, they looked like a collection of exotic wildlife. He slowed his pace.

Tessis was several meters ahead. She turned to watch his progress. "What's wrong?"

"Nothing." He lengthened his stride. "Do you know where you're going?"

"Haven't a clue," she said. "Both times I came before, it was an education tour. We were shepherded about worse than in the army. We weren't allowed to go anywhere by ourselves. Let's just follow the path."

On his left, faux-historic buildings loomed over the river, their fronts covered with ornate embellishments. He recognized the Palace of Westminster, and the Clocktower, both pressed close up against the plastone river wall. They were supposed to be exact copies of the old buildings. Big Ben towered above everything else. He'd seen all of them on the flatscreen and learned about their restoration in his history lessons. Seeing them in reality was still exciting.

Armed guards stood at all the entrances. They wore ornate dress uniforms, but their weapons looked like they meant business. Judging by their costumes, most of them were from the military.

"Is it dangerous here?" Sabre-Tooth asked.

"How would I know?" Tessis crossed the path and leaned her arms on the edge of the wall. She stared out over the water.

Sabre-Tooth joined her. "How do you think you get a job like that?"

She shrugged.

"Tessis?"

"Citizenship. And a distinguished military record? Why do you think I'd know?"

Sabre-Tooth let out a heavy disgruntled breath. Guarding famous buildings was the sort of job he'd like.

The river swirled ten feet below them, its waters dark and oily. Further out, a ferry fought its way upstream against the current. A security vessel passed it, disappearing into the shadows of a landing dock. The water rippled and a triangular fin broke the surface.

"Look." He pointed, staring as a river shark briefly emerged from the water.

It disappeared again and he reluctantly lifted his gaze to the dark buildings dominating the opposite bank.

She nudged him with her elbow. "Come on. You don't want to stare at that for too long."

He turned and followed her slowly along the edge of the river wall. "Have they told you what you'll be working on yet?"

"No." She shook her head. "No one's mentioned it. I think we'll all be told at the same time." Her eyes followed a young couple emerging from one of the cafés. "Look over there."

Sabre-Tooth looked.

He'd never seen anything like the pair before. Not in real life at any rate. They were both tall and thin. The man had waist-length blonde hair streaked with metallic gold and copper. He wore a close-fitting skinsuit in some shiny fabric, a calf-length cape and high-heeled boots. The woman had dark skin and a halo of chocolate-coloured corkscrew hair, streaked with gold to match the stain on her lips. An ankle-length cloak covered everything but her head. As they walked past, Sabre-Tooth gaped. The woman looked like the star of one of the space operas he liked to watch.

"Do you think they're vid stars?"

"Maybe." Tessis watched them stroll slowly along the river walkway, cloaks swirling around their legs. "I wonder what it's like to be them. To live here and have a proper job. Not to be scared - ever." She turned to walk in the opposite direction.

He could barely hear her. "I don't suppose we'll ever know. Anyway, they must be scared of something." Everyone was.

"We might as well be on different planets." Tessis's mind worked along the same lines as his. "Let's get some coffee. Our credits should stretch that far. Even here."

They chose a small café perched on top of the river wall, overlooking one of the ferry landings. It was crowded, but they managed to find a table close to the water. A queue of people waited for the next boat and Sabre-Tooth leaned his elbows on the table, watching them. "Where do you think they're all going?"

"Security Central?" Tessis glanced at the queue. "Smart clothes, so I shouldn't think they're industrials. Maybe they live in the inner city."

A woman approached the table, dressed in a blue skinsuit. Deep blue face paint covered the sallow skin around her eyes. "What can I get you?"

"Two coffees." Tessis held out her wrist while the waitress scanned her chip.

The waitress's eyes widened as she met Sabre-Tooth's cat-like gaze. She said nothing until she returned to the counter where she bent and whispered in the barista's ear. All three members of staff turned in his direction.

Sabre-Tooth ducked his head, wishing they wouldn't stare. They had no right. He wasn't the only person who looked different. The waitress's face was blue. That was weirder than his eyes. He glowered at her when she returned with the drinks, watching her over the rim of the cup as he took a first sip. She hurried away.

The coffee was good, nothing like the substitute the mess served; rich and creamy, with powdered chocolate on top. It fizzed along his nerves and did a lot to disperse his annoyance.

"Where do you want to go next?" Tessis dipped her finger in her cup to remove the last of the foam.

Sabre-Tooth thought about the places he'd been told of, back in the lab. "The palaces? The zoo? They've got some exotics there, haven't they?"

Tessis pulled a face. "I think you need a pass to get into the palace gardens. The zoo's expensive."

"I've got some credits," he said.

"I don't really have enough," she said. "Maybe next time? Or we could split up?"

"No. Next time's fine." He sifted through his memories of lessons, calling up the images of London his history teachers had shown him. "What about further along the river. The Old Tower? The one where they do the public executions. Have you seen it?"

"Four years ago," she said. "On the school trip. I wouldn't mind seeing it again though. I think they keep some exotics there. We could find out if you want."

The Tower was about forty minutes' walk away, past the government buildings, past a couple of entertainment arcades, a few restaurants and several ferry terminals.

"That's the Department for Defence," Tessis said, pointing at one of the buildings. Two military guards flanked the entrance, both wearing formal dress uniform of gold-trimmed green, and armed with enough lethal weaponry to win a small war. Between them, heavy plaschain links blocked the doorway. "I bet Diessen's in there."

"Let's keep away from it then."

The river walkway was busy with a variety of people; the fashionable elite strolled slowly amongst lower-level citizens, delivery workers, street cleaners, entertainers and disembarking ferry passengers. Sabre-Tooth slowed down to listen to one of the street singers, a teenage girl with a high, pure voice. She played a small stringed instrument and sang about the futility of love.

"Come on Sabre-Tooth. What are you waiting for?" Tessis shuffled her feet impatiently.

The singer finished the song, and he lengthened his stride to catch up with Tessis.

Every hundred yards or so, civilian law enforcers patrolled, weapons slung across their bodies. Most of them eyed Tessis, and more particularly, Sabre-Tooth, with suspicion.

"I wish they wouldn't stare." His shoulders prickled with irritation. Other people in the crowd looked strange, so why did everyone gawp at him? He glared at a man with deep red spider tattoos round his eyes.

"You're going to have to get used to it," Tessis said. "Although, maybe you could get some eyeshades? I bet they keep them in supplies at the barracks and they'd help you fit in."

Sabre-Tooth nodded. Many of the passers-by wore dark shades.

"And if you grow your hair just a bit more and style it right, you could hide your ears," Tessis continued. She glanced at him nervously. "We're not regular army, so they won't make us shave our heads."

"Thanks."

Tessis was much more forthcoming without Cyrus and Laszlo hanging around. A lot of her sullen hostility had disappeared. No one else got much of a chance to talk when Cyrus was present, and Laszlo was enough to silence anyone.

The Tower loomed ahead of them, its white stone turned golden by the morning sun. Neatly clipped grass surrounded it and paths made from real stone snaked around the base of its walls. Two highly visible men, dressed in ornate red clothes, guarded the entrance.

Sabre-Tooth only recognized them as guards because of the weapons they carried. Small, unobtrusive nerve shockers; killing weapons. He'd learned about them in his army classes. They were tiny, but lethal if they hit the right target.

"What are they?" He turned to Tessis as a source of information.

"They're replicas of the original tower guards," she said. "One of them gave us a tour when I came with school. They come from the regular army; mostly the officer class. It's supposed to be a reward for good work. Apparently they live in there." She nodded at the tower building. "It's a safe and comfortable posting."

"Do you think—?"

"Not for us," she said. "We'll never be officer class."

Sabre-Tooth's ears twitched as he became aware of footsteps approaching him. He swung round. Two Civilian Enforcers marched up to them, weapons dangling from their arms. They looked like twins, both tall and bulky with muscle. Under their cropped hair, their faces expressed a mixture of hostility and excitement.

"ID." One of them pulled out a scanner.

Sabre-Tooth held out his wrist. The enforcer glanced up at his face before repeating the scan on Tessis's wrist.

"Well?" The second enforcer asked.

"They're from Military Intelligence," the man with the scanner said "Their passes are in order."

"Fine." The second enforcer frowned, his expression disappointed. "Why don't you people wear your official uniforms? What are you up to in London?"

"Day off, Sir," Tessis said. She lowered her gaze to his boots. "For the Speaker's wedding. We wanted to see the tower and the exotics."

"They keep wolves round the corner. And the ravens of course. For the sightseers," the officer said. "Is that exotic enough for you?"

"Yes Sir."

"Go on then. Don't cause any trouble."

"No Sir." Tessis nudged Sabre-Tooth.

"Thank you, Sir."

The two enforcers watched them walk away.

"That was lucky," Tessis said. "They could have given us a lot more hassle. It was obvious they wanted to. You know we used to call them the Sleaze? Did you see the look they gave you? You really need to get the eyeshades. Mind you, I get the feeling that Military Intelligence doesn't get messed with much."

"I don't think I'll ever understand all the army divisions," Sabre-Tooth grumbled.

"No one does. Come on. Let's go up the bridge."

"What about the wolves? I want to see them."

Tessis heaved out a sigh. "Alright."

The wolves lived in a sunken area, which must once have been part of the moat, but was now grassed over. Three of them paced along the edge of the containment wall and, as Sabre-Tooth watched, a fourth appeared from a stone den. They were all covered in a mixture of grey and tawny fur and all wore collars round their necks. Simple, identification collars, as far as Sabre-Tooth could tell. He touched a finger to his throat. "They look a bit like that dog."

"Not as big, I think." Tessis scrutinised them. "And alive."

Sabre-Tooth leaned on the wall watching them for a while.

Next to him, Tessis fidgeted. "They're not that interesting."

"They live in the wild as well." He turned to join her. "We might have seen some in Wales if we'd stayed longer."

"They'd have eaten you." Tessis hurried away.

Steps led up towards the high-level bridge. Bracketed by two pale stone towers, it was the only remaining bridge across the rapidly changing river, and more ornamental than functional. Ferries were the best way to cross from north to south normally, and less trouble. More armed men in the distinctive red uniforms guarded Tower Bridge at both ends.

Tessis and Sabre-Tooth climbed the steep flight of steps up onto the bridge walkway and followed the crowd to the centre, where they fought their way to the railing and peered eastward down the river to where it widened in the distance. Dark barrier walls lined the banks, and cargo ships, many with wind turbines, stood on the horizon, silhouetted against the low grey sky.

"It's going to rain soon," Tessis muttered. "Let's get inside. You can pay for the coffee this time."

Sabre-Tooth moved to the opposite side of the bridge and looked at the westward view. The black mass of Security Central dominated the south bank. It was hard not to keep turning to gaze at it.

"This place feels so old," he said.

"It's not that old. They told us that it had been restored after the disasters of the twenty-first century," Tessis said. "Most of it isn't original."

A heavy raindrop landed on Sabre-Tooth's head and he ran after Tessis as the tempestuous downpour started.

ALLIANCE NEWS CORP – keeping you informed

Crime

The assassination of Councillor Einerson, Head of the Department of Defence of the British Islands and Defence Councillor for the Eurasian Alliance, is under investigation. The Chief Inquiry Officer informs Alliance News 'that progress has been made in identifying the perpetrators'. At present, the inquiry points to an assassination squad from one of the Alliance's traditional enemies. Suspicion falls on the Americas or the Indian Republic. The head of Alliance Security, Commander Rho Shin Hahmid, states that 'the investigation is one of the most encompassing our group of nations has seen. This sort of international terrorism will not be permitted to flourish on Alliance soil.'

News Corps has spoken to Einerson's colleagues on the Council. All are in shock. Councillor Krewchek's statement reads: 'While Viktor and I did not always see eye to eye, he was my esteemed colleague and I am horrified at his death. I support the Security Services in their hunt for his murderer.'

Dissension – the struggle against injustice

November 12th 2452

Who does the Alliance think they are fooling? This murder was an inside job. The Council is a nest of vipers. Councillor Einerson was an oppressor of the people and as such, we cannot regret his death. However, the finger of retribution needs to point at the real culprits.

ALLIANCE NEWS CORP –keeping you informed

Politics

The Alliance Council has put out a statement on the death of Councillor Einerson. 'While it is too early to speculate on the identity of Honorary Commander Viktor Einerson's successor, citizens may be assured that the Council is reviewing potential candidates. Voting will take place within the National Councils at the beginning of the New Year. For now, all thoughts are with his family.'

Dissension – the struggle against injustice

November 12th 2452

Barely a day has passed since the murder of Councillor Einerson, but word in the Department of Defence suggests that competition for the top job has already narrowed to two candidates. The first is an old school military supporter of Einerson, General Henry Myerton, a man who has risen, like scum on water, to the top levels of the army. The second candidate is the younger, and less traditional, Stefan Oroz, whose reputation is *that of a dangerous degenerate, and whose only qualification for the job appears to be his connection with the royal family of the British Islands. Are these the best our nations have to offer?*

Chapter 17

The sky had cleared and the sun had set by the time Tessis and Sabre-Tooth arrived back at Woodgreen barracks. As soon as Sabre-Tooth entered his cubi-unit, his desktop comm pinged at him with a list of messages. The most important one was a summons to the senior officers' mess at 19.00. Diessen demanded to see him. His heart began to pound in his chest.

He quickly changed into a clean uniform coverall and left again, almost colliding with Tessis. "Diessen commed you?" he asked.

She nodded, her face puzzled. "What do you think he wants?"

"How would I know?" Sabre-Tooth glanced up and down the corridor at the closed doors. "I wonder where Laszlo and Cyrus have gone."

"Probably found the bar," Tessis said.

The two of them presented themselves to the guard outside the senior mess, and were taken to Diessen, who sat at a table with a fashionably dressed civilian. The stranger's dark blue, high-collared tunic contrasted with golden hair swinging loosely onto his shoulders. He smiled as Sabre-Tooth and Tessis approached; a smile that warmed his blue eyes and gave him the face of an angel.

"Stefan, this is the creature I told you about." Diessen waved his hand in Sabre-Tooth's direction. "He's proved himself to be quite useful. I thought you should meet him."

"Mmm." Stefan rose to his feet and circled around the two newcomers, elbowing Tessis aside as he passed. He was slightly taller than Sabre-Tooth in his stacked boots.

Sabre-Tooth stared straight ahead. The stranger made him uncomfortable, he was willowy, not big and muscular like Obi, but he was too close. He felt like a threat.

"He could almost pass for human." Stefan peered into Sabre-Tooth's face, his breath sweet with alcohol. "Except for the eyes." He stroked one ear.

Sabre-Tooth flicked it, forcing himself to keep still.

Stefan ran a finger over the other. "And these."

"You like him?"

"Fascinating." Stefan smiled at Sabre-Tooth, his bright blue eyes sparkling with interest. "There're a couple of chimeras in one of the clubs on the River Walkway. You must have seen them. Snakey things. They dance in a cage, hanging from the ceiling. I bought them out once. Kept them overnight and had some fun with them."

"I wouldn't know," Diessen said. "I don't spend my nights in that sort of place."

"Such pretty pussy cat eyes. Can I have him for a day or two?" Stefan's heated gaze moved over Sabre-Tooth's body. "I like exotic."

"Better not." Diessen picked up a glass of amber liquid and took a sip. "He's a highly trained military asset. I'm not sure he wouldn't kill you."

"Vicious, is he?"

"Very. And if he harmed you, I'd have to kill him. I'd rather not at the moment."

What was Diessen talking about? Sabre-Tooth didn't want to hurt anyone, except maybe Diessen, and possibly Sergeant Murkhal and Corporal Obi.

Stefan laughed. "Another time, then. Who's the other one? What's she?" He stroked his forefinger down the side of Tessis's cheek.

"Human, I'm afraid," Diessen said. "She's part of my team as well."

Stefan stared at her, before shaking his head. "Boring. You can keep her." He sat down again.

"You can relax," Diessen said to Tessis and Sabre-Tooth. "This is Stefan Oroz. He's a senior administrator in the Department of Defence. He reported to Councillor Einerson." A slight smile crossed his face. "Do you know who that is?"

"No Sir." Sabre-Tooth's pulse picked up speed. He forced himself to remain expressionless. He wasn't supposed to know who he'd killed.

"He was Councillor for Defence, Sir," Tessis said.

"Very good," Diessen said. "He was Councillor for Defence. Now he's dead. Stefan will be standing for election to the Council, in the light of Einerson's tragic death." His smile widened. "What do you say to that?"

"Congratulations, Sir." Sabre-Tooth and Tessis spoke in unison.

Sabre-Tooth wished he knew what was going on. It sounded as though Diessen had removed Einerson to create a job opening for his friend, but why was he telling them?

"We've trained them well," Diessen said, with a sidelong glance at Stefan. "They know how to obey orders. Better than the other two."

Stefan raised an eyebrow.

Diessen leaned his elbows on the table, the smile fading from his face. "You two are in trouble. Your colleagues are in jail. They forgot they're here on sufferance."

"Sir?"

"Laszlo attacked another soldier, a young woman. He hurt her quite badly. Cyrus tried to lie for him."

So why was that a problem for him and Tessis? Sabre-Tooth slid his glance sideways to meet Tessis's eyes. She raised them slightly to the ceiling.

"At my request, the camp commandant spared them a court-martial," Diessen said. "If he'd been court-martialled, Laszlo would have been executed. As it is, he'll get the maximum penalty allowed without trial."

"Pity," Stefan muttered.

Diessen glanced at him. "All four of you will lose a month's pay. Cyrus loses all camp privileges for a month. Laszlo will be whipped. The punishment takes place on the parade square at eight o'clock. You'll be there to watch."

"Yes Sir." Both of them answered at once.

"So will I." Stefan leaned back in his chair. "An execution would be better entertainment, but I'm interested in your little team."

"Yes. They might be useful to you as well. We'll have to see." Diessen waved Sabre-Tooth and Tessis away.

Sabre-Tooth waited until they were outside again before speaking. "What were they doing? They've only been here a day."

Tessis blew out a breath. "Didn't you think Laszlo was a bit stranger than normal this morning? Losing his credits to Murkhal must have pissed him off. He's always been a volcano waiting to blow."

"What do you mean?"

"He's a predator," Tessis said. "You know they threatened him with chemical castration?"

Sabre-Tooth frowned. "I thought that was just one of those threats they gave us all."

"No. He'd been in trouble before for rape and other assaults," Tessis said. "I think he started with non-citizens and no one cares much about them, but I heard he killed someone he shouldn't have. Remember Cyrus warned me to stay away from him?"

Sabre-Tooth nodded. Sergeant Murkhal had said none of them were strangers to murder.

"I asked around. He's got a reputation as a sexual sadist. That's why this team was his last chance."

"What do you think he did?"

Tessis shrugged. "Something bad enough to warrant a public whipping. Bad enough that Diessen intervened."

Sabre-Tooth kicked at the ground. "I didn't like that man. The blonde one."

"Stefan Oroz?"

"Mmm.

"He was pretty," Tessis mused, "but I didn't like him either. He might be a high-level citizen but he reminded me of Laszlo."

Sabre-Tooth shivered. He hadn't liked Stefan Oroz's interest in him at all. What sort of man viewed an execution as entertainment? Other than Laszlo of course.

~~~

At eight o'clock, Sabre-Tooth and Tessis stood to attention on one side of a uniformed and medal-hung Diessen. Stefan Oroz slouched on the other side, hands in deep pockets, his high fashion suit dramatically out of place amongst the black-clad figures of Military Intelligence.

In front of them towered the whipping post, a nine-foot pillar with a hook at the top. The rest of the camp lined up, stiff and immobile, in ranks around the edges of the parade square.

Eventually the gates opened and the prisoners appeared. As well as Laszlo and Cyrus, five enlisted men marched in.

Sabre-Tooth's attention focussed; he knew who they were. They were the ones from the morning skytee. The ones Tessis called screamer freaks. All of the prisoners had their hands secured in front of them, and were accompanied by two military enforcers. Laszlo was as expressionless as ever, but Cyrus wore a scowl that filled his whole face.

Cyrus was marched to stand on the far side of Diessen, next to Stefan, and pushed roughly into place. The enforcers escorted the other six prisoners to the centre of the square. They looked small. Helpless and harmless.

"Line up. Attention." One of the enforcers bellowed the command loudly enough for the whole assembly to hear. The prisoners stepped rapidly into position, their faces a mixture of fear and resignation. Laszlo stared straight ahead.

The second enforcer walked along the row, unfastening the tops of their uniforms, while his colleague answered a signal from the commandant and read out the list of crimes and penalties. Four of the enlisted men would receive five strokes of the whip for their drug offences; their ringleader and Laszlo would receive ten; the maximum punishment permitted without a court-martial.

An enforcer grabbed the first of the men, pulling his coverall down past his waist. He pushed him against the post and secured his bound hands to the hook at the top.

Sabre-Tooth tensed, the claws on his toes flexing against the end of his boots. All he could see of the prisoner was his back. Next to him, Tessis breathed slowly in and out.

The camp Commandant approached from the corner of the square. He stopped a couple of metres in front of the whipping post and read the charges out. "Do you understand?"

"Yes Sir." The prisoner's answer was amplified so the whole company could hear it.

"Your punishment is the taserwhip. Five lashes."

There was a syncopated intake of breath from the whole gathering as the first enforcer pulled the whip from his weapons' belt. He uncoiled it and gave it an experimental crack. Sparks flew into the air.

The prisoner screamed at the first blow, his body writhing in his bonds. After the second blow, Sabre-Tooth wished he could turn off his hearing. The whip left raw wounds across the man's back. Singed flesh-smells mixed with the metallic scent of blood and drifted through the air. After the fifth blow, the prisoner was taken from the post and hauled away by two more military enforcers.

The fifth enlisted man, the one who'd wanted to cut off Sabre-Tooth's ears, was given ten strokes and had to be carried off the field afterwards.

Nausea pooled in Sabre-Tooth's stomach as an enforcer pushed Laszlo forward, and secured him to the post. His face was frozen, but his eyes darted around, searching for an escape route. The enforcer pulled down his coverall.

Sabre-Tooth stared at his back. Laszlo's pale skin was ridged and discoloured; a mass of ugly scars.

The enforcer cracked the whip.

Sabre-Tooth swallowed.

The first blow laid a red line diagonally across Laszlo's shoulders and twisted him off balance so that he hung from his bound hands. His screams started after the third blow.

Sabre-Tooth closed his eyes. He couldn't block out the smell and sounds. The odour reminded him of the roasting sheep's leg in Wales.

He counted the blows, waiting for it to be over. Laszlo's screams grew hoarser and turned to whimpers. After the whip landed for the tenth time, Sabre-Tooth opened his eyes again. Laszlo's back was a mess of blood and burnt, torn flesh.

The enforcer slipped the taserwhip back into the loop of his belt and released Laszlo from the hook. He staggered. His gasps for breath were audible from metres away, at least to Sabre-Tooth. Two enforcers seized him by the arms and half-dragged, half-carried him away. His face was stained with tears.

The camp Commandant marched off the square. Diessen and Stefan left.

Sabre-Tooth blinked rapidly in an attempt to get rid of the aftershock from the whip. Flashes of light played over the back of his eyes. "That was horrible."

"You've never seen anyone whipped?"

"Only on the vid. And it wasn't like that."

"No." Once they were away from the square, Tessis slowed her pace.

"And Laszlo. Did you see his back before they even started?"

"I told you he'd done this sort of thing before. How do you think he ended up here?"

"But why would he…?" Sabre-Tooth's voice trailed away.

"He can't help himself. He's sick."

"Poor Laszlo, can't—"

"Poor Laszlo?" Tessis halted, her brown eyes blazing. "Serves him fucking right. I mean he's a sick fuck. I… He'd have…"

She took a breath and shrugged, her voice dropping back to its normal level. "He'd better pray that woman doesn't die."

ALLIANCE NEWS CORP – keeping you informed

News Update
January 12th 2453

New British Islands

Terrorists have made a number of raids on non-military Defence institutions throughout the New British Islands. Two research establishments lost equipment as well as valuable samples. Security staff were incapacitated during the attack, but no fatalities have been reported. Alliance Security is searching for anyone who might have information about these incursions.

Dissension – the struggle against injustice

January 12th 2452

Freedom fighters in the New British Islands have succeeded in rescuing illegally held prisoners from the Council's military research establishments. We do not know who these heroes are, but we congratulate them. Dissension has uncovered evidence that the Alliance Council has been complicit in activities which break their own human rights laws, as well as contravening legislation around population stability. We suspect heads will roll in an effort to shift blame. Watch this space.

ALLIANCE NEWS CORP – keeping you informed

News Update
January 12th 2453

Politics

Early this morning, The Alliance Council announced the appointment of General Henry Myerton to their ranks. General Myerton will take on the role of Councillor for Defence, a position left vacant after the unsolved murder of Councillor Viktor Einerson.

Dissension – the struggle against injustice

January 12th 2452

General Henry Myerton is the new Councillor for Defence, however, an un-named informant tells us that the voting was extremely close. The same informant claims that Stefan Oroz lost the election due to serious security concerns flagged up by Civil Intelligence. Readers will no doubt be aware that Mr Oroz, a scion of the first families, has a very murky reputation. General Myerton is thought to have the same conservative views as his predecessor.

ALLIANCE NEWS CORP – keeping you informed

News Update

August 1ˢᵗ 2453

Weather

Temperatures in Southern Europe have reached an all-time high. Environmental restoration work, in central Spain, is now on hold for at least a month. Dr. Maria Laquiere, head of RiverCare, told our journalist, 'Significant progress has been made around the river system. Planting of desert tolerant species along the course of the river is well under way, and we have seen water in the riverbed for at least two months of the year. I am optimistic about future work. Our climate team think this summer's temperature is an anomaly. We will not give up."

Chapter 18

In the Recreation hub, Sabre-Tooth slumped in the corner of the sofa, legs stretched out and arms behind his head.

On the adjacent flexi-chair, Laszlo lounged, eyes half closed. It was nine months since his public whipping, and eight since he and Cyrus were released from the camp prison. He was as enigmatic as ever.

Cyrus watched him all the time. Both of them would be lucky to get a quick execution if he stepped out of line again. Rumours about his crime, his victim's injuries and his past history flowed through the camp. Sabre-Tooth still couldn't help flinching in sympathy when he remembered the scarring on Laszlo's back. Laszlo was a conundrum. He was lucky Diessen had a use for him.

Sabre-Tooth lifted his legs, flexing the muscles in his calves. They ached from the four hour run he'd just completed, circling the London Inner Ring Road. The plascrete was much harder on his legs than mountain paths and worse than even the most inhospitable cross-country. The air had been hot and humid as well, typical August weather. Next time, he decided, he would run north, through the ruined streets and the encroaching New London forest. At least the trees would give some relief from the heat.

He had more freedom than he could have dreamed of, but even without the constant reminder from the collar, the walled barracks, and his tiny cubi-room made him feel trapped.

He wondered what Tygre and Sugar were doing and where they were, cut the thought short before it could take shape, and nudged Laszlo. "Where's Cyrus?"

Not that he cared; it was just unusual that he wasn't hanging round his partner.

Laszlo opened one eye. "Don't do that." He closed the eye again.

Sabre-Tooth sighed. Cyrus and Laszlo had recently returned from an overseas assignment. They tended to work together, mostly in regions of unrest.

"We're tools of terror," Cyrus told him. He laughed.

Sabre-Tooth didn't.

His own next assignment was due to start the following morning, a surveillance job on a couple of officials from the Department of Urban Planning. He suspected they were marked for termination.

Commander Diessen had moved into the business of political campaigning. Extreme political campaigning. He'd been furious when Stefan Oroz lost the election, but had come out as a strong supporter of the present Councillor for Foreign Affairs. The Councillor, Andrei Krewchek, had declared his intention to challenge Sifia Hong for the position of Speaker for the Alliance, promising his support to the more aggressive factions in the military if he won. Diessen was part of his campaign group, a cadre composed of senior military leaders, determined to push their own agenda.

Rumour around the barracks, said that certain politicians wanted to go to war with the Americas. Or India. Everyone in Military Intelligence liked gossip, almost as much as they liked drinking, gambling and sex.

Sabre-Tooth saw and heard far more of Diessen than he was comfortable with. He was one of Diessen's instruments of terror. Assassination was one of the Commander's favourite tools, but he wasn't above blackmail, bribery and threats either.

Making the world a safer place? It was laughable.

Diessen had enemies, rivals, failed staff, and limited ways of dealing with them. Lethal ways. Sabre-Tooth's view was that the word would be a massively safer place for most people if Diessen were removed. Why had no one done anything about him? Assassination was a common tool for the elite, and a common tool in government, but on this scale? Sabre-Tooth had committed his fifth murder thirteen months after his conscription, and they were all people who stood in the way of Diessen's ambitions.

Sabre-Tooth wanted to live though. The memory of the collar shock was enough to make him obey his superior officer. He forced himself to forget that his victims wanted to live too. Sometimes, especially when they knew what was about to happen, they fought back. Their desperation to live was almost tangible. Sabre-Tooth blanked his mind and killed them as quickly as possible. It was better if he found them asleep. His determination to survive grew as he saw how easy it was to die.

Tessis slumped at the other end of the sofa, arms folded and legs stretched out in front of her. She'd joined him for the last hour of the run, coming in ten minutes behind him.

"What?" She snapped at him.

Her disposition had grown worse as the months progressed. She was more willing to talk, but her moods swung from angry to morose with little in between. He focused on her face, trying to read her expression.

"Do you know how creepy it is when you stare like that?"

"Creepy?" He frowned, puzzling over what she meant, before deciding to ignore it. "I'm off again tomorrow morning. Back to Inner London." The city was familiar now. "How about you?"

She slumped lower on the sofa. "Diessen wants to see me. That man gives me the shudders."

"Me too."

Tessis was the only other one of the four of them to have multiple active assignments in civilian areas. Sabre-Tooth didn't think she was enjoying the job any more than he was. He needed to talk.

Her gaze slid sideways, to rest briefly on his face. "I don't think about it."

"But—"

"And I don't want to discuss it." She bent to pick up the warm coffee substitute from next to her feet and leaned back again, staring at the info screen on the opposite wall.

Sabre-Tooth heaved out a sigh. "Do you think you'll ever get used to it?"

"No. Will you just fucking shut up?" She took a deep breath.

Sabre-Tooth waited.

She lifted her caffa to her lips, grimaced, and put it down again. "Sabe? I really don't want to talk about it. All I can think, is that if I don't do it, I'll spend the rest of my short life chained to a bunk, servicing any soldier with a pleasure pass. It keeps me awake at night. If I sleep, I have nightmares."

Sabre-Tooth screwed his eyes shut as he thought about that.

"And even if that doesn't happen, they're never going to let me go. I won't be discharged. I'll be terminated." After a second, she nudged him. "So I hate it, but I do it. And I'll have to deal with it. So will you. Otherwise what's the point? We might as well be dead now." Her voice rose.

Laszlo turned his head towards her without opening his eyes. "Do you mind? I was almost asleep."

She made a scoffing noise and slouched deeper into the sofa.

Sabre-Tooth plucked at his collar. "I don't sleep much either."

"If we didn't kill them, someone else would," she said.

That was a great comfort. Sabre-Tooth picked up his drink.

"Hey." Tessis jerked to attention. "Look." She pointed at the info screen.

Sabre-Tooth looked. A news broadcast filled the screen, an item featuring a young and glamorous female presenter with lots of artificially red hair and a serious expression. A news update ran in cursive script along the bottom of the image. Sifia Hong was thought to be pregnant. Neither item looked particularly interesting.

"What am I looking at?"

"There's someone like you," Tessis said. "On the screen."

"Her?" He was nothing like the red-headed woman. "She's not—"

"Just wait. There was a chimera. She had eyes like yours. You're the only one I've seen."

At least Tessis never referred to him as a mongrel, unlike Laszlo and Cyrus, who insisted on using it. There was respect in both their voices nowadays though, and no contempt in the name, so he let them carry on. Putting his cup down, he paid attention to the broadcast. The presenter continued to talk about constitutional rights and humanity.

He curled his lip. "What on earth is she on about?"

"People like you." Tessis stuck a sharp elbow into his ribs. "Shut up and concentrate. There it is."

The screen widened to encompass the whole of the wall and a small woman appeared next to the presenter. A girlish woman, with short, tawny hair tucked behind pointed ears.

"Sugar!" Sabre-Tooth jumped from his chair and walked to the screen. He touched the image. After a moment, Tessis followed him.

"You know her?"

"We grew up together."

"She looks younger than you."

"We're the same age. Exactly, I think."

The presenter turned to Sugar and asked her a series of questions.

"I never knew my mother 'til a week ago." Sugar's voice was as husky and sibilant as ever, and a pang of homesickness hit Sabre-Tooth. "I never even knew I had one. I was born in a lab. I was never allowed out and never saw daylight until we escaped. I was a prisoner."

Sugar was out of the lab. How had she managed it? And she had a mother. He'd had no idea any of them had mothers. He'd grown up assuming they'd been nurtured in artificial wombs. And what about Tygre?

The presenter patted Sugar's shoulder sympathetically. "Why? What did the lab want from you?"

"I don't know their reasons, just that we were a research project." Sugar widened her amber cat's eyes and gave the presenter a shy, frightened smile.

Sugar was the most fearless person Sabre-Tooth had ever met. What was she doing?

"The army paid for us to be made," she continued. "They came for Sabe over a year ago. I don't know why, or what happened to him. Maybe he's dead."

"Sabe?"

"Sabre-Tooth. He was like my brother."

Tessis nudged Sabre-Tooth. "She's talking about you."

"Yeah."

"The soldiers took him away a few months before we escaped," Sugar said. "Then the scientists were going to kill Tyg and cut him up. They said it was the end of the experiment."

Sabre-Tooth dragged his hands through his shaggy, chin-length hair. "I hope Tyg's alright. Why would they want to kill him?"

Tessis frowned. "Why are you asking me?"

"It was a rhetorical question." Sabre-Tooth held up his hand. "Shh. I want to listen."

"So how do you feel now? After your dramatic rescue? Now your mother's found you?" The presenter leaned towards Sugar encouragingly. "Now you know what your real background is, how does it feel to be free?"

Sabre-Tooth frowned, wondering if he might have a mother too. If so, where was she? Who was she?

"It's not really freedom, is it?" Sugar nibbled on a delicate fingertip. "We're still illegals. I have to stay in hiding. I don't know what to do or where to go. They still might kill me."

Her image faded, and the presenter stared out at the camera. "We're now going to talk to a Human Rights Lawyer, who feels that these creatures have been treated heinously and have a good case for appealing for citizenship and financial restitution. I'm pleased to introduce Nahmada Scott."

A tall, middle-aged woman in formal legal robes materialised next to her. "People, not creatures. Please use the correct terms."

Sabre-Tooth tried to follow her speech, but it was full of legalese and all he grasped was that there was a campaign to give chimeras the right of citizenship. Sugar's newly found mother had started the process. It was something that had never occurred to him, that one day he could be free and legally entitled to citizenship. Tessis, Cyrus and Laszlo weren't citizens either, although they had talked about the different levels and how they hoped to climb the ladder one day. Sabre-Tooth doubted it would ever happen. Laszlo's unsavoury tastes meant he'd most likely end up executed for his crimes, and he'd probably drag Cyrus with him. The only reason they'd survived this far was Diessen's protection. Once he had no further use for them, they were finished.

Tessis sounded to Sabre-Tooth as though she was walking a narrow path between control and breakdown. She wouldn't last long either if she didn't do something about it. He didn't have high expectations for his own lifespan.

At the end of the speech, the image of Sugar appeared again. She was curled in a chair, looking small, sad, harmless and cute. When she faded, Sabre-Tooth returned to the sofa.

He sucked the back of his knuckles.

Tessis trailed behind him. "Does that mean you might be free?"

Sabre-Tooth leaned forward, elbows resting on his knees and his head down, letting the residue of hope drain from him.

"Sabe?"

"I doubt it. Cyrus and Laszlo are stuck here, and they were volunteers. They should have been given level one citizenship years ago. You too. And we all know too much now."

"Cyrus and Laszlo are psychopaths. No-one's going to give them citizenship. Anyway, they wouldn't last a month outside the army."

"What about you?"

"They're not going to let me go and if I wasn't here, I'd probably be dead by now. I'm still under sentence of death and even if it's commuted, army whores don't live long." Tessis bit her lip and darted a quick look at Laszlo.

He was asleep, eyes closed and mouth open.

"I killed one of my officers."

Sabre-Tooth's head jerked up. He stared at her. "You did what?"

"He tried to rape me."

He let the words sink in. It wasn't a surprise; abuse was rife in all levels of the army, but he also knew that killing the perpetrator wasn't going to have a good ending. Officers could do what they liked to cadets, especially non-citizen cadets. Why hadn't Tessis been executed? Made an example of?

"Accident?"

"I battered him to death with a chair. I had a temper in those days."

Sabre-Tooth warmed with admiration. If it wasn't for the collar, maybe he could have done something like that to Commander Diessen. Or Corporal Obi. "That's good."

"Not that good. They arrested me." Tessis's lips flattened. "Sentenced me to death, but then Commander Diessen came along and offered me this. He said I had an interesting psychological profile."

"You—"

"I thought it was a trick. I said no." Tessis's brow furrowed. "Then he told me he was having the death sentence reduced to life imprisonment. In a military brothel. He said I'd be chained to a bench for fourteen hours a day, and locked in a cell the rest of the time. I'd never see daylight again."

Sabre-Tooth shot a quick glance at her. "If I have to kill anyone, I wouldn't be sorry to kill him."

"Me neither. I don't mind killing my own enemies, but Diessen's? I'd love to stick a knife in his throat. I'm glad your friend escaped." Tessis shrugged, and stood up. "Don't tell Cyrus what I said. Or him." She nodded towards Laszlo.

"No." Sabre-Tooth got up as well. "Would you do the same again?"

Tessis chewed on her lower lip. "I don't know. I hope not, but... I... He made me so mad. I hate feeling powerless."

"Me too."

~~~

Two days later, as night fell, Sabre-Tooth returned to the barracks after his surveillance mission. The two young officials had shown no signs of wrongdoing. They'd spent their days at work and their evenings in their homes or in a respectable dance club.

Sabre-Tooth was disappointed. He'd hoped they might go to the one with the dancing snake chimeras. He'd been curious about them ever since he'd heard of their existence and it was better to think about them, rather than the fact that he might have to kill one or both of the people he'd been watching. Both came from high-level families. That would be the problem, he thought. They were too inconsequential to bother Diessen, but something about them had rattled his cage.

It could be one of a whole pack of reasons; their family connections, their work, anything. Diessen was out of control.

"Sabre-Tooth?"

He turned to see one of the camp aides approaching him. "Yes Sir?"

"You're wanted in the Commandant's office. Immediately."

Sabre-Tooth frowned. He still wore the civilian clothes he'd dressed in for his assignment, a cleaning operative's coverall and cheap fashion eyeshades. No one ever noticed the cleaners.

"Now. Go on. At the double."

He picked up his pace. Diessen. He always took over the Commandant's office when he visited the barracks.

The two guards on duty outside the office announced him. Cyrus and Laszlo already stood to attention in front of the desk. Sabre-Tooth fell into position next to Laszlo. Tessis trailed in a moment later.

The officer behind the desk was not Diessen. She wasn't the site Commandant either.

Her black Military Intelligence coverall fit her as though it had been personally tailored to her body and a double row of medals broke up the solid darkness of her chest. She rose to her feet, arms clasped behind her back. Slightly shorter than Diessen, she was half as wide, with the darkest skin Sabre-Tooth had ever seen. She stared down at the four of them from narrowed brown eyes, which dominated a face bisected by a wide, full-lipped mouth and topped with a centimetre of tightly coiled, iron-grey hair.

The silence dragged out.

Sabre-Tooth squashed the urge to flex his claws. He'd grown out of that.

"I've called you here to let you know there will be a change in your command structure." Compared to Diessen's bullying bellow, this woman's voice was a low drawl. "My name is Commander Gibousset and I'm now in charge of Military Intelligence. I believe the four of you reported directly to Commander Diessen?"

"Yes Sir." Their voices rang out in unison.

"Until I say differently you'll report to me. Through my aides."

Sabre-Tooth's mind raced round the implications of Diessen's absence. Did it mean he could stop killing people?

"Any questions?"

"Yes, Sir." As usual, it was Cyrus who spoke up.

"What is it?"

"Where's Commander Diessen?"

Sabre-Tooth waited impatiently for the answer.

"Forget Commander Diessen. He's no longer your business." The fierce stare discouraged any further questions. "You'll follow orders from your officers as usual. I'll talk to you individually later. Dismissed."

"What the hell's going on?" Tessis asked, once they were out of the admin building. "I've just come in from the South Bank."

"Me too." Sabre-Tooth said. "From London Central."

"I talked to Diessen a couple of days ago," Tessis said. "He was still in charge then."

"Let's get a drink." Cyrus turned towards the small bar that served Military Enforcement. "We can swap what we know."

~~~

"I heard Diessen was one of the people arrested in the chimera case." Cyrus leaned on the bar, twisting round to look at Sabre-Tooth. "Apparently, it happened after your little mutant sister was on the media. I thought it was just a rumour, but looks like it might be true."

Sabre-Tooth shrugged, not wanting to indulge in too much hope. "Why did you ask if you already knew?"

"A rumour's a rumour. Could've been a load of shit," Cyrus said.

"It has to be true," Laszlo said. "I heard the military head of the project got arrested as well as some of the scientists. That has to be Diessen. The work they did on you lot broke a whole load of laws."

"Diessen? Couldn't have happened to a more deserving man," Cyrus said. "If that's what happened. Anyway, his mistake wasn't breaking the law. It was getting caught."

"I suppose it'll come out officially," Laszlo said. "Eventually."

"Maybe," Cyrus said. "Maybe not. Depends who else is involved."

Sabre-Tooth picked up his drink, wondering whether the arrests had included Professor Rizzi and Rashelle. He hoped so. "What'll happen to him?"

"He'll disappear," Cyrus said. "Either that or be used as an example. Last time someone important got arrested, they showed him on the media a couple of weeks later. They'd done a chemical interrogation. He was a drooling idiot when they executed him."

"Wonder if they'll show Diessen's execution," Laszlo said. "That's something I'd really like to see."

Cyrus ignored him. "Diessen's embarrassed the Council so I doubt he's got any friends there." He changed the subject. "I saw the media show about those other chimeras. Your sister's cute, even with the pointy ears."

"She's not really my sister," Sabre-Tooth said. "At least, I don't think so."

"So, she might—"

"I'm just glad they took the whitecoats." Sabre-Tooth thought about someone tasering Professor Rizzi, and a thrill of pleasure ran through him. The professor must have been arrested. "Serves them right. Sadistic bastards." Worry about Tygre festered in the back of his mind.

"Do you think things might change for us?" Tessis asked.

Cyrus shrugged. "Doubt it. Why should they?"

"Well we won't be Diessen's personal hit squad any longer," Sabre-Tooth said.

"Laszlo and I always did more sanctioned stuff than you. Official undercover work, so we're okay. Maybe. You and Tessis…" Cyrus sucked his upper lip. "You were Diessen's personal assassins. You might be all right. Every high-up needs a clean-up team."

ALLIANCE NEWS CORP – keeping you informed

News Update
August 3rd 2453

Law and Order

Following last December's terrorist raids on a series of military research labs, a number of arrests have been made. Yesterday evening, head of Alliance Security, Commander Rho-Shin Hahmid put out this statement:
'A senior officer in Military Intelligence has been revealed as a sponsor of unsanctioned experiments involving the human genome. He is now in custody at Security Central, along with the Principal Investigator from each lab. In addition, a number of junior employees are under question. The Alliance has zero tolerance for those who break the laws of reproduction. Investigations into alleged human rights abuses are underway.'

Dissension – the struggle against injustice

August 3rd 2453

Our sources inform us that a certain senior officer in Military Intelligence is to be the scapegoat in the Council's latest clusterfuck. We understand that their labs near Oxford have been engaged in prohibited research for at least twenty years. This unfortunate Commander cannot be the only senior figure involved. We wait impatiently for further fallout.

Chapter 19

Loud banging on his door pulled him out of the story he was reading. A louder thud landed at the bottom of the door, sounding as though someone was about to kick it in. What the hell was going on? It was barely seven o'clock. Slowly closing his palm-unit, he jumped from his bunk and flipped open the simple door latch.

"Commander Gibousset wants to see you." A black-uniformed junior aide slammed the door open and barreled into Sabre-Tooth's cubi-room.

"Now Sir?" Sabre-Tooth winced, still not reconciled to loud voices. He pressed himself against the wall. The room wasn't large enough for two fully-grown people.

"No, next month." The aide rolled his eyes. "Yes. Now. I hope we aren't disturbing you. Get some clothes on, will you?"

"Right Sir." Sabre-Tooth pulled on his coverall, glancing at the silver marks on the aide's uniform sleeve. "What does she want, Sir?"

"She hasn't shared that with me. Hurry up." He glared at Sabre-Tooth, who bent down to fasten his boots.

"Yes Sir."

Sabre-Tooth took his time. If the officer didn't have his collar control, he couldn't hurt him. Maybe it had disappeared with Diessen. No one had used it since Murkhal had his meltdown and coerced him into his first murder. Now that he was an active operative, the officers treated him less like an animal they could abuse, and more like a person. As much as the bottom ranks of the army were ever treated like people, anyway.

The aide marched with him as he headed across the square. "You need a haircut."

Sabre-Tooth raked his hand through his mop of tawny blonde hair. "It hides the ears, Sir."

The aide glanced at him. His own hair was cut to a millimetre in length, revealing a perfect pair of biscuit-coloured ears, rounded at the top and lying flat against his head.

"You might be right." He knocked on the commander's door and waited for permission to enter.

Commander Gibousset sat behind the desk scrolling through a document on the desktop screen. Sabre-Tooth halted a foot in front of the desk and stared straight ahead, wondering again, why he had been summoned.

Gibousset eventually raised her head. "Sabre-Tooth?"

"Yes Sir."

"Where did you get that ridiculous name?"

"I don't know, Sir."

"You're not quite what I expected." Gibousset tilted her head to one side. "You look almost human."

"Yes Sir."

"I've been going through your file."

"Sir?"

"It makes interesting reading."

Sabre-Tooth tried not to blink.

"Don't you think so?"

"I don't know, Sir." How was he supposed to know that? He'd never read the thing.

"Very interesting. Do you realise that your work, since you qualified, isn't documented? What do you say to that?"

"I'm sorry, Sir."

"It means that for all we know from the records, you've spent the last year sleeping in your bunk." Commander Gibousset rose and walked round the desk until she stood behind Sabre-Tooth. "Fortunately for you, Commander Diessen shared his knowledge with us."

Sabre-Tooth suspected that the sharing hadn't been voluntary. Everyone broke under interrogation with its mixture of drugs and pain.

"You're a killer, aren't you?"

"I'm a soldier, Sir."

"Diessen's attack dog?"

What the hell was he supposed to say to that? He kept quiet.

"Aren't you?"

"I obey orders, Sir."

"You shouldn't exist." Gibousset rested a heavy hand on his shoulder. "Manipulation of the human genome is forbidden. You're not even an animal, you're an obscenity. It might be best to kill you and hide the evidence of wrongdoing."

Sabre-Tooth froze.

"It's too late for that now though. Thanks to Diessen, the whole world knows what went on at that research station. He deserves everything he gets. Don't you agree?"

"I don't know, Sir." There was no right, or safe, answer to that sort of question.

"You and the other three in your little dream team did jobs for him, didn't you?"

"Yes, Sir."

"I've been told that the four of you are psychopaths."

Sabre-Tooth's eyes widened. He wasn't a psychopath. The others maybe. Not him, though.

"You'll keep that sort of behavior reined in, while I'm in charge. Do you understand?"

"Yes, Sir."

"The jobs you did for Diessen – I'll want more details. I'll talk to you about them later."

"I obeyed orders, Sir." If he repeated the words often enough, someone might take notice. Gibousset returned to her chair. "And you'll carry on obeying orders, won't you?"

"Yes, Sir."

Gibousset picked up the collar control from the desktop. "I assume you know what this is?"

"Yes, Sir." So it hadn't disappeared with Diessen.

Gibousset's fingers hovered over the buttons.

A pulse pounded in Sabre-Tooth's temple.

"Don't make me use it."

"No, Sir." He had to force his voice to remain steady.

"You can go. You'll be watched. You'll do the jobs you're given. I don't want you stepping a millimetre out of line. If I'm reminded of your existence, I might decide to end it. Dismissed." Gibousset dropped the control on the surface of the desk and reactivated her screen.

Laszlo was leaning against the wall outside the office. Sabre-Tooth joined him, his legs weak and his head light with relief that he was out of the office. Unharmed.

"Well?" Laszlo gave him a sidelong look.

Sabre-Tooth shook his head, any words trapped in his throat.

~~~

Things were quiet for the next few days as everyone in Intelligence and Enforcement found themselves confined to the camp while Commander Gibousset took over.

Boringly quiet, but that was good. Sabre-Tooth exercised, ate and lay in the sun reading modern updates of old classic novels on his palm-unit. The collar lay heavily against his throat, reminding him that he might not have much of a future. He found it hard to sleep.

Dark shadows lingered in Tessis's eyes, but neither Laszlo nor Cyrus showed much concern over the change in leadership.

"Why aren't you worried?" Sabre-Tooth asked Cyrus.

He shrugged. "Commanders come and go."

"But—"

"And I've got a little pharmaceutical help. You should try it."

Hairs on the back of his neck rose at the idea. The withdrawal day had felt like the longest day of his life. A year afterwards, the memory still counted as one of his nightmares. He didn't want to be punished like the screamer addicts either. The muscles in his shoulders twitched in response to the idea of the taserwhip.

"You're still a pussy, aren't you?"

~~~

Gibousset hadn't gone away. She'd occupied the commandant's office for nearly a week, her senior aides visible most of the time, scurrying around the camp and summoning various groups in to see their boss. They staged unannounced inspections often, as well as formal parade reviews. Two mid-level officers disappeared, and at the beginning of the week, the senior aide sentenced eighteen soldiers to five strokes of the taserwhip. Each.

At least it amused Laszlo. Cyrus escaped being caught with contraband. He had a sense for trouble and hid his stock somewhere only he knew.

"No fights this Friday," he said, in the recreation hub on Wednesday night. "Probably nothing until that fucker has gone back where she came from." He glowered at his beer. "She should be in London. Like Diessen was. She doesn't know her place."

"Interfering bitch." Laszlo pushed his drink around the table. "I'm bored."

Cyrus sat up in alarm. "Laszlo—"

"Don't panic." Laszlo stretched his arms above his head. "I don't want another whipping. I'd rather be in the audience."

"Good," Cyrus said.

Laszlo relaxed. "Let's hope she goes away soon. They can't keep us locked up for much longer." He poked his glass with one finger, watching as it slid into a patch of liquid, teetered on the edge of the table and crashed to the ground, spraying Tessis with stale beer.

She pushed her chair away from the table and jumped to her feet. "For fuck's sake, watch what you're doing."

Laszlo smirked.

Tessis stalked off, shoulders rigid, swearing under her breath.

~~~

The next morning, loud pounding on the door woke Sabre-Tooth again. He glanced at his communit. It was five-thirty.

"Commander Gibousset's office in ten minutes." The voice was unfamiliar. Heavy footsteps hit the ground as whoever it was marched away.

Sabre-Tooth bumped into Tessis as he left his room.

"You as well?" she said. "What the hell does she want at this hour of the morning? Doesn't she ever sleep?"

"Yeah." He frowned into the darkness. "Dunno." Nothing that happened this early could be good.

"She called me a sociopath, told me I'd only got a temporary stay of execution." Tessis echoed his worries. "She warned me not to make waves. Like I'm going to stick my head above the parapet?"

"Me neither."

"She's probably nervous that she'll be arrested as well," Tessis said as they crossed the square. "Guilt by association. I'm surprised they haven't swept you under the carpet."

"No more surprised than me." Sabre-Tooth bared his teeth at her. "But I wouldn't feel too confident if I was you. If they get rid of one, they'll probably get rid of all."

"Yeah." Tessis glanced sideways at him, her voice unsteady. She chewed on the edge of her thumbnail. "Do you think that's it? They're going to…?"

"No idea." His heart thudded against his ribs.

The door to the Commandant's office stood open. Gibousset waited until they were inside and pressed a button to close it behind them. "Sit down." She waved the two of them to the chairs in front of the desk, circled it, and took her own seat. Leaning back, she placed her hands flat on the desk surface.

A minute ticked by. Sabre-Tooth realised the woman was trying to intimidate them, but it took more than a hard stare to wipe the blankness from Tessis's face, and even more to make him show visible distress. He gazed at the wall behind Gibousset, and waited for her to speak.

"We have a problem." Gibousset paused again, this time as though waiting for a reply.

She didn't get one.

"Well?" Gibousset glared at Sabre-Tooth.

"What problem, Sir?"

"It's a problem that you've caused."

"Me Sir?" Not possible. Sabre-Tooth made a point of never causing problems. He was too aware of his vulnerability.

"You and your maverick commander. And your mutant friends."

"Sir?"

"This move to give you citizenship isn't generally liked. Once we start handing it out, who knows what will come next?" Gibousset scowled. "Challenges to the population laws? Citizenship for every illegal?"

"I don't know Sir."

"Of course you don't. It's none of your business. None of mine either. We just have to make it go away. Understand?"

"Yes Sir." How were they going to do that? He didn't know where Gibousset was taking the conversation, but he wasn't going to argue with the woman who controlled his collar.

"We have a troublesome lawyer. She calls herself a human rights lawyer. I call her a shit-stirrer. We need to silence her."

Tessis flinched.

Sabre-Tooth wondered who had problems with the lawyer. Gibousset had used the word 'we', so any orders probably came through the military hierarchy or through the Council.

"You will silence her. Succeed and you'll give me a reason not to get rid of the pair of you."

Sabre-Tooth moved his stare back to the wall. "Both of us, Sir?"

He'd always operated alone, and he was sure Tessis had as well. Cyrus and Laszlo mainly worked together; they were viewed as a stable partnership, especially when they were deployed as part of a larger team. Even their commanding officers knew that Cyrus kept Laszlo in check and Laszlo kept Cyrus focused.

"Both of you." Gibousset tapped her fingers on the desktop. "Any more stupid questions?"

"Who is she, Sir? The lawyer, I mean." Sabre-Tooth knew Tessis wouldn't ask.

"You don't need to know that," Gibousset said. "You'll be given enough information to ID the target and that's all."

"Yes Sir. Why two of us?"

"Because that's what I'm telling you to do." She pushed her chair back from the desk and leaned back in it, steepling her hands on her stomach. "I'll tell you this much. This lawyer claims to be representing the rights of some extremely dangerous people. If you can call them people. I don't. I call them terrorists. For the sake of everyone, she has to be removed."

Everyone was a terrorist in the eyes of the military. They were paranoid.

"We're less likely to make a mistake if we work alone," Sabre-Tooth said. "That's what we're used to, Sir."

"And I say you'll work as a pair. We have strong suspicions that she's linked to Dissension. You know who they are?" She raised an eyebrow.

"Yes Sir." Dissension was one of the most vocal opposition groups. The organization itself wasn't illegal, but many of its associated activities were viewed with suspicion by law-enforcement.

"Her clients may be with her at the site of intervention. Someone's supporting them, and whoever it is, will probably have protection. One of you will have to deal with that, while the other takes care of the lawyer. If you have to kill them all, that would be viewed as a satisfactory outcome." Gibousset glanced at Sabre-Tooth, while she turned the collar control in her hand. "Some of them come from the same background as you do, Sabre-Tooth, but while you've been civilised and trained in useful skills, these others are just animals. Do you understand?"

"Yes, Sir." Did she think Sabre-Tooth would forget Gibousset had called him an obscenity? It was worse than being called an animal. He kept his mind as blank as his expression; he could think about things later.

"If she's surrounded by these animals, she won't be an easy target," Gibousset said. "They're efficient guards. You need to remember that and to be careful. You can do that?"

"Yes Sir."

"And you?" Gibousset asked Tessis.

"Yes Sir."

"Both of you prove to me that you're valuable and loyal members of my team and you'll be rewarded. Let me down and you won't like the consequences. Is that clear?"

"Yes, Sir."

"Good." Gibousset smiled, revealing perfect white teeth. "Intelligence will brief you on the details. Location, ID and potential hurdles. You can go."

As they reached the door, she spoke again. "I don't trust either of you. If one of you makes a mistake, you'll both suffer the consequences."

Tessis stalked out ahead of Sabre-Tooth, waiting for him to catch up once she was outside and away from the Commander's office. She blew out a heavy breath. "What was that about?"

"I don't know." Sabre-Tooth slowed to a stroll, wondering whether Gibousset didn't know that he and Sugar had grown up in the same lab. Maybe she did know and didn't care. Maybe she thought that animals didn't have feelings.

"You're growling." Tessis glanced up at him.

"I hope it's not the lawyer who was on the news," he said. "Suppose it's Sugar she's got with her? I can't kill Sugar. And what if Tygre's there?" He still hoped Tygre had escaped.

"I'll do it if I have to," Tessis said. "Who's Tygre?"

"Another chimera like me. The one Sugar talked about on the newsflash, remember? Tyg? You can't kill him." He ran one finger over the front of his collar.

"If it's him or me, I can," Tessis said. "Look, Sabe—"

"I hate this shit." He kicked at the stone pathway, aware his claws were out.

"Me too." Tessis's voice was so quiet that Sabre-Tooth had to strain to hear the words. "Do you think she means to kill us afterwards?"

"I don't know." He hesitated. "She doesn't seem as mean as Diessen, but..."

"You always know the right thing to say," Tessa walked faster. "Why don't we just kill ourselves now? Save her the bother?" Her voice was heavy with sarcasm.

~~~

The conference with Intelligence brought bad news. Two desk officers waited for them in the briefing room. Both had the silver insignia of mid-rank staff embroidered into the collars of their black uniforms.

The image they brought up on the wall screen was that of Nahmada Scott, the lawyer who'd appeared on the newsflash with Sugar. Although Sabre-Tooth hoped that her present location would be somewhere Sugar wasn't, he suspected the hope was vain. Nahmada Scott's present official home was a residential building in Outer London, between the inner and outer walls. A picture of the house appeared on the wall screen. It wasn't where they were expected to attack her.

"We think it'll be too well-guarded," the senior officer told them. "A few respectable citizens have places out there, and even if you could get in, it's highly likely you'll be seen. Besides, if you get her outside the walls, we could blame her death on terrorists. The Council doesn't want to be seen to assassinate highly regarded lawyers. That sort of thing unsettles everyone."

"So why tell us about it?" Tessis snapped. "I don't give a shit where she lives."

"I wouldn't be seen." Sabre-Tooth folded his arms. If he could persuade them to kill the woman in her own house, it would be much less likely that Sugar would be there. "I've worked in residential areas before. No one's ever seen me. I could get her in her bed."

"Shut up, both of you." The officer glared. "We know that she'll be meeting with her clients at a place situated about a mile the other side of the outer wall. That's where you'll target her. We don't have images of their safe house, but no more than four or five people should be present, and none of them need saving. Our source says that she has close links with Dissension. They're all traitorous scum. Finish them off as well if you like."

Sabre-Tooth rubbed his hands over his face. "How do you know that's where she'll be?"

"Intelligence," the officer said. "That's what we do. We think. We plan. You just need to follow instructions. Dismissed."

The two of them walked back to the Recreation hub.

"Dissension?" Tessis scowled. "Really? Why don't they just outlaw the lot of them? They could arrest this lawyer then, legally. They could drag her over to SecCen and strangle her in one of the cells."

Sabre-Tooth picked up two drinks from the autodispenser. "I haven't a clue. You'll have to ask Gibousset."

Tessis accepted one of the drinks and carried it to a small table in the corner of the room. "It looks like your friend's going to be a problem. If it's her or me, then I'm not going to be the one to die."

Sabre-Tooth took a gulp of his coffee substitute and sat opposite her, holding her gaze. "You'll have to kill me first. If you think you can. You'll have to, because I'm not going to let you kill Sugar."

"Sabe—" Tessis avoided his eyes. "Let's take one thing at a time."

He dropped his voice to a threatening growl. "Tessis—"

"Why are you two looking so gloomy?" Cyrus slipped into a seat at their table.

Sabre-Tooth dropped his face into his hands.

"Come on, it can't be that bad."

"We've got an assignment," Sabre-Tooth said, when Tessis showed no sign of answering.

"So have we." Laszlo joined them. "Southern Europe again. Back in the desert."

"Where are you going?" Cyrus asked.

"Not far. Not as far as you."

"How not far?" he persisted.

"Can't tell you," Sabre-Tooth said.

"Shit, Mongrel you're as big an arsehole as ever."

"I'll tell you," Tessis muttered. "Then I'll have to kill you. It'll be a pleasure."

Cyrus blew a kiss at her. "Be like that then."

ALLIANCE NEWS CORP – keeping you informed

News Update
September 13th 2453

Environment

Alliance Scientists have published a report on developments in the wildings around the New British Islands' city of London. Evidence has been presented of colonisation by previously unseen species, such as large crocodiles and other non-native reptiles. A two metre specimen was recorded in the old residential area of Enfield, but this pales in comparison to their saltwater cousins, congregating around the Thamesmouth, where eyewitnesses claim to have seen beasts of up to five metres in length. The assumption is, that the freshwater species will prey on medium sized mammals, such as the numerous capybara and beavers. It is thought that the ancestors of these creatures escaped from captivity during the triple disasters. The population will be monitored but, for interested parties, the Department of the Environment is offering wildlife tours.

~~~

Political

Councillor Andrei Krewchek claimed to be astonished and distressed by the arrest of Commander Diessen for crimes against humaity and abuse of the population laws. 'Commander Diessen always appeared to be a loyal and committed servant of the Eurasian Alliance. I couldn't be more shocked,' he told News Corps. He added, 'Given that some of these experiments were initiated at least twenty years ago, it is inconceivable that Commander Diessen is the perpetrator. Of course this does not excuse the fact that he turned a blind eye to the ongoing crime.' Readers will remember that Commander Diessen was a close political ally of Andrei Krewchek.

Chapter 20

Sabre-Tooth pressed himself into the gap between the bushes and the featureless sidewall of the sagging building. The house was a ruin, a pile of damp red bricks, covered with rampant plant growth. Anything could be hiding in it. Why couldn't they ambush Nahmada Scott in her Outer London home?

He pushed a branch away from his nose, brooding over how he could have made the murder look like a heart attack. Poison was part of his repertoire, his skill set. He could have broken into the lawyer's house, which was one of twenty medium-sized residencies in a walled community, protected by a private squad of lethally armed guards. There were a large number of fortified homes round the northern perimeter of the city, all of them with high protective fencing, security eyes, and visible and invisible security forces. They were supposed to be impossible to break into without the help of a major force team. Sabre-Tooth knew he could do it, despite what Intelligence said.

Instead, he was outside London, in Tottham Woods, an ex-residential area that had been abandoned four hundred years ago. He'd researched the area out of curiosity. It was once a commuter zone for central London before fighting, flooding and disease caused catastrophic population collapse. No one lived in it now.

Catastrophic. Sabre-Tooth shaped the word in his head. It had a satisfying sound. The word described his life perfectly.

Nowadays, Tottham Woods was a hotchpotch of broken down buildings, encroaching swamp and forest. None of it had been reclaimed, or cleansed. It was difficult terrain to navigate, as the tangled undergrowth hid piles of rubble and huge sinkholes, where underground services had once run. Occasionally, ragged and weathered pipes, constructed from archaic plastic, stuck out from the vegetation. Rustling sounds from within them suggested that while human life was scarce in the area, other things made their home there. A large brown rat moved from a heap of decaying plants and disappeared into the open mouth of one of the pipes.

Only desperate people clung to survival in places like this; their existence constantly at risk from the military, or from citizens who craved excitement and found it by preying on the less fortunate. The environmental laws protected rats, insects, snakes and other wildlife, but unlicensed people and non-citizens had no such protection.

He hoped Sugar wasn't living here.

His ears registered small rustling sounds from Tessis's direction. If he hadn't known better, he might have mistaken them for normal nocturnal noises. She was good, better than he'd thought she'd be. She had disappeared around the corner of the building, looking for the best entry site and checking on the level of security round the building itself. Sabre-Tooth waited, alert for any sign of the lawyer's guards. Moisture trickled down from the leaves of the almost tropical vegetation and slid off the surface of his skinsuit. A warm drop landed on the tip of his nose, almost the only part of his body that wasn't covered by the military grade chameleon plasskin.

He wiped it off before it could make him sneeze.

Nothing larger than the rat stirred; no one had entered or left the house since they'd arrived. A small personal groundtran was locked to the wall of the building so someone must be inside; a valuable vehicle wouldn't have been left here otherwise. Despite the seeming emptiness, it would be a strong lure for hopeful thieves.

Rustling of the leaves between two of the bushes signaled Tessis's return. She leaned against the wall next to Sabre-Tooth, holding the branches back with one arm. Night-vision specs covered her eyes.

"Everything's locked up; there're alarms on all the doors and windows," she whispered. "I think someone uses this place regularly. There wouldn't be plasglas in the windows if they didn't. And there'd be no need for all the alarms."

Sabre-Tooth swung the kitbag from his back and opened it. He crouched down in the damp to search through the contents. "Did you see anyone? Guards? Sentries?"

"No." Tessis watched the slow progress of a large beige slug as it slithered over a mossy stone. She shuddered. "I didn't see any sign of your friends either, if that's what you're asking."

"So we don't know if the target's here?"

"We know what we were told. That lawyer comes here for meetings. There's a fifty percent chance she'll be here tonight." Tessis kept her eyes on the slug. "I hate those things."

"So we go in, look around." Sabre-Tooth ignored the slug. It wasn't hurting anyone. "If she's not here, we leave and try again tomorrow."

Why would Nahmada Scott meet any of her chimera clients this close to London? Surely, they would be hidden somewhere safe and inaccessible. Why didn't they organise virtual meetings? They must know that they were targets and if they were removed, then their lawyer wouldn't have a case. Intelligence might be wrong. It wouldn't be the first time.

The possibility of seeing Sugar filled him with anticipation. He still didn't know if Tygre was all right, or even alive. No way was Tessis harming either of them. He'd kill her first.

He pulled a small laser knife and a flat black keyfob from his pack.

"Give me that." Tessis took the fob and edged around the side of the building, forcing the wet branches out of her way. "There's a window that might do, at the back of the house. I looked through and the room had nothing in it, except a few broken bricks. It was covered in slime, like it was never used."

Sabre-Tooth followed her.

Holding up the black fob to the window, she scanned it over the heavy glass, taking extra care around the edges. "Alarms on the window are off."

Sabre-Tooth frowned, immediately suspicious. "We should be careful."

He positioned his knife, and directing its beam into the corners of the window, cut the glass away from the brick and the crumbling concrete, targeting the join and taking care to keep the cuts smooth. They might have to put it back, and make it look untouched. He caught the pane as it toppled loose. "How do you want to do this, Tessis?"

"I'll lead," she said. "You look out for any guards. You're much faster than me."

"Right." Sabre-Tooth slid after her, through the empty window, more worried about her than about invisible guards. He didn't trust her not to strike a killing blow first and question identities second.

"Be careful," he repeated.

Tessis was quiet in her movements but her breathing disturbed the air. The fall of her feet echoed as she crossed the room.

As she had said, the room was empty; its walls a mixture of rotting wood and crumbling plaster, the disintegrating concrete floor uncovered by anything other than moss and algae. There didn't appear to be any internal alarms, so he followed her through the loosely hanging door and into a narrow corridor. Several more doors opened off on both sides, and they slowly walked past them, Sabre-Tooth flicking his ears to catch any sounds. All the doors were intact and closed, fitting their frames as though new. A few treads of a broken staircase rose at the end of the hallway, leading into empty space.

They were walking into a trap; he just wasn't sure what it was. The door they'd come through was the only one in poor condition and that was enough to make him suspicious.

He stopped Tessis with a hand on her arm.

"What?" She shaped the word.

"I can hear voices." Sabre-Tooth mouthed back at her. He nodded at the next door. "That way. They're too quiet to be in the next room, but be careful."

"Stop telling me to be careful. It's getting annoying." Tessis turned the handle and pushed the door open. "I can't hear anything."

"Shh." He bared his teeth at her. He could hear at least three people talking.

Tessis glared at him before she edged round the door and into the room.

Sabre-Tooth followed her, touching her arm again. He pointed at one of the two closed doors on the opposite wall.

Tessis rested her ear against the door. "Yes. You're right." She pulled a needle laser from her belt. "I'll go through and hit everyone in that room."

Sabre-Tooth placed a finger on his lips, wishing she'd be quiet. If Sugar were on the other side of the door, her augmented ears would catch every breath they took.

The voices were low murmurs, absorbed by the stone of the wall. He didn't recognize hers among them.

"No." He formed the word carefully, lifting the corner of his lip in threat. "You concentrate on the target. I'll deal with the rest."

"I still think—"

"Shh." He continued to shape his words silently. "And if you kill Sugar, I'll kill you myself. You know I can do it."

Tessis narrowed her eyes at him. "If you get us killed..." She listened for a moment longer.

Sabre-Tooth clenched his teeth, furious with her. He wasn't the one who would get them killed. "Will you be quiet?"

"I am." She snapped almost silently.

Her heartbeat whispered in his ear. He tilted his head to block it out and to catch the whispers from the other side of the door. "They're to the left."

She kicked the door open and spun through it, needle laser pointing in the direction of a small group of people.

A hand flew out from behind the door, grabbing her wrist and twisting it until the weapon fell to the floor. She bent from the waist, exhaling with a hiss of pain.

Sabre-Tooth slid his own weapon from his belt loop and peered round the edge of the door, halting at the sight of Tessis's assailant.

Sugar.

Dissension – the struggle against injustice

September 13th 2453

Alliance Security arrested senior corporate lawyer, Timon Van Melin, yesterday, on suspicion of the murder of his wife, Lyssa. Dissension suspects this is a cover-up. Lyssa Van Melin was in the process of searching for the whereabouts of a child she gave up for adoption, eighteen years ago. Her enquiries had led her to a military research site close to the University town of Oxford. Regular readers will remember that the director of this site was taken to Security Central some months ago, on charges of abusing the human genome. There are too many coincidences surrounding this recent arrest. Timon Van Melin may be many things, but we do not believe he murdered his wife.

Chapter 21

His feet refused to move.

She *was* here. That small hand, those claws belonged to Sugar.

Tessis fought against her grip, face wrinkled in concentration, free arm flailing at her captor.

He should help her, but after a quick glance, Sabre-Tooth barely noticed her. He took a shallow breath, dropping his weapon into the holster. He wasn't going to shoot Sugar, no matter what happened. He forced his legs to propel him through the door.

Sugar pulled Tessis backwards and wrapped her free arm round her throat, kicking at the backs of her knees until she sagged. She looked up and met Sabre-Tooth's gaze, the long pupils of her cat's eyes rounding in shock.

"Sabe, tell her—" Tessis choked.

"Let her go." Sabre-Tooth edged towards Sugar as he ran his eyes over the rest of the room.

A woman, wearing the uniform of a private guard, pointed her weapon at him. "Stop right there."

Sabre-Tooth held up his empty hands. The situation had the potential to turn into a catastrophe.

Catastrophe.

His word of the day.

The lawyer from the news vid stood in the furthest corner of the room, three short, thin, almost identical youths in front of her. The bodyguard stepped forward to block them all. The voices must have belonged to these people. No wonder he hadn't recognised Sugar. She hadn't spoken. His eyes returned to her.

"Make a move and I'll break her neck," Sugar said. Her voice still had a slight lisp.

Sabre-Tooth spread his hands in surrender. "I'm not going to do anything."

Tessis's face flushed as she tried to breathe through the pressure of Sugar's fingers.

"What are you doing here?" Surprise roughened Sugar's husky voice. "I thought you were dead."

"You know these people?" Nahmada Scott asked her.

"I know Sabre-Tooth."

Tessis jabbed at her midriff with her free elbow.

"Don't do that." Sugar flexed her fingers. A drop of scarlet dripped from Tessis's wrist onto the floor.

Sabre-Tooth's nostrils filled with the metallic blood smell. He hoped Sugar was pleased he wasn't dead. It was hard to tell.

Tessis gasped.

Sugar bared her teeth in a snarl.

Another drop fell, spreading into a stain as it hit the damp concrete.

"You made enough noise coming through the woods." Sugar's pupils filled her eyes. "Or at least she did."

Tessis bit her lip as Sugar relaxed her hold. She drew in a ragged breath. "I'm sorry. I never saw her."

Sugar tightened her grip again. "Shut up."

Tessis wheezed. Her eyes fixed on his. Her sallow skin had a pink tinge.

Sabre-Tooth pulled his thoughts together fast. "Sugar? Let her go. Please?"

"Rhys?" She beckoned to the group by the wall. Sabre-Tooth had almost forgotten there was anyone else in the room. "Get her weapon, will you?"

One of the three young men stepped forward and swiped the needle laser from where it had landed. He was a thin, athletic youth with white-blonde cropped hair, a narrow face and light blue, almond-shaped eyes. His fingers were long and slender. He didn't look entirely human.

"Just finish her off, Sugar," he said, glancing contemptuously at the bodyguard, who at a signal from the lawyer had lowered her weapon. "Don't mess about. I'll deal with the sidekick. I could shoot him with her gun." Turning it in his hand, he inspected the firing mechanism.

"Let Tessis go," Sabre-Tooth repeated.

Sidekick?

It was almost funny. He glanced briefly at the lawyer.

"You came to kill us." Sugar kept her grip on Tessis, but turned her huge amber eyes to focus on him. "Why Sabe?"

"Not you. I wouldn't kill you. You know I wouldn't. She's the one I was sent for." Sabre-Tooth nodded at Nahmada Scott.

The lawyer was younger than she'd looked on the flatscreen or in the surveillance images, thinner and smaller without her legal robes. She wore a grey and green weatherproof coverall, had sleek black hair pulled tightly away from her face, and carried herself with an air of authority.

"But why do you want to kill *her*?"

"We were told to," Sabre-Tooth said. "Let Tessis go. Please?"

"Why should I?"

"Please?"

Tessis's pupils darkened in panic.

Sugar was going to kill her if she didn't let go. She didn't look as though she cared.

"Sugar." The interjection came from Nahmada Scott. "Let the woman go. I don't work for murderers."

Sugar took her arm away from Tessis's throat, dropped her bleeding wrist, and shoved her away. Tessis staggered, falling to her knees. She scrambled to her feet and backed away.

"If she tries anything, she's dead." Sugar's eyes tracked her movement.

"Thank you," Nahmada Scott said.

"You don't work for me anyway," Sugar said. "You work for my mother."

"I work for Dissension," she said. "Human rights. Your case is an add-on, a favour to your mother."

Sugar's lip curled, exposing needle teeth.

The lawyer raised an eyebrow.

Tessis doubled over, gasped, coughed a couple of times, tried to talk, choked again and finally managed to croak. "Well? What do we do now?"

"Nothing," Sabre-Tooth said. He didn't want her to end up dead. She was lucky Sugar hadn't slashed her throat.

"Who told you to kill us?" Sugar focused on Sabre-Tooth.

"Sugar?" The youth she'd addressed as Rhys, took a step forward. "Don't talk to them. We should kill them."

Nahmada Scott folded her arms. "Rhys? Put that gun away."

Rhys glanced at the armed bodyguard, sneered, and slipped Tessis's needle laser into a pocket.

It looked like Nahmada Scott was in charge.

"Come on, Sabe?" Sugar peered into his face. "Who was it? Who wants to kill us?"

"Our Commander," Sabre-Tooth said. "We're from the military. You know those soldiers took me."

"You're a soldier now?" Her kittenish face took on an expression of contempt. "Do you always do as you're told?"

"Yes."

"What happened to you?" Sugar closed in on him, pupils widening as they fixed on his face. "You were never vicious. Not like me."

He dropped his head, ashamed.

"You turned into a hired killer? Was it those drugs they gave you?"

Tessis coughed again. "It's not his fault." She shuffled sideways until she stood next to him. Her voice wasn't quite back to normal. "They punish him if he disobeys. They'd kill him."

"I want to live," Sabre-Tooth said, returning Sugar's stare. He pulled his head covering off and tugged the neckline loose. "They put this round my neck."

Sugar reached out a finger and touched the metal of the collar. "What's it for?"

"It gives shocks. They can kill me with it."

"Nahmada?" Sugar called the lawyer over. "Have you seen anything like that before?"

The lawyer pushed past her bodyguard. "It's a control collar. They use them on political prisoners, minor criminals on day release, and dangerous animals."

"Can it kill him?"

Nahmada Scott nodded. "It'll cause excruciating pain as well. I'm not surprised he does as he's told."

"We should still kill them," Rhys said. "It's the safest way."

"We don't kill anyone unless we have to," Nahmada Scott said. "We want to prevent unnecessary violence. We don't want to turn into our enemies."

Rhys's narrow mouth twisted into a sneer. "Tell that to Krux. He said sometimes violence is the only answer."

Sabre-Tooth glanced at Tessis, who looked as baffled as he felt. "Who's Krux?"

No one answered.

"This is Sabre-Tooth," Sugar said. "He grew up with me, and we're not going to kill him. Rhys, we're not."

Rhys said nothing. The bodyguard moved closer to the lawyer.

"So what do we do with them?" Nahmada rubbed a hand over her mouth. "They're a complication. We could let them go, I suppose." It sounded as though she was talking to herself. "I don't think—"

"We could take Sabe with us," Sugar said. "You'd come, wouldn't you?"

"I can't," Sabre-Tooth said. "You've got to let me go. If I don't return from a job, they'll activate the kill button."

"Oh." she said. "Do you want to go back?"

"No." Sabre-Tooth said. "We've got to though. You need to leave here as well. Surveillance knows all about this place."

"Mmm," Nahmada Scott said. "I wonder how they found it. It looks like we might have a leak."

Sugar's brow creased. "Will you be in trouble if you don't kill us?"

Sabre-Tooth shrugged.

"They'll make us try again," Tessis said. "If they know we found you and let you go, they'll execute us."

"Not you," Sabre-Tooth said.

"They will. If they know you disobeyed an order, they'll definitely execute you." Tessis grabbed his arm. "And Gibousset said she'll hold us both responsible, so that's me as well. What are we going to do?"

"It won't be easy to kill us." Sugar balanced her weight on the balls of her feet.

"For the last time, I'm not going to kill you," Sabre-Tooth said.

"She might." Sugar pointed at Tessis.

"We weren't sent for you. Just for her," Tessis said.

Nahmada Scott shrugged. Her bodyguard's hand tightened on his weapon.

"You leave her alone," Sugar said. "Nahmada, we can't just send him back. Is there nothing we can do?"

The lawyer blew out a thoughtful breath. "We could let the people who sent him know we have him, and that he'll be part of our legal challenge."

"Would that work?"

"I doubt it. He's part of the military. If they think we have him, they probably will terminate him. We could lodge a protest based on the case for his humanity, but it'll be too late for him." Nahmada scratched her head, dislodging a strand of black hair from her tightly bound ponytail. "The best thing we could do is get that collar off."

A wave of hope washed over Sabre-Tooth. "Could you do that?" Just the idea of being free of the collar made something inside him spring back to life.

"Not without equipment and expertise which we haven't got. I could call on someone, but she wouldn't arrive for at least twenty-four hours."

"Twenty-four hours is too long," Sabre-Tooth said. "We need to be back before morning."

"We could say our target wasn't here." Tessis grabbed his arm. "That the house was empty. Intelligence weren't completely sure they'd be here tonight."

"What about your hand?" Sugar's claw marks would be impossible to hide. "And your throat? They'll know we ran into trouble."

"I'll tell them you did it," Tessis inspected her wrist, which still oozed thickening blood. "You grabbed me and forgot your claws were out."

"Would they send you back to try again tomorrow?" Nahmada asked.

"I think so." Tessis sucked at her wound. "If they believe us."

"We might be able to remove the collar tomorrow night."

"You've got to try," Sugar said.

"What about Tessis?" Sabre-Tooth asked. He couldn't let her take sole blame for a failed mission.

Nahmada returned to her corner and sat down at the small table. "Legally, that would be harder." She turned her attention to Tessis. "You aren't wearing a collar, so you aren't enslaved, so the human rights argument wouldn't work. You'd be treated as a desertion case."

Tessis kept her eyes on her bleeding wrist. "I was coerced."

"Can you prove it?"

She shook her head. "My word against theirs. And there's an execution warrant against my name."

"You could desert. I'm not advising it though. If you're caught, the penalty for desertion is death."

Tessis chewed on her lower lip.

Nahmada was silent for a moment, tapping her fingernails on the table. "There might be a way. It wouldn't be immediate of course and it would depend on the premise that the government are sending in the military to assassinate their own people. Sabre-Tooth would have to be willing to speak in evidence."

Sabre-Tooth glanced at Tessis. "I'd be willing."

"We have to get your citizenship through," Nahmada said. "Non-citizens can't testify. It could take years."

"Let's get his collar off first," Sugar said. "At least then, he'll be harder to kill."

Sabre-Tooth exhaled in relief. It looked like Sugar was still on his side. She didn't hate him.

Nahmada nodded. "If you're sent back tomorrow, we'll see what we can do."

Tessis shuffled her feet. "If we're leaving, we should go now. If we're much later, there'll be questions."

Sabre-Tooth hesitated. "What if they don't send us back tomorrow?"

Nahmada Scott blew out a breath. "We know where you are. We'll be in touch."

"Okay." He wasn't sure if he believed her.

"We won't leave you there." Sugar flung her arms round Sabre-Tooth and hugged him fiercely, rubbing her cheek against his chest. "I've missed you."

"I've missed you too." Sabre-Tooth hugged her back. She felt tiny in his arms. "And Tygre. What happened to him? Where is he? Did he get out?"

"He escaped as well." Sugar released him, and stroked her hand down his face. "He's safe. I'll tell him you're alive. We worried about you."

Sabre-Tooth turned his face to rest his cheek against her hand. He wanted to see Tygre. "Where is he?"

"If you come with us, you'll see him." She patted his cheek with an open-clawed hand.

Sabre-Tooth grabbed her wrist. He didn't trust her claws.

Her mouth curved into a wide kitten-faced smile.

"Are you coming?" Tessis stood by the door.

Sabre-Tooth forced himself to turn away. He pulled his head covering back up.

"Fuck," Tessis muttered as they left the house. "That was a disaster."

Sabre-Tooth ignored her.

"I don't mind deserting." She broke the silence again as they approached the Outer London Wall. "It's got to be better than staying. If I stay I don't think I'll last much longer."

"Maybe not," Sabre-Tooth agreed.

The new commander didn't like them. She'd called Sabre-Tooth an obscenity, and who knew what she'd said to Tessis? She'd been wound as tightly as a spring for months and he wouldn't be surprised if she killed the next person who tried to make her do something she didn't want to do.

"I hope she believes us," Tessis muttered. "If she doesn't, we're screwed. Dead."

"Why haven't you thought about deserting before?" he asked, pressing the intercom on the exterior of the gate in the wall. "You haven't got a collar. You could have gone tonight."

The gate slid open and one of the perimeter guards waved them through, into the holding area.

"It's funny." She held up her face to the retinal scanner. "It just never occurred to me. I keep having visions of going down in flames, like in one of the vids. I used to daydream about taking Diessen down with me."

"Too late for that. He's fallen by himself." Sabre-Tooth stepped up for his own scan.

The guard opened the interior gate and waved them through.

Maybe after tomorrow, he would never have to return to the army camp again. It was hard to believe that he might be free. Free of the hated collar, free of the military, free of the need to kill strangers in order to keep his own life. Maybe he could even become a citizen one day.

He suppressed the idea, along with the hope that accompanied it. You couldn't be disappointed if you didn't have hope. Tomorrow, he might be dead.

Lengthening his stride, he caught up with Tessis.

ALLIANCE NEWS CORP – *keeping you informed*

News Update
September 14ᵗʰ 2453

Society

An attack on the hydroelectric station in the tidal region of Thamesmouth has led to a temporary energy outage for parts of Inner London. The culprits have not yet been identified, but the security services are in the process of making inquiries.

Residents in the London region of Camden complain that their energy supply is intermittent on a regular basis. Councillor Rhahzad Parande, from the Department for Environmental Planning, told Alliance News, 'energy rationing is done for a reason, and it is fairly distributed over all the London regions. It is unavoidable, a consequence of the damage to several generators.' The inhabitants of Camden are primarily Level Two and Level Three citizens. One resident, who didn't want to be named, said, 'Power cuts are never an issue in the region around the river wall, where the highest level citizens live.' When this accusation was put to him, Councillor Parande told our journalist, 'Riverwall is an important commercial hub, and so is exempt from energy rationing.'

The department of Urban Planning have agreed to provide low energy lighting to the main thoroughfares of Camden, and to the local community centres, from sunset until midnight every night.

Chapter 22

"He wasn't there?" Gibousset rose to her feet and paced to the window.

At eleven o'clock in the morning, the day was already warm, the air heavy with humidity. Dark clouds covered the sun, casting an atmosphere of gloom over the camp. The first drops of rain slid down the outside of the plasglas.

"Was there anyone in the house? Anyone at all?"

"Three blonde men," Tessis said. "Young. They looked like brothers. I think they were like him." She pointed at Sabre-Tooth.

"Chimeras?" Gibousset didn't bother turning round. "Did you recognise them?"

"No Sir." Sabre-Tooth was glad he could tell the truth. It was much easier than keeping his face expressionless while he told a lie.

"Did they see you?"

"No."

Gibousset faced them, wiping drops of moisture from her forehead. "Is it worth making another attempt? In the same place?"

"I don't know," Sabre-Tooth said. "I suppose we could try. The Intelligence Team sounded like they knew what they were talking about."

"Right." Gibousset pursed her lips in thought. "We'll give it one more go. If they aren't there, we'll have to assume you were seen. We'll reconsider hitting the target in his home. I'm not comfortable with that, though. Too many things could go wrong."

"Sir?" Sabre-Tooth paused, waiting until Gibousset waved at him to continue. "Why do you want to kill this lawyer? There are lots of other human rights lawyers who cause trouble."

Lawyers often appeared on the news vids, pontificating about one thing or another. He couldn't understand why the ruling council and the military made such a fuss about this one.

"Pity we can't get rid of all of them," Gibousset said.

"But why this one in particular?"

Gibousset returned to her desk, sitting down and leaning back in her chair. "You don't need to know why. You just have to follow orders."

"Yes Sir. But, Sir—"

Gibousset sighed, wiping her forehead again. "I told you why. If one class of non-citizens can challenge the Ruling Council, then it opens the door for more of them, and that's likely to lead to civil unrest. The Council's got enough problems with the pressure on our borders. Discontent at home would be inconvenient."

"But, Sir—"

"I don't think you're stupid, Sabre-Tooth," Gibousset said. "Those creatures she's defending might be sentient, they might even be human, but they're evidence that the military used illegal technology in their research programs. If they can be registered as citizens, they can bear witness to what went on. That would embarrass our leaders. No one wants to risk the stability of the Alliance."

"Sir?" Tessis asked.

"Yes?"

"I heard Commander Diessen had already been condemned, so why does it matter? You've got a scapegoat."

Sabre-Tooth glanced at her. He hadn't heard that. He couldn't believe she'd used the word 'scapegoat' to a senior officer. He checked Gibousset's expression.

"Scapegoat?" Gibousset's mouth curved in amusement. "Maybe, but other people were involved and the whole situation needs clearing up. The orders have come down from the top. Besides, if they win this case, then it gives precedence."

Sabre-Tooth frowned.

Gibousset sighed. "Do you have a problem, Sabre-Tooth?"

"No Sir. But why don't you just go after the other chimeras?"

"Why? It's none of your business. Soldiers don't ask why." She tapped her fingers on the desk. "I suppose it doesn't do any harm if you know."

"Sir?"

"They aren't the problem," she said. "The possibility that they were made with the approval of the Council is the problem. Of course, that's not the case. We weren't the only ones using this technology. We were just the first to ban it. Before we closed the borders, we had a big influx from India, and from what used to be Korea. There were a few genetic anomalies amongst the human refugees. Some governments had very different views on what constituted ethical research, and some of their creations still exist outside the law. If they aren't citizens, they can be killed legally, and we can take our time exterminating the troublemakers, as well as selecting the ones who might be useful to us."

She shook her head as though wondering why she was bothering to talk to subordinates. "Read your history."

"Thank you Sir." Sabre-Tooth couldn't see why chimeras were more likely to cause trouble than full humans.

"You can go. Your commanding officer wants to talk to you." Gibousset waved them towards the door. "If you do well, Sabre-Tooth, we might employ some of the others like you. Rather than terminate them."

Sabre-Tooth considered that as he walked back to Sergeant Cooper's office. More people like him, forced to do jobs they hated, while they wore a collar and were subject to the whims of any sadistic officer? Did Gibousset think that would motivate him? Did she think she was making a generous offer? A humane one?

157

"You're growling," Tessis told him.

He hissed at her.

She widened the distance between them.

"Sorry." He took a deep breath, halted and clenched his jaw. He took another breath. "She made me angry."

"I can see that." Tessis waited for him. "She was very talkative. Do you think that means she'll kill us when we've done the job?"

Sabre-Tooth stopped again. He hadn't considered that as a possibility.

Sergeant Cooper wanted to discuss Tessis's wounded wrist.

She winced, screwing up her face as he poured disinfectant over the scratches.

If you don't learn to control yourself, then we'll have to do it for you." Cooper jabbed his forefinger into Sabre-Tooth's chest.

"Sir, he thought I was walking into a trap," Tessis said. "He was trying to save my life."

"Shut up. He should have kept his claws sheathed. Fuck knows what sort of bugs he's got on them. If this happens again, Sabre-Tooth, I'll send you for aversion therapy. I can promise you won't like that. Now fuck off, both of you, and get some rest."

"What the hell's aversion therapy?" Tessis squinted at him in confusion as they walked across the rain-drenched parade square, back to their quarters.

"I think I can guess," he said. "It's not something I want to try."

Sabre-Tooth parted from Tessis at the door to his room and lay on his back on his bunk to think.

He hadn't realized there were many more people like himself in the world. He wondered where they were and whether he would ever meet any of them. The pale men in Sugar's group were definitely different. They were chimeras but not like him. Stefan Oroz, the friend of Diessen, had mentioned reptilian chimeras, dancers in some club.

Snake-women.

He played with the idea of snake-women dancers for a few minutes in an effort to take his mind off his worries, but it kept circling back to the present situation.

What would happen to Tessis if he escaped and she went back? What if she didn't mean it about deserting? He jumped off the bed and wiped the condensation from the plasglas of the window. He was light-headed from lack of sleep, but the twitching in his nerves wouldn't let him relax. He needed to talk to someone.

Outside, rain bounced loudly off the plascrete. It was the middle of September and the air was still heavy with moisture. His head pounded. Autumn would be late this year. Maybe winter as well.

He swung round and headed back into the corridor, knocking on Tessis's door.

"What?" She answered immediately, pulling it open and blocking the doorway. Her coverall was loosened at the top, but she was fully dressed.

"I've been thinking," he said.

"What about?"

"Come for a walk? And fasten your uniform. I can see the bruises on your neck." Sabre-Tooth didn't want to talk indoors; he was sure there were ears or eyes, maybe both, in their rooms. "I can't sleep."

"I was almost asleep." Tessis sighed as she sealed the top fastening of her coverall. "I've been up all night, and we go out again in a few hours. Can't it wait till then?"

Sabre-Tooth turned towards the outer door. He didn't believe she'd been anywhere close to sleep. "Come on."

She stamped out after him.

He waited for her to catch up and strolled across the square as though making for the Recreation Hub.

"I've been thinking about what to do, if they manage to remove my collar," Sabre-Tooth said. "It's hard to imagine. I'll have to get well away from London."

Tessis glanced up at him.

"What about you? Did you mean it about deserting?"

"I think so." She kicked at a puddle. "There's no way they'll ever give me even Level One citizenship. I can't do this anymore. If they catch me, I'll be executed, but if I stay…" Her voice trailed off.

"You're right. You should get out," Sabre-Tooth said. "If you did want to stay, though, you could blame me for the job fail."

"What?"

"You can say I broke."

"Broke?" Her brow creased.

"Broke down, went off the rails. Insane. That sort of thing. You could say you've been concerned for a while."

"Why on earth…?" Tessis halted. "Anyway, I told you. I don't want to stay."

"Keep walking."

"Why?" she repeated.

"To account for me deserting and you coming back. Your arm should make it believable. They'll assume my control's slipped badly. You won't have to burn any bridges then."

"They might not believe me," she said. "Suppose they give me truth drugs? Anyway, I don't want—"

"They won't." Sabre-Tooth hoped he was right. "Most of those drugs cause brain damage and they won't want to lose another operative."

"I don't know. I think you're being way too optimistic."

"Tell them I tried to persuade you to come with me. Tell them the truth. Tessis, I don't want you to get killed because of me. Or, you know…" He couldn't bring himself to verbalise the alternative. He thought it was unlikely they'd enslave her like that. She was too dangerous nowadays and anyway, that had been Commander Diessen's threat. It was a risk though. "Maybe I should suggest going alone again."

"Question your orders? Yeah. That's really going to work. Anyway, I want out as much as you do, so stop going on about it. I don't know why you need to keep going over the same ground. I've decided." Tessis touched her palm to the doorpad, pushing through into the mess. "Let's get this drink so I can go to sleep for a few hours."

"Will you—"

"I haven't got a choice, have I? It's getting to me, Sabe. I hate feeling controlled. Whatever *you* do, *I'm* leaving."

ALLIANCE NEWS CORP – keeping you informed

News Update
September 15th 2453

Politics

Yesterday, Andrei Krewchek formally announced his intention of challenging Sifia Hong for the leadership of the Eurasian Alliance. Sifia Hong, who recently married the head of the Swiss Defence Department, has led the Council of the Alliance for the past ten years, bringing a time of stability to the civilised world. According to her supporters, 'under her leadership poverty has halved, population has continued to decrease in a controlled manner, and the rule of law has returned to the countries of the Alliance'. Her detractors claim that her rule has weakened the Eurasian Alliance. Borders are less stable, the Indian Republic and the Americas have become a threat, and her spending on defence is derisory. Andrei Krewcheck states that he 'will reassert the position of the Eurasian Alliance as the dominant global power and, in time, will bring both India and America under the Alliance umbrella.' The Council Elections will take place next year.

Chapter 23

"I wonder if they'll turn up." Sabre-Tooth stared through the plasglas into the darkness beneath them.

"Why shouldn't they?" A note of panic threaded through Tessis's words.

The airtrans lurched, tilting sideways.

She grabbed the edges of her seat. "I hate these transports. Why couldn't we walk like we did yesterday?"

"They think they're doing us a favour," Sabre-Tooth said. "I don't know why they bother. They'll have to drop us off at least a mile away *and* they'll leave us to find our own way back."

"It's stupid." Tessis shifted position as the transport slowed and descended. "They're stupid. Your friends had better be there."

Her uncharacteristic display of nervousness forced him to suppress his own worries. When the automatic door slid open, he waited until she climbed out before scrambling after her into the muggy darkness of the night.

"Suppose they *don't* turn up?" Tessis returned to the original subject.

"Then we go back and wait for the next chance." He wished Tessis would return to her normal stoic and silent mode. Maybe he shouldn't have voiced his own doubts.

"I need to get out," she said. "If they don't turn up, I'm going anyway."

"You said that before. Tessis…"

She wouldn't last long by herself, especially in her present mood. Joining an existing organisation would give her a much better chance. Anyway, if the rebels didn't turn up she'd have to go back, for his sake if nothing else. Returning to camp without Tessis might be fatal for him. Given the claw wounds round her wrist, he bet Sergeant Cooper would think he'd murdered her.

"I want to kill someone," she said. "Every time I see Laszlo, I reach for my knife. The next time Sergeant Cooper gives me an order I don't like, I'll snap again. I can feel it building up. I'm so angry."

"Let's assume they'll be there."

When he glanced across at her, her small face was pinched with worry. Shadows cast by the moonlight aged her, turning her skin sickly sallow.

161

He shivered.

Tessis pulled her night-vision shades from her belt and fastened them over her eyes, hiding her expression. She pushed her way into the undergrowth.

The airtran rose up through the trees as it departed. Tessis didn't look back.

"Not that way." Sabre-Tooth caught up with her. "You need the trail finder."

Not everyone had his ability to find their way through darkness and over unfamiliar ground, or to be able to return easily to places they had previously visited. Tessis knew that. What was she thinking of?

Tessis snorted, but changed direction and followed him. A barely detectable path led through the overgrown and chaotic remains of the abandoned outer city, and towards the house in the ruined street.

Sabre-Tooth headed for the window they'd opened the previous night.

"We could go through the door," Tessis clutched her needle laser tightly in one hand. "They are supposed to be expecting us."

Sabre-Tooth shook his head, clearing the fog. Nerves made it hard to for him to think properly.

"I'd drop that if I were you." A quiet voice emerged from the tangle of bushes growing against the walls, and one of the pale chimeras from the previous night slid out of the vegetation, silent as a ghost.

Rhys?

Sabre-Tooth hadn't heard him. He'd been too worried about Tessis to concentrate. A small rustle disturbed the leaves of one of the bigger trees. He raised his head. Something lighter than the leaves moved in the branches.

Tessis stared, swinging the laser round to point at the newcomer.

"Drop it now."

Sabre-Tooth held his breath, unsure how she would react.

She let the gun fall from her fingers.

"Step back."

Both Tessis and Sabre-Tooth retreated into the wet undergrowth while the chimera retrieved the weapon. Sabre-Tooth clenched his fists and took several calming breaths. He hoped Rhys wasn't feeling as murderous as he'd appeared at their first meeting. If it was Rhys. He wasn't sure he could tell the three youths apart.

"Another one for my collection." He tucked it into a belt-loop, before calling to his companion. "You can come down now."

The second pale chimera slid down from one of the lower branches, his own needle-laser still in his hand.

"Follow me." Rhys waved at the barely visible path.

Sabre-Tooth and Tessis stayed close to him as he rounded the side of the house towards a rotting wooden door. When he pushed it, it opened to reveal a modern door of sturdy plasmetal.

Sabre-Tooth's heart picked up speed.

The inner door opened.

"Go on." Rhys stood back.

A man waited to one side, his hand on the edge of the doorframe. He hadn't been present the night before. "Keep walking. That way."

All three rebels followed Sabre-Tooth and Tessis, down a hallway and through another door into a larger room where several people congregated at one end of a table, talking quietly. Two armed men leaned against the far wall, looking eager to shoot anything that might be a threat. The third pale youth sat on the floor, next to them, his back against the wall. As Sabre-Tooth's group entered the room, he leapt to his feet.

Sugar was one of the people at the table. She turned her head as they entered, pausing her conversation and lifting one hand in greeting. She nudged the arm of the man she was talking to, and pointed at Sabre-Tooth. "That's him."

Sabre-Tooth smiled at her.

The man lifted his head and studied the newcomers.

Sabre-Tooth returned his inspection, before moving his gaze over the rest of the small group. Three of them, including Sugar, clustered together. Of the strangers, one was a man and the other a woman, both wearing faded and shabby camouflage coveralls. The woman was tall, skinny and angular. She had dusty blonde hair, pulled back in a long plait, and pale, pink-tinged skin. The man was shorter than Sabre-Tooth, and at least twice his age, with straight fair hair, broad flat cheekbones and tilted brown eyes.

"That lawyer's not here," Tessis whispered.

"No." One of the pale chimeras pushed past her, an amused smirk on his small mouth. "We'll be meeting with her somewhere else in future. And she's taken on extra bodyguards. Tell your masters that."

Tessis shrugged, all expression wiped from her face.

"Sit there." The other youth waved them to the chairs. "Keep your hands on the table where we can see them."

Tessis sat down first. "I'm not going back anyway." She began to tap her fingertips on the surface of the table. "So I'll be telling no one anything."

Sabre-Tooth sat next to her, acutely aware of the collar round his neck. He placed his hands on the table. His claws flexed, scarring the old-fashioned plaswood.

The brown-eyed man slid into the seat opposite him, his attention moving between Tessis and Sabre-Tooth, before focusing on Sabre-Tooth. "I hear you want to join us."

Sabre-Tooth blinked. He'd said nothing of the kind. He just wanted the collar off and not to have to kill Sugar. He wanted freedom, but he hadn't thought any further than that. He sensed the pale chimeras move to take up positions behind him.

"Is that right?" The man prompted him, warm brown eyes fixed on Sabre-tooth's face.

"I don't know," he said. "I don't know who you are or what you do."

"Sabe—" Sugar leant on the back of the man's chair.

"Quiet." The man's voice was expressionless but, to Sabre-Tooth's surprise, Sugar stopped speaking. "So tell me. What do you want from us?"

"I don't know," Sabre-Tooth repeated. "I do know that I don't want to kill your lawyer. I don't want to kill anybody. I want this collar off. The lawyer said you could take it off. I don't know who you are, so how can I know whether I want to join you?"

The man nodded, his mouth stretching into a wide smile. "Good point. And you?" His attention turned to Tessis.

"I want out of the military." Tessis kept her eyes lowered.

"Mmm? Is that all? I imagine most non-career soldiers want out of the military."

She scowled.

"Who are you?" Sabre-Tooth asked.

"My name is Krux."

Someone had mentioned the name on the previous visit. Sabre-Tooth couldn't remember why. "But what do you—"

"We provide support for those who can't rely on their government to do so."

Sabre-Tooth thought about this for a brief second. "Rebels? Terrorists?"

Krux smiled. "We're revolutionaries. People who will make a difference."

Sabre-Tooth examined his face. "Which people?"

"We call ourselves Dissension," Krux said.

Tessis inhaled sharply.

Dissension was the most visible of the anti-Council groups, the umbrella organisation masquerading as a legal critic of the governing class. Its news bulletins regularly interrupted the official Alliance News Corps broadcasts. Sabre-Tooth had read their words on the flatscreen in the lab, and in the military Recreation hubs. Like everyone else in Military Intelligence, he knew the group was at the centre of a web of seditious activity, supporting actions that caused problems outside the main residential centres. All sorts of offshoots and sub-groups, some legal, some definitely not, spun out from it. According to MI, they organised themselves as a collection of almost autonomous cells. When one was closed down, two more seemed to spring up. Interruptions to the Alliance News were only one of their activities. Sabre-Tooth couldn't understand why the parent group was allowed to continue.

"You want to destroy the Alliance?"

"No," Krux said. "We want to persuade them to acknowledge that everyone has rights. Just because you're born in the wrong place and the wrong time, shouldn't mean you're classified as non-existent."

"But the population laws—"

"The laws may be reasonable. The way they're enforced isn't. Lawyers like Nahmada are working to make them fairer. We're not just a bunch of thugs."

"Are you legal?"

Krux shook his head. "I'm not illegal either."

Sabre-Tooth glanced at Sugar. "What does it mean if I join you?"

"You'll definitely be outside the law," Krux said. "You'll work with a small group. We operate on a cell system."

What did 'work' mean? Where would he go? The breathing from the pale chimeras drifted to his ears. Behind him, one of them shifted position. The one by the wall pushed himself to his feet and ambled over to join the other two behind Sabre-Tooth.

"Come on Sabre-Tooth," Sugar leaned forward, resting a hand on Krux's shoulder. "What else are you going to do? You can't go back."

Tessis stopped tapping the table. "Do you mean you fight for the rights of unregistered people? People who are unlicensed births? Non-citizens?"

"Legally?" Krux nodded. "Yes, that's Nahmada Scott and the other lawyers. We believe that everyone's life is meaningful. We have a practical arm as well. We free political prisoners.

If we can't get them out legally, we do our best through other means. We interfere with conscript or enslaved labour. We help some of the climate refugees and give shelter to those who have nowhere else to go. That part of our work is against Alliance laws, and if we're caught, it means we pay the penalties. Our people risk their lives and freedom to protect human rights. All human rights. We want more equality."

"Mmm." Sabre-Tooth propped his elbows on the table. It sounded too high-minded to be true and as far as he knew, most political prisoners were held in Security Central. No one could break out of SecCen. He wondered how many people belonged to Dissension-affiliated groups and how many of them were known terrorists. How many of them had no other options? A fair number of illegals lived outside the civilised areas. They couldn't all be motivated by idealism. "Sounds ambitious."

"Yes," Krux said. "Are you going to join us?"

"Will you take this off if I don't?" He plucked at the collar. Now he knew it might be removed, he craved that freedom.

"No."

Blackmail. So much for all the high-minded talk.

Sabre-Tooth considered. If they went back without completing their mission, the repercussions could be disastrous. Commander Gibousset had voiced the possibility of another attempt, but she hadn't sounded happy about it. It was irrelevant anyway. Tessis's eyes narrowed as she glared at him. She wouldn't go back, not unless he forced her.

"Will you use me to kill your enemies?"

"We won't make you do anything." Krux leaned back in his chair. "We're not the military. You will be expected to contribute though. We help you, we feed you. It's not a free ride. You'll be asked to take part in attacks, but with us, you'll be able to refuse."

Sabre-Tooth didn't have to think too hard. Free of the collar, he had more options. He wasn't sure whether he believed Krux, but... "Okay."

Tessis's blown out breath filled the room. At least he'd made *her* happy.

"If you join us, the price of betrayal will be death. We don't like traitors, and we know how to deal with them. You get a chance because she asked." Krux nodded towards Sugar. "She told us you could be useful to us."

Sabre-Tooth decided. "Okay. What do I have to do?" The rebels couldn't be worse than the military.

"Just do as you're told and you'll be fine."

Where had he heard that before? Sabre-Tooth gave a mental eye-roll, but kept his expression serious as he nodded.

Krux's attention turned to Tessis. "What about you? I hear you want to desert. Your human rights haven't been violated, so what do you think we can do with you?"

Tessis's fingers started to tap the tabletop again. "I'm a non-citizen. One of those you say you're fighting for. I don't have any human rights."

"If they catch you, they'll execute you."

Tessis shrugged. "If they catch me, I hope they do."

"We'd make you disappear," Krux said. "You'd owe us."

"That would work for me." Her voice sounded calm, but Sabre-Tooth had known her long enough to detect her suppressed excitement.

"It would be better if you went back."

"No." Tessis hissed at him. "If you don't help me…Sabre-Tooth, you know—"

"Why? Better for who?" Sabre-Tooth asked.

The pulse in her temple beat frantically against her skin.

"Desertion's a death sentence," Krux said. "You can still go back."

"No." This time she shouted at him.

"No." Sabre-Tooth agreed with her. Even if Gibousset let her live, it wouldn't be long before she lost control. Someone would die, and Tessis would face military justice.

Krux pursed his lips, staring at the table. "You'll have to earn your keep if you join us. Your background gives you skills we can use."

"I can do that." Tessis's whole body sagged. She leaned her elbows on the table, resting her head in her hands.

"Fine." Krux twisted in his chair and beckoned to the strange woman. "This is Halla. She'll check you both for tracking chips, and Sabre-Tooth, she'll get your collar off."

Halla pushed herself away from the wall. "Now?"

Krux nodded.

"Is it safe?" Moisture pooled in Sabre-Tooth's mouth as he remembered the dog. "They told me it would activate if anyone tried to remove it."

"I'll do my best not to let that happen." Halla circled the table and bent over him. She ran one finger along the metal, brushing the sensitive skin at the back of his neck. "It's a pretty standard model. They've got it a bit tight haven't they?"

Sabre-Tooth nodded, fighting the urge to pull away from her fingers.

She straightened and rummaged in her belt-pack, finally pulling out a small flat object, which resembled his collar control unit. "Here we go. This should neutralise the activator."

Sabre-Tooth closed his eyes, as her fingers continued to play with the metal. The muscles in his shoulders writhed under his skin. How much would it hurt?

A slight click reached his ears. He braced himself, waiting for the agony.

The ends of the collar sprang apart.

Halla stepped backwards. "There. All done."

Sabre-Tooth opened his eyes. The collar dangled from her fingers. He flattened one hand against his neck, bare for the first time since he'd left the lab. He exhaled heavily and closed his eyes again, trying to hide the euphoria. His heart thudded against his ribcage.

"Good," Krux pushed his chair away from the table. "Halla? The trackers?"

"Just about to do it."

"Look at him first," Krux pointed at Sabre-Tooth. "The collar might have been enough, but just in case."

"Best to be sure." Halla took a small pencil shaped gadget from her belt. "Stand up." She moved the gadget over his body, an inch from his coverall. It beeped once.

Sabre-Tooth had a locator chip in his armpit. He hadn't a clue when it could have been put there. Maybe he'd had it since the lab.

"Just one. We'll have it out of you shortly."

Sabre-Tooth scratched the place through his skinsuit. Now he knew it was there, it irritated.

Tessis wrapped her arms tightly round herself as Halla approached her.

"Sure about this?" Krux asked her. "Once the chips are out, you can't turn back. Your controllers will know you've tried to abscond. You'll be officially labelled as a deserter."

"I'm sure." Tessis rose to her feet. "If you don't do it, I'll desert anyway. This is better for me. There's a chance I might really get out."

Halla moved the pencil over Tessis's skull and around her face. When it reached the nape of her neck, it pinged.

"What's that?" Tessis twisted her head, trying to see what was going on.

"Tracker chip," Halla said.

"The back of my neck? For fuck's sake?"

"We'll get it out. Keep still."

She continued to move the pencil over Tessis, finding two more of the chips, one in her armpit and one under the skin of her inner thigh. "Bloody microchips. The military are all microchips. Three though? Someone must have an investment in them. Come on; let's get them out of you." She jerked her head towards the door. "We'll do it next door. It's more private."

"In case you squeal like kittens," Rhys said.

Tessis's mouth hung open. "*Three* tracker chips? In *me*?"

Sabre-Tooth scratched his armpit again and followed the two women out of the room, across the corridor, and through the nearest door. This room was empty except for a rusty metal stack of shelves along one side.

Rhys followed them, Tessis's needle-laser still in his hand. "I'm watching you both. One wrong move and I use this."

Halla rolled her eyes. "Ignore him. He's just paranoid." She pointed at Sabre-Tooth. "Pull your skinsuit down to your waist and hold your arm up. You can rest your hand on your head."

He obeyed.

She wiped liquid anaesthetic over the skin of his armpit before taking a wide-bore syringe-like gadget from her belt, and pressing it into him.

He grunted as the razor-sharp tip dug into the sensitive flesh. Nerves and muscles twitched as the chip shot into the body of the syringe. Afterwards she sprayed the bleeding hole with liquid skin repair, which dried immediately. It still stung. He scratched at the place as she moved away.

"Don't go." Tessis sounded nervous.

Sabre-Tooth pulled his clothes back into place and waited while she stripped off her skinsuit and bent her head to let Halla access the position at the nape of her neck.

She flinched as the first chip came out, followed by the one under her arm, and the one in her inner thigh. "Are you sure you got them all?" she asked at last.

"Fairly sure," Halla replied, aiming the nozzle of the skin repair tube under Tessis's arm. She grinned. "You wouldn't be coming with us if I had any doubts." She handed the spray to Tessis. "Do your own thigh."

While Tessis dressed, Halla packed her equipment away and escorted them both back to the meeting room.

"You're coming with us." Sugar strolled over, hooking her hand through Sabre-Tooth's arm. "We're leaving now."

"Where are we going?"

"Your people know about this place, so tonight, we're moving to a safer shelter. Tomorrow, we'll go somewhere more permanent."

"Tessis as well?"

Sugar scowled. "Why do you care? She's free."

"She's a comrade."

"We'll travel together to the edge of old London. Rhys, Ryan and Eddie are going to take your comrade away from the city. She'll be on the deserter list. I suppose she'll eventually join one of the guerrilla groups."

"Don't talk about me as if I'm not here," Tessis snapped.

Sugar ignored her. "She'll be in a different group to you. Tyg and I were split up at first. We sometimes work together now, though."

"Guerrilla groups?" Sabre-Tooth said.

"She means terrorists," Tessis said. "That's what everyone else calls them."

"Like the prisoners we had to kill?" Drugged and starved, they'd been pathetic.

Tessis glanced at Sugar. "I think so."

"I mean saboteurs and fighting units made up of unlicensed non-citizens," Sugar said. "That's what they are. Krux says that one man's terrorist is another man's freedom fighter."

Krux heard his name and nodded. "True. One day we'll be seen as heroes."

Sabre-Tooth did another mental eye-roll. He wondered if they had a long-term plan.

"Even deserters like me?" Tessis asked.

"I don't know," Sugar admitted. "If we win, who knows?"

"Depends what you do for us," Krux said, bending down to pick up his pack.

Tessis studied the ground. "Anything's better than where I was. I'd rather die than go back there."

"A short life, but sweet?" Rhys joined them.

"I'm not sure how sweet," one of the other chimeras said. "We're a bit low on luxuries."

The group left the building together and headed out along a narrow track north, the three pale chimeras leading the way. Sabre-Tooth walked in silence, preparing a list of questions he wanted to ask. It was weird to think that he'd never return to the barracks, never see Gibousset again, never spend another night in his small cubi-room. Gibousset was no loss, but he'd been fond of the cubicle's privacy. And Cyrus and Laszlo. They might have their faults, but they were familiar. The knowledge that he was unlikely to see them again caused a hollow sensation in his stomach.

Tessis strode along next to him. After a few minutes, she touched his arm. "They're not going to win, are they? Against the Council? Against the military?"

"Shh." Sabre-Tooth knew that their escorts' ears were as sensitive as his.

"I don't care." She was silent for a few minutes. "Do you think they'll be as bad as the army?"

"Don't see how they can be," Sabre-Tooth said. "As long as we don't betray them, I guess we can leave anytime. How could they stop us?"

Sugar poked him in the back. "We could if we wanted." She dropped back to walk with Krux and Halla. The armed guards brought up the rear.

A moment later Tessis nudged him again. "I don't think I like your sister." This time she whispered.

Sabre-Tooth climbed over the half-decayed remains of a fallen tree, turning to grab her arm as she picked her way through the mass of bare branches.

"What do you think of this Krux?" she continued to whisper. "What's in this for him?"

"Shh," he said again. She was right. No one did this sort of thing out of altruism, but he had no idea what Krux's motives were. Maybe Sugar would have some idea. For now, Tessis should keep her attention on not tripping on one of the multitude of obstacles.

One of the pale chimeras slowed at a junction in the path. "This is where we leave you." He beckoned to Tessis. "You'll come with us."

"What about Sabe?" It was only because Sabre-Tooth knew her so well that he detected the fear under her expressionless voice.

"He's going somewhere else," the chimera told her. "Do you have a problem with that?"

"No. But—"

Krux interrupted. "Until we know we can trust you, you'll be staying at a very small base, well away from London. It's the safest place for you. The authorities won't bother looking for you there. We want to separate the two of you anyway."

"We'll take good care of you." The pale chimera snickered.

Tessis took a deep breath. "Okay. Sabe? Good luck."

"You too."

"Come on." The chimera took hold of her arm.

Sabre-Tooth waited, watching until she disappeared into the darkness of the forest scrub. She didn't look back.

ALLIANCE NEWS CORP – keeping you informed

News Update
September 20th 2453

Legal

A group of London lawyers led by notorious troublemaker, Nahmada Scott, has presented a first case for expanding citizenship. The document demands that any human residing in the New British Islands is accorded the rights of citizenship. In addition, Scott states that 'chimeras, containing a significant proportion of human DNA, should be similarly judged'. The claim will eventually be expanded to cover all territories under Alliance control. A representative from the Department of Population has stated that, while the Department has sympathy with the views expressed in this document, he believes that the introduction of organisms such as pansies, and even chimeras, into the case has turned it into a document of idiocy. He has passed it on to the Department of Justice.

Dissension – the campaign against injustice

September 20th 2453

Nahmada Scott, chief legal council for Dissension, presented the Department of Population with her carefully thought out case for universal citizenship earlier today. We, like everyone else, wait eagerly for the response.

Chapter 24

Darkness had turned to dawn by the time Sabre-Tooth arrived at the temporary resting place. He found himself close to the outskirts of historic London, a landscape of thick scrubland forest, far enough above sea level to be classified as dry land but wet enough to maintain a healthy moss and fern ground cover.

Two men in camouflage suits blocked the entrance to the collapsed building. Thorny climbing plants spread over the weathered bricks and shattered concrete, almost concealing its position. A rusted piece of warped metal was propped against a chunk of rubble, flakes of red and blue paint still clinging to it.

Sabre-Tooth pushed through the spiky foliage after Sugar. Halla followed him, while Krux lingered with his bodyguards to talk to one of the sentries.

Chipped and broken tiles led into an enclosed interior, giving him a momentary flashback to his old laboratory home. He came to a halt in the middle of a wide hall, lit only by the handheld torches of his companions. Darkness concealed everything outside the ring of artificial light, but he caught a glimpse of two twisted metal stairways descending further into the earth. A faint sound came from the depths, something soft scraping against metal.

"Where is this place?" He edged into the darkness, his ears flicking with caution. "Did you make it?"

"Me?" Sugar looked over her shoulder.

"I meant your group."

"No. Someone just adapted what was already here. I think this was part of the transport system before the disasters. It's called Woodside." Sugar shone her beam up to the eroded ceiling tiles, and then down onto the rusty metal staircase, before directing it around the walls.

He'd been in some of the central London travel tunnels. Close to the river, most of the levels were flooded. He turned in a circle, evaluating the space. A broken metal arrow on the wall pointed towards the entrance. Sabre-Tooth ran his fingers over the raised letters on the bricks above it.

WAY OUT.

Another muted creak drifted up from below.

"This is where we'll rest for a while." Sugar said.

Krux pushed through the greenery and joined them. "Sabre-Tooth? I'm leaving you here, but welcome to Dissension. Halla, you'll be coming with me."

Sabre-Tooth tilted his head, listening again. "Is there someone else down there?" He nodded at the staircase.

Krux nodded. "They're a couple of people staying. They'll travel with you tomorrow. Rose and Keir," he added to Sugar. "They arrived a few hours ago."

Sabre-Tooth's gaze drifted back to the damaged staircase.

Krux cleared his throat. "Have a safe journey. Remember what I said about the consequences of betrayal." He pushed his way back out into the light, followed by Halla who raised a hand in farewell.

"Where are they going?" Sabre-Tooth stared after them.

"No idea," Sugar said. "Probably back to Central Control but he doesn't tell me much."

"Where's Central—"

"Come on, we're down here." She ran lightly down the narrow staircase.

Sabre-tooth hurried after her.

At the bottom of the staircase was another hall, which turned into a tunnel and finished up in an open space, containing a row of thin mattresses on camp beds, six of them lined up against the opposite wall. The room was empty of life and the only light came from Sugar's wrist.

Sabre-Tooth didn't like this underground place at all. Faint sounds drifted from the other end of the tunnel, rustlings and occasional murmurs.

"Where are the people Krux mentioned?"

Sugar's forehead wrinkled. "There are a couple of other sleeping places. I thought you'd rather we were more private. We can talk. We'll see the others later."

Sabre-Tooth prowled past the bunks, studying the dark hole beyond them, while Sugar made her way to a plasteel cupboard and rummaged through it. The place appeared unoccupied, but an old-fashioned paper book lay on one of the beds, next to a machete-sized knife.

"Here." Sugar handed him a small torch. "You'll need this. It'll fit over your wrist." She glanced at the knife, picked it up and put it in the cupboard. "Someone left it behind. Careless."

"I don't like this place," he said. The walls and ceilings closed in on him and the open tunnel made his neck itch.

"No. Me neither," Sugar said. "Parts of the tunnel system have collapsed. It makes me wonder about the rest." She chewed on her finger, her forehead crinkling in concern. "I wonder what happens if the flood protections fail."

"Fail how?" He swung round to stare at her. The thought of flooding, this far from the centre, hadn't crossed his mind. He'd blocked it out.

"The whole of this area is protected by the flood barriers round London, but everyone says the water level is reaching the point where they won't work anymore. It's the water table, as well as the rain."

"What happens then?" The weight of the earth above him was almost physical. While he knew about the flood barriers in theory, he'd never considered the practicalities before. His lesson modules had concentrated on the amazing feats of engineering, not the problem they dealt with.

"This might fill up with water. Further down there, it's flooded. I had a look the first time I came here." She pointed into the dark. "Here's supposed to be safe though, above sea-level and we're only here for today. You can get a few hours' sleep and we'll move out tonight." She grinned at him, showing her canines. "There is an alarm system if the water defences fail."

"Mmm." Sabre-Tooth wasn't sure he trusted any alarm system. Not underground. Not with only one way out that he could see. He wanted to explore. "So where do we go tomorrow?"

"The Thamesmouth. It's just east of London, past the barriers and beyond where the ships come. Tygre's there at the moment and a few other chimeras as well. We seem to have congregated."

"Chimeras like the three men who went with Tessis?"

"Yes. They escaped with us. Twelve of us broke out of the labs. We're the most human. Rhys, Ryan and Eddie are a bit weird. We think they've got rat in them, maybe albino. They're very pale."

He hadn't known the name of the other chimeras. The first one, Rhys, had been bloodthirsty. He'd have killed Tessis and tried to shoot him, if Sugar hadn't been there. "I don't remember anyone else in the lab."

"No, they were kept in another building. There were different mixes. Those three are true triplets. There were another five like them, two more males, and three females. The others were more canine." She dropped down to sit cross-legged on one of the mattresses.

Sabre-Tooth fiddled with his wrist-light. "What about Krux? Who is he really?"

"He's in charge." Sugar glanced up at him and pointed to the adjacent mattress. "Sit down. He formed Dissension a few years ago."

"It's been around for ages, hasn't it?" He'd heard the group talked about by the military (*terrorists*).

"It was just an underground newspaper before," Sugar said. "Krux turned it into a movement."

"Terrorists," Sabre-Tooth muttered under his breath. They raided food production sites outside London, attacked the military, were responsible for some assassinations. They were as bad as the army, but only half as legal. "I'm not assassinating anyone for them."

Sugar ignored him. "It's a mixture of direct action and campaigning. We want to make the world safe for people like us."

"Just like the military," Sabre-Tooth muttered.

"I don't know about that." Sugar's kitten face creased into disapproval. "Anyway, Krux was here to talk to Nahmada so he came along to meet you."

"Nahmada?"

"The *lawyer*," she said. "The one who's bringing our arguments to the justice department. The one you wanted to kill."

"Oh. Nahmada Scott."

"That's what I said." The dim light made Sugar's pupils expand to fill most of her eyes.

"So Krux?" Sabre-Tooth returned to his original question. "Who is he? Is he ex-military?" Authority had bristled from him.

Sugar hunched one shoulder. "I don't know. He's a bit of a mystery. I've heard he comes from one of the high-level families, the ruling elite. They say he's rich as well."

"So why—"

"It might not even be true," she said. "I don't believe it. No one with any choice would live like this." She curled up on her mattress. "Why don't you try and get some sleep?"

Sabre-Tooth lowered himself onto the narrow bed and stretched out on his back. "Sugar?"

"I'm tired," she grumbled, switching off her light.

"But don't you have a plan? What does Dissension want long-term? Do you really think—"

"Tomorrow." She wriggled onto her side, facing away from him. "Put your light out."

After a moment, Sabre-Tooth switched the torch off.

"I really don't like this," he muttered into the darkness. Why did she have to mention flooding? Walls pressed inwards from all sides, above and below, and the air was stagnant. The whispers from the strangers had faded away and for a long time Sugar's even breathing was the only sound. Eventually he drifted into sleep.

~~~

It took three days to reach the Thamesmouth. Part of the journey was through the Essex wetlands, a region of old outer London that was no longer protected from the encroaching water. Two quiet humans from the other tunnel, a male and a female, both dressed in protective camouflage and carrying heavy packs, joined them for the journey. They introduced themselves as Keir and Rose, and had a flat-bottomed boat waiting at the point where the land became impassable. The two of them took it in turns to propel the boat along, letting Sabre-Tooth and Sugar carry it where the water became too shallow.

"Be careful," Rose said. "Things live in the water. Big things with teeth." She bared her own.

Sabre-Tooth's ears flickered, his nerves jumping at every unexpected noise. He'd seen pictures of the things that lived in these wetlands. Crocodiles, they were called. Their ancestors had escaped from collections of exotics, once the waters started rising and human civilisation broke down. Some of them were seven metres long. He'd like to see one, but from a safe distance. Protected by the same environmental laws that covered everything except humans, they'd thrived and increased as humanity struggled.

"So what's Krux's long term plan?" He glanced over his shoulder at Sugar, picking up the conversation from the previous night.

"He wants to force the Alliance to recognise the rights of everyone."

"By legal challenges?" Sabre-Tooth leaned on the side of the boat, looking down into a swirl of bright green waterweed.

"Yes."

"So what's with us?" he asked. "Why are we attacking Alliance property?"

"Mostly to make sure everyone's fed." Sugar sat on a bench opposite him, next to Rose. Keir was at the back, in charge of pushing the boat along.

"But—"

"And to help people like you, who aren't given any choice. Climate refugees, conscript gangs—"

Sabre-Tooth frowned at his reflection in the dark stagnant water. "The Alliance isn't going to change its mind on population restriction."

"Krux knows what he's doing. Everyone says he's brilliant," Sugar said. "Isn't that true, Rose?"

"I hope so," she said.

East of London was a pretty depressing landscape even without the predators. Ruined grey buildings rose from scummy water whose surface was covered with a layer of green and brown algae. Thin growths of green and black clung to the surface of ancient, degraded concrete. The damp air was heavy with the scent of rotting vegetation, and busy with clouds of small insects.

"It must be a good hiding place," Sabre-Tooth said as he trailed a hand in the water, separating the surface colours. "No one with any sense would come within miles of here."

"Yeah." Keir pushed the boat away from an island of concrete blocks. "I don't think many people live roundabouts. Fever's a problem. You've got to watch the weather as well. None of this area has much in the way of working flood defences. High winds or high tides happen a lot, often without warning. It's getting close to storm season already."

Sabre-Tooth eyed the flat broken surface of the water. It was almost black, reflecting the darkening sky. The first drops of rain splashed down, spreading out in circles, which grew and merged.

"Cargo ships tend to congregate west of us, at the river mouth," Keir added, wiping one hand across his eyes. "There're docks up the coast at Shipsgrave. The river police as well. When the weather's good, we need to watch out for them. If they're having a quiet day, they get restless. They think it's fun to run off any illegals they find. Even to shoot a few."

Sabre-Tooth wiped the rain from his own face. He'd known people like that. They weren't even twisted like Laszlo, just mean and vicious.

~~~

The rebels had set up a semi-permanent camp on a rust-eroded wreck of a ship, moored where the Thames estuary turned into open sea. The hulk must have once been some sort of working vessel. Now it was a multi-storied heap of scrap, surrounded by similar wrecks, none of which looked seaworthy. Seagrasses and sparse shrubs grew amongst them, springing out of crevasses and gaps where silt built up. Mixed scents of decomposition and salt lingered in the air.

Sabre-Tooth drew in a deep breath, tasting the sea on the back of his tongue. Decaying seaweed, iron and the ghost of oil wove into the tang of the ocean.

"Some of the hulks have inhabitants," Keir said. He'd abandoned the flat-bottomed boat once they reached deeper water, mooring it in the shelter of a high, eroded wall and moving everyone to a rowing boat. "It's a ship's graveyard. People hiding from Civil Enforcement sometimes end up here. Like us. It's not ideal, but it's convenient for some of the work we've done recently."

"What work?"

"You don't need to know." Keir guided the small boat alongside the target wreck. It towered above them, casting a long dark shadow over the water. "You're just staying until someone comes to collect you."

Sabre-Tooth frowned. "What do you mean?"

"You'll be attached to a group. Didn't Sugar tell you?"

Sugar sat at the far end of the little boat, talking to Rose. Hearing her name, she looked up. "I did. Didn't I?"

He shook his head. Filtering out important information from the rest of Sugar's speech was as hard as ever. He'd always thought it was the drugs the scientists fed him, but maybe it was just her.

"Everyone's attached to a group," she said. "One of the sentries sent a message when we arrived in Southgate."

"To who?"

"Central Control. They'll assign you to a team. You'll find out soon."

Sabre-Tooth wrinkled his nose. "Who're Central Control?" It sounded vague. Still, he didn't have to stay. Now the collar was gone, he could do what he liked. He touched the base of his throat.

"Krux," Sugar told him. "Halla's there as well, and other people. They do the planning, and tell us where to go. They'll find a place for you, but you'll have a chance to see Tygre before you go." She stood up, causing the rowing boat to sway, and swung her body onto a ladder hanging over the side of the bigger ship. "Come on."

Sabre-Tooth glanced at the scummy water, then at the swaying ladder. He gritted his teeth and followed her. To his relief, the ladder felt much more secure than it looked.

Before he reached the top, the rowing boat pulled away into the channel between the wrecks, taking Rose and Keir with it.

"Thanks." Sugar leaned over the side, waving as the boat disappeared.

Rose looked over her shoulder and lifted a limp hand in farewell.

"Where're they going?" Sabre-Tooth asked. He took a step backward from the flimsy rail.

"One of the other wrecks," she said. "I think they're crossing the channel tonight."

"What for?" Sabre-Tooth grabbed Sugar's arm, pulling her away from the broken railings. Black water stretched out as far as he could see, and iron grey clouds hung low on the horizon. White caps rose and fell on the surface. Further out, the wind whipped the sea into waves. Mewling seabirds circled overhead, diving down into the water, or landing on the boats, their shrieks mixing with the sound of the wind. He'd never seen such a wide expanse of water before.

"Something to do with a problem in France. Sometimes their people come over here and ours go over there. Especially when they get labelled as a priority by the enforcers. I'm not sure what they're doing at the moment. I haven't been involved." She looked down at his hand. "Are you nervous?"

"I don't want you to fall over. Meet a watery death." He clutched her wrist tighter.

"You're so melodramatic." Laughing, she shook off his hand. "Come on. I'll show you where everything is."

A fluctuating number of people made their temporary home on the hulk, but Tygre wasn't one of them at present. One of the other residents told Sugar he was expected back in the next couple of days.

Most of the people living on the hulk were unlicensed humans. From time to time, according to Sugar, a few other chimeras stayed as well. Two of them hung their hammocks in the same bunkroom as Sabre-Tooth. They weren't present when Sugar showed him where he would sleep, but as he left the bunkroom, Sugar told him how they'd escaped with her and the pale chimeras, when Krux's men broke into their old lab prison.

"I'm amazed we never found out they were there." Sabre-Tooth said, although he remembered how incurious he'd been before Diessen took him from the lab. It must have been a side-effect of the sedatives they'd used on him, but surely, he'd have noticed the signs of other chimeras. Even Sugar's security guard friends hadn't mentioned them.

"Me too." Sugar said. "One of the labs is doing a DNA analysis, but there's a backlog. They've done the rats. There were eight of them in the building next to us. They all got out. Hopefully they'll look at us next."

"I never knew," Sabre-Tooth said again.

"They kept us separate," Sugar said. "When Krux's lot rescued me and Tygre, they got the others as well. Wait 'til you meet the dog-men. They look like werewolves."

"Werewolves?" Sabre-Tooth hadn't watched a horror film since he'd left the lab.

"Or two legged attack dogs."

"Why do they want our DNA?" he asked. "Surely knowing what we are doesn't make much difference to us."

"It's for the legal case."

As the two of them climbed to the top deck, the rain started, single giant drops rapidly turning into the morning downpour, water bouncing off the rust of the deck, the roof and the surface of the estuary. Sabre-Tooth retreated under the canopy, barely able to hear his own thoughts through the rattle of rain on metal. "What if it sinks?"

"It's not deep here," Sugar said. "The boat rests on the bottom and the tidal surges have to be high to reach up here."

"How do you know that?" It was deep enough to drown him.

"I was worried. I couldn't swim when I came here the first time." She nudged him with her elbow. "I'm still worried. I don't like water much, and last winter all these wrecks were swamped. So they say, anyway. I don't think anyone was on them at the time."

The sound of light footsteps jerked Sabre-Tooth out of his worry about drowning, and he looked up.

"It's the wind that's the real problem," Sugar continued. "Last winter it…" Her voice trailed off as she realised he wasn't listening.

A stranger approached; a very odd stranger. A green stranger who picked up speed as it sought shelter from the fierce rain.

Green.

Sabre-Tooth stared. Was it male or female? Was it really green (unlikely, he thought) or was it cosmetically enhanced? He checked out its face, its neck where skin, the colour of spring leaves, disappeared beneath a camouflage coverall, and its long, slender hands. All green. He'd never seen anyone who'd coloured themselves all over before. "Who's that?"

Sugar waved a hand in greeting. "It's a pansy."

"A what?" He kept his voice to a whisper. The name tugged at his memory.

"They were made to work on the terraforming project on Mars," she said. "Have you never seen one? They show up on the vids sometimes."

"No." He frowned. "Maybe. Something to do with the planetary colonisation?"

The green hands mesmerised him. They twined round each other in constant movement, reminding him of the way creepers wrapped tree branches in their tendrils.

"Is it really green? Not dyed? Cosmetic?"

"They photosynthesise," Sugar said. "They don't need much food, and they can hibernate when it gets cold or dark."

Eventually it noticed his interest and wandered over.

Sugar stepped protectively in front of him. "Sabe, be careful. It's—"

The green thing glided round her. "You're new here?"

He nodded, fascinated, wondering what to call it.

Thing? Person? He? She?

"Did you escape? From a lab like hers?" It nodded at Sugar, whose expression had turned wary.

"I was rescued from the army," Sabre-Tooth said. "What about you?"

"I escaped from a teaching lab on one of the food production sites. I was an aid on an agritech course. They kept me in a box the rest of the time." The green of the creature's eyes sparked.

"A box?"

"In the dark. I need light or I don't have much energy."

Sabre-Tooth nodded, trying not to think about claustrophobia.

"It was horrible, so I got out. I killed a lecturer, two students and a security guard," the thing said. "They weren't expecting it. They thought I didn't have enough sun. I'll kill anyone who tries to put me back in a box." It didn't look as though it regretted anything, but its smooth green features were hard to read.

"You got away?"

"They came after me. I can blend into the forest, but I didn't realise I had one of those tracker chip things, so they followed me. Luckily for me, some of the rebels were in the area, and they bumped into my pursuers."

"Lucky." This creature had had a worse time than him. "Are you male or female? Do you have a name?" Was he being overly intrusive?

The thing didn't seem to mind. "I'm P-3378. That's my batch number, but they call me Fly here. Short for Venus Fly Trap. I'm female, mostly, but I don't know if I can breed. I've never tried."

Sabre-Tooth couldn't help his instinctive inspection of Fly's chest. It was as flat as his own.

"Come on, Sabe." Sugar tugged him away. "You never used to talk so much."

He looked over his shoulder as the pansy walked away. "Don't you like her?"

"It's dangerous," Sugar said. "It likes to talk, but you should be careful around it. They don't think like real people and those scientists made them strong. Really strong. It killed people with its fingers."

"How—?"

"Nahmada, the lawyer you came to kill, is putting together a legal challenge to the status of chimeras. She's considering the pansies as well. They're harder, because they're classified as plants."

"That's not a plant," Sabre-Tooth said. "It... she talks. She sounded sensible."

"Yeah. But legally it is," Sugar said. "Nahmada Scott thinks that's wrong and she's keen to change the definition. It's a more difficult case though, and anyway, most of them are on Mars or the Moon base. I think they're used in the asteroid mine fields as well. I don't know if it's just that one, but I think they're weird."

"Why's the lawyer doing it at all?" Sabre-Tooth asked. The pansy had disappeared. "What's in it for her?"

"My mother found her," Sugar said. "She takes on hopeless cases, mostly for Dissension. My mother says she's a crusader. I don't understand it really. Why would anyone with a proper life take risks? Some of the men say she's just making a name for herself. She could be rich if she wanted, though, so I don't think that's it."

"I don't know." He thought about the murdered dog, and the first woman he'd had sex with. The memories had tangled together and dropped out of his mind, but he remembered wishing he could save both dog and woman. The dog was dead, the woman might be dead by now, but perhaps he could be a crusader. Perhaps he could save *someone*.

Sugar chewed on her finger. "Nahmada Scott's not the only one though. Krux has other lawyers doing similar things."

"Tell me about your mother," he said. "How did you find her?"

Did *he* have a mother; did all three of them have mothers?

ALLIANCE NEWS CORP – keeping you informed

News Update
September 25ᵗʰ 2453

Foreign Affairs

Ruling Speaker for the Alliance Council, Sifia Hong, has scrambled to rescue talks with India's Chief Administrator Aaditya Varma, after his committee advised him to walk away. The Indian Republic has proved hostile to the idea of population control, a policy that is central to the beliefs of the Eurasian Alliance. Major climate disasters have increased in the Indian sub-continent over recent years, motivating the ruling elite to reach out to their neighbours. It is widely feared among the policymakers of the Alliance that breakdown of talks may lead to all-out war. No one wishes for this. Councillor for Foreign Affairs, Andrei Krewchek, will join the talks later this week. Krewchek has challenged Speaker Hong for leadership of the Alliance Council. The Council will vote in two years' time.

~~~

Breaking News – Weather

A major storm is forming out in the mid-Atlantic. Forecasters are predicting it will move towards the coast of Western Europe. Local authorities have advised The Floating Cities to evacuate.

Chapter 25

Sabre-Tooth leaned on the railing, staring back at the flat, algae covered water. In the distance, islets covered in green broke the surface, and beyond them, saltwater marshes stretched out. After three days on the hulk, Sabre-Tooth wasn't worried he'd fall overboard. It was more likely he'd explode with frustration. The humans had gone and he was the only person on board, apart from Sugar and the pansy. The pansy would have been willing to talk to him, but Sugar turned protective, hissing under her breath, every time she (the pansy) appeared. He couldn't believe he missed Cyrus, with his annoying motor mouth. Where were he and Laszlo? Where was Tessis?

Sugar talked. She'd always talked, but she couldn't tell him what would happen to him, or when and anyway, she said she would leave soon, to join her own group.

There was nowhere to go; water surrounded them, and the wetlands extended for miles, so he couldn't work off his energy by running. He missed his old communit with its links to all kinds of information and reading matter. He didn't even have a palm-unit.

Taking a deep breath, he stroked his throat. The collar was gone and that made up for everything else.

Turning around, he bumped into Rose. It said a lot about his state of mind, that he found himself smiling at her as though she was an old friend.

"Hey." She grinned at him. "How's things?"

"I'm not used to doing nothing," he said. "Did you have a good trip?"

She shrugged. "I got back last night. We're leaving again tomorrow, me and Keir. We want to get another crossing in before the storm comes."

"Will you show me how to row the little boat?" Sabre-Tooth asked. There were a few small rowing boats tied to the side of the ship.

"What will you pay me?"

Sabre-Tooth frowned.

"I'm joking." Rose's smile widened. "Come on, then."

Rowing was easy as well as physically satisfying, and after an hour, she left him alone to practise his new skills.

"Just don't sink it," she said.

He explored the flotilla of abandoned ships, hulks and wrecks for the rest of the afternoon. The possibility of drowning didn't worry him as much, now he knew he had a way of getting back to land that didn't involve swimming for his life. He hadn't enjoyed the swimming component of his military training. The brief, heavy shower was enough cold and wet for him. At the end of the afternoon, he tied up the boat and scrambled back up the ladder onto the hulk.

Two bodies sprawled in the shelter of a tattered awning. Neither of them was green. One of them was Sugar. The other lay on its stomach, raising its head at the sound of Sabre-Tooth's approach.

Sabre-Tooth leaned back against the rusting rail, pushed his wet hair out of his eyes, and took a deep breath. The long lanky figure was unfamiliar, but the face…

He took a couple of steps forward. "Tygre?"

The figure rolled to a sitting position. He had changed a lot since Sabre-Tooth had seen him last, but it was definitely Tygre. Tygre after a growth spurt. Tawny fur still ran from his head and down his back, and when he rolled over, shorter white fur covered his bare stomach, disappearing into the loose waistband of his trousers.

He jumped to his feet, his mouth spreading into a wide feline grin. "Sabe." He flung his arms round Sabre-Tooth, squeezing him hard. "Sugar's been telling me what happened. We thought you must be dead. I'm so glad you're not."

Sabre-Tooth squeezed him back. "I worried you were dead too, especially after that vid with Sugar." Tygre was as tall as he was.

Tygre pulled his head back and grinned, revealing perfect stiletto canines. "It was a near thing." He'd changed in more than appearance. Sabre-Tooth hadn't heard him say so many words in a row since he'd been a small child. And he stood up without encouragement from the goad.

"What happened to you?" Sabre-Tooth kept his arms round him, running the palm of his hand down the silky fur of Tygre's spine. "You've grown. You're different."

"It happened this last year." Tygre arched his back against Sabre-tooth's hand. "Those drugs they gave me, they must have…" His voice trailed away and he grimaced.

"I thought I was going to die when they stopped," Sabre-Tooth said.

"I thought I *was* dead." Tygre stepped backwards.

Sugar joined them. "I thought we'd lost him. We had to keep him tied up for two days. He tried to claw his eyes out. We couldn't stop him."

Sabre-Tooth winced. At least he hadn't been able to reach his eyes. The cuffs on his wrist had made sure of that. "What happened to Rashelle? And Professor Rizzi?"

"They got arrested," Sugar said. "No one knows what happened to them after that. They disappeared into SecCen."

Tygre spat over the ship's railings. "I hope they killed them slowly."

"Where've you been?" Sabre-Tooth asked.

"On an adventure." Tygre's smile widened. "Remember those action vids we used to watch? I've been a superhero."

"What?"

Tygre told him he'd been smuggling refugees from the continental mainland and into the New British Islands. He had a few days break before he needed to return to his group. Sugar belonged to the same group and would go with him when he left.

Early evening sun shone from a clear sky, sinking damp heat into Sabre-Tooth's bones. He sat on the deck between Sugar and Tygre, resting his back on the wall of one of the engine rooms. The warmth from the wood seeped upwards. It was difficult to believe a major storm was forming out in the Atlantic. "I wish I knew what happens to me next."

"Someone will come," Sugar said. "I told you. It won't be long."

"I want to know where I'm going. I hate not knowing and not having anything to do."

"That must be the military training Sugar told me about," Tygre said.

"Maybe." It was more likely to be normal human frustration. "Tell me how you got out. Sugar told me Krux's men raided the lab, but when? What happened?"

"It wasn't long after you left," Sugar said. "One of the security guards joined the rebels. You remember Frank? The tattooed one who brought us chocolate?"

"Brought you chocolate," Sabre-Tooth replied.

"I suppose so," Sugar said. "But it was what they were planning for Tyg that made him help us."

"Tyg?"

"They were going to kill me." Tygre's voice sank to a rusty growl. "According to Frank, the military didn't want me. I wouldn't blend in very well, they said. He said he'd heard Professor Rizzi say the experiment had gone as far as it could, and they might as well do some final tests."

"Vivisection." Sugar's upper lip curled away from her teeth.

"They didn't do it," Tygre said.

"I'm glad he was arrested," Sugar said. "I hope they tortured him to death in some SecCen cell. I hope they vivisected *him*."

Sabre-Tooth twisted round, so he had a better view of Tygre, who had slid down the wall to lie on his back, eyes closed. Hatred for the lab-staff, for the military, and for Professor Rizzi in particular, blurred his vision. Sugar was right. They deserved whatever happened to them in the dungeons of the Intelligence Services.

Sugar drew in a shaky breath, her voice hoarse with fury. "Anyway, Frank suggested to one of Krux's men that they broke us out. I don't think it was for our sake so much as an attempt to embarrass the military and the Council. What they were doing was illegal, you know?"

"Yeah," Sabre-Tooth said. "My commander was executed for it. Good riddance."

"You didn't like him?" Tygre asked.

"No. He was a bastard. A worse bully than Rashelle. Worse than Professor Rizzi. I hated him."

"I heard they had to use the shocksticks on Rashelle," Tygre said. "Enforcement arrested a few of the staff, but Frank still has contacts there. They had to drag her out."

"Good." Sabre-Tooth stared up at the sky. "Wish I'd seen it. I liked the way she painted that scar though. The one you gave her. If I get a scar, that's what I'll do."

Sugar smirked. "A few months after we escaped, my mother found us. She'd been searching for a while. The legal challenge was her idea."

"I thought we were grown in incubators. I couldn't believe it when you talked about your mother in that vid. I wondered if you were making it up."

"I had a mother," Sugar said. "So did you. We weren't made in artificial wombs. The rat men were and the dog-men, but not us. I think it was because we were the first."

"What about mine?" Sabre-Tooth asked. "And his? Did they look for us?"

Tygre yawned, his green eyes narrowing to slits. "They couldn't find my mother. The lawyer looked. Sugar's mother said we could share. I liked her."

"Yours is dead," Sugar turned to Sabre-tooth. "She was looking for you though. Mine told me. They knew each other."

Sabre-Tooth sat up, drawing his knees to his chest and wrapping his arms round them. He stared at the horizon, where the sun glittered on blue-grey water. He'd always assumed that he'd developed in an artificial womb. That's what the lab tecs had told him. What sort of mother gave up her child to be an experimental animal? None of the parents in the vids would have done that. If his mother were dead, he would never know.

"Do you know what happened to her?"

"I think she was murdered." Sugar squinted up at him. "My mother said something about it, but I don't remember. You can ask her if you like. It wasn't her fault. The mothers were lied to."

"Oh."

Murdered?

Sabre-Tooth stored the information at the back of his mind. He wasn't ready to think about it yet.

A mother?

His friends in the military didn't have families. None of them, not even Cyrus the garrulous, talked much about their past, but he knew they'd all grown up in institutions. They'd all been unlicensed children, so their mothers had either been non-citizens or had unlawful pregnancies. Unlawful pregnancies had unpleasant repercussions, and the ones that weren't terminated were hidden, the offspring abandoned. If they were lucky, they were placed in institutions, fed and educated until they reached eighteen and then cast out to fend for themselves as non-citizens. If they were very lucky, they showed signs of a skill that would eventually earn them citizenship. Like Cyrus, Laszlo and Tessis, they were people with few options. Mothers had never been a subject for discussion.

He rested his chin on his knees, wondering where Cyrus and Laszlo were now. It probably depended on Laszlo's behaviour. He was a nightmare, but Sabre-Tooth hoped he managed to control himself. It would be horrible if he and Cyrus were executed.

Tessis was okay, he hoped; he still wasn't sure how much he trusted these people, but if anyone could take care of herself, she could. If she didn't have a breakdown. Tessis was tough, but brittle. The pressure might have been the only thing holding her together.

"What are you thinking?" Sugar asked.

He told her.

"No point in worrying." She sat up, mirroring his position. "Anyway, this Laszlo sounds like a menace. The sort of person the world's better without."

"Maybe." Sugar was probably right, but Sabre-Tooth didn't think Laszlo started out as a psychopath.

Tygre stayed on his back, eyes closed against the sun. "What was it like? Being a soldier?"

"I wasn't a proper soldier," Sabre-Tooth said. "They called me a stealth operative. I spied on people, sometimes I had to kill them."

"Isn't that what soldiers do." Tygre jack-knifed up and opened his eyes.

"I killed them when they weren't expecting it, while they were sleeping. Diessen forced me do as he wanted."

"I like tracking people," Tygre said. "I don't mind killing some of them. The bad ones."

"I hated it." Sabre-Tooth stared at his bare feet. "And how do you know which ones are bad?"

~~~

At the end of the week, the two dog chimeras appeared. They were in the bunkroom when Sabre-Tooth walked in with Tygre.

Sugar was right. They looked like monsters from the old werewolf films. Both were at least six inches taller than him, lean and angular. Both had shaggy brown hair growing around their faces and tapering down the back of their necks. One of them had brown eyes; the other had one brown and one blue. Their jaws were just long enough to look wrong. There was no way they could ever pass for human.

"Hey, Tygre, how's it going?" The one with odd eyes slapped Tygre on the back.

"Don't do that." Tygre's eyes narrowed.

The dog chimera laughed.

"Sabre-Tooth?" The one with two brown eyes spoke.

He nodded. "That's me."

"I'm Connor. That's Callum. We've come to collect you. You'll be part of our unit."

The two of them were friendly. Connor gave him a basic palmunit, which would also act as a comm. They even talked about the job they'd just done. Their unit had helped a small group of unlicensed people from one of the border refugee camps break out and cross into the Eurasian Alliance territory. They had fled the rising temperatures and desertification of southern Europe, only to find that the inhabitable zones defended their borders aggressively.

"They were coming up from the south," Connor said. "You can't believe what it's like down there. There are people from Southern Spain now, as well as the remnants of the North African Exodus."

"I've seen the news," Sabre-Tooth said. "I had training in León. It was hot enough to boil your blood even that far north. It's been bad for a long time."

Callum, the second dog, lifted the corner of his lip in a sneer. "News? It's all propaganda. The Alliance army are stopping most of the refugees before they get as far as the camps. Shooting them."

Sabre-Tooth sank down onto the edge of his hammock. Laszlo and Cyrus had been working with the army on the southern borders. That included Spain. He wouldn't be surprised if they'd been involved. Laszlo would have enjoyed it.

"Why?"

"Population control," Connor said. "The Councils want to keep the population to its present level, or less even. They say there aren't enough resources for many more."

"There's a bit of truth in that," Callum said, "but they need to think about the way they're doing it. It's ideological, that's what it is. Where's the moral high ground here?"

185

"Anyway," Connor said, "the group we helped have agreed to work with us if we keep on helping their people."

"If there're any left," Callum said gloomily. "That whole area is a mixture of desert and wasteland from the last wars. If the army doesn't get them, there's still no food or water. Most of them won't stand a chance."

Sabre-Tooth closed his eyes and lay back in his hammock. Maybe he'd been lucky.

"We'll leave in a couple of days," Connor said. "We want to avoid the storm, but I really need to catch up on sleep."

~~~

Two days after the dog-chimeras arrived, a human visitor brought new orders for Sugar and Tygre. It was time for them to join their units. Both were going west to where the military had a small base. The messenger was silent on why, and what they would do once they arrived.

"I'll be glad to get onto solid land," Tygre said.

"Me too," Sugar unhooked her hammock, shook it out and rolled it away. "Don't worry Sabe. We'll likely meet again, soon. You've got a comm now. We can talk."

The wind had picked up, whipping the surface of the water into waves, which crashed against the sides of the hulks. It was relentless, still not at a dangerous level, but singing through the cluster of abandoned ships and building in strength. Sabre-Tooth felt it vibrate in his bones; turning his mood restless and irritable. He'd only just found Sugar and Tygre, and now they were leaving.

He leaned his arms on the ship's railing, watching the rowing boat take them away.

Next to him, Fly wrapped one long slender arm around the top railing. "She doesn't like me." The pansy had kept her distance while Sugar was around. "She's scared."

"I don't think so. Nothing much scares Sugar." Sabre-Tooth's eyes followed the boat until it disappeared behind another rusting hulk.

"We'll be going later this afternoon." Connor leaned on the railing next to him. "Everyone's evacuating. The hazard warning went up this morning."

"What about you?" Sabre-Tooth asked Fly.

"I'm going with Keir and Rose," she said. "Back to central Europe. Where there's sun. I can't wait."

Sabre-Tooth stared at the water and the wrecks, hoping to catch a last glimpse of the boat. He wished he'd asked Sugar more about her mother before she'd left. He wanted to meet her, to ask her about his own. Now it was too late. He wondered if he had a father and, if so, how much of him came from his parents? What had the scientists done to him? What made him chimera? What made him not human?

ALLIANCE NEWS CORP – keeping you informed

Society

The Department of Population Control have responded to the refugee crisis in southern Europe by offering unconditional Level Two citizenship to selected individuals. Selection will be based on merit, in terms of ability and education. The qualified applicants will be integrated into Alliance territory on the condition that they use their skills to benefit their adopted nations. In addition, a greater number of the displaced will be offered level one citizenship with zero reproduction rights. This process will begin at the end of the year.

~~~

Inhabitants of The Floating Cities have questioned the council's decision to rehome southern refugees. Subsequent to the devastating storms of the past two years, many from the drowned coastal regions and river plains would like to relocate inland. They argue that their needs should come before those of outsiders.

Dissension – the struggle against injustice

October 3rd 2453

The Eurasian Alliance is congratulating itself on its generosity, as it invites climate refugees to apply for legal entry to the nations of the Alliance. Dissension says it is barely scratching the surface of the humanitarian crisis. Fewer than 50,000 of the displaced millions will be offered sanctuary in the habitable territories. Of these, only ten per cent will have any chance of achieving full citizenship. Millions in the camps have been abandoned to a slow death from thirst and starvation. This is a shame on all of us. Dissension's lawyers are preparing to fight for the rights of these people.

Chapter 26

The journey from the estuary to the Forest of Epping took four days, mainly because of the weather. The first day was trouble-free; Callum, Connor and Sabre-tooth took it in turns to row the small boat. On the second day, the high winds turned the rain into a hostile force, and the three travellers were forced to shelter in a ruined house, on a patch of higher land.

For twenty-four hours, the wind uprooted trees, tearing them from the earth and hurling them across the landscape, together with any other loose debris. Every gust shook the walls of their refuge and attacked the remains of the roof. The storm's fury died down, a little, the next day. Connor, restless and unsettled, insisted on moving out, but it was still windy and wet enough that Sabre-Tooth was grateful for his high-spec chameleon skinsuit. A spare coverall would be good, but he'd taken nothing with him when he left the military.

Epping itself was a mixture of old town rubble, trees, ferns and ferocious undergrowth, all springing out of damp, squelchy moss-covered ground. Bare branches of deciduous trees overlapped with the towering evergreen conifers, and birdsong melded into the continuous sound of water dribbling and dripping through the leaves. The terrain was treacherous underfoot, making it impossible to tell where ancient, man-made hazards lay. Moss and lichen hid the remnants of an earlier civilisation. Sabre-Tooth caught a glimpse of the pale rump of a deer as it disappeared into thicker vegetation, glanced after it and almost fell into a gaping hole.

"Careful." Callum watched him jump across the gap, mouth wide with amusement.

The morning's downpour stopped abruptly as the three of them emerged from the forest into scrubby swamp and more broken buildings. The wind died back suddenly.

"We're here," Connor shouted.

A small man and a smaller woman materialised from behind a green lump and came forward to greet them. The man lifted a weapon, lowering it when Callum waved.

"It's us." Connor jogged towards the couple.

"We've been expecting you. Took your time didn't you?"

"How long have you been here?" Connor asked, looking down on the man, who was short enough to fit under his arm.

"A couple of days."

"Do you know what we're here for?"

"I've heard we're helping with an attack on an agricom. Further north."

Connor frowned.

"They've used non-citizens as labour. They haven't paid them and they haven't processed any applications for level one."

"What's new about that?" Connor asked.

The man ignored him and stared at Sabre-Tooth.

Connor turned, sighing. "Sim, this is Sabre-Tooth. Sabre-Tooth, meet Sim."

Sim nodded.

"And that's Kezia."

The woman waved.

"So how does it work?" Sabre-Tooth asked. "The attack? How did you decide on this agricom as a target?"

Sim shrugged one shoulder. "It's really an excuse to do a food run. Our central organization has a list. It's this place's turn. We'll take anything we can and share it out. It's mostly rice, but they've got a small amount of maize, and some root vegetables. Have you ever seen those farms?"

Sabre-Tooth nodded his head.

Sim ignored him and carried on. "They're labour intensive. Officially, they take unregistered teenagers from the institutions and pay them a pittance in exchange for helping them get Level One citizenship. This lot aren't even doing that. They deserve to be burnt to the ground."

"Is Maisi here yet?" Callum changed the subject.

Sabre-Tooth tuned the speakers out and turned in a circle, inspecting his surroundings. This new life was just another job, like the military but without the collar. He scratched his neck.

The area must have been an urban settlement once, part of the outer reaches of the city of London. The remains of buildings were visible amongst the sparse trees and tangles of thorny climbers. Some of them were merely piles of weathered brick and stone, while others had managed to stay mostly upright. All of them were well disguised by rampant vegetation.

A woman emerged from a gap in one of the ruins. A projectile weapon hung loosely from her left hand.

Callum waved to her.

She picked her way through the debris towards them. "I heard you were on your way. Storm hold you up?"

"A bit." Callum smiled, showing pristine, and very canine, teeth.

She smiled back, before turning her attention to Sabre-Tooth.

"You're our new recruit?"

Sabre-Tooth nodded.

"I'm Maisi. I'm in charge, so as long as you do as I say, we'll get on fine."

Maisi was a tiny woman. Everything about her was dark, deep brown skin, short black hair, large brown eyes and dark greenish-grey coverall. She bristled with energy.

"I'm Sabre-Tooth."

"So I hear." Reaching up, she stroked Callum's cheek. "I'll show you where you're sleeping. I'm afraid it's a bit of a dump, but we won't be here long."

Sabre-Tooth followed his companions through a small gap into one of the bigger piles of brick. Maisi was right. It was definitely a dump. The interior was huge and dim, despite holes in the walls where windows must once have been. Now they were blocked by shrubs and branches, which expanded into the room turning the limited daylight into specks of brightness and large patches of shade. Four temporary camp beds had been set up around the inner walls. They were the only furniture. The stench of decay drifted in the air and the floor was almost as squelchy as the boggy forest.

Maisi activated the small light on her wrist, pointing it at Sabre-Tooth. "Welcome."

Sabre-Tooth blinked at the sudden brightness, silenced by the suspicion in her voice.

"You can use the bunks in here," she said. "I wouldn't put anything on the floor. Everything's damp, and when it rains, the ground's just a big puddle. It's rained every morning since we got here. That storm—"

Callum laughed. "You do give us the best, Maisi."

"You can share with me." She slipped her hand through his arm. "Just as damp, I'm afraid."

Sabre-tooth watched the two of them, trying to work out the dynamics of their relationship. He sat on one of the low beds, still restless.

Connor threw his small pack onto the adjacent bed. "Let's explore. Sabre-Tooth? You want to run?"

Sabre-Tooth nodded, although he wasn't sure how easy it would be to run in the dense woodland. "You don't think we'll be sucked into some swamp?"

"You might. I won't. Just watch where you're going. Sim? Callum?"

"I don't think so," Sim said. "I'm saving my energy for tomorrow. Sabre-Tooth's right anyway, it's soggy out there."

"Call me Sabe."

"I'm going to catch up with Maisi," Callum said. "Besides, I've just hacked my way through spiky bloody plants for two days. I want a day off."

Connor shrugged. "Come on Sabe. Let's leave them to it."

"Be back in a couple of hours," Maisi said. "We need to talk."

The run wasn't so much a run as a struggle through an enemy landscape. At one point, they encountered a barrier of thorns, giant brambles and dead trees, all surrounded by a pool of stagnant water.

Connor paused, barely panting. "This is fun."

Sabre-Tooth halted next to him, studying the obstacle. His skinsuit would be fine although he'd have to watch his eyes.

"You're in good shape," Connor said.

Sabre-Tooth shrugged. After the stay on the ship and the slow journey, he fizzed with energy.

"It's good to have someone to run with. Callum's having a thing with Maisi. He'll be nose to nose with her until we have a job to do."

"Callum and Maisi?" An oversized imitation werewolf and that tiny woman? Sabre-Tooth tried not to examine the idea too closely, but it gave him hope that he could find someone as well. He looked much more human than Callum. "I don't mind running by myself."

"You're a cat," Connor said. "I'm a dog. I need a pack."

"I'm not a cat," Sabre-Tooth said, wondering if his companion was serious.

"What are you then?"

"Human."

"Right." Connor gave him a pitying look. "Embrace your differences, that's my philosophy. Come on, let's tackle this thicket."

On the other side, Connor stopped, brushing a thorny branch out of his hair. "Why do you want to be human, anyway? Look how they treated you."

"I don't want to be. I just am." If he wasn't human, he had no idea what he was.

"I'd never pass for human," Connor said. "I don't care."

When they returned to the damp room, the others were waiting. Sabre-Tooth counted them; with him, they were a group of six, Connor and Callum, Maisi, Sim and Kezia.

"We're leaving at dawn," Maisi said. "I've got the directions. We're meeting another unit at the target location in two days' time."

"Won't it be guarded?" Sabre-Tooth asked. All the big food producers were protected by small armies.

"We'll cause a distraction. The plan is to take the power out. Someone in the other unit is an expert in electronics and sabotage. Trained by the Alliance army, he was." Maisi pointed at him. "Just like you. I want you to stick close to Connor. He'll show you how we do things."

Sabre-Tooth wondered if he should mention his training. He wasn't an explosives expert, but he'd done his share of blowing things up. Transports with Diessen's enemies in them. He decided to keep quiet.

~~~

The raid on the agricom was successful. The electronics expert performed his magic, cutting out power across the whole site. The majority of the guards sprinted to the north side's control centre, leaving only two men to patrol the southern perimeter. Kezia and Sim stunned both, while the labourers watched, doing nothing to stop the intruders as they searched through the storage bunkers. Sabre-Tooth's unit escaped with as much food as they could carry.

~~~

He spent the next few months taking part in similar raids. The rebels seemed to spend a lot of energy feeding themselves. It all felt a bit pointless but he had nowhere else to go.

His most exciting expedition was a trip thirty miles northwest to an area of low wooded hills, where a small army squad were hunting down a group of illegals who had set up semi-permanent residence. It brought back memories of his first trip to Wales, only not as wet and now he was on the opposite side, saving the dispossessed from the guns of the Military.

A group of local insurgents joined the mission. Ten of them arrived at the meeting place.

Maisi passed out heavy duty stun weapons as they waited to ambush the hunters. A runner from Central Control had delivered them the night before.

"Keep them on light stun," she said to Sabre-Tooth. "Just enough to knock them out and keep them uncoordinated for half-an-hour, while the people they're chasing get away."

"We don't kill them?"

"Of course we don't kill them," she said. "We don't want them to get personal over hunting us down. Central Control says we might need allies one day. No point killing them if we don't have to."

"How did you know they'd be here?" Sabre-Tooth asked.

Maisi gave him a sidelong glance. "We have spies. Even in the military."

Maisi's group split into two; Maisi, Connor and Sim in the first group, Sabre-Tooth, Callum and Kezia in the second. The two groups would flank the soldiers as silently as possible. There were twelve armed men in the military squad. The local fighters waited in the woodland ahead of them, armed with the borrowed weapons.

Sabre-Tooth leaned against a tree trunk, ears tuned for the sound of the approaching soldiers. He heard them long before they appeared. They probably thought they were quiet, but to Sabre-Tooth's ears, they crashed through the undergrowth.

The first four soldiers fell without knowing they were under attack. Their companions spread out, taking cover.

Sabre-Tooth's group opened fire.

The soldiers had needle lasers and started to fire them randomly into the thick scrub. A beam cut through the trunk of the tree next to Callum

"Shit." He dodged as the tree sagged towards him, remembering the first time he'd seen a similar weapon drill a hole right through its target's skull.

The soldier aimed his weapon again and Sabre-Tooth leapt at Callum, pushing him out of the way. At the same time, Kezia stunned the shooter and a burning pain shot along Sabre-Tooth's upper arm. He swallowed his instinctive yelp.

"Get off me," Callum hissed. "You're squashing me."

Sabre-Tooth slid away from him, shaking his arm loose and twisting his head to inspect it. The skinsuit was shredded and the burnt ends hung loose about his arm. His skin felt as though it was on fire, but the wound was shallow.

"You got hit?" Callum pushed the cloth aside and peered down. "It doesn't look too bad. I don't think you'll even have a scar."

Kezia joined him, after checking that there were no stray soldiers around. "I bet it stings."

Sabre-Tooth glared at her.

She grinned.

Maisi made her way through the trees. "You were hit?"

Sabre-Tooth let out a shuddering breath. "I'll be okay." It *was* only a scratch, but he'd been in the army for over a year and never been shot. He didn't like it at all. He needed to be more careful.

"What happens to those people now?" he asked Maisi, trying to distract himself from the throbbing in his arm. "The ones the soldiers were after?"

"They can go where they like and try again, or they can ask to join us." She shrugged. "Most will just move on. The hunters will likely get them in the end."

Sabre-Tooth rubbed his arm. Why did they even bother? An uncharacteristic wave of depression washed over him.

ALLIANCE NEWS CORP – keeping you informed

News Update
January 27th 2454

New Beijing

A third colony ship was launched from the New Beijing spaceport yesterday night, carrying five hundred citizens, thirty working pansies and the equipment needed to set up a third habitable dome. This will be built two hundred kilometres equidistant from the two existing Mars colonies, and once it is established and running self-sufficiently, underground transport routes will be constructed. The Interplanetary Exploration Department has put out a notice: 'Non-citizens, looking for opportunities to better themselves, should register now, with agencies specialising in off-planet construction.'

The planetary colonisation programme is one of the greatest achievements of the Eurasian Alliance scientists, and evidence that our nations are well ahead of any rivals. It is over four hundred years since the Americas had anything approaching a space initiative, while the attempts of the Indian Republic were brought to a halt by the first of the triple disasters.

Dissension – the struggle against injustice

January 28th 2454

Dissension congratulates the Eurasian Alliance on its expanding space programme. It does however, feel that the Council should concentrate on its main work of creating and governing the emerging civilisation of Eurasia, where human rights abuses are still rife.

According to Dissension sources, the Security Services of the Alliance are spying on loyal citizens of their own nations. The Justice Courts, the Food Security Department and Civil Security are among the organisations targeted by the spies of the Alliance Council. Employees of the organisations in question support these allegations. Workers have seen their colleagues arrested on the basis of information obtained from nanodrones. This sort of surveillance of the Alliance's own citizens is intolerable. While it exists, none of us, living in the Eurasian Alliance, can claim to belong to a civilised society.

Chapter 27

Sabre-Tooth's group set up a semi-permanent camp in the ruins of a shopping market just outside the outer boundaries of old London, far enough from the centre that the patrols ignored it, but close enough to reach the Wall in a half day. It was a place to return to, and to store food, as well as spare clothing and weapons. They protected the outer perimeter with a wide circle of broken glass and sharp metal, hiding it in the lush growth. It would be hard for anyone to approach without making a huge racket.

Soon after they'd settled in, another band of illegals arrived. They brought their own watchers with them, two women who each had an infant toddling after them, an older man and a woman with a broken leg. These four shared guard duties, and stayed in the camp while the active groups travelled.

~~~

The morning after Sabre-Tooth returned from a trip to New Midland, one of the watchers came to find the team. Maisi, Sim and Sabre-Tooth were in the central room, sharing a warm protein mix and coffee substitute.

Sabre-Tooth looked up. A small child peered out from behind his mother's legs, staring at him. He stared back. Children were a novelty, and this one was the result of an unlicensed pregnancy.

"Krux is here," the woman said. "He wants to talk to you. Where are the others?"

Maisi shrugged and rose to her feet. "I think they're still asleep."

Sabre-Tooth smiled at the child, exposing his pointed teeth. The boy's eyes widened. He giggled and hid his face against his mother's leg.

Krux and his escort had set up a temporary camp in a small space, still inside the main complex. It was in even poorer shape than the one Sabre-Tooth's team lived in, but it didn't look as though they planned to stay for long.

Krux sat on one of the camp beds, elbows resting on his thighs. Two men in military grade protective coveralls flanked him. A small solar powered lamp cast a circle of artificial light around the group.

Sabre-Tooth had never seen the two men before and next to Maisi, they appeared gargantuan, all height and muscle. A woman and another man sat on two of the neighbouring beds.

"Sabre-Tooth. How are you settling in?" Krux raised his head. The skin around his eyes crinkled as he smiled.

"Fine, Sir." It probably wouldn't be a good idea to criticise the accommodation.

"You look in pretty good shape."

Sabre-Tooth held himself rigid. "Thank you, Sir."

"You aren't in the army now," Krux said. "Relax."

Sabre-Tooth nodded. "Yes Sir."

Sim elbowed him in the ribs.

"You don't need to call me Sir, either," Krux said. His smile faded. "Am I right in thinking you were trained as a stealth operative?"

Sabre-Tooth nodded.

Krux turned to Maisi. "We've got a delicate job. We could use his expertise."

Sabre-Tooth rubbed his throat and wondered if it was time to disappear. "Who do you want me to terminate?"

"I don't want you to kill anyone," Krux said. "I want you to rescue someone. It would be a straightforward grab and run, if it wasn't inside the wall. But as I told you last time we met, you don't have to do anything you don't want to."

Behind him, Maisi snorted.

Sabre-Tooth blinked. He'd never rescued anyone before. "I don't know. Tell me about it." He was sure a refusal wouldn't go down well.

"One of our friends has a problem. She's a citizen at a high level, an insider with links to Dissension. Very useful to us, but—" Krux frowned as a newcomer squeezed through the damaged doorway into the room. "Here she is. Petrian. This is your problem. I'll let you explain."

Petrian was a tall woman, whose blonde hair contrasted with the rich tones of her skin. Her clothes were a fashionable civilian version of combat clothing and her hair trailed down her back in an intricately woven tail. Dark-blue perma-dye glowed around her eyes, merging with the milk-chocolate of her face.

Sabre-Tooth closed his mouth, realising he was staring.

She set her jaw as she glanced at Krux. "I told you I was sorry. These things happen. It was a disaster and I know it was my fault, but now we need to fix it."

"Just tell them what happened," he said. He jerked his head towards Maisi and the rest of the team. "Convince them to help."

Maisi's mouth was a thin line.

Petrian surveyed the small group. Her posture stiffened as she met Maisi's unfriendly gaze. "Just these?" She lifted her chin, returning Maisi's stare with hauteur. "Only six? Are you sure—"

Krux folded his arms, mirroring her position. "Maisi's very competent and it's none of your business who's in her team. I don't want you meeting too many of my operatives. It's not safe for them. Not safe for you either."

"That's not fair." Petrian pushed a strand of silky blonde hair behind her ear. Iridescent blue jewellery spiralled round the outer curves before dripping from the lobes. "I wouldn't—"

"You already have. And you know as well as I do…" He blew out an exasperated breath. "Get on with your story."

"Three of our people were taken by the military a couple of days ago," she said. "They launched an attack on a new construction site, west of London. The army caught them."

Maisi frowned. "I didn't know about that. Krux, I'm supposed to be told what goes on in this part of the country. Why haven't I heard?"

"Because it was an unsanctioned operation," he said. "Central Control had nothing to do with it. I only heard about it once it had all gone to hell. That's why I called you in at such short notice."

Maisi's frown deepened. "So why did they—"

"I asked them to do it," Petrian interrupted. "One of the construction workers on the site was a friend of mine. He was conscripted. The gangmaster uses slave labour. The whole construction team are unlawful labour. I would have asked for approval but there wasn't time."

"So you planned an intervention?" Maisi glanced at Krux. "And how come someone like you had a friend who wasn't a citizen? A construction worker?"

"Someone like me?" Petrian's expression should have turned Maisi to stone. "He was a citizen anyway, until… He just got sentenced to—"

"What makes you think—?"

"Maisi." Krux snapped at her. "And Petrian, you know you should have talked to me first."

"There wasn't time, and I didn't think it would be a problem. All they had to do was grab him and run. He was out on one of the edges of the site. Everything went wrong though. A military guard died. After that, the rest of them caught three of our people. The last one managed to get away. She told me what had happened."

"Why aren't I surprised?" Maisi rolled her eyes.

"How could I have known?" Petrian spread her hands. "I didn't know they'd got reinforcements up there. No one knew."

"That's why we plan things," Maisi said. "We gather intelligence and plan."

"There wasn't time," Petrian repeated. "The construction group was moving to a war zone and—"

"And now they've got more of our people." Maisi oozed contempt. "They're bound to interrogate and execute them. For fuck's sake."

"Maisi, that's enough." Krux said. "Petrian knows she made a mistake. These're our people. We need to get them out."

"Won't they give her up?" Maisi pointed at Petrian.

"They don't know my real name," she said. "And I never met them in person. But if they get questioned hard, they'll name the person they were trying to rescue, and he knows who I am." The shaking in her voice was almost imperceptible.

Sabre-Tooth's ears flickered, catching her uncertainty. "Why did they do this for you?"

Petrian turned to face him, ready to answer. She met his feline eyes, raised her eyebrows and closed her mouth again.

Krux shrugged. "Don't worry about that, Sabre-Tooth, you don't need—"

"I want to know," Sabre-Tooth said. He didn't like being patronised.

Krux exhaled loudly in exasperation. "Petrian's a high-level citizen with a senior position in the Justice Department. We need to influence opinion amongst citizens as much as we need to use guerrilla methods. Petrian's a major asset for us. She's been part of our group for a long time. She knows the codes, so the operatives would have assumed she was legitimate."

Petrian rubbed her eyes. "I have contacts and my family are well thought of. I have links with the official part of Dissension. Most people in Justice do, but no one would suspect—"

"Unless they interrogate this newly non-citizen friend of yours." Krux interrupted, turning back to Sabre-Tooth. "Only a few people in the organisation know about her, but this group worked with her once before. She had the correct passcodes. They thought she had the authority for this sort of operation. She doesn't. They thought she knew what she was doing. She didn't."

Petrian took a deep breath. "I said—"

"Petrian's involved in information gathering, not operations." Krux interrupted her again. "She shouldn't have done this, but the team didn't know that. The attack was unsanctioned by us. If we'd planned it properly, it might have worked."

Sabre-Tooth nodded, wondering who would suffer for the disobedience. He bet it wouldn't be her. She looked like one of the models from the vids.

"They were caught," Krux said. "I'd say it serves them right, but we can't just abandon them, to be executed. And we certainly don't want to risk Petrian."

"Okay." Sabre-Tooth was relieved he didn't have to kill any more strangers. "Why does it serve them right?"

"If they'd thought about it, they'd have checked with the other units. They should have found out what sort of presence we had in the area and asked for support. They didn't think."

"Krux…" Petrian's voice rose.

"Petrian? Just shut up for a minute." Krux turned back to Maisi. "This could be a difficult extraction. It's within the outer wall. You'll need to take the prison transport almost as soon as it leaves the base, get the prisoners, and get out as quickly as possible."

"Sounds dangerous." Maisi kicked at the dirty floor.

"They were sent to the WoodGreen military camp," Krux said. "You know it very well, don't you, Sabre-Tooth? That's why I thought of you."

Sabre-Tooth nodded.

"Could you break into the camp and get them out that way?"

"No." He didn't have to think about the answer. The WoodGreen base was huge and well-guarded. He might be able to get in and out by himself. Three illegals would make it impossible. They'd have no chance; they'd end up dead or captured. Captured would be worse. He rubbed his throat again.

"So how easy would it be to take the transport down before it reaches the inner wall? They're supposed to be moved to SecCen tomorrow."

"Easy to take it down," Sabre-Tooth said, wondering where Krux got his information. "To get prisoners out and away before backup arrives? Not so easy."

"Maisi?"

"It looks like we don't have much choice."

"Maybe, but another option is to destroy the prisoner transport, with the prisoners in it. That would be safer for you," Krux said. "Safer for Petrian too. They can't be allowed to talk. If Petrian's caught, she'll lead them to a lot of other assets."

Petrian sucked in a loud breath.

Maisi glanced at her. "We'll try and get them out alive, but I think we should take the firepower to wipe the transport out if we fail. If it was me in there, I wouldn't want to end up in SecCen."

After a moment, Krux nodded. "Good thinking." He looked round the others. "Well?"

Sim shrugged. "We can try."

"Sabre-Tooth?"

"Yes." He must have had more dangerous jobs. He couldn't remember at the moment, but this beat being sent out to assassinate strangers. It sounded more interesting than doing food raids on agricom businesses.

"Good. Maisi will tell you what to do. She's in charge."

Maisi rolled her eyes.

"You'd better go. Tomorrow morning's when you have to be in position."

Sabre-Tooth repressed the urge to salute and, at a nudge from Sim, ambled out of the room. Behind them, Krux and Petrian continued talking in furious whispers. From the outside, they appeared to be equals.

"No." Krux's voice rose. "I'm not discussing it any further."

Maisi paused, glancing over her shoulder. "Sim? Find Callum and Connor. And Kezia. They'll be involved as well. Let's all meet in my quarters in half an hour." She turned as Petrian emerged, gave her a look of contempt, and walked away.

Petrian watched her go. "Shit. Shit." She rubbed her forehead.

Sabre-Tooth lingered.

She lifted her head and saw him.

He backed away.

"Wait." She inspected him from his boots, to the tips of his ears, before meeting his eyes. Hers were an iridescent blue, almost matching her ear ornaments. "I haven't met you before, have I?"

He was mesmerised by the unusual colour of her eyes, and the deep blue paint around them.

She snapped her fingers. "You're like the doggy-werewolf things, aren't you?"

"A bit." He wasn't going to argue about it. They were no more alike than the humans and chimeras, but it didn't really matter. She must have met Connor and Callum and seen that they looked nothing like him.

"I didn't catch your name."

"Sabre-Tooth." He studied her face again. "Your eyes? Are they—?"

"Cosmetic. You've got something in your hair." She plucked a small twig from his head, her fingers brushing his ear. Her eyes lingered on his clawed hands.

He jerked his head away and sheathed his claws. "Thanks."

"What about yours?"

He frowned.

"Your eyes," she said.

"Not cosmetic." He reached for the dark glasses he kept in his belt.

Her interest sharpened. "Come and talk to me for a minute?"

It sounded like an order, so Sabre-Tooth followed her into the remains of yet another house, almost hypnotised by the swaying of her long tail of hair.

She pulled a small bottle out of her pack, unfastening the top and taking a sip from it. "Here. Try this."

Sabre-Tooth sniffed it suspiciously. It smelled a bit like cleaning fluid, so he drew a very small amount into his mouth. The fumes went up his nose and he choked, spitting the liquid onto the floor. The taste was foul; worse than anything Cyrus had offered him.

Petrian raised her eyebrows. "That's the best vodka you can buy. It's imported from New Latvia. Don't you like it?"

"It tastes like poison."

She grabbed the bottle back, raising it to her lips again. "I really needed that. Sit down."

Sabre-Tooth sat on a rickety crate. "What do you want?"

Petrian perched on the edge of a fold-up bed. "Nothing really. I just wanted to talk to someone and Krux is furious with me. He flat out refused to let me help with the rescue."

Sabre-Tooth stared at her. She couldn't really expect to be involved, could she?

She shrugged. The tension in her body suggested she was more bothered than she was prepared to show. "He'll get over it. We go back a long time."

Sabre-Tooth shifted on his crate, uncomfortable with her inspection. He'd never met anyone like her before, unless he counted the strangers he'd occasionally seen on the river wall when he was based in London.

She narrowed her eyes. "You're different from the others. What are you?"

"Human."

"But what else?" She leaned forward, placing a hand on his knee.

"I'm a chimera." He watched her hand as though it was a snake. "Like Connor."

"I know that. What sort? There are two working as dancers in one of the London clubs. They're not like you though. They've got scales and forked tongues. You look more human than the others."

"Than the snake women?"

"Than Callum and Connor." Petrian pushed a strand of hair away from her face. "How Maisi can... He's twice her size."

Sabre-Tooth had wondered about the odd pairing himself, but didn't say so. It was rude and none of his business. Or Petrian's. "Why did you do it? You must have known it could go wrong."

"The job? It didn't appear that difficult, and I had to try. I was tired of sitting in my office while other people took risks. I've done it for years." She looked down at her hands. The nails were tipped with the same iridescent blue as her eyes and ears. "The man I tried to rescue was someone I'd known for a long time. I met him on a routine visit to one of the justice courts and I recruited him as an informant. He helped me with things I passed to Krux. Not directly of course, but..." She sighed and sat back, taking another sip from her vodka bottle. "He had other criminal tendencies as well. He was caught with contraband and lost his citizenship. He didn't deserve that, so I thought I could help him." She sighed again. "What a mess. He's been shipped out to the eastern border now."

199

"I'm sorry." The eastern border meant nuclear clean-up. Clean–up duty of any sort was highly dangerous, especially for convicts who had little in the way of protective clothing. He had no idea why she was telling him all this.

"I feel responsible. He wasn't twenty-five yet and…" A bleak expression crossed her face before she shrugged. "Oh well. I tried. There're others like him out there. Maybe in worse situations. Have you done this sort of thing before?"

"What sort of thing?"

"Rescued people from the Security Services?"

"Not—"

"Sabre-Tooth?" Callum called his name.

Sabre-Tooth stood up as Callum's shadow appeared in the doorway.

"Come on. Maisi wants to talk to you. Hi Petrian."

"Callum." She nodded at him, touching Sabre-Tooth's arm as he moved away.

"Come and see me later?" She smiled, revealing small white teeth. "We can talk some more."

His heart rate picked up speed.

"When your meeting's over?" Her finger trailed down his arm.

"Hurry up." Callum leaned into the room. "What are you doing?"

"She knows you," Sabre-Tooth said as they picked their way through the rubble.

"We met a couple of times," Callum said. "Nahmada Scott knows her quite well, through the Justice Department. She's the one you were going to kill, isn't she?"

Sabre-Tooth followed him to their building, without answering. Inside, Maisi, Connor, Kezia and Sim sat on the temporary beds. Behind them, Halla leaned against the wall, shrouded in the shadows.

"Where've you been?" Maisi asked. "We looked for you."

"Talking to Petrian."

Maisi raised her eyes to the sagging ceiling. "You don't want to listen to her. She's a nut job."

"A what?"

"She's got too high an opinion of herself. She comes from one of the high-level families."

"High-level?" Sabre-Tooth frowned. Diessen had been high-level. It hadn't helped him much. "What's she doing here, then?"

"She shouldn't be here. She likes pretending she's a revolutionary." Maisi's voice dripped contempt. "She's pretty well set in the Justice Department, so Central Control thinks she's useful. She must have got the job through contacts 'cos she's incompetent. And she can't follow orders."

"You don't like her?"

Maisi snorted. "No. And now she's landed some of our people in trouble. I'd shoot her."

Sabre-Tooth flinched.

"Krux won't though. I don't know what his link with her is, but he lets her get away with too much."

Sabre-Tooth sank onto the ground by Connor and crossed his legs.

Connor leant down whispering in his ear. "She's not that bad. She and Maisi—" He shut up when Maisi glowered at him.

"Now you've finally joined us, we can start." Maisi turned her glare on Sabre-Tooth.

Sabre-Tooth squinted into the darkness, waving at the woman leaning on the wall. "Halla?"

Halla nodded. "I was in the area. Krux thought you might find me useful."

"This is the team," Maisi said, still frowning. "The six of us, plus Halla."

Sabre-Tooth stared at her. "Seven is too many to take over the wall. Too dangerous."

"Are you suddenly in charge? Maisi's frown deepened.

"No, but—"

"So you need to do as you're told."

"But—"

"Can *you* obey orders?" Maisi asked him.

"Sometimes." What the hell was wrong with her? He wasn't following orders that would get him and everyone else killed. He didn't wear a collar any longer. She couldn't make him do anything.

Maisi swore under her breath and stood up. She paced to the other side of the room, turned and paced back. She sat down again. "Sorry. That woman annoys me."

"I can see that," Sabre-tooth said.

Maisi dragged both hands through her hair, pushing the short strands away from her face. "What did you want to say?"

"The prisoner transport will pass over a populated area. There are residential buildings just south of Wood Green. They're spread out, but we still need to be careful. We don't want anyone to see us, so the fewer of us there are, the better. Just enough to bring the flyer down and get the prisoners out would be best. We've got to get over the wall as well. That's a point where we're likely to be seen." An image of the wall sprang to life in his mind. "There're a couple of places it might be possible. Not seven of us though."

"Might? How did you manage to do jobs inside the wall, then?"

"I didn't have to get in, I was already there. If I wanted to be invisible, I wore a chamsuit. A chameleon skinsuit, I mean."

Halla pushed herself away from the wall and sat on the edge of Maisi's bunk. "I think we can rustle up a couple of those, and I've got one. I'm wearing it."

"I've got mine," Sabre-Tooth said. "It's got a tear in it from when I got hit with that needle laser, but it should still work."

"So we could send two people, as well as you and Halla," Maisi said. "Do you think that would work?"

"It might." One to help each prisoner, and Halla because they needed her skills. They'd probably get in okay; it was getting out with prisoners that would be hard.

"I hope you know what you're doing." Maisi sucked on her knuckles.

Sabre-Tooth glanced sideways at Connor, hiding his exasperation with difficulty. He'd been doing this sort of job for months. What the fuck did Maisi think he'd done in the military?

Connor grinned.

"Who to send…" Maisi pursed her lips. "We'll all go as far as the wall. Sabre-Tooth will lead after that because he knows the area. Halla, because she's the only one who has the tech to incapacitate the flyer." She hesitated. "Connor and Callum? You should go as well, in case the prisoners are hurt. You and Sabre-Tooth have twice the strength of the rest of us. Once you're back on this side of the wall, we can help get them away."

"Will the suits fit us?" Connor pointed at himself. "We're bigger than most people."

"They adapt," Halla said.

"When do we leave?" Sim asked.

"An hour after midnight." Maisi suggested. "We don't want to hang around the wall for longer than necessary. They have more patrols down there."

Sim frowned. "They'll have had our people for three days at least."

"I can't help that," Maisi said. "I hope it'll teach them to be more careful in future."

"Do you know them?" Sim asked.

"Never met them. They're mostly based up near the New Midland development site. Krux knows them." She flipped a virtual screen from her communit and displayed a map, which had the WoodGreen base as a dot at its centre. "He knows everybody. Let's talk about the practical aspects." She enlarged the map and focussed in on a section of the road, about half a mile south of the base. "This is where we'll strike. There's heavy woodland and not much in the way of housing."

An hour later, she brought the briefing to a close. "That's all. We'll meet here at midnight."

"They still can't help treating us as animals," Connor said as they left. "I mean, you look almost human, but they talk to you as though you'd got the intelligence level of algae. And Maisi's sleeping with Callum. You'd think she'd know better."

Sabre-Tooth shrugged. "In the military, they talk to everyone like that. It used to give me a headache. Now, I don't care. I barely notice."

"We were made and trained to be at the high end of human intelligence," Connor grumbled, ignoring him, "and they know that, but still—"

"So have you done this sort of rescue before?" Sabre-Tooth interrupted him before his complaint could turn to a rant. "It sounds complicated."

"Never," Connor said. "It sounds fun though."

"Maisi didn't sound as though it was fun." Sabre-Tooth raised his eyebrows. It didn't feel like fun to him either.

"It's her job to worry." Connor's mouth spread in a wide, toothy grin. "We're action men."

ALLIANCE NEWS CORP – keeping you informed

News Update
February 17th 2454

Foreign Affairs

The number of refugees from the Indian sub-continent has increased exponentially over the past five years. Experts in population studies assign this phenomenon to destabilization of the climate, in an area where population growth is still on an upward curve. Sifia Hong is in talks with the political elite of the Indian Republic in an attempt to find a solution to the problem. Flooding, in the coastal regions and across river plains, has exacerbated the situation, while desertification in parts of the north has been blamed for food shortages. There have been a number of populist uprisings against the ruling classes, followed by wide suppression of dissent and violations of human rights. A spokesman for the Alliance Council told our journalist, 'The situation, which is causing tension at borders with the Alliance, cannot be allowed to continue The Council will consider all solutions.' Andrei Krewchek, in his role of Councillor for Foreign Affairs, will bring his own team to the talks.

Chapter 28

Sabre-Tooth crouched in the bushes above the road, glad of his military-grade chamsuit. He glanced up in the direction of the WoodGreen military camp. The transport was supposed to be a hover-tran, capable of rising just high enough to clear the trees. He thought it would follow the route of the road though; that's what they always used to do. Next to him, Connor breathed slowly and deeply. He was kneeling in a heap of wet moss and rain-drenched ferns, but the damp didn't appear to bother him. He stroked the sleeve of his borrowed chamsuit fondly.

"Sabe?"

"What?"

"Did you spend the night with Petrian yesterday? You weren't in your bunk."

"I didn't sleep last night," Sabre-Tooth rolled stiff shoulders. "Remember? We were trekking to the wall and sneaking over it."

"Before that. Come on, tell me."

"Maybe," Sabre-Tooth said.

"Maisi doesn't like her," Connor said.

"Maisi doesn't like me much either," Sabre-Tooth said.

"It's just the way she talks," Connor said. "She likes you fine. So Petrian? What's she really like?"

"You said you'd already met her."

"I've never spoken to her," Connor said. "Come on. Give me a clue."

"She's okay." She was the first woman who'd had sex with him voluntarily, the first he hadn't paid to do it. "It was one night. Only a couple of hours really."

"Sabe?" Connor punched him in the arm.

He smiled to himself, remembering. "She's nice." She was a bit intimidating. Sabre-Tooth had never been so close to such a perfectly groomed human being before. She had all that hair on her head and none at all on her body. Her skin was silky smooth. Her toenails matched her eyes. She'd wanted *him*.

"How big an escort do you think this prisoner transport is going to have?" He changed the subject.

Connor heaved an exasperated sigh. "You'd know that better than me. And if she'd known, I'm sure Maisi would have told us. I'm bored. Tell me about Petrian."

"She talks a lot," Sabre-Tooth said. "She told me that Krux had once been a legal citizen. That's how she knew him."

"Really?" Connor's interest shifted away from Sabre-Tooth's sex life.

"Really. High-level too, until he turned to revolution. Years ago, she said."

"I don't believe it. Why would he give that up for this?" Connor plucked a handful of greenery and tossed it at Sabre-Tooth. "He's been around forever. Or so I hear."

"How would I know?"

"Will you see her again?" Connor asked.

"Doubt it." He wasn't sure he wanted to. He'd had a good time with her, but she was more like a character from one of the vids than a real human being, and she made him feel like a different species. She fascinated him as much as the wolves in the London tower had.

Connor subsided into silence and Sabre-Tooth let the chatter of birds and rustling of vegetation wash over him. If he were lucky, the job would be done before the morning rain started. There was no sign of any military convoy yet, but he didn't move. On the other side of the road, Callum lurked in the woodland edge. Sabre-Tooth's enhanced eyes caught a tiny movement. If he concentrated, he could locate all three of them. Halla was somewhere close by, better hidden than the others. She was the least expendable of all of them.

A tiny vibration in his comm warned him that something was about to happen. He glanced sideways at Connor, who gave a small nod.

The two of them pushed through the undergrowth down towards the road, arriving on the verge ahead of a slow-moving vehicle that floated above the trees and resembled a giant cockroach. It was a heavily armoured hover-car, with two protrusions at the front that looked like they could morph into gun turrets. Sabre-Tooth had trained in various military vehicles during his first months as a recruit, and he had once piloted one like this. They were named after the insects they favoured (roaches to the soldiers who used them), and were almost as indestructible. Halla needed to disable those guns quickly.

A flash of fire came from the other side of the road, hitting the vehicle but causing no discernible damage.

The vehicle slowed to a stationary hover, descending until it rested a metre above the road. The protrusions elongated, just like insect antennae.

"They're stopping," Connor whispered. "That's just stupid. If they kept going, we'd have no chance of harming them. They always stop though. You'd think they'd learn."

Sabre-Tooth gave him a sideways look. "Does anyone?"

"I do." Connor practically bounced with excitement. "Come on. We need to be in position, for when Halla incapacitates the thing." He stepped out onto the road.

Sabre-Tooth followed.

The gun towers revolved towards them as they emerged from the bushes. He locked his knees to stop himself from running back into the woods. Even a military grade skinsuit wouldn't help him much if those guns were fired in his direction. A cloud of ash would be all that was left of him.

The guns froze and the vehicle sank slowly onto the road.

"Halla." Connor nudged him. "She's done it."

"Where the hell is she?" He'd never had a really big gun pointed at him before and the ones on the flying roach could have brought down a row of houses. His heart thudded painfully against the wall of his chest.

"Around."

The front top of the vehicle skimmed away from the bottom, revealing the occupants struggling from their seats.

Callum burst from the trees opposite. Like Connor and Sabre-Tooth, he carried a needle laser in his belt and a stunner in his hand.

Four armour-clad military guards stood back-to-back in the exposed interior of the vehicle, their personal weapons drawn. A fifth sat in the front driver position, his fingers desperately flying over the console. The mounted guns stayed frozen.

Sabre-Tooth, Callum and Connor sprinted towards the transport.

"Drop your weapons." The leader aimed his gun at Callum who slid down the embankment without pausing.

Callum ignored him, and the leader fired. The weapon hissed pathetically. The guard frowned down at it. His three companions raised their weapons, pulling on the triggers, confused and alarmed when they didn't work.

Callum aimed his stunner, fired, and the guard collapsed into the vehicle. He stunned a second one before the two remaining dived under cover. The last one still struggled with the console control.

"Safe to enter?" Connor whispered to Sabre-Tooth, who nodded and crept forward.

When Sabre-Tooth leapt onto the roach-tank, balancing on its side, the two stunned guards were motionless in the bottom of the vehicle, only the pupils of their eyes moving. Sabre-Tooth examined their features. He didn't recognize any of them.

By then, Callum had followed him in, and barrelled through the vehicle towards the two remaining guards. One of them was at the rear, standing in front of a reinforced prisoner's cage, and still checking his weapon. The other turned to face Callum, who dropped his stunner into his belt holster, wrapped his arms around the guard and hauled him over the side of the vehicle, dropping him to where Connor waited.

Sabre-Tooth stunned the remaining soldier from behind, while he still struggled with the lock on the cage door.

Callum pulled the limp body away from the cage. "We make a great team."

"What about him?" Sabre-Tooth gestured at the sealed console compartment.

"Have you finished up there?" Halla climbed over the side of the roach.

"We're just—"

She pointed her fob at the door of the cockpit.

It clicked open. The man at the console twisted in his seat, reaching for his useless weapon.

Halla shot him with her stunner. "There you go." She turned and made her way to the back of the transport.

Two people huddled in the prisoner-cage at the rear of the vehicle, a man and a woman, both wearing yellow prison coveralls.

"We're here to rescue you." Halla's voice was soothing as she elbowed Sabre-Tooth aside and fiddled with the door. The locking mechanism dropped away. She stood back.

The woman prisoner gingerly pushed at the door.

"Hurry up, will you?" Callum dragged the door fully open.

Both prisoners edged past Sabre-Tooth and, with Connor's help, scrambled down to the ground.

"I thought there were three of you," Halla said. She slid out of the vehicle after them.

"They killed Carla." The man rubbed a hand over his face. "They told us she died of natural causes. We all know what that means."

He and the woman were thin, pale and heavy-eyed. Both wore collars round their necks.

Halla pointed her tech stick at each of them in turn. The collars fell away.

Sabre-Tooth stamped on them, damaging the fastenings beyond repair. He picked them up and tossed them into the trees.

Connor, Callum and Sabre-Tooth lifted the stunned guard from the ground, shoving him back into the vehicle with his companions. "They'll shake off the effects eventually," Connor said. "We'll be well away by then."

"You don't kill them ever?" It was good they didn't need to kill the guards; after all, they might have been no more willing to serve in the military than he was.

"No. Not worth making more enemies than we need." Connor turned his head to answer him. "That's what Krux says."

Halla was staring at the prisoners. "How are we going to get these over the wall without being seen? Bright yellow?"

Sabre-Tooth's heartrate picked up again. This was going to be the hard part. "We'd better get moving."

Callum hesitated. "Can you drive one of these things?" He gestured at the roach.

"I know how," Sabre-Tooth said. He'd piloted this model before and he was sure the memory would come back to him. "They need a code, though, to unlock the mechanism. Why?"

"I thought we could take it and get over the wall before anyone realizes we aren't an official flight," Callum said, "but if it's locked, that's no good."

Halla turned away from the prisoners. "I can unlock it." She frowned at Sabre-Tooth. "Why didn't you tell anyone you knew how to fly these things?"

"I didn't think—"

"Never mind. You can tell us later. Help them in." She pointed at the prisoners.

Connor and Callum hoisted the two of them back into the interior of the roach. Sabre-Tooth and Halla followed. Sabre-Tooth dragged the occupant of the console seat free and dropped him in the bottom of the vehicle.

"Are we taking them with us?" Callum gestured at the stunned crew.

"Why not? They'll be out of action for at least an hour," Halla said. She was doing something to the console. "We'll be miles away by then. Sabre-Tooth? Come up here. I need your input."

Sabre-Tooth joined her, while Connor and Callum stopped the prisoners kicking the stunned guards.

He sat down at the console. Halla leaned over his shoulder, watching him nervously as it hummed into life. Dragging one finger over the screen-panel, he lifted the flying roach into the air, swung it round and took it back the way it had come, deviating from the road as they approached the military base. He peered down through the plasglas as they flew over, trying to spot his barracks, wondering who slept in his cubi-unit now.

The hover-car passed over the wall with no problems and Sabre-Tooth set it down a mile from where they'd left Maisi with the rest of the team. It would be bad if their own people attacked them.

"That's better than walking," Connor said.

"Better than being fried as we tried to get over the wall." Callum helped the prisoners down before jumping himself.

Both wobbled as they tried to walk.

"Drugs?" Halla asked.

The woman shrugged and nodded.

"We need to hurry." Sabre-Tooth checked the stunned guards. It looked as though they were beginning to recover.

Connor took the woman's arm, supporting her as she walked. After a few steps, he stopped and threw her over his shoulder. Callum did the same with the man. Neither argued.

Maisi emerged from the bushes, followed by Sim and Kezia. A huge smile spread across her face. "Well done. I was worried. A hover-car came over the wall half an hour ago."

"That was us," Halla said. "We'll explain later. We need to get as far away as possible now."

The small group set off, Sabre-Tooth and Maisi taking the lead, picking a way over the roughening ground. Adrenaline fizzed through Sabre-Tooth's bloodstream, adding speed to his legs until his pace increased to a jog.

"Wait." Halla caught up. "The man's been sick."

Connor joined them, lowering the woman to the ground. She clutched at his arm.

Maisi studied her. "Are you going to be able to carry on?"

"We'll have to." She grimaced, shifting her weight and favoring her left leg. "They starved us, and kept us in underground light cells." Her face was lined with fatigue. "We weren't allowed to sleep for more than an hour, and I'm pretty sure they put something in the water. I can't tell what's real any more."

"Did they interrogate you?"

She shook her head. "The ones who caught us were just run-of-the mill security guards. Military of course, but nothing special. You know one of them got killed? They weren't questioning Carla. They just…" Her voice trailed off.

Callum arrived with the man, who staggered towards them on his own feet.

Maisi scratched her chin. "Let's move on, while you still can." She dug in her pack and pulled out a stack of energy bars. "Eat those while you walk. We'll help you."

Night was falling by the time they reached the Epping base.

Three watchers materialised out of the dusk. They checked identities before taking the exhausted victims from their rescuers and helping them into the safety of a ruined building.

"Where will they go now?" Sabre-Tooth swallowed the last of his energy bar as he pushed his way between two dilapidated buildings.

"Now?" Maisi said. "I'm not sure. They should be okay here while they recover. No one will look for them so close to the centre of government. Let's go and find some proper food."

"I'm starving," Connor said. "At least in the lab they fed us regularly."

"You'd better be joking." Callum slapped his head.

Maisi rooted around, under one of the bunks, until she pulled out a pack of military-grade high-protein rations. "Just as well these things are waterproof. I'd love to go somewhere dry, even a week would be good. A week without rain and with real food." She sighed.

Sabre-Tooth thought of Cyrus and Laszlo as he chewed on his share of the nut and paste mixture. Were they still working in the heat of the New Spanish Desert, he wondered. "Do you know what we're doing next?"

Maisi shook her head and shrugged at the same time. "We'll be told soon enough."

Connor patted his shoulder. "Relax."

Afterwards, Sabre-Tooth lay on his camp bed indulging in Petrian fantasies. Her skin had been so smooth; flawless and a perfect rich brown. He'd wanted to unfasten her hair and examine its length and silkiness. She'd protested, telling him the style had taken ages to finish and she couldn't do it for herself. She had a personal stylist.

She existed in a world Sabre-Tooth had never seen. He hadn't even realized it existed.

Personal stylist?

He didn't understand why she had wanted him. A woman like her could have anyone. She was imperious and it was obvious she expected to get what she wanted. Would she want to see him again? Did he want to see her? He shifted uncomfortably, turning onto his back and sliding his hand down his body.

ALLIANCE NEWS CORP – keeping you informed

News Update
May 6th 2454

Foreign Affairs

Sifia Hong and Councillor for Foreign Affairs, Andrei Krewchek, released a joint statement last night. They have reached an accord with the leaders of the Indian Republic on the subject of border containment. Chief Administrator Aaditya Varma has agreed, in principle, to some degree of population control, in return for increased access to Western Europe and Eastern China's habitable regions. Sifia Hong told our journalists that the details have yet to be finalised, but she is adamant that progress will be made. Councillor Krewchek is cautiously optimistic, but warns that there are still hurdles to be overcome. 'The present population of the Indian sub-continent is unsustainable, and land in Alliance Territory is limited,' he said in a recent interview. 'Anyone who lives within the Eurasian Alliance must accept its laws limiting reproduction.'

Dissension – the campaign against injustice

May 6th 2454

Dissension welcomes the positive tones of the recent meeting between Alliance representatives and the administration of the Indian Republic. The major problems in the world are global in nature and can only be solved by international cooperation. We would like to see the Indian Republic welcomed as a full member of the Eurasian Alliance.

Chapter 29

Life took on a rhythm, irregular but broadly predictable. Most of his unit's actions felt unproductive to Sabre-tooth. He was restless but there was nowhere else to go. He didn't want to be alone, he didn't want to lose Sugar and Tygre again, and he had no idea what he would do if he left the rebels. It wasn't the sort of life he would have chosen, but he supposed it was better than the one where he'd worn a collar, and better than the one where he'd lived in a cage.

Military action outside London increased as rumours spread about plans for the new residential centre. Official news releases from the Alliance Council focussed on rising water levels, and the difficulty of keeping London free of flooding. High protective walls corralled the river, but surface runoff and encroaching salt water were becoming more of a problem. Drainage pumps were pushed to capacity as the water table rose, and while the central riverbank areas inhabited by the highest-level citizens remained trouble-free, dwellers in the outer housing complexes frequently appeared on the media, demanding to know what was being done about their drainage systems.

Petrian's message reached Sabre-tooth as he returned from a sabotage trip to New Midland. He'd left the rest of the team to meet with some of their old comrades and returned alone, wondering what the aim of the mission had been. Surely damaging building sites was pointless.

"Sabre-Tooth?" One of the watchers called to him as he picked his way across the protective circle of debris.

He turned.

It was the woman with the broken leg. Her bone had almost healed and she hurried towards him, balancing on a makeshift crutch. "There's a message for you. A Level Two citizen brought it."

Sabre-Tooth frowned. "Where is he now?"

"Headed back for town without even waiting for a drink. He said he'd be missed if he didn't hurry."

"How did he find us?" Sabre-Tooth's frown deepened. Were they safe if people could find them so easily?

"He's been before," the woman said. "I've seen him. He passes messages from our people inside the walls. He's one of us."

Most of Sabre-Tooth's orders came via Maisi, and he had no idea who else was likely to contact him. Who else knew he was here? Only Sugar and Tigre, and they had his comm details. "Who sent it? Why didn't it come by comm?"

Maybe it was from Tessis. He hadn't heard from her since the night they'd deserted from the military. Anticipation swirled around his mind. He hadn't realised he missed her moody awkwardness.

"It's a package from your girlfriend. You must have forgotten to give her your comm."

"From who?" What the hell was she talking about?

"The one with high-level citizenship. She wants to see you."

Petrian? Sabre-Tooth didn't know any other citizens at any sort of level. "She's not my girlfriend."

"Not what I've heard." The woman smirked. "She's sending some sort of transport to meet you at the AllyPally gate."

"I can't go near the gate. I'm wanted by the military."

"That's your problem." The woman shrugged, handing him a pristine kitbag. "She sent you this. It's to get you through the gate."

"When?"

"Tomorrow afternoon. Don't get caught." She tucked the crutch under one arm, patted his cheek and limped back to her post.

Inside the shelter, he opened the bag. It contained an expensive civilian skinsuit in graduated intensities of indigo, some fashionable eyeshades, a thin translucent strip and a handwritten note. The note instructed him to fasten the strip around his left wrist, where most citizens had their ID chips embedded.

He took an energy bar from his belt, chewing as he considered the empty bag. What the hell did she want? He couldn't go into the city, just to meet a woman. Could he?

He stretched out on the bunk, closing his eyes. An image of Petrian, as he'd last seen her, burned the back of his eyelids. Naked, lithe and exotic, with sparkling blue eyes; the shining gold of her hair contrasting with the rich brown of her skin. A fierce jab of wanting made him gasp.

The next morning he went for a run as soon as it got light. For once, the rain held off and sunlight broke through the canopy of leaves, dappling the ground and turning drops of water into sparkling crystal. It didn't help him clarify his thoughts. If Maisi found out he was even thinking about doing this, she'd kill him.

Maisi hated Petrian, who she viewed as everything that was wrong with the established order. She'd pointed out her flaws to Sabre-Tooth when she found out about the night they'd spent together. Petrian was spoilt, entitled, arrogant, foolhardy, and if it hadn't been for her friendship with Krux, she would have been a definite enemy of the revolution. She was responsible for the capture of at least one unit, and Carla would still be alive if Petrian had kept her nose where it belonged.

Sabre-Tooth had listened. It would have been rude not to. He could tell that Maisie's real grudge was because Petrian had mocked her relationship with Callum.

Sabre-Tooth liked her arrogance and the self-confidence gained from a privileged life, but he wasn't sure how much he trusted her. Petrian obviously expected him to accept her invitation without argument. Maisi was right about her sense of entitlement.

He'd enjoyed the sex though. It was different with someone who didn't do it as a job. Better. He still didn't understand why she'd wanted to do it with him. She was a high-up, wealthy citizen and whatever he liked to tell himself, he wasn't even properly human.

She was insane. Of course he wasn't going to answer her summons.

At fourteen o'clock, he dressed in the skinsuit. It fitted him perfectly, the luxurious material soft against his body. After a rapid assessment of the weather, he pulled his military coverall on top of it. He wrapped the strip around his wrist where it took on the hue and texture of his skin. Excitement bubbled up through his bloodstream, fighting with his nerves.

A small civilian airtran waited out of sight of the gate, on the unprotected side. It looked like a private vehicle. Petrian had to rank very high in the hierarchy of citizenship, even higher than he'd originally assumed, if the airtran belonged to her. Private transport was actively discouraged and only the top layer of society had access to it. He climbed into the back.

"Ready?" The human pilot turned his head.

Sabre-Tooth nodded, peeling off his protective coverall. "Do you work for Petrian?"

"Miss McIntyre? Yes."

The airtran lifted above the treetops, hovering for a moment before it dropped down towards the city gate checkpoint. Sabre-Tooth's stomach dropped with it. If this went wrong, he wasn't going to allow anyone to capture him. He wasn't letting anyone put a collar around his neck again. They'd have to kill him first. His skin twitched and he clenched his fists around his flexed claws.

They landed on a small square of black plascrete. The top of the airtran slid open. A guard leaned in. Sabre-Tooth offered his wrist, heart thumping against his ribs. The guard scanned it and moved onto the pilot.

He released the breath he'd been holding and examined the city wall as the pilot chatted with the guard. It was high, and topped with a mix of razor wire and eye spies. There was no way he could climb over it here. He'd scaled the wall before, with Callum, Connor and Halla when they rescued Petrian's friends, but this time, he was too close to the official AllyPally gate. If he tried and failed, he'd be in real trouble. He clutched his chameleon skinsuit, wondering if Petrian was worth the risk.

The airtran lifted again, cruising over the scattering of outer London buildings, before halting at the inner wall. Again, they were waved through and ten minutes later, the airtran dropped onto a flat, enclosed courtyard.

Sabre-Tooth climbed out and surveyed his surroundings. Medium height residential buildings surrounded the courtyard on all sides, their walls covered in green scrambling plants. Wide stairways led up to the higher levels, where terraces ran along the building's façade. These too were covered in plants, many of which were in flower, filling the humid warmth of the air with their scent. The sky above was clear and blue, the air heavy and claustrophobic. Fountains splashed in each corner of the square, small trees grew in pots, and café tables stood in groups on the faux stone terraces.

Close to the top of the wall, a door opened and Petrian appeared on the terrace, waving to him, before running down the steps, gold hair streaming behind her. She was dressed in a short tunic and flat sandal-boots, which displayed her painted toes. Sabre-Tooth stared down at them. They were the same iridescent blue. She still wore the cosmetic lenses, covering her eyes, and hiding her thoughts.

"You look good." Standing on tiptoes, she kissed his cheek. "That colour suits you." Bright rays of sunlight shone on her face, emphasizing the small lines around her eyes and the deep shadows under her cheekbones. She must be around the same age as Krux; years older than Sabre-Tooth. He wanted to stroke her.

He backed away, hands clasped behind his back. "What am I doing here?"

"It's been a while. I wanted to see you."

Sabre-Tooth stared. "Have you any idea how dangerous it is for me to come into the city?"

She shrugged. "No one knows you're here. I've taken care."

"But what do you want? It's been months."

"What I said. To see you." She pushed her loose hair behind her ears. "Come on. I'll give you some decent food and we can talk. You must be tired of that army ration stuff."

"I wondered if you needed me to do something for you." He couldn't believe he was here for no reason. "Like you got people to try and rescue your friend."

Her brows rose. "No. Nothing like that. I wouldn't try that again."

She couldn't want him just for sex. A woman like her could have anyone, and their last encounter hadn't been that good. In his experience, any sex was amazing, but she must have masses of better and safer options. "But—"

"I wanted to spend some time with you." She touched his face with a slender finger. "Why don't you take off the shades? I can't tell what you're thinking."

His body jumped to attention.

Stroking the finger down his cheek, she moved closer, reaching to take his sunglasses.

He jerked his head away.

"You're different," she said. "Relax, Sabre-Tooth. I just want to get to know you."

He still couldn't believe it. Was she making a fool of him?

"I'd better get back." He swung round to face the airtran, anger, at himself as well as at her, almost overwhelming him.

She grabbed his arm. "Stay till tomorrow morning? I'll make sure it's safe."

When she dropped his arm and jumped backwards he realised he was growling.

He took a deep breath. "What do you think Krux would do if he knew about this? What do you think would happen to me if I were caught? Maisi's going to be furious as it is."

"It'll be fine. Come on Sabre-Tooth? Don't say you don't need a break. Have a meal with me at least." Her voice wasn't as assured as before. "And Maisi has no room to talk, not with the way she keeps Callum on a leash."

Sabre-Tooth's anger turned to reluctant amusement. Petrian knew nothing about Maisi's relationship with Callum. She knew nothing about the way they lived.

His eyes lingered on the way her turquoise tunic clung to her body. The intense colour contrasted with the silky-smooth brown of her skin. Temptation pulled at him until he gave in, stretching his hand out to run his fingers down her bare arm.

She smiled, a small triumphant smile, and turned away.

He followed her up the stairs to the fourth, and top, level of the building.

It wasn't just the promise of food and sex that drew him. He was curious to see how she lived; to see how privileged citizens lived. He'd taken the risk already; he might as well get something out of it. He'd never been in a private home before; at least not without breaking in, creeping through the dark, and killing the occupant.

"I really thought you needed me for something serious." He wondered if he was fooling himself. His mind swirled in confusion. "You shouldn't do this. Suppose next time you really need help, no one comes?"

"Don't be silly." She tossed the words over her shoulder as she placed her palm to the door lock. Her confidence had returned. "There are proper channels if I want to call for help."

Sabre-Tooth raked his claws though his hair, barely containing his irritation, mainly at himself. His mood ricocheted all over the place. Excitement, anger, lust, irritation, all cycled rapidly round his head, and under them lay curiosity and anticipation. Her interest in him made his chest swell with pride.

The apartment was amazing. Slotting his shades into his belt, he gazed around the reception room, unable to believe that people actually lived like this. Characters on the entertainment vids maybe, but surely not real people? "Can I look?"

She nodded.

Petrian had several rooms all to herself, dry, warm and comfortably furnished. There were separate ones for sleeping, eating, and bathing. She threw herself onto a long scarlet sofa, waiting while he paced through the rooms, examining everything.

"Does anyone else live here?"

"Like who?" The expression on her face conveyed puzzlement. "This is my home. My personal maid has a room in the servant's complex, but not in here."

"I just wondered." He remembered her telling him she had a stylist to do her hair. Was that the same as a personal maid?

He wandered over to the windows. On one side of the apartment, they looked out onto the wide river, and across to the South Bank. Fortunately, for his peace of mind, the angle meant that the Security Central buildings were hidden. He leaned his face on the plasglas and stared down at the dark oily water while Petrian used her communit to order food.

ALLIANCE NEWS CORP – keeping you informed

News Update
December 1ˢᵗ 2454

Politics

The two main contenders for the position of Speaker for the Eurasian Alliance are well into their campaigns. Next year's election was triggered by a challenge from Andrei Krewchek, Councillor for Foreign Affairs in the New British Islands domain of the Alliance. During the past three years, Andrei Krewchek has been an enthusiastic campaigner for more assertive use of the military, and has strong support in the higher levels of the armed forces. Sifia Hong, who has steered the Alliance for over ten years, issued a statement claiming she has no fear she will lose this election. Her strong and conservative leadership has increased the stability of the Alliance group of nations as well as expanding their sphere of influence.

Alliance News Corp will be bringing you coverage of the run up to next year's elections, with a close focus on the two main contenders.

Dissension – the struggle against injustice

December 1ˢᵗ 2454

While Andrei Krewchek's aims may be laudable, Dissension fears that his political ambition could embroil the Alliance nations in expensive and unpopular conflicts. Is this worse than the tyrannical governance of Sifia Hong's Council? It remains to be seen. Dissension is not blind to the self-serving lies of our leaders, but a change in regime may be an opportunity to push for other changes.

Chapter 30

Sabre-Tooth woke before first light, immediately aware of the softness of the mattress, and the body lying asleep next to him. The room's sensor registered his movement as he sat up, and the overhead globe gradually cast a dim illumination over the bed. Petrian sprawled on her side, ribbons of shining hair covering her face and much of her body. He touched it, gathering up a handful and running the silkiness through his fingers. It couldn't all be real but he liked it. Everything about her was a feast for his senses. Even the perfume she used didn't hurt his nose. He sniffed at the place where her neck met her collarbone, inhaling deeply.

She didn't wake, so he climbed out of the bed and headed for the bathroom. Last night, he'd discovered the pleasures of hot water. Cold water was horrible, but hot water was almost as satisfying as sex. He'd never had a hot shower before and, since he'd left the army, he'd had very few showers at all. Once he found the best temperature, he stood under the powerful stream of water until he heard Petrian call his name. He switched the shower off and stepped into the warm drying area, squeezing the excess damp from his hair.

"You must have used my energy allocation for the entire day," she grumbled. "We only get so much free, you know? Then they charge us."

Sabre-Tooth shrugged. Judging by the way she lived, Petrian could afford it.

She slid from the bed, brushing her hair behind her shoulders. It slithered down her back, glistening gold in the dim light.

"I've got to go," he said.

"Must you? Already? I've got a free day." Her fingers reached for his hair, sliding through it and stroking his ears. "I love your ears."

He jerked his head away. He'd hated people touching his ears since his first day in the army.

"And you have the prettiest cat eyes. All golden and amber."

"I have to go." He slid his hands over her naked shoulders.

Azure eyes sparkled up at him through outrageously long lashes. "Really?"

He lowered his head, rubbing his face against her hair. "Soon."

After they'd done the sex thing again, this time with her on top, he used the hot shower once more. He pulled on his new skinsuit before leaving the bathing room.

217

"Honestly, Sabre-Tooth." Petrian scrambled off the bed. "What is it with you and that shower? That's the third time you've used it. Your skin'll fall off."

Sabre-Tooth inspected his image in the full-length mirror. He'd never seen an entire reflection of himself before. The fashionable garment made him look almost as good as the vid models. He twisted to check his back view. "I might never get another hot shower," he said. "You don't know how lucky you are."

"It's just a shower. I'll have mine later." She pulled a deep blue robe from a hook by the door. It covered her from collarbone to ankle. "Do you want some coffee before you go?"

He nodded. "Then I *really* have to go."

The coffee was nothing like caffa, the substitute he was used to. He hadn't tasted anything like it since he'd visited London with Tessis and they'd drunk the expensive real thing. It felt like an age ago, another lifetime. Petrian's coffee was even better than that. He closed his eyes, inhaling the rich scent. There were pastries as well. It was almost worth the risk of being discovered, just for the pastries.

"You're such a sybarite." Amusement filled her voice as she nibbled on the smallest portion.

Sabre-Tooth took another croissant from the plate. Melting chocolate oozed from the centre of this one. He knew he'd never come close to the sort of luxury Petrian enjoyed, but maybe if Nahmada Scott managed to win the citizenship case, he could have a life that involved comfort. Maybe he'd occasionally be able to drink real coffee and afford chocolate. One day. A pang of loss shot through him as he admitted it was never likely to happen.

"You mustn't do this again," he said to her, before climbing into her airtran. "It's wrong and stupid and far too risky. I won't come." He told himself he meant it.

"Who says I'll invite you?"

"Petrian—"

She folded her arms and scowled at him. "Where's your sense of adventure? And curiosity? You're a cat, aren't you?"

"I'm human." He scowled fiercely at her, lifting his lip to show his teeth.

She patted his cheek. "Of course you are, sweetie."

"You don't know…" He let the words trail off. How could she, with her privileged life and her comfortable living space, and her unlimited food, know what it was like not to be safe. He hoped she never found out. "Thanks for everything."

"Till the next time." She waved as the airtran lifted.

"No next time." Sabre-Tooth whispered the words under his breath. The pilot glanced over his shoulder and raised an eyebrow.

~~~

Meeting with Petrian made Sabre-Tooth even more restless. He envied her comfortable, secure home. He was used to moving around now, settling in easily to the series of temporary camps. He stayed for a few weeks, did a few jobs, before moving to another one, usually with Maisi's team. Only rarely did he get to spend a night at the original north London base. At least in the military, he'd had a permanent home, where the door closed, giving him privacy. It was the only thing he missed. He didn't like feeling rootless. He didn't like it when his friends weren't close by.

Occasionally, he managed to catch up with Tygre and Sugar when they were in the same part of Outer London. Their unit travelled a lot more than his, as far as the Spanish desert where they helped the resistance groups supporting the southern refugees. Sabre-tooth wondered if they were ever in the same area as Cyrus and Laszlo. He hoped not. Cyrus and Laszlo might not even be alive.

Tygre didn't like travelling much. Sugar did.

"She's not a real cat," Tygre grumbled to Sabre-Tooth, a week after his visit to Petrian's home. "They probably mixed migrating wildebeest into her DNA."

Sabre-Tooth laughed.

Sugar tweaked Tygre's ear. "Don't you want to see the world? All those places we saw on the vids in the lab?"

"No." Tygre pushed her hand away. "Practically everyone in those vids got killed. What's the point of being a dead hero? I don't want to be a hero at all. I want to stay in one place. Somewhere no one shoots at me and I can sleep and eat as much as I like."

"What about you, Sabe?" Sugar asked. "Your unit stays south of New Midland. Don't you want to see more of the world? You could ask for a transfer."

Sabre-Tooth wrinkled his nose. He could think of nothing he wanted less. He remembered the Spanish desert from his army training.

"What are you all talking about?" Connor arrived and flopped down onto the ground next to Sabre-Tooth.

He explained.

"What does it matter where you go?" Connor asked Tygre. "We've got beds. We've got friends. We're part of a team. No one beats us. Why do you need to stay in one place?"

"I just do." Tygre insisted.

"I know what you mean," Sabre-Tooth said. "I'd like to stay in the same place for a month at least."

"But why?" Connor looked confused.

Sabre-Tooth shrugged. "I don't know." It was hard to explain that he wanted a home. He'd never had one, so he had no way of putting his feelings into words. He wanted somewhere permanent, somewhere of his own, a door he could close. Somewhere like Petrian's apartment. He wanted the people he cared about, like Sugar, Tygre, even Tessis, nearby. He wanted a safe place. He wanted Petrian's life. "Dogs are wanderers. Cats stay in one place." He was only half-joking.

"I thought you were human." Connor mocked him.

"I am," Sabre-Tooth said. "Mainly. Anyway, lots of humans stay in one place forever."

"Not the ones we know, and it's not safe to stay too long in one place. You must have seen how the military raid any permanent settlement of illegals?"

"Yes." He'd been part of the raids.

"That last place up near New Midland? They burned it to the ground. I don't know how many were killed." Connor shuddered. "That's why it's not worth having permanent camps."

"I know," Sabre-Tooth said. "They shouldn't have burned it. That's unlawful. That lawyer told me. Nahmada? Remember? The one I was supposed to kill?"

"Nahmada Scott? Yeah." Connor rolled his eyes. "And they've been prosecuted for it, have they? Anyway, killing illegals isn't unlawful."

"Burning things is. It's a crime against the environment." Sabre-Tooth scowled, sprang to his feet and stalked off. Of course they hadn't been prosecuted.

~~~

Soon after Sugar and Tygre left, he had another invitation from Petrian, then another. Despite a nagging worry in the depths of his mind, Sabre-Tooth returned to her every time she called. He couldn't stop himself. The way she lived fascinated him. He loved her confidence and assurance. He loved her assumption that nothing would interfere with her life, her assumption that safety, protection and comfort were her right. When he was with her, he could pretend that this was his life as well.

She sprawled on her scarlet sofa, wrapped in her blue robe, while he sat cross-legged and naked on the floor, staring at her entertainment screen. Her fingers moved through his hair, lightly scratching his scalp. He half-closed his eyes, uninterested in the soap-vid she liked to watch. When the episode ended, he turned to look up at her.

She stretched and sat up. "Food?"

He nodded.

After she'd placed the order, she curled up in the corner of the sofa. Sabre-Tooth pushed himself to his feet and joined her, sliding one hand into the opening of her robe. When she didn't protest he pulled it open and nuzzled the flawless skin around her navel.

She squirmed, gasped and laughed. "What are you doing?"

"I like the way you smell."

"Hmm?"

"And the way you taste." He dipped his tongue into her navel.

"Don't spoil your appetite." Her fingers clutched at his hair.

When the food arrived, she placed it on the small table in the kitchen. Sabre-Tooth dressed himself in the tawny skinsuit she'd given him and joined her, hoisting himself onto a small circular stool, which was almost as uncomfortable as the crates he normally sat on.

Petra pushed one of the bowls over to him. She swept her loose hair over one shoulder and picked up a set of antique chopsticks. "Eat."

He took the second set of chopsticks and poked at the rice in the bowl. It was bright with a mixture of vegetables and beans. Steam rose from it, bringing a mixture of aromatic spice scents. "Nice."

"I don't know how you survive on those ration packs." She lifted a tiny amount of food to her lips.

He shrugged, and asked her about her week. He liked the way she talked about herself, about her role in the Justice Department, about the social circle she moved in. He'd much rather talk about her life than about his own. He liked the occasional hint of vulnerability she showed. Her glittering cosmetic eyes hid most of her thoughts, but sometimes she revealed more than she intended. She was as difficult to pin down as a wild animal and he had no idea how much she thought about him when he wasn't there. He knew he wasn't her only lover.

He interrupted her as she talked about a conference she'd attended. It was about legal cases involving under-age citizens and the best way to deal with them. Sabre-Tooth was interested in everything, but now he wanted to know more about Petrian.

"Petrian? Why did you get involved with Dissension?"

She put her chopsticks down and gave him her wide, social smile. "I don't really remember."

"It's dangerous. You have a pretty good life," he said. "Don't you think—"

She frowned down at her almost full bowl. "I have a pointless life," she said. "I don't have children. I live alone. I wanted to do something useful. Something that wasn't just about me."

"There are other things," he said. "Rich people do charity work. Some of them volunteer on environment improvement teams. Some of them—"

"I wanted to do something *real*. My family thinks I'm worthless. My coming of age medical was a disaster. The analysts found a mutation that meant I could never have children. They've never forgiven me. My brother has his two, but that's not enough for my parents."

"Is that why you're risking your life?"

"I don't like the citizen classifications. I don't like the way people get judged by their place in the hierarchy. I can't help the fact that I don't have reproductive rights. Why should I feel less because of that?" She picked up her chopsticks and pointed them at him. "Things have to change."

"That's it?"

Her robe slipped from her shoulder as she shrugged. "Krux asked for my help. He gave me a purpose. I can make a difference."

Sabre-Tooth lifted a stalk of broccoli to his lips. He still didn't get it, but she sounded serious, another of Krux's followers. He finished his rice, and when she pushed hers away, he cleaned that out as well.

~~~

Sugar disapproved of Petrian almost as much as Maisi would if she knew. He met up with her again, after he'd finished a job on the western outskirts of London. She was alone, and excited over some sabotage trip to one of the London checkpoints. After she'd finished telling him about it, she folded her arms. "Is there something you want to tell *me* about?"

"No." The two of them sat side by side on one of the bunks in the upper halls of their old transport hub hiding place, sharing a drink. "Do you know how the legal case is coming along?"

"Legal case?" She frowned.

"You know? The one to give us citizen rights?"

Sugar should know; after all, it was her birth mother who had stirred things up, and demanded legitimacy for her daughter. Sabre-Tooth still hadn't met this mother of hers. He nudged her with one shoulder. "Well?"

"Yeah," she said. "It's going on. These things take ages. You should talk to my mother."

"I'd like to. Do you see her?"

Sugar shrugged. "Sometimes. It's not safe though. Not for her. We're still classed as illegals. Or animals. According to Nahmada, it's not clear. She's optimistic though." She held out her hand, demanding her share of the drink. "I'll try and arrange for you to see her."

"Thanks." He wasn't going to hold his breath.

"Give me that coffee." She jabbed him in the ribs with her forefinger. "And tell me what you've been up to. I want to know about this citizen you're involved with. Romantically. Is it true?"

He passed the coffee tube back to her and stretched out on his back, staring at the sagging ceiling. "Not really."

"How do you mean? Not really?" She twisted round and poked him in the ribs again.

"You haven't changed," he grumbled. "Still as nosey as ever. I'm not involved. I don't think it's romantic. It's dangerous. It's just that I don't know how to say no. And it's not like there's anyone else. Petrian is…"

His voice trailed off as he thought about her. He'd found that the more he had sex, the more he liked it, and the more he wanted. He wasn't at all sure how he felt about Petrian. His feelings changed every time he saw her. She was fascinating, charming, demanding. Sometimes he liked her, sometimes he didn't. Sometimes he resented her. He wished she wasn't so entitled. He wished he didn't feel so intimidated by her. Most of all, he wished she wasn't so careless of her own safety. Sometimes he was overwhelmed by a wave of affection for her.

"I'm not as nosey as you." Sugar poked at him again. "You should find someone else. I've heard about her. Maisi's right. She's a liability. You know why she's sleeping with you, don't you?"

He closed his eyes. "Of course I do."

She ignored him. "It's because you're different. I bet she tells all her high-level friends about how she has a chimera as a lover."

"She's sleeping with a mongrel." Sabre-Tooth's lips twitched.

Sugar laughed. "Seriously though Sabe, you need to be careful. Everyone knows, and it doesn't come from you. She's an idiot."

"I know." He opened his eyes and focussed on the ceiling. Arguing with Sugar was pointless, but Petrian wasn't an idiot. She was pretty clever, really. She just had no grasp of personal danger. He thought she'd been doing the undercover work too long. That was why she was careless. Krux needed to persuade her to retire. He wouldn't though; she was too useful.

"Next time I really will say no," he said. "Although she has amazing food."

Sugar's laugh turned to a giggle. "You'd risk your life for chocolate?"

"Hot showers and coffee." He turned onto his side, facing her, and propped himself on one elbow. "You should try her coffee."

ALLIANCE NEWS CORP – keeping you informed

News Update
December 1st 2454

Crime

The Justice Department has announced a crackdown on anti-social behaviour. No one is exempt from the rule of law. Arrests have been made in the Department for Population Control, where officials have been issuing residency permits and granting citizenship to people who can afford to pay for them. This has affected immigration from both our neighbours to the west of China and to the south of Europe. The mid-level officials in question are under investigation and if the charges are verified, they will suffer full penalties under the law.

Dissension – the struggle against injustice

December 2nd 2454

It appears that the Alliance Security Services are flexing their muscles. These arrests of middle managers will not serve to eradicate the corruption that lies at the heart of many of the Alliance's institutions. Dissension asks its readers to consider why this is happening now. What do our leaders hope to conceal?

Chapter 31

By the time he visited Petrian for the seventh time, Sabre-Tooth was almost blasé about passing through the London checkpoints. She sent him expensive fashion wear with each invitation. Two weeks before the midwinter holiday, he received a parcel containing a skinsuit in green and gold. When he arrived at the apartment, she was dressed in similar colours. Her eyes and nails matched; emerald with flecks that sparkled when they caught the light.

"We're going to a party." She smiled at him.

He opened his mouth, but closed it again immediately, lost for words.

"You'll enjoy it."

"No." There was no way.

"Come on Sabre-Tooth. You can show off your new clothes."

"Call your pilot," he said. "I'm not staying."

"Don't go." She sank onto the scarlet sofa. "I'm leaving in a couple of days, to spend Midwinter with friends. I won't see you for a while."

"No party, then."

"You've never been to a party. It'll be a new experience."

"It might be my last experience."

She pursed her lips, studying his face.

"No." She could persuade him to do many things, but this was much too far. He stared back at her. "You need to be careful. If they catch me and find out I was with you, then you'll be in serious trouble as well. Do you want to end up in a prison cell in SecCen?"

She shrugged. The artificial green of her eyes hid most of her feelings.

He knelt on the floor next to the sofa, resting his hands on her thighs. "Seriously Petrian? I'm not doing this. What's wrong with you?"

"I…"

"What?" He wished he could read her expression.

She shook her head. "All right. We'll have our own party."

Leaving the city the next morning, he worried over her state of mind. Something about it reminded him of Tessis. Petrian must know how dangerous her behaviour was, though. She wasn't stupid.

~~~

A week later, Sabre-Tooth's ears flickered as he heard a disturbance around the entrance to the camp. Recognizing the voices, he didn't bother moving from his position in the winter sun.

One of the speakers was Krux. Sabre-Tooth hadn't seen him since he'd met Petrian for the first time, but he'd heard a lot about him. Gossip surrounded him. His supporters viewed him as a revolutionary leader. Some of them talked as though he was a god.

Sabre-Tooth didn't believe there would ever be a revolution. He wasn't even sure how much point there was in Nahmada Scott's legal battles. He'd thought about Krux's motives, but the man's mind was a complete mystery to him.

Nothing would change. The Alliance Council allowed Dissension to exist, but they swatted anyone who might be a real threat to the status quo as carelessly as they would kill a mosquito. More carelessly. Mosquitoes were part of the protected biosphere. He knew he should be grateful to be free of the collar and the military, and he was, but he was also edgy and it was hard to see an end to his nomadic, hidden way of life.

Two other voices joined Krux's.

No one knew where Krux originally came from, but after talking to Petrian, Sabre-Tooth had a half-formed idea. According to Petrian, he'd grown up in the city and had friends there. High-level friends. She said he'd run away from his home at seventeen, and had been in hiding ever since. She didn't say why.

A rumour circulated of how he'd built up a fortune in credits, based on illegal recreational drugs. Sabre-Tooth wasn't sure he believed that.

Gossip said that he'd first emerged as a leader among the rebels about five years ago, and organized them into a force of protest. Gossip said that he was one of a group of people who had founded the present version of Dissension, years earlier, when the organization had been set up as an alternative media outlet.

Petrian said that he was campaigning to change the laws surrounding rights to citizenship, and that Nahmada Scott's case for the chimeras was one of several. She said that there were others in the Justice Department who helped him, besides her. She had told Sabre-Tooth a little about Krux's high-ranking family. It didn't seem important, especially as she wouldn't say who they were, and couldn't or wouldn't say why he'd abandoned them.

Sabre-Tooth frowned, thinking about her escalating heedlessness. She was indiscrete. Krux would be furious if he knew how much she talked about him. Rumour said he had a fiery temper, and while Sabre-Tooth remembered his charisma, he also remembered the streak of ruthlessness when he'd mentioned the consequences of betrayal. Petrian was playing with fire.

Within five minutes of Krux's arrival, the heavy stamp of boots thudded towards Sabre-Tooth.

"Don't you people do any work?" The henchman nudged him with the toe of his boot. "Krux wants to see you."

Sabre-Tooth pushed himself up and fastened the loosened top of his coverall. "What does he want?"

The man shrugged. "He doesn't share his thoughts with me."

Sabre-Tooth followed him through the debris, down a tunnel, into the main hall. His eyes adjusted to the change from bright daylight to the dim gleam of personal wrist lights. Krux sat cross-legged on a plas-sheet on the floor, two more of his men standing guard behind him.

"Sir?" he said. He still hadn't managed to shake off his instinctive need to include 'Sir' in his sentences. "You wanted to see me?"

"Sabre-Tooth." Krux acknowledged him with a worried smile. "Sit down. We have a problem."

"What sort of problem?" Sabre-Tooth sank to the ground opposite Krux.

"I've heard you've come to know Petrian very well." Krux raised his eyebrows.

"Not that well," Sabre-Tooth said, his heart rate speeding up as he contemplated what Krux might do about it. "We've met a few times."

Seven times, not counting the first. After the last meeting, seven was probably more than enough. He hoped she wasn't in trouble. He hoped he wasn't in trouble.

Krux shook his head. "You shouldn't have met at all. She knew that."

"I—"

"I'm not blaming you and anyway, never mind that now. She's been arrested in this new crackdown. I don't know how she came under suspicion, but I suspect... I think Intelligence must have been watching her for a while. She's always been reckless, but..." He rested his elbows on his knees and cupped his face in his hands. "She's a fool. I don't think she realized her own danger. She's done a good job for us for a long time, given us a way into the Justice Department, but the stress..."

"What? Could you say all that again?" Sabre-Tooth had lost the thread of the conversation when he'd heard the word 'arrested'. His stomach clenched. Petrian? In a cell?

Krux repeated what he'd said.

Sabre-Tooth rubbed his face. Why was he surprised? It was baffling that she hadn't been arrested before. He'd warned her. Why hadn't she listened? He jumped to his feet and paced across the floor. Surely, her status would give her some protection. He swung round and faced Krux. Status hadn't protected Diessen. "What will they do with her?"

"Sit down." Krux pointed at the ground in front of him. "I haven't finished. I'm assuming you want to help?"

Sabre-Tooth sat down. Krux hadn't answered his question.

"She never used to be so careless. I don't know why... Anyway, we need to get her away. She was staying with friends on an estate north of New Midland, but they're bringing her down to SecCen for questioning. Apparently, they arrested her host as well. One of her colleagues in Justice contacted us. I hope..." Krux's voice drifted off again.

Sabre-Tooth couldn't stop thinking about Petrian in a SecCen cell. Very few people ever left Security Central and those who did were never the same afterwards. "We've got to—"

"She'll be interrogated, of course. Maximally, given her status." Krux jerked back to attention. "That's a risk to all of us. She knows the names of several mid-level citizens who are sympathetic to our cause and may have broken the law for us. We need to get her out. If we can't get her out, we need to kill her."

"You want *me* to kill her?" Krux must be mad.

"I'd rather you got her out," Krux said, "but if you can't, you'll have to silence her."

"No!" Heat rushed to Sabre-Tooth's face. He clenched his fists. "How can you think—?"

226

"You don't want to do it," Krux said. "I understand that, but do you know what maximal interrogation means?"

Sabre-Tooth winced. Everyone had heard of the techniques the security forces used. They made sure their methods were widely known. That sort of knowledge kept most of the population in check. Sabre-Tooth had seen the reality. He'd watched an interrogation as part of his training. It hadn't even been maximal, but it had ruined his sleep for a week.

"I'm not killing her." He'd hated killing strangers. He'd done it to survive, but killing someone he cared about was a completely different thing. No way could Krux make him.

"She'd be dead when they finished anyway. Or as good as. I don't want SecCen getting their filthy hands on her. She deserves more from me than that. At least you would end her quickly. She wouldn't suffer like…"

Sabre-Tooth chewed on his lip, remembering the last time he'd seen Petrian. Her transformed eyes had glittered with emerald life. If they'd been real, he would have described them as feverish. "No. I can't."

Krux folded his arms. "Don't imagine this is an easy decision for me. I've known her since we were children. Let me tell you about Petrian."

Sabre-Tooth took a deep breath. Whatever Krux had to say wouldn't change his mind. "Go on."

"Petrian's family and mine had adjoining country estates outside London," Krux said. "We were friends as children. Good friends. When I had to leave home, she helped me."

Sabre-Tooth looked up. So it was true about Krux's past. "How?"

"If you repeat any of this, I'll have you killed." Krux's intense gaze burned into Sabre-Tooth's face.

"I won't."

"My father had violent tendencies. He beat me, and my brother, frequently. He was a top-level citizen, just one rung below the first family, so no one would have interfered with him. When I was nearly eighteen, I refused to obey an order. He attacked me with a taserwhip. As soon as I could move, I left. I hid in an outbuilding on Petrian's family estate."

"How did you manage to do that?" Laszlo hadn't been able to walk for a week after his beating.

"I had help," Krux said. "A family servant got me away from my father's house. Petrian brought me food and water until I could travel. Once I'd established myself outside the wall, I got back in touch. She's always been a good friend. Her family weren't easy on her either."

"Established yourself?" Sabre-Tooth wanted to keep him away from the subject of killing Petrian.

"I made some credits, illegally of course, and… but all that's irrelevant. I just want you to know how much I owe her. She's almost a sister to me."

Sabre-Tooth rubbed his eyes. Sugar was a sister to him. He couldn't imagine giving up on *her*. He wouldn't order *her* killed if she became a danger. He growled under his breath.

"She can't be interrogated." Krux's head sagged and he contemplated his knees. "I *told* her to get an anti-interrogation implant."

Sabre-Tooth nodded. He was familiar with the technology. Some of the implants killed the wearer when their pain levels reached a certain level.

"It can cause massive brain damage if it reacts with a couple of the drugs they use. That scared her so much, she wouldn't do it. And now—"

"Maybe she never thought she'd be caught." Petrian had never grasped that her security wasn't absolute, or that her links to people at the highest level wouldn't always keep her safe. Despite her sophistication, she had a basic core of naivety.

"Of course she didn't. No one ever does." Krux rubbed his face. "I should have cut her loose a couple of years ago. Up 'til then she was fine. Calm, organized, careful, but this past year… I'm very fond of her and—"

"Give me the details," Sabre-Tooth said. He didn't think much of the sort of affection Krux displayed. "I'll get her out."

He considered what she might look like after a day in a SecCen interrogation room. They'd shave off all that luxuriant hair before they even started to question her.

His claws flexed into his clenched fists. She mustn't become another person he couldn't save. She mustn't join the dog, the sexscort and all the assassinations that populated his dreams. He pressed his lips together. Poor Petrian. She would be so scared.

"She's being brought down by a prisoner transport from New Midland Security. They're moving her in two days' time."

"Won't they already have questioned her?"

Krux frowned. "I hope not. I imagine they'd save it for SecCen. Given her social standing and the fact that they might get leverage on other influential citizens, senior intelligence would want to do it themselves."

"Are we all in danger from what she might say?"

Krux frowned. "Us? Not really, not anymore than we already are. I'd rather the Council assumes I'm dead, but it's not as if I've any plans to take up my old life. I might get reclassified as a non-citizen but it wouldn't worry me that much."

Sabre-Tooth wrinkled his brow, wondering how the Council knew of Krux. "So why do we need to kill her?"

"The Council lets us exist because we're an outlet for any dissatisfaction in the citizenship. Alliance Security thinks differently. They'd like to make a few examples from the higher-levels. It's our undercover contacts I'm worried about. Petrian knows a number of her fellow citizens are involved with us, and if she names them, they could point out others. She'll give them up; everyone does in the end. Besides, I meant it when I said it would be kinder to kill her ourselves."

"I see."

"Are you okay with this?" Krux stared into his eyes. "I know you had enough after you came out of the military, but if you—"

"No, it's fine," Sabre-Tooth said. He would get her out. There would be no need to kill her.

"Maisi says you're turning into one of our best operatives. I'd like you to be involved, but I don't want any hesitation."

Sabre-Tooth grimaced. "If it was me, I'd rather be killed than taken to that place." The image of Security Central sent a shiver through his entire body. Petrian wasn't going there.

"I understand you care for her," Krux said. "That's one of the reasons I'm asking you."

"I'd do it for any of our people." Sabre-Tooth avoided Krux's gaze. His feelings were no one else's business.

"Good," Krux said. "I'll send some of our most experienced people with you."

"What about Sugar and Tygre? They're both—"

"Sugar's efficient but she has a tendency to be reckless. Tygre's a good spy, but he's not a killer. I'll send Callum. You're used to working with him. He's solid." He hesitated. "Sugar would kill Pet without thinking about it. So would a lot of my other operatives. I know you'll get her out alive if it's at all possible." He rubbed a hand over his head.

"Okay." Sabre-Tooth knew Krux was right about Sugar. He was wrong about Tygre though. Tygre had no problem with killing his enemies. Callum was nowhere near as ruthless.

"It's not going to be a routine extraction," Krux said. "There are problems. First, the military will be extra vigilant. Petrian's an important arrest. Not many citizens at her level end up in custody. They might expect her family to try and rescue her."

"Won't they?"

"No. She hasn't spoken to them in years. When they find out about this, they'll distance themselves even further. Disown her."

"Okay. What else."

"They'll be on the watch for us as well. We've seized prisoners several times in the last year, and like I said, Petrian has higher value than most."

"I'll be careful," Sabre-Tooth said.

"Her colleague in the Justice Department told us she'll be brought from the military base near the New Midland development, down to Central Security, where she'll be interrogated and possibly, if she's still alive, put on trial. It's a joke, they already know what they'll do with her, but she's an example. She's connected to a wide number of people who think they're untouchable." Krux squeezed his eyes closed and pinched the bridge of his nose. "We haven't long."

"So do we rescue her at the Midland end, or here?" Sabre-Tooth asked.

Krux was waffling, deviating from the necessary information. Maybe he was more upset than he looked.

"Halfway between New Midland and London," Krux opened his eyes again. "It'll be you, Callum, Halla, a couple from my personal team and Maisi. The others met Maisi and Callum earlier today. Maisi will lead the attack on the transport and cause a distraction. You'll come in behind them and snatch the prisoner."

"Is that all?"

Connor's casual sarcasm was having an effect on him. Not a good effect, if the expression on Krux's face was anything to go by.

"No." Krux leaned back against the wall. "Did I already say they'll be using a military skytran? One of the new high-flying roaches."

"How on earth—" Sabre-Tooth had never attacked anything that wasn't earthbound, or at least low-flying before. "I haven't got bloody wings." Krux wasn't the only one who was upset.

"It won't go that high," Krux said. "Not for a short journey, and one of my people is a marksman. She's another chimera, like you, and she'll bring down the roach with minimal damage. We might even be able to salvage it."

"What sort of chimera?" he asked.

"A mixture, but her eyesight and spatial awareness are outside anything I've seen before."

What if Petrian was killed in the crash? Sabre-Tooth pushed his hair away from his face. Almost anything could go wrong. "They'd need to be."

"We want a quick extraction. Unobtrusive if possible," Krux said. "The escort won't be large, just one ground vehicle, I'm told. Normally you'd be able to do it with no problems." He hesitated. "We both know there're always problems."

"Do you know what sort of ground transport? What sort of weapons?"

"No. It's a prisoner escort though, so the crew will be trained to deal with this sort of attack. They'll be heavily armed, but Halla's bringing the tech to deal with that."

Sabre-Tooth considered. "Hmm."

He hoped it would work. If nothing went wrong, it might. Apart from the skytran component, it should be more straightforward than the last rescue he'd been involved with. At least it was outside the walls.

He pictured Petrian as he'd seen her last, half asleep, her pale hair spreading over a pillow, her mouth curved in a small smile as she watched him leave. His stomach cramped. He couldn't kill her. He couldn't bear to think of her in the cells at SecCen either.

"Is that all?" He needed to be by himself.

"Make it work," Krux said. "You can do it. I've heard a lot about you. When you come back, we can talk about your future. You'd be a useful addition to our central control group."

Sabre-Tooth nodded. He could think about that if he came back.

"You'd better go. You'll be on foot, so it'll take you most of the time available to get there."

As he left, Sabre-Tooth glanced back over his shoulder.

Krux pinched the bridge of his nose. "It's my fault. I dragged her into this. Get her out if you can. If you can't...don't let them have her."

ALLIANCE NEWS CORP – *keeping you informed*

News Update
December 14th 2454

Crime

Subsequent to raids on the Department of Population Control, several officials from the Department of Justice were arrested last week, their crimes: betrayal and treason. Senior staff have been accused of selling information to enemies of the state; information that has facilitated acts of terrorism, both domestic and international. The Council have promised that these people will be publicly tried, and if found guilty, will be punished to the limit of the law.

~~~

Social

Musicians and performers from the many Alliance nations are gathering in London for the Midwinter celebrations. This year, a highly regarded dance company from the Indian Republic joins them. The publicist for 'The Zenith of Lost Mumbai' talked to our journalists last week. 'This is Zenith's first tour outside of the Republic,' he told us. 'The performers, as well as their proud fans, are beyond excited. We would like to thank Sifia Hong and her Council for the opportunity.'

Chapter 32

The sky was darkening to a deep flame-edged blue when Sabre-Tooth left the camp, heading along one of the partially cleared paths north. He wanted to stay well away from the main official road, as the military used it, and recently, their surveillance traffic had increased. There were usually a couple of patrols somewhere along its length, even when things were quiet. Sabre-Tooth was distracted. He didn't want his lack of focus to lead him into trouble. He picked his way carefully; it would be easy to turn his ankle on the shifting debris.

Several hours later, he caught up with Maisi and the others.

"Sabre-Tooth." She sounded tired. "Good to see you. I believe we're liberating your fuckfriend." Disgust wound through her tone.

Sabre-Tooth tossed his pack to the ground, growling in the back of his throat.

Maisi had said nothing before. Sugar had told him the affair was common knowledge, but she had a tendency to exaggerate. He should have known though. The rebel groups were just as addicted to gossip as the regular military.

"One of our assets." He hissed at Maisi, baring his teeth. "We're liberating a compromised asset."

Maisi snorted, unintimidated. "Right. We'll move as far as we can tonight, rest, and then cover the remaining ground tomorrow night." She tossed him an energy bar. "Here. You'll need this."

He accepted it as a peace offering. She must know he had his own supplies.

"I'm sorry," she said. "I don't like her, but I wouldn't want this to happen to anyone. We'll get her away, Sabe."

The others already sat on the ground, eating quietly. The two men sent by Krux were strangers. Neither one of them was the chimera. The female stranger was as small as Sugar and just as harmless at first glance, but she had the eyes of a hawk and black hair that looked more like feathers. She might have come from a lab like him or, more likely, arrived in the New British Islands with one of the refugee groups.

~~~

Night faded into dawn as the group moved into positions in the woodland at the side of the main road. The skyroach would follow the line of the road, to accommodate the single carrier of ground troops escorting it.

Sabre-Tooth curled up in the damp undergrowth and rested. As the sun rose, he scrambled to a kneeling position, and peered around him. None of the others were visible, but he knew they were there. Maisi, Halla, Callum and the rest of Krux's people would deal with the ground escort first, while the sniper brought down the skyroach. Sabre-Tooth's role was rescuer; he would snatch the prisoner. It sounded easy when he said it quickly.

The sky gradually brightened, the temperature climbed higher and the atmosphere thickened with moisture. Sabre-Tooth took a breath, testing the air; it would rain soon. Overhead, patches of blue broke up the sparse green-brown of the treetops. He kept his eyes half-closed while his ears waited for the sound of the expected skyroach. The dominant noise was that of the morning bird cacophony, underlined by the rustle of a light wind sifting through the branches. Occasionally, he detected movements that could have come from a small mammal, but was more likely to be one of his companions, disturbing the vegetation with a slight movement.

The sun was almost at its zenith when the vibration of an approaching vehicle disturbed the woodland. It had to be the groundcar, the prisoner escort. His companions moved quietly down towards the road.

The tone of the birdsong changed to a staccato note of alarm. Sabre-Tooth tensed. He couldn't see much of the sky, as the lush canopy allowed only small shafts of sunlight through, so he listened hard, judging when the vehicle skimmed the tops of nearby trees. Maisi had told him that the sharpshooter would be in position on a branch of one of the higher trees. When the sound of the pressure rifle reached him, it was no more than a small disarrangement of the air. He tensed.

As soon as the rhythm of the overhead machine changed, Sabre-Tooth rose to his feet. After less than two seconds, there was an ear-splitting screech, several loud bangs, and a wave of movement rippled through the undergrowth. The birdsong stopped.

He ploughed through dense vegetation towards the source of the crash. The shot must have forced the vehicle away from the road. As he moved, shouts echoed from the road, followed by the low rumble of active weapons.

The downed vessel rested in a tangle of greenery, like a giant, iron-grey beetle. One of its solar power panels had broken loose, and was wedged in the forked branch of a nearby tree. Beyond it, on the road, was the stalled ground escort. It didn't move. The guns were frozen, half in, half out of their firing position and its occupants were trapped inside. Halla must have done her tech magic.

Sabre-Tooth rolled his eyes, amazed by the incompetence of the military. They must know about the rebel tech by now. They had something similar themselves, so why weren't they prepared for it?

Ignoring the groundcar, he edged forward, eyes focused on the prisoner transport vehicle. The skyroach. He'd never seen one before. No one moved around it, but Petrian, if it was her, must still have at least one guard with her. And what about the driver?

The side door hung open, distorted and damaged by the crash. Low conversation drifted from inside. Sabre-Tooth crept closer.

"Nervous?" A male voice drawled. "There's nobody out there. They're fighting your escort in the bloody jungle. Why don't you go and join them?"

"Shut up." Another male voice snapped.

"Letting yourselves be shot down? That'll fuck up your promotion prospects, won't it?"

The sound of a fist, striking flesh, broke through the sounds of the forest.

"Ow. What did you do that for? I think you've broken my jaw."

"I told you to shut up. You should remember you're a prisoner."

"Difficult to forget." The voice shook.

"Soon to be a dead prisoner. If you don't keep your mouth shut, I'll shoot you myself. You're not the important one here."

"That'll really help your career."

Sabre-Tooth considered. Two voices. Two men. One sounded like a prisoner, a male prisoner. So where was Petrian? It wasn't like her to keep quiet.

The voices identified the positions of the two speakers. Grabbing the edge of the door, Sabre-Tooth leapt into the interior of the vehicle, his clenched fist striking the guard on the side of the head. The man wore a solid helmet, but the blow was hard enough to knock him sideways. Sabre-Tooth shook his hand out. He was going to have a bad bruise across his knuckles.

The guard regained his balance, swayed and fumbled with his weapon. Blood trickled down his face, behind the clear visor of his face-protector.

Sabre-Tooth hit him with his other hand. The faceplate crumpled. Blood spurted from his nose and he collapsed onto the floor. Sabre-Tooth watched him for a moment, before nudging him hard with the toe of his boot. He didn't move. Sabre-Tooth turned his attention to the other occupants.

The pilot of the vehicle sagged in the driver's seat. Small groans came from her, signaling she was alive. After a brief check, Sabre-Tooth decided she must have hit her head in the crash. She wasn't in any condition to cause trouble.

He spun round to examine the rear of the transport. Two people occupied the cage seats and both were restrained by heavy-duty plaschain, which attached their shackled wrists to the cage structure. The male prisoner watched him, alert despite the trail of blood running down his chin from his broken lip. He wasn't supposed to be there. No one had mentioned more than one prisoner.

The other occupant was Petrian, almost unrecognizable. She sagged in her bonds, unconscious, asleep or dead.

ALLIANCE NEWS CORP – keeping you informed

News Update
December 15th 2454

Western Eurasia

The local sub-committees of the Alliance Council have published their final decisions on the location of new government centres for the New British Islands. The conclusions will come as no surprise to most of our readers. The planned city will be situated in New Midland, safely above predicted sea-level rises. It escapes the worst of the inland river floods, which plague the highland regions of the islands. The early phase architects and designers have worked closely with the military in the first stage of the project, clearing significant numbers of illegal squatters from the site. Building works will start in January. This is the biggest construction project seen in the New British Islands since the regeneration of the southern flood defences, over a hundred years ago. The most vulnerable regions of London will move to the new city within the next ten years.

~~~

Social

Sifia Hong and her husband, General DeWitte, will spend this Midwinter in London. Their arrival will be heralded by a reception at the Royal Buckingham Palace, hosted by the King and his Consort. Speaker Hong's colleague and rival, Andrei Krewchek, will join the festivities before departing for his family estates in the hills north of Midland.

Dissension – the struggle against injustice

December 15th 2454

Dissension is concerned by the increased abuse of human rights and the retreat of freedom as Midwinter approaches. It fears that the Alliance is exploiting the holiday season to mask its attacks on its own citizens. Dissensions' lawyers and investigative teams will not be fooled.

Chapter 33

Petrian's head drooped onto her chest, multi-blonde hair falling forwards in a tangled mass.

"Petrian?"

She didn't move. He reached out and touched her throat. Her skin was cool and clammy. Beneath it, the throb of her pulse was barely detectable.

Taking out his needle laser, he burned through her bindings, pulling her free from the seat cage before dragging her to the damaged doorway.

"Hey." The male prisoner called out.

Sabre-Tooth cast an impatient glance over his shoulder.

"Aren't you going to get me out as well?"

Sabre-Tooth surveyed the carnage of crushed vegetation outside the transport. He couldn't see any human life at all. The sounds of fighting had died away. It looked safe to leave.

Slowly he turned back into the interior, steadied his grip on Petrian and aimed his laser at the point where the man's manacles attached him to his chair. Nothing in his orders had mentioned a second prisoner, but he couldn't leave anyone behind to continue the journey to SecCen.

The man pushed himself shakily to his feet, rubbing one hand across his face. Blood from his mouth smeared across his chin.

Hoisting Petrian over one shoulder, Sabre-Tooth scrambled down from the transport and carried her away. The stranger followed, breathing heavily.

Once he was a few metres from the vehicle, Sabre-Tooth lowered Petrian's limp body onto the ground and bent over her. Her lips were slack, and a painful wheeze came from between them.

The other prisoner caught up. He leaned his back against a tree, bending forward to catch his breath. Exhaling heavily, he straightened to meet Sabre-Tooth's gaze.

"Do you know what's wrong with her?" Sabre-Tooth crouched at Petrian's side. She lay still.

"Drugged," the man said.

Sabre-Tooth raised his eyes. "Why her and not you?"

"They haven't bothered with me yet. Not important enough." He licked a bead of blood from the corner of his mouth. "She was off her head from the interrogation." His eyes closed and he took another shaky breath. "Fuck knows what they dosed her with, but she wouldn't stop screaming and thrashing, so they gave her a sedative. She's been like that ever since. For two days. Bunch of amateurs. They were supposed to leave her for SecCen. MI will do the same to them if they've broken a prisoner already."

Two days? She'd been in this state for two days?

One of her hands drooped at an awkward angle and it looked as though her wrist was broken. Bruises stained her brown skin with red, yellow and purple. A trail of dried blood ran from one nostril down the side of her face. Her half-open eyes were all white, the pupils rolled up under her lids.

Sabre-Tooth checked her throat again. The skin was still cool, the pulse still shallow and irregular. He stroked his fingers over her moist skin.

"Who are you?" He didn't look up.

The man shrugged. "Another prisoner."

"Who? We were told there'd just be her."

The man bent at the waist, pressing one hand against his side. "She was staying with me, when they came for her. I don't even know what she's supposed to have done. Now look at me? I've lost my citizenship, and it looks like I'm on the run." Anger filled his voice.

The comm in Sabre-Tooth's ear buzzed.

Maisi's voice followed the signal. "We're on our way to you. Stay put."

The team arrived a minute later, pushing back the undergrowth. "We checked your prisoner transport," Maisi said. "One barely conscious pilot and one unconscious guard?"

"That was me. What about the groundcar guards?"

"They won't be a problem. And their vehicle's stuck for at least another hour. They'll still be there when the salvage team arrives."

Sabre-Tooth nodded. "There was another prisoner on the skyroach." He pointed at the stranger whose back was propped against a tree trunk. He hadn't caught his breath completely.

Maisi eyed him. "Are you hurt?"

"I'll be okay." He pressed his manacled hands over his mouth, suppressing the cough.

Maisi raised an eyebrow and beckoned to Halla who produced her detector and ran it over the man's body.

It buzzed twice.

"We're going to have to dig your chips out," Maisi said. "Brace yourself. We haven't got much in the way of anaesthetic with us."

She passed a multi-bladed knife to Halla who used the narrowest blade to pry the chips from under the skin on the prisoner's shoulder and thigh.

He winced, clenching his jaw and squeezing his eyes closed. "My life's completely screwed."

After she'd finished, Halla released his hands.

She turned her attention to Petrian's limp body. "What the hell have they done with her?"

A trail of perspiration ran down Sabre-Tooth's face as he crouched next to Petrian. "He says they drugged her."

Halla knelt down and passed her detector over Petrian. It bleeped once. She dug a chip from Petrian's thigh before standing up again and returning the knife to Maisi. The wound bled sluggishly.

"Who are you?" Maisi dug a finger into the stranger's ribs as he wiped the blood away from his shoulder.

"A friend of hers," he repeated, tilting his head towards Petrian.

"What's your name?"

"Mario Fazelle."

"And why are you here?" Maisi paced round him, her aura bristling with suspicion.

"He cut me out of the cage." Mario pointed at Sabre-Tooth.

Maisi heaved out an exasperated sigh. "I meant, why did they arrest you?"

"Seditious activities."

"What the fuck does that mean?"

"I entertained a person of interest to the security services. How the fuck was I supposed to know what she—"

Halla looked from him to Maisi. "Hadn't we better get going?"

Maisi nodded, but pointed her knife at Mario. "I've got my eye on you. If I think you're lying, I'll kill you."

"I'm sure you will." He wiped more blood from his thigh.

"Believe it." She slotted the knife back into her belt. "Right, let's move. Sabe, can you manage Petrian?"

Sabre-Tooth nodded and hoisted her over his shoulder, where she hung limply. The broken wrist would have been agony if she'd had any consciousness at all. She didn't even flinch.

He followed behind Halla and the others, careful not to let the whipping branches hit Petrian's inert body.

Callum brought up the rear. The sharpshooting chimera had disappeared. Sabre-Tooth couldn't be bothered to care.

The sky darkened and heavy drops of rain soon turned to a downpour. After a mile or two, Maisi slowed until she was level with Sabre-Tooth. "Any sign she's coming round?"

"No. No change at all."

Petrian's hair was a wet mass that hung limply from her skull, slapping at the back of Sabre-Tooth's legs. The rest of her was completely inert. He tightened his grip on her thighs.

"Are you sure she's still alive?"

"I checked her pulse. It's irregular but still there." He told Maisi what Mario had told him.

"Drugged with what?" Maisi blew out a deep breath. "It doesn't matter. Even if we knew what it was, we couldn't do anything here. It'll have to wait till we get back."

"I hope they've got a medic ready." Sabre-tooth shifted Petrian to a more comfortable position.

"They will." Maisi touched his arm. "It's Woodside we're going to, remember. There's always a medic on call. Krux will have everything sorted."

Sabre-Tooth's neutral opinion of Krux had turned into strong dislike. "What about the flooding? I thought—"

"I don't think it's that bad there. Not yet. Come on. Let's keep going."

Sabre-Tooth shifted his burden and flexed his fingers. There was no point in constantly feeling for a change in her pulse rate. "We should have waited for the clean-up team to fix the skyroach."

Maisi huffed in sour amusement. "How long do you think that would take?" She pushed ahead of him again. "And we can't keep it. It's far too noticeable. As soon as we got it above the trees, some sniper would bring it down."

Sabre-Tooth grunted. He couldn't fly it anyway. It was a new model. His mind was wandering.

By the time they arrived at Woodside, worry filled Sabre-Tooth's mind. Petrian's condition hadn't changed; her pulse was sluggish, her skin drenched with cold sweat and her body limp as a puppet. The hand at the end of her broken wrist was hot and swollen; purple tracks snaking from it, up her arm, to disappear under the sleeve of her yellow prison coverall. He was afraid it was infected. God knows with what, but he doubted their medic had anything strong enough to kill the sort of bugs she might have picked up. She might lose the hand, possibly her arm.

Krux appeared before Sabre-Tooth could put her down. "You got her out. Alive. Well done." His mouth widened in a relieved smile. "There's a bed prepared for her and a medic waiting." He ushered Sabre-Tooth to the entrance to the underground hideout. "How's she doing?"

"I don't know."

"Bastards." Krux's brow wrinkled in concern as he registered her comatose state. "They didn't need to…" His voice died away as he stamped down into the darkness. Seconds later, his wrist light activated and Sabre-Tooth followed.

He placed Petrian on the narrow bunk in an alcove, stepping back as the medic bent over her. She hadn't regained consciousness at all.

"Is she going to be all right?"

The medic glanced up. "How the fuck would I know. Bugger off and let me get on with it."

Sabre-Tooth hovered just outside the alcove. He was sorry for the bad thoughts he'd had about Petrian. She looked so much older, limp and lifeless, nothing like the vibrant woman who'd mesmerised him. Her mass of hair was tangled and dark with rain water.

"Go away." The medic didn't look up.

"Come on." Krux gave him a small push. "Nothing you can do now."

"What do you think?" Sabre-Tooth tried to find meaning in Krux's expression.

Krux shook his head. "She doesn't look good. Someone messed up with her. We'll know more later. I'm going to have a word with the other one you brought out."

He strode towards where his guards waited with Mario.

Sabre-Tooth's stomach growled and he hurried off to find some food. He was starving, but at least, when he found Maisi, he found food. She'd already located the ration supply. She, Halla and Callum sat on the ground in another alcove, backs against the rough wall, each with a military ration pack. Sabre-Tooth sat down, crossed his legs and took a pack from the small pile.

Once he'd eaten, he returned to check on Petrian.

"How is she?" He peered over the medic's shoulder, determined not to be scared off again.

"Worse. I'll know more tomorrow." The medic sank down onto the floor next to the bunk. "I wish I knew what they'd given her. Just look at the state of her."

Petrian's whole body quivered.

"They don't bother to test those drugs before using them in interrogations," the medic said. "Fuck knows where they come from."

"Is that what's wrong with her?" Sabre-Tooth remembered the horror of his own drug withdrawal. At least Petrian didn't know what was happening.

"She started to fit." The medic jumped up, holding her down as her torso jerked and her neck arched.

She bared her teeth, before relaxing into limpness again. Her eyes rolled up and the trembling resumed.

"Like that." The medic rested one hand on her forehead.

"Is she waking up?"

"How would I know? Come back tomorrow."

"What about her wrist?"

The medic sighed. "I've given her the antibiotics we had, but…" His voice trailed off. Most antibiotics were useless, a placebo to reassure the patient.

"Thanks." Sabre-Tooth waited for a minute. When the medic showed no signs of saying more, he crept away to find a bunk. He was so very tired.

Lying on his back, sick with exhaustion, he fell into a fitful sleep.

~~~

A loud bang jerked him awake. He sat up, activating his wrist light. The other bunks were all empty. Sounds of running feet echoed from the tunnels. He leapt out of his narrow bed, fastened his coverall, slid his feet into his boots and sprinted for the central hall.

Krux and another man stopped him halfway down the passage. "Don't go that way. We've got a situation. Hostiles. The main exit's blocked by the military. We can't use it, but there's a passage from the second bunkroom. It goes down to the next level, then comes up again about a hundred metres away. Let's hope it's not flooded."

Sabre-Tooth frowned. "You're going the wrong way." They were heading towards the crashing from the central hall.

"We need to spread the word. Some of the others are just down here and—"

"I'll do that," Sabre-Tooth said. "If I send them this way you can get them into the passage. Go on."

Krux spun on his heel and disappeared towards the flight of stairs leading further underground. Hopefully, the flood defences would be adequate. Woodside was on the higher edge of old London, and the tracks had never been very far underground.

Sabre-Tooth circled the sleeping quarters in the adjacent alcove, where the occupants were already awake and preparing to evacuate.

"Yeah. We know where the other exit is," the medic said.

"What about Petrian?" Sabre-Tooth asked as Halla pushed past him.

"She's still unconscious." The medic picked up a backpack. "I can't drag her through the underground. She'd slow us down."

240

"I'll get her," Sabre-Tooth said.

The medic shook his head. "Don't be stupid. There isn't time. She's not going to make it anyway. She won't be telling any secrets."

"I'll try. What about Maisi?"

"She left earlier, with Callum and the other prisoner." Halla looked over her shoulder. "Come on Sabe. You'll be trapped if you don't get moving."

The crashing was getting closer. Halla and the medic disappeared into the tunnel and Sabre-Tooth turned into the last alcove. He couldn't just leave Petrian, not knowing whether she'd live or die. It would be worse if she lived and they caught her again. All the effort would have been for nothing.

Petrian lay on her back on the bunk. When he bent down to pick her up, her eyes half-opened and she muttered some words.

"What?" Sabre-Tooth bent over her, scooping her into his arms. "I can't hear you." She was smaller than he remembered, her face drained of its habitual confidence. Deep lines fanned out from her eyes and her body was slick with sweat and shaken by bone-deep tremors. A sweet chemical odour rose from her pores.

"Tracker on me." She forced the words past clenched teeth before closing her eyes again.

"Shit. Where?" What had Halla missed? There was no point running if they took a tracker with them.

"Hhhair," she stuttered. "Flea."

The sound of heavy boots grew louder and Sabre-Tooth glanced over his shoulder at the entrance that led back to the hall. The hunters were already in the tunnel. There was no escape that way. He ran towards the other exit, unsure where it led, other than downwards.

A loud crack echoed in the chamber behind him; a silver pellet flew through the air, landing in the tunnel ahead. It started to effervesce, the fumes snaking upwards, visible in the light from his wrist.

Gas.

Desperation gave him speed.

He shifted Petrian, balancing her on his shoulder. Her body stiffened.

"Go." Her voice was tiny. A brief convulsion shook her again, and a high-pitched whine came from her mouth. She sagged. "Dying." Her breathing roughened.

"You're not going to die. Just hold on."

There was no way he'd leave her. He didn't want to add her to his memory of the dog and the sexscort, and if there was one thing he'd learned from the entertainment vids, it was that a soldier didn't leave his comrades behind. He worked his hand through her hair in a frenzied search for any locator chips. Too much hair. If – when - they escaped, he'd have to cut it off.

As he ran, something slammed into the back of his leg. His knee crumpled under him and he collapsed headlong onto the ground, spilling Petrian's body into the darkness. Falling forward, he sprawled on hands and knees, half covering her as he landed.

She didn't move.

A fine white vapour oozed along the tunnel towards him. Panicking, he tried to stand. Pain stabbed into his leg and it folded underneath him. Reaching behind him, his hand encountered something long and metallic protruding from his thigh. He no longer had control of his movements. His body lurched to one side while his mind slowed. Hands grabbed his arms and hauled him backwards, before dropping him back onto the ground.

"The woman's dead." A strange voice echoed in his ear. "Someone's going to be in trouble for that."

He reached out to touch Petrian, but the white mist thickened and his hand flopped loosely to the ground. He gasped for breath, choked and the world faded into darkness.

ALLIANCE NEWS CORP – keeping you informed

News Update
February 10th 2454

Weather

This winter has seen cataclysmic weather events throughout the Alliance territories. The latest mega-storm is forming in central Europe today and tomorrow, and is predicted to move southwest over the next week. Hurricane force winds will bring torrential rain and flooding to many areas. Major construction projects in France and the New British Islands will be temporarily halted, delaying work on Seine river walls and the New London development. In addition, a massive typhoon is forming off the coast of China. Precautionary measures are in force, and shore workers have been told to move inland. Experts in atmospheric physics predict that these will be the last major storms of the season. The Alliance has developed considerable expertise in coping with this sort of climate challenge, and consequently plans are in place to keep damage, and casualties, to a minimum.

Chapter 34

How long had he been in this cage? Sabre-Tooth opened his eyes and stared at the white plascrete ceiling. Nothing had changed. Everything was white; walls, floor, bunk, his own prison coverall.

It should be yellow. Prison uniforms were always yellow, weren't they?

He'd have been glad of any colour. Faint regret leaked into his mind. He'd never liked white.

Worst of all, a control collar circled his neck again.

Days and nights merged into each other. He wasn't sure how much time passed, but it must have been a long while. The wound in his leg from the projectile had left a roughly circular scar, so he estimated a month at least, maybe two, but he healed quickly. Arching his back, he stretched out until the leg twitched in protest. The pain lasted no longer than a fraction of a second. He relaxed again, letting his body sink onto the solidity of the bunk.

This white tomb would probably be his home until they executed him. Or killed him with their truth drugs.

The memory of Petrian's condition made him shudder. It joined with his memory of the murdered attack dog, back in training camp, as one of his recurrent nightmares. He wished he knew whether the others had escaped. After he passed out from the gas, he had no idea what had happened. He'd regained consciousness as four black-uniformed men pulled him out of a prisoner transport and dragged him onto the ferry that served Security Central. The journey across the river towards the looming black plastone prison made him want to jump overboard. Unfortunately, he was securely fastened to the bench seat, and anyway, the occasional dorsal fin of a river shark cruised alongside the boat. The river currents were notoriously powerful and life was still better than death.

Petrian had to be dead. And what about Maisi, Halla and the rest? What had happened to them? Had they caught Krux?

Sabre-Tooth couldn't understand why he was still in the cell, or why he hadn't been interrogated. Maybe he was being saved for something else, but what?

Where was Tessis now? And Sugar and Tygre? He had no way of finding out. His mind circled constantly round the same questions. He closed his eyes, blocking out his view of the smooth white ceiling.

The weight of earth piled onto him. His prison was even deeper underground than his old cage in the laboratory. His memories of daylight and the rich smell of the outdoors twisted him with longing. He banished both from his consciousness, but as soon as he relaxed, the images and yearnings returned. Disinfectant dominated the scents down here, the acrid odour underlaid with the smell of urine and the faint coppery tang of old blood.

Sometimes the light was bright enough to hurt his eyes; sometimes there was no light and the darkness pressed down on him like a thick blanket. The lights were at mid-level now; bearable, which probably meant someone was watching him. He stayed immobile, stretched out on his back. The time slipped by with the speed of a wandering snail.

The sound of a door opening at the end of the corridor pulled him out of his half-trance. His ears rang as the pressure of the air changed. Someone was coming; maybe with food and water.

Sabre-Tooth didn't allow himself to think about such things normally. The gaps between meals were erratic and unpredictable, and often his throat seized up from thirst. He didn't allow himself to think about fresh, moving air, or the sunlight on his bare skin either. If he did, he'd go mad. One hand drifted automatically to his hollow stomach. He ignored his parched throat, keeping his eyes on the ceiling as the two sets of footsteps approached. One had the familiar stamp of army boots. The other was more slithery, with the rhythm of soft-soled shoes.

"This is him." The voice was one he recognised. A guard.

"Can you get him to stand?" The new voice was smooth.

Mellow and seductive, it stirred a memory. Somewhere, he'd heard that voice before.

Sabre-Tooth remained still, opening his eyes and letting his focus swing sideways to check out the visitor. A tall man, slender and fair, and dressed in expensive high fashion, slouched gracefully on the other side of the bars. Recognition flooded his mind. It was Commander Diessen's friend. What the hell was he doing here?

His gaze returned to the ceiling.

"Sabre-Tooth? On your feet." The guard's voice snapped out. "Now."

Sabre-Tooth ignored him.

"On your feet, or I'll press the button."

Experience had taught him that defiance would only bring pain, and he'd have to obey in the end. It wasn't worth it. He sat up, swinging his legs to the floor, and slowly pushed himself to his feet.

"What does the button do?" The visitor sounded intrigued.

"Gives him an electric shock through the collar. He doesn't like it."

"Let me have it." The stranger held out one hand.

"Mr. Oroz—"

"Now."

Stefan Oroz. The name returned to his memory. Sabre-Tooth hadn't liked the man when he'd encountered him the first time. The guard, who was stupid and sadistic, appeared to be afraid of him. That couldn't be good.

The guard handed over the collar control.

"What's this?" Stefan Oroz indicated the red button.

"Termination. It's disabled in case someone kills him by accident."

"And this one?"

"That's the shock button. We use it to control his behaviour."

"Hmm." Stefan smiled, his face pure and angelic as he looked up at Sabre-Tooth through long sooty lashes. He pressed the button.

Sabre-Tooth collapsed, convulsing as the shock hit him. He managed to suppress the cry that bubbled in his dry throat, but couldn't help scrabbling at the solid floor with his unsheathed claws. He twisted round, steadied himself against the barred door and pushed himself to his knees, glowering at his tormenter. One day, if he had the chance, he would kill him. He was obviously going to die anyway, so he would take as many of these sadists with him as he could manage. The bars held him back as well as supporting him. He realized he was hissing.

"I see." Stefan pushed a strand of silky blonde hair out of his eyes and turned to the guard. "Let me in the cell. I want a closer look."

"But Sir, you—"

"Now. Or I'll make you as sorry as he is."

The guard held one hand to the pad and punched in a code with the other hand. The door to the cell slid back. Sabre-Tooth released the bars, scrambling out of the way.

Stefan crouched next to him. "I love his animal ears." He stroked his fingers over them. "So soft."

Sabre-Tooth shivered at the touch, sniffing as the chemical scent of cosmetics mingled with the cell's antiseptic stench.

Stefan laughed, inserted the tip of his little finger between Sabre-Tooth's lips and pulled up the corner of his mouth. "And fangs." He pressed his forefinger against the tip of one. "Sharp. I'd like to see him use them."

Sabre-Tooth kept as still as he could, desperately wanting to bite down on the finger, twist it off and spit it onto the ground. This pretty, delicately formed man made his skin crawl.

Stefan straightened. "Get up." He fingered the control. "Unless you want more of this?"

Sabre-Tooth pushed himself upright, his legs still weak. He kept his gaze on the ground, his hands clenched into fists.

"He's lost weight." Stefan turned to raise a questioning eyebrow. "Mostly muscle tone. It's not a good look."

"He's been on minimal rations," the guard said. "It's policy for long-term prisoners. Keeps them quiet."

Stefan switched his attention back to Sabre-Tooth. "Show me your claws."

He opened his fingers, his razor claws already fully extended.

"Very nice. Very useful. I might have a job for you."

Sabre-Tooth's head jerked up in an involuntary movement. His eyes clashed with Stefan's intense blue gaze. He turned his face away, trying not to hope.

"Aren't you going to ask me what sort of job? You're a cat. Where's your curiosity?" Stefan caressed Sabre-Tooth's cheek.

Sabre-Tooth said nothing.

"If I hadn't come along, you'd have been terminated." His tormentor's finger hovered over the button. "What do you say?"

For a very short moment, Sabre-Tooth contemplated risking the collar shock again.

"Thank you, Sir." It was the first time he'd spoken since he'd been taken prisoner. Even then, all he'd said was his name. His rasping voice sounded unfamiliar to him.

Stefan patted his cheek. "Good boy. You're going to be a personal guard; a present from me for a friend of mine. He's a very important man, with enemies as well as dangerous friends. I think you'll make a good bodyguard. What do you think?"

Sabre-Tooth had no idea. He eyed the collar control. "Very good, Sir."

"He won't admit it, but my friend's got a taste for exotics." He ran his hand down the side of Sabre-Tooth's face to his neck, before leaving the cell. "He'll love you."

Sabre-Tooth stayed frozen in position as the door slid closed.

"Take care of him." Stefan handed the control back to the guard. "I'll be back to collect him on Monday." He smiled over his shoulder at Sabre-Tooth, his perfect features alive with charm. "And give him some food and water. I want him looking better than that. I'll keep him for a day or two before I pass him on to Andrei."

When the door slammed shut behind his two visitors, Sabre-Tooth returned to the bunk and stretched out, flexing his feet as the muscles of his legs quivered from the aftershock of the collar.

It sounded like he might be getting out. That was good. At least it should be an improvement on his present situation. The ghost of Stefan Oroz's fingers drifted along his cheekbone. He clenched his jaw. He could put up with whatever the man planned for him if it meant he would be out of this cell.

Once he was outside, he might have other options. He'd escaped once; he could do it again. Anything would be better than festering in all this white for much longer. He might find out what had happened to the others. At any rate, it looked like he wouldn't die just yet, and he might even be fed. His stomach lurched, caught between the shock-induced nausea and a desperate need for food.

He would make them sorry.

He ran his forefinger along the edge of the collar and closed his eyes, thinking of Sugar. She'd told him he'd never been vicious. Things changed though. They hadn't needed to hurt Petrian like that.

He would survive this.

He would escape again.

He would rip them all apart.

Dissension – the struggle against injustice

February 23rd 2454

Election season has started in earnest. Sifia Hong has a tried and tested campaign team, but challenger, Andrei Krewchek, has the support of the military. Readers of Dissension News may remember disgraced head of Military Intelligence, Commander Diessen, was part of Krewchek's early network. Councillor Krewchek must have felt a sense of relief when Diessen disappeared into a SecCen cell. His relief must have strengthened at the rumour that Diessen died there. Krewchek has also been seen to distance himself from Stefan Oroz, one of the more dissolute offshoots of the royal family of the New British Islands.

ALLIANCE NEWS CORP –keeping you informed

News Update
February 23rd 2455

Social

Andrei Krewchek invited his supporters, as well as many from Sifia Hong's campaign, to a glittering party at his Hampstead mansion on Saturday night, signalling the beginning of his serious campaigning for the top job. His wife, Melissa Hussayn-Kalidi, brought her own family to the event, along with their considerable political influence. She was resplendent in an indigo drape, designed especially for her by London fashion guru, Sen Watson. Councillor Krewchek's cousin and fixer, Caradoc Krewchek, was a visible presence, also in Sen Watson indigo. Queen Consort, Liljas Oroz-Stuart arrived in the company of her distant cousin, Stefan Oroz, a long-time acquaintance of Councillor Krewchek. Both wore midnight blue skinsuits, and silver over-robes.

Also in attendance, were many senior figures from the military, including top Alliance generals, Richard Rivera, and Chaloem Mookjai. Councillor Krewchek made a point of welcoming Sifia Hong's husband, General Manuel DeWitte, who is touring the New British Islands at present, as part of his wife's campaign. A scattering of figures from the Security Services moved through the crowds, their black dress uniforms contrasting with the glitter of the civilian finery.

As a matter of curiosity, one of Councillor Krewchek's personal bodyguards appeared to be a human chimera. The councillor had no comment other than, 'I have many indentured servants in my household. Some of them lack citizenship and are my personal responsibility.' While it is illegal to use human genetic material to create chimeras, News Corps is not aware of any stricture against ownership of one.

Alliance News Corps wishes both contenders the best of luck in the coming election.

Afterword

Almost Human is a book in the 'Degrees of Freedom' series, set on an Earth (mostly) recovering from a series of cataclysmic disasters. Three hundred years in the future, civilisation is rising again, but for many of its inhabitants life is a continual struggle. This series tells some of their stories.

Acknowledgements

Many people inspired me while I wrote this book. I put the idea for the series together while I studied for an MA in Creative Writing at Lancaster University. The first book in the series (tentatively entitled 'This Same River') was written during the course, and 'Almost Human' followed from that. I would like to thank everyone in my MA writing workshops for their help and support and their useful feedback. 'Almost Human' benefitted from the comments of Lancaster Writers, Gary Flood, Mandy Bannon, John Rutter, Adrian Horn, Teresa Garanhel, Judith Sowter, Paul Atherton, and Inés Gregory Labarta. My very grateful thanks go to Inés who read through two versions of the completed manuscript and gave detailed, thoughtful and informed insights on the plot and characters. Mandy Bannon did the final edits, and finally, Helen Dunning produced a great cover.

About the Author

Anne Cleasby lives in Cumbria in the UK, with two Birman cats. If she leans out of her bedroom window she can see over the rooftops to the waters of Windermere. She has written short stories in a variety of genres, and a series of fantasy romance novels under the pen-name of Annalisa Carr. She is presently working on her 'Degrees of Freedom' series, as well as writing the first draft of a space opera. In her free time, Anne Cleasby works as a contract biophysicist, reads widely and explores the mountains around her home. She would like a dog.

Visit Anne at her website, where you can sign up for her newsletter:
www.annecleasby.com

Made in United States
North Haven, CT
29 September 2023